WHAT LIES BENEATH

The Bloodstone Chronicles – Book Three

DECEMBER 14, 2020

A NOVEL BY SAM BEACH & L. DEE WALKER

Walker & Beach Publications 2020

What Lies Beneath
The Bloodstone Chronicles – Book Three
Sam Beach & L. Dee Walker
Copyright 2020 by Sam Beach & L. Dee Walker
Illustration by: L. Dee Walker

Novels by Sam Beach
The Rise of Seth – The Bloodstone Chronicles
Guardian of Antiquity – The Bloodstone Chronicles – Book Two

Novels by L. Dee Walker
The Rise of Seth – The Bloodstone Chronicles
Guardian of Antiquity – The Bloodstone Chronicles – Book Two

Special Dedication
To our fans. We're deeply sorry that it took so long, but… 2020.

1

Egypt in a desolate church

It is painful burying a friend. More so when he saved your life countless times. That agony tore at Sir Francis de Molay's heart the day they laid Sir Miles Garioch to rest. Only the tried-and-true knights he served with attended the humble service – the Noble Templars only accepted rootless men into their ranks who had no ties to use against them in times of strife.

Per his request, the knights set fire to the headless body in a blaze of glory. Those who attended, did so in silent prayer, hoping that his spirit would find eternal life in the kingdom of Heaven. Only Francis knew that his friend's soul – damned for all time – would be on its way to a far different place. That knowledge – added to the weighty chain already crushing his usually optimistic essence – gnawed at him like a rabid wolf.

When the service concluded, they gathered the ashes and placed them in a simple bronze urn, handing it over to Francis. "I've tried reaching out to Duncan," one of the knights said, "but there's no answer, and his voicemail is full. Should I keep trying?"

"No," a backlog of warehoused tears clogged his throat. "I'm quite sure Duncan already knows, and he's probably well on his way over here as we speak." Holding the urn as if it were a newborn fawn, misty eyes looked up at the man. "See you back at the church. Miles would wish us to continue this fight with all haste."

Giving the three-finger salute – the peace sign with a thumb added – the man walked off, leaving Francis to his remorseful thoughts. *Did I do the right thing? Should I have killed the beast while we had the chance? Would Miles still be alive if I had?*

The hour-long ride back to their church riddled Francis's mind with such doubts; grief-stricken guilt ate away at his insides – so much so, that when he arrived, he could hardly make his way into the well-appointed office. Still clutching the urn, he fell into a large chair, spinning it to face the morning sun pouring through the window. A parade of tears streamed down his gloomy face, pinging onto the container's surface; granting himself permission to finally mourn.

"Save your grief for the afterlife, Francis," came a low, guttural voice from behind him.

His heart lurched into his throat, beating out of control, causing him to take a second to compose himself before turning. Setting the urn carefully on the desk, his lower lip quivered. "Duncan. I *knew* you'd come. I am *so* sorry."

Red eyes bore down on him as enraged laughter shook the small room. "*Sorry*?! You have no *idea* of sorry!"

"I feel the same as you, and I–" suddenly suspended in the air, the vice grip wrapped around his throat, choking off his supplicating words. Shaky fingers pulled at the clamp around his neck – hyoid threatening to break in two. His face turned beet red as aching lungs strained to find breath.

"You know *nothing* of what I'm feeling! Tell me why I shouldn't snap your mortal neck like a twig." Ivory fangs slowly descended as the fury within threatened to take over. Duncan managed to just scrape by with his struggles against the beast, but with the traumatic emotions in a whirlwind of jumbled chaos, he found it almost impossible to curb the calling of his bloodlust.

Trying to capture enough air to speak, Francis sputtered. "He… was my… friend *too*."

Duncan Garioch snarled, his fingers gripping tighter, before slamming him back into his chair. "*He was my brother!*"

"Of course." He coughed between precious gulps of air. "We were brothers 'til the end, but he and I–"

"*No*, you fool. He was my *twin* brother!" Turning, he eyed the window – curling his hands into fists that cut into his flesh before releasing them as they instantly healed – trying to bridle his resentment.

Through coughs and shallow breaths, Francis eyed the man in silence, until he felt Duncan's rage subside. As the severe ringing in his ears fell silent, his forehead creased. Not wishing to reignite the man's anger, he spoke in low tones, massaging his tender neck. "*Twin*? That's not possible. We have never allowed–"

"*Allowed?*" His hypnotic gaze snapped back, as irritated laughter once more filled the room, like a mad scientist in his lab. "That tidy little rule book, tucked away in that mass of dogma you call a brain, is *not* a neatly paved road to salvation." Taking the seat opposite him, Duncan ran a set of long fingers through his tousled light hair. "Miles and I were born to the same parents on the same day."

"Then how–"

"Orphaned at the age of six, we learned how to survive on our wits, but we had no sense of purpose. Street urchins, they called us, and we were damn good ones. Being so young, people took pity on us, willing to spare a coin or a bite to eat. Hell, some gave us shelter for a brief time. We learned how to steal, survive, and live on barely enough to feed a bird. Some days were better than others. We did," he heaved a heavy sigh, "*whatever* it took to get by. One day, out of nowhere, knights rode into our village, spouting off about how God sent them to recruit able-bodied men for their fight against evil in the Holy Land. By then we were eighteen, and those words... those *promises* of food, shelter, never having to live on the streets, turned our heads, but the glory on Earth *and* in Heaven..." shaking his head, a blood tear coursed down his cheek as his eyes glanced at the copper-colored urn, before shooting back to Francis. "We were hooked. Having already served our time in Hell, we joined up, trained, bought into the whole "*we're right, they're wrong*" deal."

"We were right *then* and still are to this day." Francis pointed at the Bible. "Ephesians six-eleven; Put on the whole armor of God, that ye may be able to stand against the wiles of the devil."

"*Amen*. Five hundred strong we went into battle without so much as making a sound. With the blare of the trumpet, we sang loud and clear, *not to us oh Lord, not to us but to thy name give glory* and with our lances, we charged the enemy. We never yielded. We either destroyed them... or we died. We *never* backed down. Though injured, countless fought until they no longer could. Upon our return, the weak and injured set the pace for the rest of us in front... as we would leave no one behind... and the stronger of us took up the rear, still protecting them from anyone who might attack God's warriors... protectors of the faith."

"Yes. King Louis the seventh, Richard the third, and Louis the ninth *all* trusted us. We brought order to the royal army." Francis spoke with pride.

Memories of the past filled his head. Sneering, Duncan jumped up, leaning over the desk, setting his balled fists flat against the top. "*We* spilled the blood of *thousands* of Muslims. Men, women, *children*. Didn't matter to us one bit. We even slaughtered their livestock. Why? Because *God* ordained it to be. We became wealthy. Plundered gold, silver, jewels. You name it. If it had value, we took it because the *Vatican* told us that God approved. They were enemies of the Lord and therefore ours as well... their blood spilled for a worthy cause. It was righteous. That is... until King Philip the fourth… the *Fair*," he snorted, "*engineered* the election of Bertrand de Goth, making *him* Pope Clement the fifth."

"I've heard the stories."

"I *lived* them!" The glaring daggers hit their mark. "He bought cardinals, pulled strings from behind the curtain for them to do his bidding until the number of French cardinals in the Vatican's College of Cardinals equaled the Italian ones. They elected the person of *his* choosing. Bertrand. Philip wanted full control of everything… *including* the church that had cast a bad light on him after killing Boniface. In time, he moved the papal court to Avignon. Philip knew of the vast wealth we accumulated… and *wanted* it. That's when we found out about our beloved, *spineless* Vatican, and *God* didn't have *anything* to do with it. Pope Clement the fifth abolished the order."

"Yes, but the confessions–"

"They spun us as heretics, tried us, made several write *false* confessions. Then again, a man will say *anything* to stop someone from torturing him. Day in. Day out. Nothing but pain until your soul *screams* for a death that never comes. Did you know that you can break almost every bone in your body and continue to live?"

"No. That sounds painful."

"*Painful* is an understatement. It's like red-hot lava coursing through your body, igniting every nerve, every muscle, every blood cell. Then… *then*, just to make a point… they burned us at the stake. No more were Templars respected and held in high esteem. Catholics and Muslims alike hunted us, so those of us left went into hiding. Self-preservation, you might say. Miles and I… must have been about… thirty, I believe. We found out the horrible truth about the *real* enemy. It wasn't a fanatical religion that didn't agree with ours, or a king who had more power than brains. Hell, it wasn't even *our* religion. We found out about the *undead*. Immortals, who lived off the blood of human beings, even making more of their kind. Vampires. We saw a way to return our order to power. We'd rid the world of these vile creatures, save mankind, and become heroes."

"A true knight doesn't worry about being a hero," pride tinted his tone. "Our mission is and will always be the same. Destroying the evil that infects our world. That's why we captured the beast who will–"

"Shut up. You don't know the whole story, only what those who indoctrinated you into the order *wanted* you to know. You're as bad as *we* are with your lies, secrets, and betrayals." Sitting back down, Duncan took a deep breath, smoothing his trousers before continuing, resting his elbows flat on his legs. "We *tried* fighting them, thinking our faith would protect us. It didn't. Our numbers dwindled. When there were only a few hundred left, we gathered in secret at Stonehenge. We needed a plan." Turning a saddened gaze to the urn, his jaw jumped as he clenched his teeth. He tightened his hands into fists, knuckles turning white, once more cutting deep into his flesh, before slowly exhaling. "Miles brought up the idea to infiltrate their ranks. It would be easier to find out their weaknesses. *If* they even had any. Then we could exploit them. *Destroy* them. We had one way to do that… to *become* them. *Few* volunteered. That's giving your *soul* over to Satan."

"Not necessarily. God will forgive his warriors if their heart stays true." Francis crossed himself before kissing the silver crucifix around his neck.

Seeing the action, Duncan let out a small laugh. "I don't remember seeing *that* in the commandments. Perhaps you can show it to me." Waving a hand, he cut him off. "*Whatever*. It didn't *matter* to us. Our souls were a *small* price to pay to save humankind from the evil trying to destroy it. *Eighty* of us agreed to the plan. We would become one of them. Live their lives. Learn their powers. Find their weaknesses and exterminate them. That made us double agents."

"A dangerous plan, but it should've worked. What happened?"

"It didn't go as *smoothly* as we planned. Several of us were able to fight the temptation of the power compelling us to do evil. We did whatever was necessary to survive, but we were always able to keep one foot, sometimes just a toe, in the door to our humanity. Most of the others gave in and became what they hated."

"If they *truly* went to the dark side, why didn't they turn you in?"

"Maybe brotherly loyalty, or a little goodness still found within the evil… who knows." Looking off to the side, Duncan rolled his shoulders. "We made a pact at the beginning, that no matter what happened, we would *never* turn on each other. We were brothers to the grave and beyond." Looking up at Francis, Duncan's eyes turned from deep brown to a hypnotic gold.

His mind filled with sadness, alternating from the funeral service to trying to visualize what Duncan told him. Without warning, a bloody massacre began all around him. Adrenaline flooded his already frazzled nerves, confusion caused his heart to beat faster, and his breath came in short gasps.

What's going on? Where am I? How did I get here?

Spinning around, every muscle tightened as he found himself without a weapon, unable to help anyone. One man stood on a hill, laughing as the terrified people ran from him, screaming in fear. In the blink of an eye, the man appeared in front of a woman. His face twisted as sharp fangs descended. Grabbing her by the hair, he shoved a hand into her heaving chest. Shock settled in as her shrieks stopped, staring at him with wide eyes. When the man ripped out her heart, she sank to the ground with a silent thud. Turning, he began eating the still-beating muscle, her blood dripping down his arm, pooling at his feet.

Francis's stomach lurched, threatening to spill his breakfast. Beads of perspiration broke out on his forehead, running down his face as if in a marathon. His whole body shivered from head to toe as the gruesome images continued, blanketing his thoughts with never-ending horror.

As if taking a step off of a steep cliff, he fell until he landed back in his office. Grasping the chair's arms, his shattered mind tried leaving behind the remnants of the nightmare. Wiping away the sweat, Francis shot frightful eyes at Duncan. His words barely above a whisper. "*What* was *that?*"

"Evil. It isn't easy resisting *that* call. Feeling your victim's terror wash over you like a gentle breeze. Hearing the frightened heartbeat of someone in front of you," sharp incisors extended, a low menacing growl murmuring from deep within, "wanting to rip it out of their chest. Drain them of *every* drop of blood. It's an addicting drug that fills you with a sense of control. You long for it. It takes more than *just* willpower to resist. It takes gut-wrenching restraint. You feel as if your head is about to explode. Many of us couldn't deal with that kind of pressure. Then again... satisfying the need is so easy. Just reach out and take what we want. Like taking candy from a baby." Point made; his fangs retracted as he let out a deep sigh.

Francis felt the exact moment when Duncan released the mental grip on him. Shocked by how easily he crept into his mind, he rubbed his jugular protectively, clearing the terror-ridden phlegm from his throat. "I'm sorry for what you suffered for the sake of mankind. You *are* a hero. I only wish people *knew* what you sacrificed."

"As you said... a knight doesn't do things to become a hero. There are those in everyday life who do things to *better* mankind. Firefighters, police, doctors, EMT's, the military, and anyone else who rushes *into* danger to help others... instead of *away from* like cowardly mice... are the modern-day knights and heroes... and get little reward and recognition. It's who we are deep down. The true evil are those individuals fighting and doing *anything* to hurt another being. Because like any other villain, they target the weak and defenseless. *That's* why we have heroes. To protect those who don't stand a chance."

"True. I don't know of *any* who could deal with that. I know *I* couldn't." Sad eyes glanced at the urn before falling back on Duncan. "Moving on to the present. About the beast. Perhaps we skipped ahead a bit. Our emotions were on overload as we wanted to jump at the chance to capture, interrogate, and–"

"It didn't occur to you, that *maybe* you should take Miles along." His gaze fell on the urn, once more releasing a pain-shattering sigh. "In case the big bad vampire got the drop on you?"

Straightening in his chair, Francis cleared his throat again. "We discussed bringing Miles along. Just in case. However, I felt it strategically to our benefit to leave him behind. I didn't want the creature knowing vampires were working with us, nor did I feel that information needed to be divulged to his mortal victims, who I now realize are his accomplices, in case a clash happened."

"I don't normally call people idiots," his eyes snapped back at him, "but *you're* an idiot. In that puny brain of yours, you never *once* thought about how Miles could have affirmed, or refuted, your conclusion that Jonas Sparx was *the one*?"

"I saw no need to chance that because Brother Dominic's drawing was–"

"Wrong," he growled. "*Who* beheaded Miles and took it as a souvenir?"

"Sparx, I assume. Since the death of Miles, we could use your help finding him. Next time, we–"

"There won't *be* a next time, Francis." Eyeing him, Duncan tapped his fingertip against the edge of his chin. "You *assume* it was Sparx? You haven't looked at the security footage to make sure?"

"Well… not yet. I–" Realizing his error, Francis slid his laptop over. Turning it so they both could see, the men watched as a woman appeared in the frame. "His female victim. Or rather accomplice."

Duncan's eyes never left the screen, taking in all key points. When Dusty came into the picture, he allowed a slight lift at the corner of his lip, pride filling his eyes. As his brother entered the scene, he held up his hand. "Stop it there! Why doesn't she shoot him? Her weapon's drawn. Miles doesn't use guns. She has him dead to rights and has the ammunition to end his life."

"Well, I–"

"Continue."

That question, among others, egged Francis's mind as the screen fell back into motion. Miles drew his sword. A brief exchange of words between them ended when the knight turned into a statue, poised to slice the woman in half.

Continuing to watch the scene play out, Duncan's face paled – if it could get any whiter – as another man appeared. "You impotent son of a–"

"What is it? Is *this* man one of their followers too?" Having never seen Duncan afraid of anything made the tiny hairs on the back of his neck stand straight on end.

His lips pursed not wanting to witness the death of his brother. "Speed this up."

Francis's jaw almost hit the floor when the man took Miles's head. "H-how did he–"

"*That,*" Duncan said, rising from his seat, pausing the video, "is your beast. *Not* Jonas Sparx."

Unease – like seeing a toxic asp – wrapped around his spine as Francis looked hard at the solemn image on the monitor, committing the man's features to memory. "Then we will concentrate on finding *him.*"

Once again, the mad scientist took over as Duncan burst out in ironic laughter. "How many men are under your command, *Sir* Francis?"

Arching a brow at the eruption, his tone turned indignant. "Seventy-five loyal men, willing to die to prevent this apocalypse."

"Really? *That* many. If you go after *this* vampire, you'll need to dig seventy-five holes." Pointing at the figure on the screen, Duncan glared. "*That,* my dear Francis, is *Seth.* And before he kills your men, he'll make sure you watch them die. Slowly. In agony. Then, he *might* let you go so you live the rest of your life hearing their screams, or he'll turn you into a youngling and make you live with the regret for centuries."

Crinkling his brows together, he scrutinized the image. Everyone in the order heard the frightening stories about Seth. "*That's* Seth?"

Glaring at Francis, Duncan stepped back. "If you would've used your head, my brother would *still* be here. I'm holding *you* responsible." Turning to leave, he stopped at the door. "If you're serious about going after Seth, you might want to find Jonas Sparx. Maybe *beg* his forgiveness and ask to help *him.* If *anyone* is going to stop that bastard, it will be Jonas… *and* Dustina."

Before Francis could answer, the man vanished. Staring into the empty room, Duncan's strange words echoed through his mind. Seth's involvement turned this into a far more dangerous mission than before; he didn't think *that* could be possible. Curiosity got the better of him and he hit *play,* watching the glimmer of silver as the woman withdrew a shiny necklace from her shirt. She kissed it, lovingly, before tucking it back into place, hidden from the world once more. Blinking in surprise, blue eyes grew wider as his rapidly beating heart leapt into his throat.

No! It can't be!

Taking a screenshot, he enhanced the image, narrowing in on the gold and silver crucifix. His face blanched as recognition lined his features. His knees shook before losing all strength, falling back into the chair. "God help us all!"

2

The malicious storm outside paled in comparison to the wintry gale going on in Dusty's tattered mind. As she sat, half-heartedly stroking Hooch's ghostly fur, she tried not beating herself up about letting Travis in. Unbeknownst to her, when they dated, he got through the extra protective casing guarding her heart. Combination? Psh. He didn't need one. Travis just snapped his fingers and all the iron-clad locks and complicated gizmos, holding everything tucked in tightly, broke open, allowing him in. When the two of them were together, they were great; two best friends meeting for a night of passion that would make anyone envious.

Those smoldering hazel-green eyes had a way of staring into her soul, pulling her into his charismatic spell. Maybe his sexy baritone, dumb hillbilly act – letting her take point in their joint investigations *and* take all the credit for figuring things out – appealed to her. Then again, it could be how the two of them fit perfectly in bed, both satiated and neither able to walk right for hours. If a soulmate existed for her in this crazy world, it *had* to be Travis… that is… until he shot her. From that moment on, he stamped: *Request Denied* on *anything* the two of them *might* have had.

Staring out the window, the bloody battle continued, duking it out with herself. With every punch, Dusty felt her defenseless heart shatter a little more. Travis used to call her every other day *just* to hear her voice. It didn't take much convincing to turn that phone call into a face-to-face meeting. All he had to do was mention trouble with a case and she was all in. Soon after he arrived, it turned into the two of them having fun together with Hooch. Cheerful memories filtered through her mind; half of them made her laugh and smile, others made her want to cry. Oddly enough, she could easily see herself settling down with Travis Knight, popping out a cute little brat or two with his eyes and her hair.

"Never had to worry about that. Don't plan on it either."

"Why do you say that with such certainty? I didn't expect to fall in love. Sometimes you can't help it. Just happens."

"Meh. Maybe for some, not me. My heart's in a fire-proof safe with a complicated lock. Men have sex on the brain, not frustrating locking systems." Shrugging, she turned to the white sheet staked over the body. *"Sounds more like a debilitating disease. Stops people from thinking, much less living."*

She didn't lie. Travis had wormed his way into her heart without her even knowing it.

A dull ache started between her eyes. The recollection of that conversation – trying hard to compete with the loving memories of Travis – had no chance of ever winning. Sighing, she slumped further into the seat. She wanted to open an escape hatch in her mind so she could get far away from those tear-jerking memories. If possible, she would throw them into a roaring inferno, making them yesterday's ashes, and watch them float away. She didn't need any complicated locking systems because her heart already belonged to Travis.

Hating herself for thinking in that forbidden venue – *he shot her* – she banged her head back into the soft chair, trying to delete that ugly thought, angrily running a hand through her hair. Tears threatened to break through in a torrential monsoon, making her wish to curl up in a bed, and cry it out. As a stray tear journeyed down her cheek, she quickly swatted it away.

Antoine fidgeted in his window seat as the weather played a game of hacky sack with the jet. *"Can't* this thing go *above* the storm? I feel like I'm in an elevator, and it can't make up its *damn* mind!"

Not affected by the tumultuous shaking of the jet, Dusty glanced out the window, her mind a million miles away. "It's *just* a storm, Antoine. I'm sure the pilots have flown through these a *million* and one times."

"Are you *sure?* How do *you* know?! Did you interview them *before* we got on this plane? Did *any* of us *meet* them? *How* do *we* know they aren't part of Seth's crew?" The roiling maelstrom of wind pounded on his window as shards of blinding fury raced past, each tendril of white-hot electricity-producing a larger detonation of super-heated air. *"Oh my God!* Did you *see* that? I'm gonna be sick."

Snapping her head in his direction, Dusty frantically tried looking out his window. "What is it? Is the *engine* off? A *fire*? Something wrong with the *plane*?"

Looking out the window in stark fear, Antoine spun around, shooting a wide-eyed gasp at Dusty. "*What* made you ask *that*? Does *that* happen a *lot*?"

"Well… no." Inwardly, she winced for putting more erratic thoughts into his head. "Just asking the *worst*-case scenarios because… well… you look scared out of your *bleeping* mind. If it's not a worst-case scenario happening, what are ya freaking out about then?"

"That *lightning* just turned the blacker than night sky into broad daylight. *Broad daylight! BLAM! Daylight*! Then it quickly faded back to darkness so I could *see* how *close* the lightning is to us when it cuts through the clouds! *Jesus, Lord, save me*!" He clutched at the armrest, his head rolling back and forth against the back of the seat. "*We're going down*! *I just know it*! *Abandon ship*!"

"It's a *plane*, Antoine." Jonas chuckled softly.

"Doesn't matter, *Jonas*! It's the end, *that's* what it is! *We're gonna die*! I'm *never* gonna have another cheeseburger."

"This is the captain speaking," the voice crooned over the PA. "We've run into a *little* storm that just jumped in front of us so it's going to be a *slight* bit bumpy. I need you to remain in your seats and buckle up. Don't worry. We've handled *much* worse."

"*Buckle our seatbelts?* They *only* tell us to do that when there's trouble. Or they think we're gonna *crash*!" Antoine quickly buckled in. Tiny beads broke out on his forehead as his facial expression screamed out his words. "Dear Lord! We're gonna die!"

"Oh, Antoine." With the rocking of the jet, Dusty staggered over – looking like a drunk after a weekend binge drinking session – collapsing into the chair beside him. "We're *not* gonna die." Snapping her belt in place, she reached over and secured his. "God *wouldn't* allow this plane to go down in flames when *we're* needed to *save* the world."

White knuckling his armrests, he shook his head heatedly back and forth. "*Nope*! I'm not buying it! *How* can you be so sure? Are ya having meetings with God now? Next time pull me in. I have a thing or *two* to say to Him about *how* we're being treated!"

Taking a soothing tone, one used on Hooch, Dusty ran a soft hand over his tightly clenched fists. "Antoine, calm down. It's gonna be okay. God's been watching out for me since I was born, and He won't stop now."

Still shaking his head, his eyes flickered around the jet, fingers continuing to death-grip the armrests. "*How* can you say that with so much *conviction*? You lived a life of *hell*, worse than *both* of us put together, and it *hasn't* gotten any better *yet*!"

Canting his head to the side, Jonas scrunched up his brows. "I'm not so –"

"If *that's* looking out for you, *I* don't wanna be on His shit list," Antoine screamed.

"I'm still *here*, aren't I?" Clearing her throat, she pulled the side table out. "*He* didn't make my uncle a crackpot. The *war* did. Some… life or death war. Not sure which. He didn't like talking about it. All he ever spoke about was *how* I needed to be prepared in case of some natural disaster that rocked the planet."

"Still! *He* could've made it easier on you!"

"That which doesn't kill us makes us stronger. Had I *not* lived the life I did… I *wouldn't* be able to deal with all *this*. I'd be off living an easy life somewhere, unaware of the dangers surrounding my happy home." Then she thought about that for a moment. "On second thought…"

Antoine cringed at a blast of white lightning in the dark sky. "Lord have mercy! We're going into the *Bermuda Triangle*!"

Unable to keep from laughing, Jonas shook his head. "We're nowhere *near* the Bermuda Triangle, Antoine. It's only storm-related turbulence."

"No, it's not!" Antoine argued. "*Something* is trying to pull the damn plane apart! I swear I can hear the bolts jiggling! This ain't normal. Now I see why Dean freaked out on the plane when the demons were taking it over."

Dusty's brows shot up into a question mark. "Wait, what?! When did *that* happen? I'd think Cider Lake would've been gossiping all day and night about that! Churches overflowing with new members. I wonder how I missed it!"

"Supernatural," Jonas offered, finding the whole scene comical. "He's talking about a TV show."

Nodding, Antoine's voice raised an octave. "Yes! And it *looked* the same as *this*!"

Taking a deep breath, she took his hand, speaking in a calming tone. "Antoine, this *isn't* a TV show. Lord have mercy, with the way you both talk about them, it's a good thing. We think we have it rough *now*? Just imagine if we had to worry about demons too. *This* is reality. We're not gonna crash. There's nothing wrong with the plane. It didn't come alive and nothing is attacking us. It's *just* the weather." Pulling over the satchel, she took out the quatrain. "Now, let's figure this thing out."

"*Now*?!" Antoine's face went pale as he looked out the window again. "You wanna work at a time like this when we're about to die?!"

"We're *not* about to die. *Man*! You'd think you *never* flew in a plane during a storm before. *Stop* looking out there and look at *this*!" Tugging the shade in place, she pointed down to the riddle. "Yes, let's work on it *now*. It's in English this time so that'll make it easier. Surely, we can figure this out."

"*Okay*! And don't call me Shirley."

"*What*?! I didn't call you *Shirley*! I know what your *daggum* name is."

Snickering, Jonas looked over at the two. "*Airplane*!"

With a puzzled expression, she shot a glance toward Jonas's window. "An *airplane*? *Where*?! Coming *at* us?"

Laughing, he shook his head. "No, it's… um… never mind. Not important."

Struggling with the desire to give him a tongue lashing, she turned back to Antoine, pointing at the quatrain. "Come on now. It'll take your mind off what's happening out *there*."

After redirecting his death-defying scenarios onto the brain-twister, the two were like a comedy act – arguing as a father and daughter would. At first, he found it amusing, seeing the adorable bond they shared, then it grew boring. Gazing out the small window, Jonas tried stilling the million different thoughts flying around his head – as if on their own turbulent path. Closing his eyes, he tried relaxing for the long flight.

The turbulence faded as the jostling ride smoothed out. Turning to Antoine with a sarcastic quip, Jonas opened his eyes. The jet disappeared. Seated beside Bacchus, the sarcastic 'here we go again' trailed across his face as he pivoted his head. He sat in a darkened movie theater with only two seats.

"Is this business or pleasure?" Getting comfortable, he stretched out his long legs. "At least it's front row seating."

A disapproving scowl creased the ancient's face. "How cocky you've become. Reel in the attitude. You need to understand what Kanis is capable of."

"I *know* what he's capable of." His voice took on a hard edge. "I know more than *anyone*."

"You don't know the *half* of it. The *rumor* about him killing off the vampire council is *nothing* compared to the truth."

"*Rumor*? So, it's *not* true?"

"Oh, it is *quite* true. Watch and pay attention. You *might* actually learn something."

As the words started across the movie screen, like the beginning of *Star Wars*, Jonas nudged Bacchus. "Reading?! You could've at *least* supplied some buttered popcorn with this."

Bacchus shook his head. "Younglings."

...

Stupid, dumb luck. It happens all the time. Someone walks into a store for a six pack, drops a buck on a small slip of paper, and the next day they have enough money to buy a round for the entire city. Luck doesn't care if you're good, bad, or a vampire. It falls where it will... when it will. On a clear September day in 2001, luck – good and bad – fell on vampire and human alike. The world of both changed forever.

The eastern headquarters of LaDevia Enterprises – only tenant on the eightieth floor of the South Tower – buzzed with deal makers and breakers, working in a frenzy. Different aftershaves and fragrances filled the air, from overpriced perfumes to bargain-basement Eau De Toilette. Security cameras lined the entire floor as if Fort Knox itself moved there. Just a normal Tuesday, except for *her* presence.

Katarina Breen, dressed in her dark, gray, business suit, stepped from the elevator, instantly quieting the entire floor. A well-cared-for briefcase – with a seven-digit numerical lock – swung from the end of her arm, gripped tightly as if it were the nuclear football. Employees shared concerned glances. The talk around the water cooler flourished with vicious rumors about how *The Ice Queen*, assistant to the council, only came in for a major shakeup to record the minutes or dispose of a body. Black heels imprinted the plush, dark, wall-to-wall carpeting, as she strode past a line of occupied workstations divided by Plexiglas. The tinted, exterior windows distorted her reflection.

Emergency meeting. Come at once.

The urgent text came in just minutes after she stepped out of the shower, hurrying her along. Foregoing her usual large, Caramel Macchiato, double shot, she made it to the office within seconds.

Glancing over her shoulder, penetrating gray eyes told gawkers to *get back to work*. Catching that knowing look, idling personnel ran into each other in their haste. Scurrying off in opposite directions, they desperately searched for something productive to do.

Placing her thumb on the fingerprint reader, she leaned forward, eyeing the retinal scanner. "Katarina Breen. G-seven-nine-four-B-X-one-one-zero-eight." A green laser shot out.

The voice-recognition software spoke back. "Katarina Breen. Accepted."

With a whoosh, the heavy doors opened. Once inside, they quickly closed again. Soundproof entrances stopped the bleeding echoes from oozing through.

The darkened headquarters of the central administration held an odd mix of contemporary and Gothic decor. Twin dragon water fountains stood on either side, filling the room with the gentle sound of flowing water. Priceless works of art by Van Gogh, Monet, and Renoir adorned the office wall. The glass shelving held Crown Royal to an ultra-rare bottle of Glenmorangie from the mid-eighteen-hundreds. The twelve swords, representing the elders, hung on the sable paneled walls. Fifty-inch screens adorned two of them with one tuned to *Wall Street,* with picture-in-picture showing the latest in the stock market exchange, while the other showed black and white episodes of *The Untouchables.*

A large 'U-shaped' desk, hewn from seven-hundred-year-old Bloodwood, functioned as the centerpiece with a podium at the midpoint. Twelve council members sat in front of their open laptops – the LaDevia insignia on the front covers – waiting for the days wheeling and dealings to begin. An armed bodyguard stood at attention behind each of them.

Respectfully, Katarina bowed her head to the man at the crest of the table. "Please forgive my tardiness. I came as soon as I got your message."

The man smiled. "Think nothing of it, my dear. Please set up so we may begin."

Katarina opened the briefcase, removing a handful of manila folders. After turning the steno machine on – an archaic way to keep records but she preferred hard copies – her fingers swiftly moved over the keys, starting the minutes, dictating those present, date, and time. Once complete, she nodded, glancing to the one standing in the center whose gruesome reputation preceded him.

After seating himself, Darius Novak, head of the vampire council, looked around, gray eyes surveying those within the room. "Thank you all for arriving so quickly. I apologize for the dramatic flair. I call this emergency meeting open for new business. The first order is a request from Kanis Vorteck." That said, he turned his attention back to the man standing. "Kanis, we will now hear your motion and argument."

The tall man took his place at the podium. "I move we start the prophecy so stated in the elder scroll. I found the three mentioned.

Now that we know their location, we *must* take any and *all* measures to keep them safe. This may be our *only* opportunity."

The room erupted with clear laughter as half of those present relaxed in their seats, talking softly amongst themselves.

"How *absurd*!"

"To think, I sat here worrying about *that*!"

"I know! A *joke*. Nothing but a joke."

"A good one, but a *joke* all the same."

Wide-eyed, shocked into silence, the other half didn't mock the *ridiculous* motion. They knew the daunting reputation and capabilities of the man requesting it and looked paler than usual.

Darius gave the man a pitying look as he quieted the outcry with a raised hand, before running it through his dark hair. "Kanis, you cannot expect this council to even *consider* your proposal. It is not only *ludicrous* but also self-destructive."

Nodding in agreement, staggered murmurs echoed from the others.

Letting out a disgusted snort, Kanis's deep-set eyes angrily scanned over the group. "You have *all* grown complacent. *Fat* in your success. Can you not see we are *destined* to rule? The day of man's grip is over."

A disapproving frown creased Darius's forehead. "In all my thousand years, I do not believe I have heard *anything* so ridiculous. Let sleeping dogs lie. We should *not* disrupt the peace we share. They have *no* knowledge of us, save handsome, charming, fictional characters they *adore*. If they knew otherwise, it would do no good for them *or* us."

Kanis's anxious expression flat lined. "You call this *peace*? Why... we are nothing more than *pets* doing *anything* to please them."

"Staying in the shadows is *far* different than being a *pet*."

"Do *none* of you see what this means for us? We will be powerful beyond our own dreams." Excitement traced his features as Kanis spread both hands out. Mesmerized with their own fantasies, a few of the council members smiled. "Imagine what we can do with *that* kind of power. We will rule the *world*! They will cower like diseased *rats* while we dine openly… as we *should*. No longer will we be scavengers, but *rulers* of the jungle. *Predators*. Marking our prey. Hunting them. *Reveling* in their fear. Once again, we will have kings in place of presidents, keeping world order among our slaves. For *that* is what will become of them! To do with as we please *without* ramifications for our actions because *we* are the law! No longer will we allow them to destroy the planet with their petty wars."

Like a rogue virus, the savory thought marinated with those seated at the table. They remembered how it *used* to be, before having to blend into the darkened shadows. Fictional creations, romantic idols, all shoved into the make-believe section of the public libraries. Tucked into the closet, bound into hiding, demented authors turning them into nothing more than sparkling fantasies or bloodcurdling nightmares.

"You're right. We *could*." Darius waited until everyone looked at him before taking back control, hitting home with his point. "Then they would join ranks, stop fighting amongst each other, and bring war to *our* doorstep. We are *not* invincible. They would kill *each* of us. *We* would be their enemy. Nothing brings mortals closer than fighting the same foe. Need I remind you how much they sorely outnumber us? *That* war will bring out the knights and *this* time… they will win. *No* one wants to go through *that* again."

As if watching a challenging tennis match, the council turned from one to the other with renewed sparks of interest. Those magically drawn into Kanis's speech saw an imaginary world; rich, powerful, vampires running everything. Darius brought out the reality of that pipe dream. If they tried bringing an ancient prophecy on to mankind, the Knights Templar would all come together – out of their hidden sanctuaries – and war with them again.

Over the years, bold vampires grew uninhibited, divulging critical secrets. Most agreed with Darius. Though treacherous beyond a mere mortal's scope of possibility, they weren't invincible. The possible gain would be far less than the cost. The few still siding with Kanis, cast wary glances at him.

Seeing he had lost the remainder of those ready to join him in battle, Kanis clicked his tongue in disgust. "You make it sound like they would have the upper hand. Need I remind you that we have learned things since the *last* battle with mortals and will not *easily* die."

"Need I remind *you* of the vampires who still care for the mortals?"

"One should not play with *food*."

Darius released a heavy sigh. "Kanis, we *all* agree it sounds heavenly. Ruling the world again. Not breathing to blend in when it's unnecessary. Never shielding our *true* selves for fear of destruction."

"Then join me! We can change things for the better!"

"*But*… we *also* know it would *never* be that simple. Mortals have changed. They are more offended and insulted over the slightest little things. Not all, but *some* are offended at their *own* skin color, warring with others because of it!"

"Because they're so miserable, *they* would join *us*!"

"And infect us with their stupidity? *That* would be the *end* of our race as we fight each *other*! It isn't worth the gamble. As a friend, I'm *asking* you to take back your request. Withdraw this *ridiculous* notion."

Irritated, Kanis's eyes snapped in Darius's direction. "You call me *friend*, yet will not sway this council on my behalf?"

"This council exists for the well-being of us *all*. What you are asking jeopardizes not only *that* welfare but our *very* existence. You cannot put your own selfish agenda before our race. Leave that to the humans." Walking over, Darius placed a hand on Kanis's shoulder. "Once… we called each other brother, bonded by *more* than blood. I *beg* you, abandon this quest. We exist in peace with mankind. With Deva's help, we –"

"*Deva!*" Kanis lurched from Darius as if his touch burned. "She should be *dead*, or in Torpor. *You* fear her! *I* do not! She is a nobody. Worse. A flea on a mongrel, scraping for a meal! When Seth has risen, he will make sure *she* is no longer a thorn in my side."

The air crackled as if the fabric of time shifted. "*That* doesn't sound good." Darius backed away, eyes widening.

A rotating black twister dropped from the ceiling into the center of the room, causing the neat piles of papers on the desk to blow around the room. With a shriek that only dogs could hear, Katarina frantically raced behind, clawing at them. The water from the fountains, flying laptops, pens, bottles of liquor, pencils, and chairs all joined the swirling mass. A priceless Ming Vase forced the group on high alert, streaking over their heads, easily avoiding outstretched hands.

Tendrils of lightning spread across the ceiling, making everyone duck again. The intense heat promised to burn anyone standing too close; instantly making the office a sauna. The room filled with the biting odor of sulfur.

A thunderous roar threatened to tear the building apart with an earthquake so wicked it growled like a rabid dog, pulsating the massive windows, threatening to explode them outward.

Just as suddenly as it started, the vexatious squall stopped.

Twisting pages fluttered back into place, to the amazement of the woman still feverishly trailing behind. Liquid streamed across the ceiling returning to each of the fountains, once more filling the room with the soft sounds of bubbling water. Unharmed, all objects miraculously went back to their points of origin as the room's fever dissipated, along with the odor. Except for mussed hair and clothing from those trying to capture the flyaway artifacts, everything returned to normal.

Almost.

Deva LaDevia, dressed for more of an evening out than a business meeting, stood between the two fountains, a heated scowl on her beautiful face. Darting eyes cast sidelong glances in her direction. The plunging, laced neckline of her leather romper gave the men an eyeful of her titillating peaks and valleys. The long fabric in the back dusted the floor. It opened in front, revealing a pair of long legs that porn stars would kill for, poured into four-inch stiletto-heels, caressing perfect feet. Three laces wrapped over blood-red toenails, before snaking around her ankles. Only one thing surpassed her power – her beauty. Vampires made Hollywood seem like a leper colony.

Ignoring the gawks and serpentine grins, bright blue eyes glared ice daggers. Dressed in the finest Armani suits, the council mirrored an ad out of a GQ magazine instead of twelve of the deadliest creatures to walk the Earth. Even their goons sported tailor-made outfits, though not with the equivalent high price tag. Seeing all the nonessential bling, Deva made a mental note to cut next year's clothing allowance from the budget – they could pay for their own exorbitant tastes.

The uninvited guest did not go unnoticed as the guards stepped her way with all intentions of seeing her out.

Snapping her head in their direction, a devious grin lined her lips, stopping them in their tracks. "Oh, I *wish* you would. I am feeling," she winked, "*hungry.*"

Sighing, Darius gestured the men back to their posts.

Finely shaped brows crumpled, eyeing each council member with revulsion, curious to which one had the kind of power to razzle dazzle her into the room, not to mention chutzpah. "Of all days for you to interrupt me." Keeping her anger in check strained her usual alluring British accent. "I was right in the middle of an *important* corporate meeting. What is so bloody pressing with," she waved her hand in annoyance, ignoring the constant ringing of her phone, "whatever *this* is."

Everyone in the vampire community knew of Deva – and her lethal reputation – and most feared her. The slow murmur started as concerned council members began discussing the sudden disruption. When Deva unexpectedly showed up – unannounced and uninvited – for an impromptu meeting, it usually meant someone's death. Vicious rumors and speculations scattered around the world, but nothing beat the real deal. It made everyone at the table uneasy and they weren't afraid to share that with each other, watching her cautiously.

Darius glared. "Deva –"

"Kanis *Vorteck.*" Deva's lip curled fastidiously, dropping her tone an octave, pronouncing his name like an ancient curse. The unclouded irritation poured from her eyes as she appeared before him.

"Deva *LaDevia.*" He repaid the favor.

"I should've *known* it was *you*, of all people, responsible for the disruption in my schedule." Glancing at her pricey watch, she motioned for him to continue, turning those icy glaciers back in his direction. "Get on with it. I've got other... more *important* things to deal with. What nonsense are you driveling on about *now*?"

Unimpressed, Kanis returned her disapproving expression. "I was not aware that *you* would be present for the meeting, but no worries. I have located the three mentioned in the Elder Scroll. With them, I will empower Seth to his destiny. He will sweep aside *any* who stand against him." Brazenly staring her in the eyes, he smirked. "Even his *whore*."

Unaffected by the intended insult, she reached up, slapping his face with a mocking, hurtful expression, before squeezing his cheeks together. "Aw. You're *still* upset he chose *me* over you? Jealousy is such a dreadful *mortal* emotion, Kanis."

The heat rose under his collar, pouring out onto his face, as he brusquely shoved her hand away. He turned to strike, but with a snap of her fingers in his face, paralysis struck him, leaving him rooted in one spot.

Turning to Darius, she stifled a yawn. "You called me here for *him*? If *you* cannot control this," moving her hands in erratic motions, she roughly messed up Kanis's hair, "ignorant imbecile, I assure you *I* can. Would you like me to show you *how*?"

Darius's lips clamped into a thin line as he turned his crossness on her. "The council will deal with Kanis. As for calling you here, I have *no* idea what you're talking about! We –"

The large oak clock on the wall stopped at eight thirty-five. All twelve council members froze. The room turned silent. Coffee waterfalls from pot to cup stalled. The fountain water stopped moving, frozen in time, creating a Daliesque scene.

Unaffected by the sudden change, Deva glanced out the window at the birds stopped in mid-flight. Staring at the frozen Darius, Deva's brow arched. "You cannot blame this one on *me*! I had *nothing* to do with it."

"Now Deva," came a sexy baritone from the shadows.

"Ugh." A frustrated groan puffed out her cheeks. "I should've *known* that none of *these* imbeciles had *that* kind of power. I'll have you know that you yanked me from a crucial meeting. I'm going to have to play *hell* in explaining how I just *Houdinied* out of the room! Good thing there were only a *few* mortals in there."

"*You're* not playing nicely."

Rolling her eyes, she held up a hand. "Save the lecture. As agreed, *I* stayed away from him, but he just couldn't keep his mouth shut! *He* started it, and *this* time," she bore crimson eyes in his direction, "*I'm* bloody well going to *finish* it!"

A hooded figure stepped forth. Removing the cowl revealed a very handsome man with brown hair and silver eyes. In his presence, *everyone* appeared homely. Turning to Deva, he smiled. "You *know* Kanis has to do this. Now, I realize he called you a whore –"

"Among *other* things," she grumbled.

The corner of his lip lifted. "And you'd like nothing more than to *end* his infuriating existence."

"So, let me."

"Can't. We *need* him to play his part. Without him, it *won't* happen."

"Fine, then get on with it. *Why* did you call me here? *What* is so *bloody* important?"

Reaching into Kanis's calf-length overcoat, the man carefully withdrew an ancient piece of writing. Unrolling it, he read aloud. "So, it is written, in the blood of our king when Marduk is attacked for six days and nights, a single mortal soul will be split thrice. Each part will find rest near the others, and breath will fill their lungs as the sun rises in the ninth month after. They will bear the mark of Zeus's fire and by this mark, shall we find them. At eighteen cycles, and unknown to man, must they be brought forth, to the one worthy enough. He shall consume them, joining the three to one, and thus empower himself to assemble the Bloodstone. From his seed will rise the promise made to our maker. A world of the damned, created to destroy the pale God. Mark well this scroll, for should the time pass, it will not come again, and we shall perish forever."

"*That's* what he ranted on about? He doesn't have a *clue*." Taking a deep breath, a knowing look crossed her features, before exhaling slowly. "So… *it* begins."

"Yes." Rolling up the scroll, he replaced it. "Pretty wordy, isn't it?"

"They always are. Let me teach Kanis a lesson. Just a small nibble. It will make him respect," an evil sneer lit up her face, "or *hate* me even more. I'm fine with both."

After staring at Kanis for a moment, the man nodded back at Deva. "If you *must* but do it quickly. From what I have gleaned, you do *not* want to be here in twenty-eight minutes."

Nodding, she swiftly retraced her steps. "Very well. I will make this brief. Meet me back at the castle."

"As you wish. Pay attention to what you see," he said, bowing slightly before vanishing as the second hand on the clock resumed its march.

"– did *not* call you," Darius erupted, finishing his sentence.

Feigning ignorance, a confused expression traced across Deva's face. Opening her mouth, she fumbled for the right words before wide eyes glanced around. "Wait. Y-you didn't?"

"No." Darius didn't hide the questioning look on his face. Usually, Deva knew about every event happening in the vampire world. This threw him – and the rest of the council – for a loop and it showed.

Running a hand through blonde strands, she nibbled on the inside of her cheek. Furrowing brows traced lines in her face as she appeared to be working it out in her head. "Then who –" As if a light bulb exploded, she snapped her fingers, turning apologetic, wide eyes back to the council. "Oh my! That *stupid* girl did it *again!*" Deva looked at Darius through half-shaded eyelashes, giving him an embarrassed smile and a slight giggle. "My *sincerest* apologies! I'm training a new girl and she has my schedule *all* messed up. You wouldn't know what that's like." Turning, she smiled at Katarina. "You've got the *best* assistant."

Beaming from the compliment, Katarina nodded her head in acknowledgment and thanks.

"If *ever* you need a job, my door is *always* open." Winking, she turned back to the council. "*Please*, forgive this unnecessary intrusion. I did not mean to just barge in here uninvited. You have your own... issues, it would seem. I'll read all about it in the minutes, yes?"

Not exactly convinced by her performance, Darius nodded. "As always, your majesty."

"Very well. Now, what should I do with the troublemaker?"

"Release him, please."

Walking around Kanis, the sneer turned to a pout. "Are you *sure*? If I keep him like this, you won't have to listen to him prattle on about things –"

"*Now*, Deva."

Sighing, she lightly shrugged. "Fine. If you insist, but before I do." Without another word, she grabbed Kanis, a fistful of black hair twisted between her fingers, clutching tightly to his skull. White, glistening fangs poised over his jugular, making her purr. "I'm just going to teach him a little lesson on what happens when he goes against me, so that he doesn't try it again." Yanking his head back, she plunged deep into his vein.

Wide-eyed, the council winced at the utmost humiliation and violation. Deva's actions – using Kanis like a juicy box drink – went against their laws, not to mention being downright rude. Instinctively, all of them put a hand protectively to their own necks.

"*Opprobrious*!" Darius shouted in shock. This action alone – though well-deserved – could undo centuries of disciplined behavior and ruin the fine, upstanding reputation the council held. A place of peace where they guaranteed no harm would befall any who stood before them. Well, there went *that* promise.

It only took one drop for her to withdraw, spitting on the floor in revulsion. "Ugh! *That* is the most *disgusting* thing I've *ever* had the misfortune of putting into my mouth! Talk about a rotten soul. *This* man is tainted to the *core*." Arching a brow, she dismissively waved her hand. "Doesn't matter. I have a busy schedule and must return. Good day, gentlemen," turning to Katarina, she winked, "and lady."

In the blink of an eye, she disappeared.

Released from the spell, a mortified Kanis instantly covered the bleeding wounds before they sealed on their own. "Where is she? I will –"

"*Enough!*" Raising a hand, Darius stopped any further outbursts. "*This* day is turning into a bloody *circus* act! *No* more! *This* is your *last* chance, Kanis. Turn away from this ridiculousness or it *will* be your demise!"

Scowling tightly, Kanis made a sweeping motion with his hand. "I would rather die under Deva's boot than tie myself to a bunch of *sniveling* weaklings. It is *you* who will crawl and beg. *Beg* for Seth's mercy. It is *I* who will laugh when he *rips* your cowardly hearts from your chests."

Darius emitted a heavy sigh. "As you wish. The council will now vote. All in favor of Kanis's motion, please signal with a raise of your hand."

Only Kanis raised his hand.

"All opposed?"

Twelve hands rose, though a few did so slowly.

"It is unanimous. Twelve against. Having lost your position in the council, *your* vote no longer matters."

"I will see that *your* vote means *nothing* to this prophecy," Kanis snarled.

Taking on a distant stare, Darius walked back to his seat. "It saddens me *more* than I can say, but you leave me *no* choice. Kanis Vorteck, you, your children, and *any* who follow your demented ideas, are hereby *exiled* from the vampire community. *All* will shun you. Further attempts to fulfill this *prophecy* of yours will result in your death. Am I understood?"

"I understand that you are *fools*. Fat and lazy, willing to coexist with our *sworn* enemy. Know this… when the time comes –"

The room shuddered, silencing Kanis as everyone peered around in surprise.

"What just happened?" Quickly rushing to the window, Darius glanced in all directions, but nothing appeared out of the ordinary. Turning back to Kanis, he pointed to the door. "Go now before you say something you *will* regret."

Turning on his heel, Kanis made his way out. "It is *you* who will regret your words." Slamming the door behind him, his mind worked out the details of the council's demise. People quickly moved out of his way. Seeing the hysterical, large crowd gathered at the elevator, he turned toward the stairwell.

A bike messenger stopped him. "Man, it's like eighty-hundred floors down or something."

"Good for my cholesterol," Kanis told him before vanishing.

"Fuckin' A! You're like that Criss Angel guy!"

An apocalyptic scene greeted him. Loud sirens sounded as police herded bewildered people away from the area. A terrified woman ran past him. Reaching out, he grabbed her arm. "What happened?"

One minute she ran as if her life depended on it, and the next she came to a complete stop. It rattled her grief-stricken mind and took a moment for the traumatized nerves in her legs to get over the radical change in course. Angrily looking up at Kanis, ready to let loose on him, she found her expression easing to a friendlier one. "Only the worst thing you could fucking imagine! I was just sitting over there, on my fucking lunchbreak, minding my own business… when BAM! There was this loud ass explosion. For fuck sake! It was fucking *horrible*! A fucking plane just flew into the *tower*. How the fuck does a big ass plane just fly into the fucking tower?" Shaking off a delayed full body shiver from his touch, she turned back on her way. "I think there's been a fucking war called. I gotta get my kids. Stay safe!" That said, the agitated New Yorker ran off as if he hadn't stopped her.

Kanis excitedly looked up to the plume of thick, black smoke rising from the North Tower. His face fell instantly. "Wrong building." Watching humanity face a horrifying disaster proved luscious. Tornadoes, hurricanes, floods, earthquakes – he had seen them all, but when people died by their own design *that* thrilled him to the core. Finding a good vantage point, he settled in to enjoy the show.

"Mm. The smell of death takes me back to the good old days," a feminine voice cooed. "Back when corpses littered the streets and rats ran among them. All we had to do was snatch one into an alley with no one the wiser. Just another dead body tossed among the many."

Seeing Amelia Vargas – full-time vampire archivist/part-time psycho bitch – take a seat next to him, Kanis pointed to the smoldering building. "My dear, if *only* that had happened to the *other* tower. We could be rid of –"

A roar split the air – the deafening sound of a screaming engine stuck in the wrong gear – followed by a loud explosion. Debris hit the street like projectile weapons, taking out cars and people along the way. It added chaos to panicked New Yorkers – crying, calling home, screaming about war. Off in the distance, an isolated few cheered on rooftops for the brutal victory of the suicide pilots.

Kanis's brow rose. "There *is* a God after all."

Amelia's face lit up as she watched the chaos unfold. "So much beautiful death." Her eyes, pools of smoky gray, turned lavender. "It's almost orgasmic."

"While I don't share your *personal* pleasure, I agree the aroma is *most* exhilarating. Takes me back to the Crusades. The Knights Templar thought they could defeat us with their puny weapons. Remember the delicious agony in their cries for mercy?" His eyes closed as a look of pure ecstasy lit on his face.

Kanis and Amelia sat watching the carnage, sporting mollified grins of pleasure. Christian, Catholic, Jew, Muslim, anarchist, liberal, conservative, patriot, black, white, yellow, gay, straight, and transgender. Their mundane, pissy issues – which humans fought endless wars over – none of that mattered to *them*. These *people* were cattle with one purpose; to die.

After watching for shy of an hour – making bets on how many people would jump to their deaths, getting a thrill when one did – Amelia pursed her lips. "Kanis, I hate to be the bearer of bad news," her tone held a challenge, "but the elders *didn't* die. Not *one* has crossed over. For all we know, they're not even *in* there any longer."

Staring up at the smoldering tower, his eyes flashed. "No, they are *still* there." Looking around, he spotted an abandoned soda can. Picking it up, he set it on the ground between them. Closing his eyes, he spoke an ancient tongue before flattening it with the palm of his hand. The South Tower followed suit. Grinning wickedly, he pointed. "They *won't* survive that."

The skyscraper imploded in on itself – the guts of the building dropped, pulling the exterior inward – as if the hand of God fell upon it. Terror-stricken people ran haphazardly while clutching tightly to their belongings. Large numbers looked to the sky, screaming out the same question, "are we at war?!"

Petrified people quickly made their way out of the nearest buildings, surrounding the tower, as mighty beams thrust through the structure, caving in walls. Blocks away, screaming throngs tried escaping huge chunks of concrete as they burst through the pavement. It turned reality into a virtual 'Frogger-like' game. Earsplitting cries, squealing car alarms and horns blared through the dusty area, as speeding vehicles collided into each other; running into and over people in their haste.

One man ran in a zigzag pattern, trying to avoid the heavy objects, pulling his wife along behind him. A colossal shard of glass sliced him in half, sending his ensanguined upper torso wailing to the ground. The last remaining seconds, his shattered mind strained to make sense of everything as he swam amid his internal organs in a pool of blood.

Witnessing the gory scene, the woman beside him screeched, trying to release the death grip of the hand still holding on, jumping back in horror. Devastation raked her body as sadness took over, spilling tears down her face, clouding her vision. Turning in a complete circle, her thoughts raced.

Is this a nightmare? Is this real?

Before she could take another step, a heavy column splattered her in every direction.

Stained with fresh warm blood, horrified bystanders fell to their knees wailing.

It continued in that span of time – minutes feeling like hours – as rubble fell from the sky. As the death toll increased, confusion turned to howls. The second horseman arrived with no end to his fury. Blasts of thick, gray, ash-filled smoke poured from his steed's nostrils, slamming helpless people to the ground.

A hypersensitive rush filled Amelia. No drug ever took her to such a euphoria; the aroma of death, painful wails, human suffering, all combined into sweet nirvana, but it didn't last long. One of her gifts – though she called it a curse – being the one and only gateway to Hell for any condemned, vampiric, deceased soul. At that moment, thirty 'nobody' vampires slammed into her, marking her soul with their names. Early on, she learned how to manage that without showing the slightest flinch or hiccup. Her blood recorded all their memories, children created, as well as every detail about life before and after rebirth.

None of that compared to the most powerful vampires in existence, rushing through, making her pray for death. Invisible swords pierced her convulsing body. One by one, the twelve council members raped her to the core. The cocktail of fury and despair threatened to destroy her bruised psyche. She fought for control as each tried taking over her mind and body, her limbs stretching out beyond anything possible, as if on an invisible rack. The raw surge of energy caused her to rise off the ground, spinning in a circle, living each of their lives, from creation to death, in nothing less than a heartbeat. It nearly tore her asunder. As the last vestige of force abated, the door closed. She fell, gasping, blood pouring from her nostrils. Her body violently desecrated as each member left their scar on her mind and soul.

Glancing up at Kanis with resentment and adoration, she ran a trembling finger under her nose, wiping it clean. "No, they *didn't* survive *that*."

"Good. Inform the others *I* am now in charge. If any would like to argue, they can meet the same fate." Rising, he dusted dirt from his pants, looking down at Amelia in disgust. "Fix yourself. Nothing is more important than those girls and our prophecy. Now, see to their safety. Make sure they are untouched. In twelve years, they will meet their destiny."

At the end of the movie, one line scrolled across the large screen.

Luck. It happens, even in the world of vampires.

…

The screen went black and Jonas turned to Bacchus as the room flooded with bright lights. "The world would've been a better place if you had just let Deva– Wait! The three souls in one… the missing girls Dusty looked for… *those* were the three that Seth killed?"

"The same. When the council refused to listen to Kanis and change the status quo, he ended them. That foretelling… his agenda… Kanis will do *whatever* is necessary to make it happen. No *matter* the cost. He's more dangerous than you understand. He will risk it *all* to make sure that *this* prophecy comes true."

"Yeah, but *how* did he know where those three girls were? Why did you say he had to play his part? What part were you talking about? If you *know* how deadly he is, how can you trust him to play *any* part? Why were you and Deva talking like you both shared a secret? What is going on here? *What* aren't you telling me?"

"All in due time. You might want to buckle your seat belt, Jonas. You're about to land."

With more questions than answers, Jonas opened his eyes looking around. Antoine and Dusty were still arguing over the riddle of the scroll with Hooch happily curled in her lap.

"Please buckle your safety belts, shut down all electronic devices, and prepare for landing. Thank you for flying LaDevia Air. The time is now five-thirty a.m. The temperature is a mild seventy-eight degrees. A car will be waiting to escort you to your hotel. We hope you enjoy your stay here in Madrid."

3

Antoine never experienced anything more frightening than Dusty's dare-devil driving until that terrifying plane ride from hell. It rattled his time-worn bones worse than a dangling Halloween skeleton during a windstorm. After jerking twice, rubber kissed asphalt then smoothed to a quiet roll, though he loudly swore they were going too fast to ever brake in time. Crossing himself, he glanced up, trying to slow his racing heart. "Thank you, Lord, for making sure we *weren't* part of the six o'clock news. I would like to earn my fifteen minutes of fame in another fashion!"

"Oh, ye of little faith." Her halfhearted laughter echoed as Dusty nudged him. "I *told* ya he wouldn't."

"I'm sure your faith will be rewarded someday."

"He brought *you* into my life, didn't he?" Reaching over, she released the window shade, displaying the early hour in Twilight's lingering darkness. "*That's* reward enough for me."

Leaning over, his eyes darted around conspiratorially. "Since you're on such good terms with the old guy... think he could maybe send a cheeseburger my way?"

"*Old* guy?"

"Yes, the creator of everything is pretty old, wouldn't you say?"

Her brows shot up instantly, before taking a deep breath while shaking her head. "I'll put in a request for you and your dang tapeworm. Only I'll use better, less *offensive* wording." As she reached for her seat belt, Antoine stopped her. "What's wrong *now*?"

Pointing at the flashing seat belt sign, he shook his head. "We haven't stopped yet. Hell, the pilot could accidentally hit the gas, sending us careening into the tower, and *you'd* go flying into the cockpit."

"Then we'd be dead anyway... belted in or not."

Winking, he gave her a warm smile. "Better safe than sorry, right?"

"*Safe*? Which part of all *this* do you consider safe? We're battling evil every step of the way, trying to preserve what *little* good's left in the world, and you're worried about a little thing called *safety*? I think we're *well* beyond that. Jonas, call out the National Guard. We need a squad to *immediately* search for Antoine's man card lost somewhere in Egypt... probably in that one tunnel where we had to temporarily destroy part of a wall to get in... when we were *unsafely* traipsing around *forbidden* pyramid sections!"

Jonas laughed at the huffy look on Antoine's face. "I'll get right on it."

Removing his hand from her buckle, the professor turned away, staring out the window. "*Well!* There's *no* need to get *personal*. Besides, *I'm* not the one who got shot!"

The unwelcomed memories and emotions, associated with Travis, threatened to claw through Dusty's insides like a swarm of ravenous insects eating their way out. However, doing her level best to keep Antoine calm – and concentrating on the mystifying riddle of a quatrain – had cooled the steaming waters enough not to blow a gasket, for a short while. However, those hurtful memories would once again surface. His malicious acts pierced through the safe, slashing her tender heart, leaving another permanent scar – reminding her not to let anyone *that* close again. No time for the pain, she placed it on the back burner for now; she would deal with it later.

Once the plane came to a complete stop, the co-pilot unlatched the stairs and motioned for them to exit. The first one out, Jonas stopped to shake the man's hand before descending to the tarmac. A uniformed man dressed in black chauffeur's clothing stood beside a silver Rolls. Jonas walked over, briefly speaking in Spanish.

After getting their luggage from the storage compartment, Dusty walked down the stairs behind him. Glancing up against the sun's glare, she noticed a large crowd gathered in the window of the waiting area with phones out. It brought up more agonizing memories of her and Travis. A few times, Bob loaned her out to the Sheriff's Department to assist Travis on a cold case file that took them out of Cider Lake. Many times, she had to drag him away from the ceiling to floor windows as well. He always swore he saw some famous actor or chart-climbing singer because, "who else travels in jets?" Shaking off the urge to wallow in her sadness, she continued on her way.

"I *know* you didn't just thank him for doing a great job of flying that death trap." As Jonas rejoined them, the angry, shocked expression said it all when Antoine pointed back at the plane. "Did you at *least* tell him the *truth*? That was the *worst* plane ride we've had since this whole thing started! Hell, I'd be inclined to say *ever* in my life, and I'm an old man! *Surely*, they saw that storm on their radar, or a tower somewhere hinted about it? With today's technology, there's just *no* damn excuse for that so –"

"Does he come with an off switch?" Turning to Dusty, Jonas hitched a thumb over his shoulder at Antoine.

The bored expression bled through her words. "Leave him be, Sparx. After that storm, even a muscle-bound bonehead, missing his man card, would act like an old lady with her granny panties in a bunch." Grinning deviously, she turned to Antoine, using her baby-talk voice. "Ain't that right, Antoine?"

"Got *that* right! It doesn't even matter about –" As the sarcastic words bounced around in his head, he turned his evil eye on her. "Old… *lady?*" Poking a bony finger into her shoulder, his eyes narrowed. "You best watch that forked tongue of yours, missy. Ever been hit with a cane before? Old *ladies* do that too. Saw it on CNN, so mind your manners. I *knew* I shoulda brought my damn cane! It would've come in handy for situations like *this!*"

If anyone could take her out of her foul mood, Antoine could. "Yes, *ma'am!*"

"Old lady. Humph. What do you expect? Y'all are starving me. Hurry up and find me a Snickers bar before I start looking for Bingo halls."

"Okay, George and Gracie." Jonas motioned to the car where the confused driver still held the door open. "Can you two settle this *in* the car? I'd like to be on my way before the next full moon."

"Why are you worried about a full moon?" Antoine's eyes darted from left to right, visibly going through a forbidden checklist in his mind before pure terror lit on his face. "Is *that* your way of telling us there is a werewolf problem around *here?*"

Scowling, Dusty turned back to Antoine, clicking her tongue. "*Werewolf?* Why on *Earth* would you say that? *No* one said *anything* about werewolves, Antoine. Stop trying to create issues when there aren't any. Not sure *how* you came to *that* theory."

"Because the *only* supernatural that anyone worries about during a full moon is a werewolf… or a mad scientist and we are fresh out of *those!* Nobody told me about werewolves. I didn't sign up for –"

"*If* there is," Jonas pointed to the inside of the vehicle. "Don't you think you'd be safer *inside* the car?"

Antoine bolted into the back seat as a piercing howl split the early morning air. "You might be right. Never can be *too* safe!"

After a short glaring contest, Dusty jabbed Jonas hard in the gut as she passed by. "Knock it off. He's scared enough."

With the slamming of the door, Jonas rolled his eyes. "What did I do *now?* Next thing you know she's going to blame me for the plague." While rubbing a dull ache in his gut, he caught an unwanted but familiar scent on the breeze. Sharing a concerned glance with the driver, Jonas made his way around to the passenger side. "I think we better be on our way."

"Si, Señor."

Once inside, Antoine, in pure bliss, spied the variety of sweet goodies to nibble on. Cakes, cookies, and candies all individually wrapped, as if Deva knew all his weaknesses. His empty stomach roared like ravenous animals in the zoo. Snatching a package of María Biscuits, he hurriedly opened the wrapper, shoving a whole cookie into his mouth. Chewing greedily, he turned his eyes to heaven. "Oh, my goodness! That is one tasty cookie."

"*Anything* is good when you're hungry." Looking him over, she arched a brow. "You act like you haven't eaten in days. You *just* ate on the plane."

"I have a high metabolism." Pocketing more of the treats than he was leaving behind, he held one out for her. "Speaking of delicious snacks, do you want one?" Before another word, like a rabid dog waiting to attack, the booming protest of Antoine's growling stomach echoed around them.

Laughing softly, Dusty shook her head. "Don't worry, dear one. I *won't* take your cookies."

Antoine shoved the remaining packages into his overloaded pockets. "You never know what could happen. For instance, we might get attacked by a pack of –"

"See what ya did, Sparx?" Reaching over the front seat, Dusty smacked Jonas in the back of the head. "Now Antoine's probably gonna have nightmares about *werewolves*. It's not enough that he has to worry about vampires, now ya throw some *other* creature at him. Tell him there ain't no such thing!"

Rubbing the tender spot at the back of his head, Jonas looked menacingly at Dusty while shifting toward Antoine. "You don't have to worry about werewolves. I just wanted to get you into the car so we could be on our way. The way you two were going at it over stupid shit, we'd probably start to attract unwanted attention."

Antoine pointed an accusatory finger at Dusty. "She started it."

"Did not." Once again, Jonas ignored the topic on werewolf *existence*. Dusty filed that in the crammed 'to be used later' portion of her brain, drowning in unanswered questions. Seeing how quickly he wolfed down the cookies, she reached into her pocket, offering the bag of jelly beans. "Try these. They might help more. They stick to your insides and you don't need as many. At least, until we can get some *real* food." Dusty's stomach tried rivaling Antoine's. "Come to think of it, he's got a point. If I'm getting fat, just tell me. Don't starve us."

Chewing on jelly beans, Antoine grunted. "Oh, don't start that 'fat' stuff again. Hell, you barely eat enough to keep a bird happy, so how the hell are you gonna gain *any* weight."

"That's a good thing, considering we rarely eat," Dusty told him, taking out a handful of jelly beans, popping them into her mouth. "Anyone on a diet just needs to –"

"Okay, *enough*." Turning in his seat, Jonas eyed them.

"Hey! We can talk!" Dusty protested.

"Yeah! We can talk!" Antoine agreed with a severe nod of his head. "If you want our mouths to stay closed, then feed us! You know it's serious when *little miss never eats* speaks up!"

"We'll get a delicious meal soon enough, I promise. I have something special in mind, that you're *both* going to love, but in the meantime, can you just enjoy the ride?"

Antoine sat back, turning to look out the dark-tinted window. "Fine, I'll shut up. Doesn't mean my stomach will."

The resentful expression on Dusty's face, screamed out the silent question, *what is wrong with you?* Not waiting for any sort of response, she turned her gaze to watching the landscape pass them by, running her hand over Hooch's ghostly fur.

"Thank you!" It sounded more like, "It's about time!" Turning, he faced the front.

As the miles rolled on, his uneasy thoughts turned to the past. Time flew by, standing still for no one. Before he knew it, centuries had slipped away. Everything changed. A few venues were familiar, but two centuries left the landscape unrecognizable. Ageless vampires could not stay antiquated, so they also changed outwardly. They spoke differently, dressed in whatever era of clothing helped them blend in, as well as any other necessary adjustments. However inside, where it counted most, they were no more than spine-tingling monstrosities frozen in place, held there by a cruel sadistic master.

Having been reborn for a mere click of the watchmaker's second hand, even those few centuries wore on him. Those cursed eras, forcing him to face the unbidden passage of an invisible enemy, slowly gnawed at his hollow and damned soul – once full of life and promise. With his intense training, Jonas became powerful, yet could only stop time for short bursts. He couldn't rewind, change what he had become, or escape his tormented existence. He felt sorry for Bacchus, or even Seth for that matter; moving through countless centuries, driven at first by insatiable hunger, then by the desire to live, then at last… just boredom.

Voltaire was right, Jonas thought. *God* is *a comedian, playing to an audience too afraid to laugh.*

"We are here, Señor." The car stopped as the driver pulled up to the hotel's front entrance.

Broken from his melancholy, Jonas managed a smile, turning in his seat. "I think you'll like it here."

Many distinguished celebrities chose this hotel for its impressive five-star service since it opened in 1953 – as did those who appreciated and who could *afford* its five-star rates. The Gran Melia Fenix rested at the heart of the Golden Mile in the district of Salamanca. The breathtaking panoramic views over Madrid, rated "best in the area," were worth the price of admission alone.

"Now *that's* what I'm *talking* about!" Antoine escaped the vehicle's confines first, an ear to ear grin across his dark skin.

"Wait until you see the *in*side," Jonas said, as two bellhops scurried to the Rolls.

Opening the trunk, the driver stepped aside as the men started unloading the bags.

Turning, Jonas spoke Spanish while nodding at the cart. "I told them the room would be under LaDevia Enterprises. They'll find the number, take the bags up and put them inside."

As the bustling porters started past Antoine, he reached out, snatching the timeworn satchel off the top. *"I'll* take *this.* My underwear isn't important, but *these* can't be lost."

Seeing Antoine's fast-actions, Jonas nodded appreciatively. "Good thinking. Shall we check in?"

The front doors opened to a rotunda dressed in luxury. Eight towering marble columns rose, floor to ceiling, supporting the expansive blue stained-glass dome. From its center hung a sparkling, two-tiered, crystal chandelier, illuminating the polished marble floor. Directly beneath it, four quarter-round, red-velvet couches – adorned with brightly colored throw pillows – circled a waxed, mahogany table. Plush, upholstered, Queen Anne style chairs – tastefully placed around them – waited patiently to comfort weary guests. A red-carpeted staircase wound up and to the left, leading travelers to their well-appointed rooms. All this opulence boggled the mind, but the lonely Steinway, mirror-polished in all its ebon glory, caught everyone's eyes.

Walking around it, admiringly, Dusty lightly ran her hand over the top. "Once upon a time, I thought of taking piano lessons… for about five minutes… until I realized just how much went into it. I'm way too busy with other things."

Following behind her, Jonas also admired the reflective finish. "You have a good eye. I used to have one like this." Jonas eased onto the equally smooth bench. "Beautiful, isn't it?" Raising the key cover, he smiled.

"Yes. It looks like someone really takes care of it. The way it shines." Peering over, she saw every curve in her face. "You can see every flaw you have."

"Then you shouldn't see anything. You are flawless."

"Ha!" Dusty shook her head. "*You* need glasses, but don't expect *me* to point them out if you can't see them!" When he sat down, she huffed out a breath. "Sparx, don't get us kicked out before we even get checked in." Not wanting to take her hostility out on Jonas, when it still belonged back with Travis, she joined Antoine at the seating area.

"Didn't Deva tell us to stay *under* the radar?"

"*Under* the radar? In a *jet*? *Fancy* hotels?" Dusty laughed. "Then again, I guess to *them*, it's what we're doing… in a weird kinda way. *Hide it in plain sight.* Isn't that the old saying?"

"It is." Eyes widening, Antoine sucked in a gasp, glancing at Jonas. "*Tell* me he's *not* about to play that thing."

"I *could*, but I don't think *either* of us would believe it. No telling what boring-ass Crip-crap he's gonna play. It could be from *any* century."

"I beg your pardon, little lady, there's nothing wrong with classical music." Antoine turned, watching Jonas. "It's soothing to the soul."

"If you say so. It puts *me* to sleep." Dusty laughed as Antoine poked her in the ribs. "If he starts with classical, don't blame me when everyone in the lobby just drops… in a dead sleep."

"Hush! He might surprise you."

"That'll be the day."

The excited guests in the lobby getting registered, and the frenzied workers getting all the details for their rooms, just stopped as Jonas started to superbly play the piano. Turning, they gave their undivided attention to the man singing, *Maybe I'm Amazed*, by Paul McCartney.

Jonas stared at Dusty, as if no one else witnessed him pouring out his heart in a song.

The second Jonas started, it brought up an aching, joyous memory in her life. "Seriously," she whispered. "Doesn't *anyone* know any other song but *that* one?"

…

Standing, staring at the lived-in establishment before her, Dusty shook her head, turning to leave. "Oh no! Take me home! I'm *not* doing this!"

Rushing over, Travis snaked an arm around her slender waist, hooking his thumb through a belt loop, piloting her into the money-making bar. "*Yes*, you are. I know it's a foreign thing to you… being a recluse and all… but I'm gonna show you what *people* look like. Don't worry. They won't bite."

She elbowed him in the ribs. "Seriously? You pulled me away from my work for *karaoke*?" As he half dragged her along, Dusty shook her head. "I have *soooo* much to do. I don't have time for this."

"You *always* have *soooo* much to do. That case will still be there just as you left it." Using hand signals, Travis caught the attention of the waitress to place his order; two Coronas with a lime wedge. "Make time. Dusty, we used to see each other *every* weekend, now I'm lucky if I get once a month. You need a refresher course on what you're missing."

"Yeah, but if I hogged all your time, what would the *other* ladies think?" Reaching around, she wrenched his hold off her, following him to an empty table close to the stage.

Settling in the chair, he picked up his cigarettes, lighting two, handing her one. "There *aren't* any other ladies, ya goof. Just you, and I want *this* date to count."

Sitting beside him, she accepted his offering. "They *always* count, silly. It doesn't matter what we do. We're still together, right?"

Taking her hand, he kissed the top of it before nodding. "*Exactly.* So, *stop* arguing with me since," he did a poor imitation, "*it doesn't matter what we do.*"

"I do *not* sound like that." Snatching her hand back, she patted his cheek roughly, letting out an annoyed breath. "I'm feeling played like a fiddle in the middle of a square-dancing ho-down. Ya know, like the one you took me to *two* weeks ago… claiming ya needed help with a case. The only work was to my feet!"

"Stop bitching. *You* had fun."

"Meh. Our definitions are totally different, I see."

He winked. "You weren't complaining back at your place."

"Whatever." Taking a drag off the cigarette, she slowly exhaled. "*Fine*, but they *better* serve food. I'm starving." Sidling up to him, she gently ran her fingertips over his forearm. "Ya know, *babe*, we could've stayed at my house and went over the case again with subs and a six-pack. Two eyes are *always* better than one. Not to mention the fun when we're done."

"No!" As she tried sliding away, he held firmly onto her chair. "I didn't want this to be a *working* date. Hell, we do that *every* time we see each other. Has anyone ever told you that ya work too damn much?"

"Nope. Never. Just the opposite."

"Someone who *obviously* doesn't know you! I mean, come on now. Every once in a while, ya gotta get out and do something. Besides, it keeps your mind fresh."

"That's the *biggest* load of horse patties I've ever heard."

"Nope. It's scientific facts, proven by statistics… and whatnot… that when you focus too much on one thing, ya get used to it. It becomes stuck in your brain. Ya need to get out and do something else so that it's fresh when you go back to it."

Unable to stop laughing, she took another drag off her cigarette. "*Reeeeally* now? Did ya learn that from watching a movie?"

"Yep."

"Hell, you should put that in a textbook, *deputy*, and teach a course at the college on how to investigate a missing persons' case… see how many show up."

"I just might do that! Probably be all women. You know they can't resist my southern charm." He flirtatiously wiggled his brows.

"Yeah, yeah. You're a *god*."

The waitress stopped over with their bottles of beer. After exchanging pleasantries with Dusty, then brazenly flirting with Travis, she went on her merry way.

"Besides, what's *wrong* with karaoke?"

"Nothing, if you know *how* to sing." After squeezing the fleshy lime and adding a pinch of salt, Dusty picked up her bottle, taking a deep swig.

"You know I can carry a tune better than some. I'm not saying I'd win American Idol, but –"

"American Idol? Let me guess. That's some TV show ya watch?"

Taking a deep breath, he let it out slowly. "We *really* need to sit and watch TV one night."

"Seeing what America views as an idol, after the way some of them dress in public, I'll pass."

"How have you gone through life without turning on the TV or watching *any* movie? I mean... how in the world do ya know where to eat without watching commercials?"

"Psh! Hush your mouth! I get what I need and go home and cook it. I'm not lazy... unlike *certain* individuals." She took another drag, slowly exhaling. "*Hey!* I watched that *one* movie with you. Hooch. It was the only way you got to name my dog."

"That doesn't count. You fell asleep as soon as it started!"

"I was... tired."

"Uh-huh."

"Oh, hush you. You're lucky you got me out here to listen to people *trying* to sing."

Taking a deep gulp of his beer, he rested it in front of him. "You've had *plenty* of other missing persons. What's so special about *this* case? It's like... ya can't rest until you locate her, which means putting everything else on hold. So come on, Dusty. Out with it. What gives with this *one* missing person's case?"

"Well, for one thing, it's not *just* one. There have been *six*. It's just... something tells me they all tie in with Tammy Barker."

"Who?"

"The first one to go missing. I can't help but think... Tammy isn't having any fun. She's probably somewhere alone, cold, crying, *pleading*, probably praying to God for *someone* to find her." Swallowing hard, she shrugged. "*I* am that someone. *That's* why I keep searching. I don't want her prayers to go unanswered. I have to do *everything* in my power... and then some... to find her."

"Yeah, but babe... you *know* the statistics. It's been so long... she could *already* be dead."

Staring deeply into his beddable eyes, fingers tracing the clear long-neck bottle, she let out a deep breath. "You don't think I know that?

Time's against me. That's another reason I'm always searching for her, no matter what else I'm doing. Because, until I *see* her dead body, I *will* keep searching and everything else be damned."

Losing that mega-watt smile, he reached over, placing his callused hand over her silky one, gently massaging the knuckles. "Even me?"

Pulling her hand back, she took a long pull on the cigarette as she considered those two little words. They held so much meaning she would either destroy or fuel with her response. She didn't want to lead him on with a lie but didn't want to hurt him either. Decision made, she lifted her gaze back to meet his, slowly exhaling smoke off to the side. "Even you."

That clarification brought out the despair in his long sigh. "You have a lot of dedication that's for sure, but don't worry. You can't get rid of me that easy."

"You might change your mind."

"Nope. Never. You can't resist my charms." He pointed to the stage. "*This*, however, is my *favorite* hobby."

"So why did you bring me *here*? If you wanted to sing, you could've done that in the car like you *always* do."

"Hey. This is me opening up and letting you in. That's what people do when they're dating. That's us." His finger moved between them. "We're dating. You're the only one I'm seeing, and I know I'm the only one you're seeing, despite how many times poor ole Charlie asks. We're supposed to be straight with each other. I *love* singing." Standing, he pressed a kiss against her forehead before heading to the stage. "Almost as much as you. Sometimes, it's the *best* way to communicate… when you're dealing with a *hardhead*."

"Okay, but if everyone rushes out of here with their ears bleeding, don't say I didn't warn ya."

"Oh, har-de-har-har. You're so funny." Hopping up on stage, he snatched the mic from the stand. "Hey everyone! I wanna dedicate this number to the hottest girl in town." He pointed at her. "There's no other girl for me, but my gal, Dusty. Girl, you got under my skin like a microscopic organism and infected my heart with your debilitating plague."

Taking a swig of her beer, Dusty almost spit it back out as she busted out in laughter, wiping her mouth with the back of her hand. "Such a *smooth* talker you are. Be still my heart."

Not needing to see the neon words on the big screen, Travis glided across the floor. Reclaiming his seat beside her, he belted out, a little offkey, *Maybe I'm Amazed* by Paul McCartney, while everyone cheered him on.

…

After the last few notes died off, the room burst into applause. Rising from the bench, Jonas bowed slightly before making his way over to Antoine and Dusty. "Singing is a favorite pastime of mine. This job doesn't allow me the freedom of such luxuries, so I take it when I can." Lifting his hand, he eyed his nails before buffing them on his shirt. "And you thought I'd be boring."

Jonas's silky baritone interrupted her thoughts, pulling her back to the present. "Sorry, I wasn't paying attention. What did you play?" Certain emotional triggers – such as that damn song – pushed their way past the clouds and through her titanium barricade at the most inopportune times. As the waterworks threatened to well up and spill, Dusty called upon years of training to harness them back into place, behind the overflowing dam of unshed tears. Eventually, it would break – like it did with Hooch's death – but not today, and certainly not over a song.

At the sound of a boisterous roar that any lion, tiger, or bear would be envious of, Antoine patted his stomach. "Who knew you could play the piano much less sing! You missed your calling, Jonas. You should've been a singer. I thoroughly enjoyed it, but then again, unlike my partner here, *I* appreciate good music. Now, I do believe you promised food and ya know what? I've heard nothing but good things about Aduana."

Tearing her aggravated gaze from Jonas, she focused on Antoine, squinting as if suddenly blind. "I'm sorry, you don't wanna what?"

"Huh?" Antoine returned the confused expression and after a short staring contest, he tried keeping his laughter in check. "No, no. A-D-U-A-N-A," he spelled it out. "The restaurant in this hotel is famous for its Mediterranean food. Healthy eating and wine. Then again, everyone knows that wine, in moderation, is good for you."

"Amen." The chandelier's light caught a slight gleam in her eyes before she blinked them back behind the barrier. "I have a glass before every confession… in my room… before bed."

"I'm sure you do." Giving her a scolding stare, he pointed up. "However, the restaurant is just on the seventh floor. We should pop over after we check in. Not sure I can do any more than that before passing out from low blood sugar. I feel like I haven't eaten in a month."

"You sure do know a lot about restaurants in foreign countries. You must've just sat around drooling about them on the internet."

"If you mean while adding 'eating at them' to my bucket list, then yes."

Her mouth twisted into a cynical grin. "I'm not sure *why* that surprises me… you're *always* hungry."

Figuring his warmhearted serenade fell on deaf ears, Jonas ran a hand over his face. "C'mon, let's go get checked in."

Looking over, Antoine noticed people were dropping money into the tip glass on the piano. "Right behind you," he called out after Dusty. Nonchalantly making his way over, he peeked into the crystal glass. Emptying the pesos into his palm, his mouth dropped open. "Nine-hundred and fifty-four pesos? That's fifty bucks! Man, I'm in the wrong business." As he pocketed the cash, a tap on his shoulder startled him.

"Señor?" asked a burly concierge, eyeing Antoine's pocket.

"It's okay, son," he answered, clapping the man on the shoulder. "I'm his… manager." Hurrying off, he hollered over his shoulder. "Great place you have here. I'll be sure to give it five stars when I get back. Six if I can. Yes sir! This place is top-notch! I'll even recommend you for promotion. Oh my! Yes." Turning the corner, he ran straight into Jonas's back.

After righting himself, Jonas turned, noticing the 'doe in the headlight' expression on Antoine's face. "Problem?"

"No, no. No problem. Just some folks wanted an… *autograph*." He sagely nodded. "They read my book."

"You wrote a book?" Turning, Dusty put a hand on her hip, watching him curiously. "Boy, talk about keeping a secret! Why didn't you tell me? When? What was it about?"

"Uh. You wouldn't have found it interesting. Big book. Lots of pictures. Ancient Greek For Dummies. I wrote it back for my dissertation during –" His eyes snapped forward, homing in on Jonas. "Forget that. Is it time to eat yet? Are we all checked in? I'm so hungry, I'm losing my train of thought! Not good for a professor of my lofty standards, you understand. It could be detrimental."

Tightening his lips, Jonas continued staring at him for a moment as if he didn't believe a word of it. "*First*, we get the room situated, *then* we can talk about food."

Antoine lowered his head and slumped his shoulders forward. "I'm gonna die. I just know it. I'm gonna die… in a foreign country… on an empty stomach. This is *no* way to treat your elders."

"You're *not* gonna die." Taking a hold of his arm, Dusty escorted him to the elevator. "You saved those cookies, remember? If ya finish those, before we get a meal, remember… I *always* have jelly beans."

Antoine's eyes widened about as big as the smile on his face. "The *cookies*! I totally forgot about those!" Taking out a package, he quickly opened it, cramming two in his mouth at the same time. "I knew I saved these for a reason!" With crumbs lining his lips, as others fell to the plush carpeting at his feet, they barely understood him.

"Yes, because we are *always* starving you." Stepping into the elevator, Jonas gripped the bar in the back. "I swear you have a bottomless pit of a stomach. Are you *ever* full?"

"They should put more than six in here! I could really go for a tall glass of milk!" Antoine swallowed, grabbing another one from the package. "Me? Full? Well, that one time… during the holidays… I was full to the point of busting a gut. Gabby made a mean, *juicy* turkey. It melted in your mouth and ya couldn't just stop at *one* plate." Standing in the opposite corner, he pointed at Dusty. "Little Ms. Jelly beans here ate almost *three* plates full. Turkey, stuffing, mashed potatoes, *and* gravy, with the sweetest corn on the cob you ever tasted. Don't get me started on how many desserts she ate afterward."

"*Three?*" Jonas turned a quizzical look her way. "How?"

A short laugh ripped from her throat as she sent an accusatory glare at Antoine, taking a position between them. "That *wasn't* supposed to be divulged… but… yes," she turned back to Jonas. "I did. His wife could cook. Not only was her turkey on point, but the mashed potatoes, and all those delicious desserts. I didn't eat for two days after that… just a couple of jelly beans here and there. I do believe that started my jellybean habit."

"Liar. You were munching on those things when I first met you," Antoine reminded her.

"How?" Jonas couldn't hide the stupefied expression on his face. "You couldn't eat another bite after the diner in Cider Lake. If I recall, you had a chocolate shake, heavy on the whipped cream… well done cheeseburger with everything… taters with fried onions, green peppers, mushrooms, topped with cheddar cheese and Ketchup… pickle slices on the side… order of "damn near burn 'em" crunchy fries."

"After ya turned me into an older, fat clown?" Recalling that moment made her madder than a wet hen. "Who the hell wants to eat anything when they're wearing fifty extra pounds!"

With his eyes aglow, Antoine rubbed at his belly. "Now *that* sounds like something from Bobbie Jo's! I could really go for a plate of her taters *right* now. Mmmmm!"

While eyeing the crumbs on the floor, Jonas pushed the button on the elevator. "Let's get to our room. You're making a mess in here."

Gripping the bar as the elevator headed up, Dusty echoed his puzzlement. "How the boring tater-loving plateful do ya remember what I ate that day?"

"One of the joys of being a vampire." He tapped his head. "You don't forget *anything*."

Antoine jammed another cookie into his mouth. "Didn't sound boring to me! It sounds a hell of a lot better than what I'm eating right now. Don't get me wrong, these cookies are good, but ain't got *nothing* on Bobbie Jo's taters! Mm-hmm!"

Those with deep enough pockets stayed in the Red Level rooms. The two-bedroom suite – where they were staying – had a full-sized sofa, two plush chairs in the living room, a hydro-tub in both bathrooms, and the best amenities money could buy.

Seeing there were only two bedrooms, Dusty pointed to the white, velour sofa. "Dibs on the couch." When Antoine started to argue, she shot up a hand. "I called it first. Pick a bedroom." Plopping down on it, she kicked her feet onto the coffee table. "Holy comfy critters! This is softer than my bed at home." Running a hand over the creamy cushions she leaned back, winking at Jonas. "Do that thing you do and 'hocus pocus' it back to my house. Think you can manage that?" Dusty didn't care one way or the other about that couch, but Antoine had a bad back and she didn't want him sleeping on it. Not on her watch. The man snored like Rip Van Winkle, while she barely rested long enough to close her eyes.

"Sure. I'll steal a couch from one of the premiere hotels in the world. Who'd notice?" Glancing at his watch, Jonas looked between them. "It's almost seven in the morning. Let's get settled in, rest for a few hours, then start our vacation."

Fighting off a yawn, Antoine looked down at his stomach. "I *knew* it! Guess you'll have to wait. No sense passing out halfway through breakfast." Heading toward the front bedroom, he opened another package of cookies, calling over his shoulder. "Don't kill each other while I'm asleep." Not long after the door closed, his gentle snoring came from the other side.

"You need some rest too after... well... *you* know." He winked. "Trust me, it's going to sneak up when you least expect it. Feeding a vampire can be exhausting to mortals." Jonas offered a warm smile. "See you in a few?"

His winking, smiling, and talking sweetly caused unease to crawl up her spine. After staring at him for a long moment, she patted the cushion beside her. "Pop a squat. We need to have a chat."

Choosing a chair opposite her – far enough away so he could move if she took a swing – his smile evaporated. "*That* doesn't sound good. Look, if this is about the sofa, I can ta–"

"It's not," she interrupted. "I seriously doubt I'm gonna get much sleep anyway. Too much on my mind. Besides, *some*one has to keep working on this… riddle."

"Okay, so what is it this time? According to you, there's *always* something."

Ignoring the lame attempt to sidetrack her, an impeachable glare zeroed in on his eyes. "What's *wrong* with you?"

"Is that a trick question?" After a pregnant pause, he held open his hands. "Okay, I give. Can I phone a friend? Maybe poll the audience?" Realizing the whimsical comment went over her head, he leaned forward in frustration. "*What* are you talking about?"

Ignoring the "poll the audience" comment, she pointed at him. "*Something's* wrong with you because… well… you're… acting *weird*. Are ya outta Hemosynth?"

"No. I just picked up a new supply before we left for Egypt."

"Maybe you should call your dealer… Uh… what's his name?"

His jaw tightened. "His name is Garrick, and trust me, he's the *last* person I want to talk to right now."

"Yeah, him! Well, you *should*, because *something's* not right. Do vampires need new doses over time?"

"New… doses?"

"That happens, ya know. One of my… *assignments*… ended because of an overdose in medicine. Too much at one time. She got… weird. Is that what's going on here?"

"What? *No*! What's with the Spanish Inquisition? There's *nothing* wrong with me and *nothing's* going on!"

"Not from what I've seen. Look, I tried ignoring it and wasn't gonna say anything, but you're *really* acting weird."

"I am not."

"*Yes*, you are."

"Fine! *How* am I acting weird?"

"Remember the day ya shot yourself in the head?"

His eyes turned dark. "I've tried to forget it, but thanks so much for reminding me."

"When I came to see you at the Bluestone Motel, where you explained to me about vampires. *That* day."

"Since you didn't pick up on the obvious sarcasm… yes, I remember *that* day."

"Well… *that* day you were acting all kinds of weird too. Like ya had too much to drink. Kinda like you are now!"

Running a hand through his hair, he let out a slow breath. "I *told* you. Hemosynth does that. It's one of the side effects, though it doesn't last long."

"I know, but you've been acting the *same* way since we rescued you. All… lovey-dovey and shit."

"Lovey-dove–" Staring at her as if she'd grown a third eye, he backed up a bit. "You're mistaken. Vampires aren't capable of *lovey-dovey*."

"You sure have a funny way of showing it! Well, it wasn't exactly *loving,* more like… you were the biggest horndog ready to 'get it on' under the covers."

"Nothing has changed from the first time I explained it. Hemosynth has that effect on us. Many mortal/immortal relationships started off because of that *very* thing." Not really but it sounded good.

"Well knock it off. You're like… smiling… winking… acting overprotective. Giving me sidelong glances. Puppy dog eyes. It's distracting. Annoying. Especially after… well… ya know what happened."

He shot her an icy glare. "So, you'd rather I act like you don't matter?"

"Well, ya don't have to act like a cold fish stuck outta water, but just not as… *weird*. We have a job to do. Let's finish it so we can try and find out what normalcy will be left in our lives when we're done!"

"So… you want us to be business partners. Nothing more." Standing, he walked over to the fireplace, eyeing the oil painting over it. "Business it is then. Forgive me."

It sounded better in her head and the admission of guilt on her face registered as much. "Not exactly. Jonas, I –"

"It has never been my intention to make you ill at ease. I *won't* make that *mistake* again." Giving her a slight bow, he turned and strode toward his room.

She wanted to run after him and slap him silly for confusing her so much, but his cold tone worked better than any 'Do Not Disturb' sign. Exhaling a raspy breath, she turned to Hooch, shaking her head. "There's just no winning with that man. Or *any* man, for that matter."

'Are you trying to drive him away?'

Wow! You've been gone for a long time. Was there a meeting for imaginary friends or something?

'Something like that. I am *dealing with much more than* just *you. What's the matter with you?* You're *the one acting weird. He* was *trying to be nice.'*

No, he *was overdoing it.*

'And this is a crime, why, exactly?'

Because I'm not in the mood for games! Travis might as well have ripped out my heart and stomped all over it. It doesn't give me warm and fuzzy feelings to realize that he played me.

'He didn't play you. He honestly cares deeply and there's more than meets the eye right now that you'll find out about in time. Okay, so you're mad at Travis. Why *take it out on Jonas? Are there feelings for him that you don't like?'*

I dunno. Maybe. Jonas gives me the worst case of heartburn in history.

'Heartburn huh? So, eat some Tums and stop being such a bitch.'

I'm up to my eyeballs in confusion with him. One minute, he's loving as all get out. The next, he's keeping secrets from me while expecting me to be open and honest with him.

'You need him as much as he needs you in this. Believe it or not, you both need each other. You can't work together well when you're at

each other's throats. You need to trust each other more than you ever have.'

That's not gonna be easy. I have serious trust issues. And... well... there is *something else.*

'What? Spit it out. I do have other *people to deal with.'*

When I gave him my blood... something happened between us.

'Something? As in?'

Sexual.

'Vampires taking blood can be just that. Erotic. Mortals can't handle what it does to the nervous system. What of it?'

I don't know if that was the reason, maybe because we were so close... but it gave me this feeling that I've never felt before.

'What type of feeling?'

Which part of "I never felt before" escaped you? I don't know. I do know that... every time I look at him, I just want to finish what we started... twice.

'So, what stops you?'

Travis.

'You're definitely a complex creature. Torn between two lovers. Feeling like a fool. Loving both of them is breaking all the rules.'

No one said I'm in love with either of them. Right now, I hate them both for lying to me. It seems my whole life that's all anyone ever does is lie to me and I'm sick of it. It's downright mentally exhausting trying to figure out what the truth is... from everyone. What is it about me?

'You don't make it easy.'

Look at the life I've had! If I were a dog, I'd be biting everyone I meet, so I think I'm doing damn good! Explain to me why my *life had to be so harsh?*

'What doesn't kill you only makes you stronger.'

I see loving family moments and I wonder... why couldn't I *have had that too? Why was* I *chosen to have such a crappy life?*

'Goodnight, Dusty.'

"Ugh. So evasive. Goodnight, imaginary friend. Stick around this time."

'Quit being such a hard ass.'

Kicking off her shoes, she collapsed on the couch, patting the empty space at her side. Hooch snuggled up, feeling the sorrow she refused to admit. Wiping away the tears, she gave him a peck on the forehead. "You're the luckiest one of us all, boy."

He didn't think so.

In the space between sleep and conscious thought, a set of sea-green eyes flecked by gold and silver, haunted her every move, trying to make her see the world through them. As much as she wanted to, it didn't compare to what lurked in the background. *That* reminded her of what would happen if she allowed anyone too near that well-protected box around her heart. In the past, Travis had figured out the combination… forcing her to change it… that Jonas now threatened to solve as well. Confused, her head began to pound.

Slamming the door shut to both, the blissful sleep of the dead welcomed her into its comforting arms… for a brief time, at least.

4

That didn't go at all as expected. For a split second, he considered going back, trying to explain why he acted like a lovesick schoolgirl. Then again, if he acted on impulse to snatch her up off that couch, take her into his arms and make mad passionate love until they both collapsed from pure satisfaction, she wouldn't walk straight for weeks. That thought tickled his brain until the corner of his lip lifted – more for the dumbstruck look on her drop-dead gorgeous face if he did that. Hell, after that, they could tell all the nameless players in this pointless exercise to piss off.

I could blame it on the nonexistent Hemosynth. She bought it before. Then again, who am I trying to fool? It won't matter. She's not interested, Sparx. Get that nonsense out of your head! That's never going to happen. In all her lifetime. She's made that perfectly clear.

Shaking his head, he walked to his bedroom door, ready to just kick back and relax. Stopping short, skepticism lined his features as someone – or something – opened his door. Knowing Bacchus wouldn't do something so foolish, and Deva would make a grand entrance, his first thought went to Dusty's safety, above all else. His second thought ventured in the direction of Antoine.

Quickly entering the room, his eyes turned a deep crimson as glistening-white incisors lowered. Turning the lock behind him, he scanned the small room. "Show yourself," he snarled.

A green mist seeped from the opposite wall, slowly taking the form of a man. "Ello, mate."

"*Garrick*!" Anger threatened to overcome reason. "I should –"

"Whoa there, cobber." Garrick didn't act his normal, cheerful self. Raising his hands defensively, he looked almost weary. "I come in peace."

After a slight staring contest between the two, Jonas nodded. "You have five minutes. *Why* are you *here*?"

"Can't a bloke look in on an old friend from time to time?"

Friend? Biting back the acidic retort, Jonas looked at his watch. "Four minutes, fifty seconds."

"Fine, fine! If you're gonna put me on a bloody schedule, it'll be faster to show you." Glancing around, Garrick spied an empty glass, snatching it off the nightstand. Dragging a sharp nail across his wrist, he allowed the dark blood to coat the bottom before handing it over.

Eyeing the enticing offering, Jonas tilted his head. "If this is some trick of Kanis's to trap me –"

"Just drink already, will ya? Christ, didn't ya learn *nothin'* from Deva?"

Taking the donation, he brought it to his lips, whispering, "T'rak ugthas n'invay," before draining the thick liquid, ignoring the invigorating kick that came with it.

The door vanished as gray stone replaced the walls and silver bars slammed over the single window.

Looking around with a mixture of pride and concern, Garrick nodded approvingly. "I stand corrected. Ya *did* learn something from 'er."

While keeping his eyes on Garrick, grainy images – like old film reels – flashed in the background of his mind. Twin young boys, filthy and ragged, roaming the hectic streets of Paris, living hand to mouth. Years later, the same boys grew into good-looking men, listening to an honorable knight speak.

Jonas felt the emotional intoxication when they joined the incorruptible Knights Templar. He witnessed the brutal slayings – guilty and innocent alike – as they slaughtered in God's name. Soon enough, the red tides turned, and a hard-hitting sense of torturous betrayal struck him in the gut. The hunter became the hunted. They made a pact; a hero's plan to infiltrate the undead by joining their unholy ranks.

Everything about Sir Duncan Garioch died the night a Russian vampire brought him over. After weeks of learning to control the lethal bloodlust, Duncan finished the second part of the heinous deal. Keeping his wits challenged him, but he successfully brought over his twin brother. As agreed from the beginning, Miles remained in the care of the knights, learning how to control the beast, drinking only from the brotherhood contributions. Even when the unbridled beast ravaged his fragile psyche, he refused to harm a living soul. His new meat and potatoes diet turned into a cup of vital fluid. Looking through Garrick's eyes, anguish and rage washed over Jonas, seeing Miles losing his immortal life to Seth's deadly stroke.

The scene faded.

"Nah'gila." Once more, they were in Jonas's fancy hotel room. No longer enraged at Garrick's presence, Jonas rested his eyes on him. "So… you're actually one of the good guys. After your actions, that's a frightening concept to swallow. I'm sorry for your loss."

With a heavy heart, ignoring the "good guys" comment, Garrick nodded. "Yeah, mate. Me too."

"You're French not Australian. You can lose the fake accent. That's almost as bad as Seth pretending to be Doc Holliday from Tombstone."

"The joys of this God-forsaken world. You can be whoever you wish to be. Even Crocodile Dundee. With social media, most people put on a façade anyway, pretending to be something they're not. Brave. Righteous. Victim. Hero. Villain."

After rinsing out the glass – didn't need Hooch catching the scent – he set it back on the nightstand. Taking a seat at the small table, Jonas kicked the other chair out, motioning to it. "Sit. You still haven't told me *why* you're here."

Running a hand through blonde spikes, Garrick eased his lanky frame down. "I need ya to do me a right solid, mate."

Not wanting Garrick to figure out that Jonas knew about Hemosynth turning vamps into dopeheads, he leaned back. "If I can. What is it you want?"

"I'm done. Tired of the fighting. I want ya to kill me. I know ya want to for turning ya into a junkie, even though that wasn't *my* call. I want ya to know, Jonas. I really did think of you as my mate. I fought for ya. I told everyone involved that you were strong enough to fight the beast on your own. They weren't having any of it. Kanis wanted you on a leash… a short one at that."

Narrowing his brows, he pursed his lips. "The only other person who knows that *I* know the family secret is Deva. *She* told it to me, so I seriously doubt she would *ever* divulge it. Even Dusty thinks I'm still taking that crap, so how do *you* know?"

While laughing, a gleam sparkled in his eyes as he pulled out a joint. Once lit, he took a deep toke before exhaling slowly. "One for the road, as it were." Holding out his hand, he offered the reeking doobie to Jonas.

"I'll pass."

Rolling his shoulders, Garrick polished off the aromatic weed, before leaning back in the chair. "Been a vampire for about a thousand years, mate. Picked up a few tricks along the way. Oh, not as many as you have from darlin' Deva, but still… point is, now that *I* know, so will Kanis. That will be bad for you and… *others*. Am I on the mark?"

"You *could* say that, but if that's all you're worried about… as you said, I learned a *lot* from my training."

"The way ya masked old Charlie's thoughts?"

Speechless, surprise found its way to Jonas's forehead.

Garrick shot Jonas a look of resignation. "No thanks. Ya know that's only gonna fool *Sethie-poo* for so long. Eventually, he's gonna realize he's been had, and… well, let's just say I don't wanna be Charles F. Thomas, officer of the law, when he does. Ain't gonna be pretty."

How the fuck does he know about Charlie and China? Did he get that from me? Without me noticing. If so, then he's –

"Dangerous, mate," he finished Jonas's thought. "Makes me too dangerous to keep alive. Don't you agree?"

While trapped behind silver bars in Deva's dungeon – going through a detox that made his blood boil – Jonas imagined this meeting going entirely in a different route.

Folding his hands onto the table, the sorrow in his expression rippled through Garrick's words. "Look, I have a few tricks, but I can't keep Kanis outta my head for long. Besides, I'm tired of all this… *immortality*. Like I said, I'm done. My brother's gone home, wherever *home* is, and I'm ready to join him. If Seth wins, all of us are gonna end up slaves to him and his kiddies, or we're dead. If you guys win, there's no place for me here. At one time *that* was my hope… not anymore. Not after what I put you through." Easing back, his expression held nothing but friendliness. "It's a win-win. You get what mojo I have and… as payment for giving you some good shit… I get to finally walk off the chessboard. C'mon mate. It would do *no* one any good if Kanis got into my head. There are things there that *you* need to see, but *not* him. Besides, it's the *human* thing to do."

"I have no humanity left."

"Then what ya doin' back home?" Turning his head to the window, Garrick hefted a sigh. "Way I see it –"

Duncan Garioch never uttered another sound.

Swiftly and precisely, Jonas drained Garrick's life force without spilling a drop, robbing him of all his phenomenal powers. Afterward, striving to keep the willpower to compose himself, he gently lowered his friend to the floor before diving onto the bed. He didn't want anyone to hear the disfiguring torture about to happen. The first spasm took hold of his body, stretching him in every direction as if on an invisible rack. Then his muscles retracted as it tried turning him into a shape-shifting pretzel. Jonas held in the growls and inner screams as the pressure in the back of his head, slowly moving inward, felt like two thumbs trying to press his wide eyes from his skull. Never having taken a vampire as old as Garrick, it took ten full minutes of expanding and recoiling before he won the battle.

Taking a deep breath, Jonas sat up, swinging his legs over the side of the mattress. He held onto his head fearful it would fall off if he didn't. "Wow, what a kick. Deva should bottle up *that* and sell it." Glancing down at his one-time best friend, he sighed. "You weren't as bad as I thought you were. May you now find peace." Standing, he closed his eyes, holding out his hand. "Infernum Mortes Ex."

Garrick's lifeless form instantly engulfed in a green flame, leaving only dust behind as it subsided.

With a flick of his wrist, the window opened, and a gentle breeze drifted in, gathering the pile, and scattering it to the outside, before closing shut again. "Rest well, mate."

Climbing into bed, he closed his eyes and set about the task of combing through Garrick's memories, arranging them – as Deva taught him – in order of importance. Starting in the beginning, he scanned through them on fast forward, before he came to an unexpected one.

He bolted upright with eyes wide open. "*Katherine!*"

5

The limousine's enormous, black leather seats swallowed the little girl. Troubled caramel eyes peered through loose brown strands at the man, dressed in all black, wearing scuffed black boots seated opposite her. "Where are we going?"

"To your… uncle's. He'll take care of you." Spoken in a very gentle, almost caring way, he cracked a soft smile. "You're too young. This wasn't supposed to happen for a few years yet… but… it can't be helped."

"Where's my mommy and daddy?"

"Gone."

"What do ya mean… *gone*?"

"You saw it. They burned in the fire."

Sadness crept into her voice. "No."

"Yes. Sorry, but they were still in the house. We couldn't get them out."

Tears filled her eyes. "Why not?"

"Flames were too hot. Too high. We barely got *you* out in time. No one else survived," he told her, nonchalantly.

"Why?" Tears cascaded down her cheeks as she sobbed out the word.

"Who knows? Electrical short? Gas leak? You name it. Anything could've happened."

"How come?" Barely able to see him through the tears, her body convulsed with deep sobs as emotions machine-gunned her words. "That's not fair! Go back and save them! My daddy is Superman! He can do anything."

He shot her a warning glare of his waning patience. "No, he's not. It's time you realize the reality of the situation. No one can save them, Dusty. They're gone. Burned to ashes. There's nothing we can do about it."

"Yes, you can!"

"Dustina! Stop it! They're dead. Don't worry, though. Your uncle is going to take great care of you. You'll be taught the ways of old."

"No! No! No! I don't want any uncle! I want my mommy and daddy!"

"Settle down, Dustina."

"I want my mommy! I want my daddy!" Her cries turned into full-blown sobs. She didn't see it coming, but the slap spun her head around, silencing her. Blood trickled down her lip as she stared at him in shock.

"I said, settle down. You're too emotional. Emotions aren't your friend, Dustina. The only one that will be is anger. Harness it. Push it down into your soul. Allow it to burn slowly. When needed, it will add power to your punch. However, don't let anger consume you. Angry people don't think, they just leap. Do not make me repeat myself. You won't like it if I do. Stop blubbering. Nothing more annoying than a whiner. You're not a baby, so stop acting like one," he growled.

The weeping stopped as disbelief, resentment, and sorrow lined her facial features. "I'm sorry." Tears welled up in her eyes as one side of her face turned red, showing the outline of a hand. It stung like hell, but she held the tears in check, refusing to give him the satisfaction of acknowledging the pain.

Wiping the blood from her lip, he suckled his finger, smiling down at her. "Much better. My name is too hard for you and I hate how you butchered it earlier, so just call me, Sir G. Do you understand?"

"Yes, Sir G." She wiped at her eyes, trying not to make him angry.

"Good. Dustina, you're a brave little girl. You've lived your whole life being sweet. You have a kind heart and a good soul. You also have a long, hard road ahead of you. I wish it didn't have to be like this, but it is. Your lineage goes back all the way to the beginning of creation. Not many can say that. But *you* are the *last* one in your line."

"What's… *lineage*?"

"It means where your family came from. Your bloodline. The beginning of your family tree." Taking out a necklace, he carefully put it around her neck.

Feeling the weight of the cumbersome object against her chest, she looked down at it, furrowing a brow. "What's this?"

"A special necklace handed down from your… *lineage*. Being that you are the last… it now falls under *your* care. *You* are now the guardian of this necklace. Do not let anything happen to it. Never take it off. Ever. Protect it with your life because it is more valuable than you are. We will teach you how to be a fighter… a warrior… a survivor in all situations."

Taking the bulky pendant between her little fingers, she studied it for a moment before looking up at him. "It's heavy."

"You'll get used to the weight. Remember, Dustina, you're a special girl and that requires special training."

…

Gasping awake, Dusty sat up, gripping the necklace. She did, in fact, get used to it. Fighting the sudden dryness in her throat, she blinked, slowly releasing her hold.

What was that?

'You tell me.'

That face. Right after my parents died… Sir G had come and picked me up.

'Why would that surprise you to see him again?'

I don't have any memories of that time or anything before it. It's as if they were just erased. That's the first one… that I can ever recall having.

'Maybe it's time that you start. Something in your past might help this mission progress faster.'

I don't see how, but why now? What is it about Spain that makes me remember something so long ago?

'Maybe you're just looking forward to the Caparrones?'

Shaking off that featherheaded thought – they had more important things to worry about than a weird dream of hers – she shoved a handful of jelly beans in her mouth. Stretching out, she felt cramped knots release from sleeping on the couch. After turning on the laptop, she headed into the kitchen area to make a strong pot of brewed delight. Another yawn escaped. All these catnaps were going to catch up to her eventually. The human body was not made to run forever on only a few hours' rest. That memory tossed shards of broken glass into her heart, making her eyes well up with a river of harnessed tears. It killed all hopes of ever going to back to sleep.

With a steaming cup in hand, she pulled her laptop closer, looking over at Hooch. Taking a sip, the heat warmed her to the core, as she breathed in the delicious vanilla scent, making her more alert. "Nothing like a good cup of strong coffee to make you right again. That dam has to be in a country that uses English for a language, Hooch. The two main ones that come to mind are the United States and the United Kingdom. Then again, would they really put two in the United States? That seems... rather odd."

Sitting beside her, it looked as if he understood, nodding in answer before emitting a low growl.

"Well, if neither of those pan out, then I'll just move onto the next English-speaking country on my list. First things, first." After giving him a belly rub, she pulled up the largest dams in the US. The slight mist of a forgotten cigarette burned out in the ashtray as she began her search.

6

After going through Garrick's distressing memories, Jonas had nothing but questions no one could answer. Needing a break from Garrick's thoughts raping his mind, he tapped on Antoine's door. "I'm heading out to Toledo. It's gorgeous this time of year. Care to join me?"

Bleary-eyed, still half asleep, the professor patted his stomach as it rumbled. "Aren't we gonna eat first?"

"No. It's ten-thirty in the morning."

"That's considered brunch to most people. Maybe because you don't *have* to eat, you've forgotten a little thing about eating *schedules* and how important they are to us... *mortals.*"

He offered the most he had for a smile with a slight lip raise. "Don't worry. We'll eat when we get there. I have something *special* in mind."

Stifling a yawn, Antoine stepped aside, letting Jonas in. "Man's gotta eat, but I'll forgo breakfast if ya promise to treat us to some *gen-u-ine* Spanish cuisine."

"Deal."

As Antoine dressed, the conversation turned. "Ya know, while I'd *love* to go sightseeing, convincing Dusty might be a different matter."

"It's not my place to convince her of *anything*, though I *can't* understand the constant need to *always* be on point." Recalling their cataclysmic difference of opinions, Jonas gazed out the window at the sun.

Antoine looked from a light blue shirt to a green one, trying to decide between the two as he casually glanced over at Jonas. "Speaking of always being on point… did she ever tell you how we met?"

"Vaguely. The CIA went through every language specialist in the world after discovering something with odd inscriptions on it. When their experts failed, she tracked you down."

"Yeah. I couldn't figure the damn thing out either." Reaching in, he settled on the blue one.

"That's what she said."

"Hell, I knew the second I saw it that there wasn't a snowball's chance in hell of solving it."

"Really? I could've sworn she said you tried."

"Naw. I gave the impression of trying, but I dragged it out for a month. Many times, Gabby invited her over for dinner. Dusty always declined. Too busy. Raincheck. However, if I called, the same exact day, with a possible update to the case, she came with bells on."

"Yeah, she works *too* much."

"Take the incident on the plane. She used the *only* thing she could relate to for calming me down."

"Which is?"

"The only thing that works with *her*. *She* turned it into work to get my mind off the fear that we were gonna crash. When she did, it also took *her* mind off Travis. Do you know *how* I knew that would work?"

"Because she works too much," Jonas reiterated, leaning against the chest of drawers by the door.

"No. When I first met Dusty, I could tell there was something special about her. I know you can sense it too."

Running a hand through his hair, Jonas averted his eyes. "Not sure what you're talking about."

Antoine scoffed, waving a hand in the air. "Bullshit! You know *exactly* what I mean."

His eyes snapped back to Antoine. "I thought you were happily married."

That brought a smile to the old man's face as Jonas finally admitted his deep fascination for Dusty. "Not like that. For me, it was more like… have you ever seen a litter of puppies, but you were instantly drawn to the runt because no one really cared for it?"

"Yeah."

"I saw it the *moment* I laid eyes on her. They put her on such a strict regime that it was flat out child abuse. *No* child deserves to live like that."

Shifting his weight, Jonas huffed out his cheeks. "Is this story going somewhere?"

Sitting on the bed, Antoine reached for one of his loafers, sliding it on. "Did you *really* think I was terrified on the plane?"

Remembering the absolute fear in the man's eyes and how he broke out in a sweat, Jonas nodded. "Yes. The worst case of aerophobia I've ever seen. You should be medicated."

Buffing his nails, Antoine winked, giving his best 'Elvis' impersonation. "Why, thank you. Thank you very much."

Crinkling his forehead, Jonas stared at him. "*What* are you talking about, Antoine?"

"Maybe *you* didn't see it, what with you two being at odds with each other, but *that* girl is hurt. Even though she *claims* no one has gotten close enough to affect her heart, Travis did. She loves that boy – even though she won't admit it to herself – and what he did hurt."

Jonas felt a forbidden twinge in his chest. "I know you two are close, but she told me she's *never* been in love. I think she would know better than you."

"How?"

"What do you mean, *how*? You're the professor, surely you can figure that out."

"When you were younger, you had a mother's love, right?"

"Yes."

"You watched the relationship between your parents."

"Sure. Even though my father cheated on my mother left and right, she only saw him for who he was in her eyes. She adored him. Faults and all."

"That's how a child learns. If it's not a caring relationship between the parents, *that* takes a *whole* different route."

"One of the many problems with the world today."

Antoine cleared his throat. "To hear Dusty talk, she didn't have anything close to *any* sort of relationship with anyone. Her parents died in a fire. Her uncle really didn't give a crap and blamed her for everything."

"Yeah, he didn't sound like a nice guy."

"No, he didn't. Dusty's been in training since she was just a small child. Never shown an ounce of love, tenderness, or caring. A prisoner on Death Row has *more* freedom than she did. Duty and orders are the *only* things she's ever known. A vacation to her – when she's never been on one – is as foreign as a Martian's language would be to me, though I would love to meet an alien."

"Just like realizing that vampires are real… and meeting me. She thought we were nothing more than mosquitoes," Jonas admitted with an understanding nod.

"Exactly. I've been a firm believer in the supernatural – blame Sam and Dean for that one – so it was easier to grasp once it sunk in. Demons. Angels. Vampires. Werewolves. Creatures from the dark. Witches. *Chuck*." He chuckled. "Watching TV and movies starts the ball rolling with imagination. Reading fictional novels is another way to create fantasy in the mind. It makes you think… what if? The Bible, though filled with its own… *stories*… isn't exactly imagination inspiring."

"True, but I *have* offered to sit down and watch movies *and* TV shows with her. She refuses."

"Apparently, so did Travis. She mentioned many times it was the only way that he got to name Hooch. That right there should tell you something. She trusted him to name her new little baby. She and Hooch hit it off with a deep emotional connection right away. Like the two of them were put into each other's path by a higher power."

Jonas rolled his eyes at the mention of his rival. "Whatever."

"Accept her for the person she is… *right* now. Unlike others, she hasn't been loved… save for me, Gabby, Hooch, and… evidently… Travis. You can look in her eyes and see that she's hurt by what happened. That means he wormed his way inside like a summer cold and she didn't even realize it. She might've *thought* it was just sexual, but her heart begged to differ. He offered her something missing in her life and she accepted it and him."

"Yeah, I see what you mean."

"*Most* people would've figured it out, but they also would've had something to base it off of. Dusty's flying blind… and has been solo for most of her life. What seems normal to us is foreign to her. You know how it is… people always try to change what they don't understand… fix something they think is broken… try to make the abnormal… normal. Travis didn't do that. He loves her for who she is and accepts all her quirks. It was the best time of her life. He didn't try to change her but loved her instead."

"I'm not trying to change her, Antoine. I just wish she would ease off the gas once in a while. Enjoy what possible little time we have left on Earth."

Antoine couldn't hide the smile as he stood, moving his pajamas to the top of his bag still packed in the corner. "Maybe she will, maybe she won't. That's not for you, or me, to push."

"Well, *I* won't be pushing her in any direction at all from this point forward." Heading for the door, Jonas paused. "I'll be down in the lobby waiting."

As the door closed, Antoine stared at it in surprise. "What the hell?" Shaking his head, he finished dressing, splashed on Aqua Velva, and headed out to the living room, rapping on the wall. "Knock-knock." Popping around the corner, he saw her hunched over the laptop, exactly where he thought she would be. "Did you sleep at all?"

"Enough." Reaching over, she butted out the cigarette filter, smoldering in the ashtray. Shoving her hand into the bag of candy on the coffee table, she grabbed a fistful.

His stomach protested loudly again. Reaching down, he patted it like he would Hooch, before moving to take a seat beside her, snatching a handful of jelly beans. "Settle down. I'll get you something real shortly." Looking around, he saw the tablet of paper between the laptop and overflowing ashtray, with words underlined and then crossed out. "It looks like you've been at this for a while."

"Long enough. There are a craptastic number of dams in the US and UK."

"*Why* are you concentrating on just *those* two places?"

"Because the quatrain's in English."

"English is recognized by a lot more than just two countries."

"I know, but I went with the obvious first. If these two don't pan out, I'll start checking other areas. I already ruled out the UK. None of them match."

"Well, considering *you're* the only one of us who saw it, only *you'll* be able to recognize it."

"True. Hopefully, *I* will before Seth does."

As the old man sat down, Hooch bounded over, begging for attention. "Ya know, you're gonna drive poor Hooch away if ya don't take him out for some play time."

"He gets plenty of play time. Remember, he sleeps with me. I pet him until I fall asleep."

"You mean what *little* sleep you get." Giving the ghost dog a good belly rub, he looked over her work area. "Damn, woman. You're gonna burn yourself out."

"We *have* to figure this out before Seth does."

As the puffs of smoke drifted in his direction, he moved the ashtray to one of the other end tables. "That's just gross. You *really* should stop that nasty habit. It stinks. All the perfume in the world can't mask that funk! You never know when a fella's gonna wanna kiss you. *No* one wants sloppy seconds from the Marlboro man – that's like sucking on a dirty ashtray. Ew."

"Ya been sucking on dirty ashtrays lately to even *know* what it's like?" The irritation on her face screamed out her annoyance with the same rerun again. "Hell. That's just *more* reason to keep smoking if you ask me."

"Regardless. It's a nasty habit."

"I'll take it under advisement."

"Not to change the subject... but... Jonas is gonna visit his birthplace. It's a gorgeous morning, and he's promised to treat us to authentic Spanish food. Why don't you and Hooch set aside your work, just for a little while, and come with us."

After the squabble with Jonas, riding anywhere with him would be awkward – especially where they left it. Motioning to Hooch, she continued looking through pictures of dams on the internet. "I got a better idea. You take Hooch. That way, I can stay here and keep working. I feel like I'm close. Once I figure that out, we can be on our way to the next location."

"He'll never leave your side and you know it."

Pausing, she faced him. "How do you even know Jonas wants me there? Earlier, I said harsh things to him. Pretty sure, he doesn't want me along. But don't let that stop you guys from having a good time. I'm *determined* to figure out where this crack-a-lacking dam is if it kills me."

"You two are worse than a married couple. I swear I don't know which one is which. You know damn well he wants you there." Reaching over, he closed the laptop's screen. "We're a *team*. We do things *together*! Don't make me sling you over my shoulder like a caveman grabbing his woman, because I will. I haven't even *looked* at the scroll since I got here. You can set this aside for a little while. Besides, he *did* invite you... through me. He felt like *I* might be able to convince you better than he could. After all," buffing his nails on his chest, he offered her a smile that screamed of his teasing. "Everyone knows what a good *convincer* I am."

With tongue hanging out and tail beating against the floor, Hooch looked at her like only a loving pet could... even a ghost dog... with the saddest puppy dog eyes, begging her to go.

Glancing from one to the other, she scoffed, pushing the pad of paper back on the table. "*Convincer* is not a word, mister." Grabbing the jelly beans, she shoved them into her pocket. "Fine! I'll go! I need to get more jelly beans, anyway. I'm running low."

"How many did you bring for the trip?"

Shoving her notes and laptop under the couch, she cleaned up the area, making it look like a living room again. As he gave her an odd stare, she grinned. "Just in case someone comes in while we're gone, they won't find *anything*. And in answer to your question, dang near the entire bulk section of 'em from Costco's."

"So, instead of packing clothes, you grabbed jelly beans?"

"No, but unlike *most* women, I don't need a lot. Just my jeans, T-shirts, jacket, *unmentionables*, cigarettes, and jelly beans. The latter makes up most of my luggage." Picking up the cigarettes and lighter, she held a finger up to Antoine. "Not *one* word about the cigarettes." Walking to the door, she opened it, looking back. "Well, come on!"

Giving Hooch a big 'thumbs up' sign and a wink, Antoine followed them both out the door. "*That's* the ticket!"

"Yeah, yeah." Closing the door behind them, she put out the *Do Not Disturb* sign before following Antoine to the elevator.

7

As they rode down to the lobby, the cookie crumbs from earlier already vacuumed away, Antoine gently put a hand on Dusty's arm. "You *need* to cut Jonas a break. Whatever this stupid rift is between you two... draw a peace treaty already. Just for the day anyway."

An accusatory glare landed in his direction. "Why?"

"First off, it's getting old."

She narrowed her eyes. "So… you're choosing *his* side. Figures."

"Oh stop! I'm not sure *why* you're so furious at *him*."

"*He* knows."

"Does he? Really? The only thing *either* of us know… *Travis* has you miffed."

"Well –"

"Think about *this*. Jonas hasn't been back here since he left… *ages* ago. *Today* he wants to visit the only place he ever called home… to see his *mother*. It's *gotta* be affecting him. He's gonna need *our* support, though he would never in a *million* years ask for it."

"Yeah, but why after all this time? Now? With us?"

"Only *he* can answer that but do me a favor. Don't ask. I'm not sure if you've noticed, but he's not as cold as the others. He actually *cares* about human life."

Taking a deep breath, she recalled the heartrending pain when Jonas shared the tragic memory of his last day on earth with his mother. The adoring way that Isabella stared at her only son, forever etched into Dusty's mind. So tender. Exhaling, she offered a temporary peace treaty. "Okay. So… stop being a bitch?"

"You said it. Not me."

Actually, the little voice in her head did, but she didn't need to share that with the rest of the class. They wouldn't understand. Hell, half the time, neither did she. Rounding the corner of the lobby, she saw Jonas. Handsome, standing by the door with a stoic expression, his body firm like a statue – his mind elsewhere. "Ya okay?"

"Well as can be expected, I guess."

"Good. So, Antoine says ya wanna go for a little drive. How far is this place?"

Feeling a flutter in his chest at her presence, he nodded, opening the door for them. Even though he wouldn't admit it, he got a thrill that she decided to come along for the ride, even if he didn't know why. "It'll take about a half hour to get there."

Either the guilt from Antoine's speech, the shared memory, or the dream from earlier triggered something within. Reaching out, she wrapped her arms comfortingly around Jonas for a tight, heartwarming hug. It sounded like he needed one. God only knew *she* did. "It'll be okay. We're here for you... *always*. Don't forget that. I might not like you at this moment, but I will *never* desert you." Her face buried into his chest, but the words were still audible. "Ever."

Closing his eyes, savoring the moment, he returned the hug. Hearing those words gave him more joy than he cared to admit. "Has anyone ever told you that you're bi-polar?"

"Among *other* things."

"I don't doubt it. After we visit my home, we'll get some Caparrones."

Quickly drawing back, the smile on her face matched the sparkle in her eyes. "Caparrones? *Really?*"

"Yep."

"I've been *dying* to try those since you teased me with them!" Turning, she headed out the door.

Wide-eyed, shaking his head at the dramatic change in her demeanor, Jonas turned to Antoine. "I'm not sure *what* you said or did but thank you. I *think* all has been forgiven... or she's doing a great job of driving me insane."

It did his old heart good to see Dusty acting like a loving human being. *There might be hope for these two after all*, he thought. "Women are *always* trying to drive us insane, Jonas. Since the beginning of time. You should *know* that after five hundred years."

"You'd think I would know a *lot* after five hundred years, Antoine. Doesn't mean I do, *especially* where women are concerned. No man will *ever* understand them."

Antoine laughed. "Sealed. Stamped. Delivered. *No* one does. Not even *them*."

Giving directions to the driver, Jonas got in the passenger's seat, facing the front. Along the way, he pointed out certain landmarks which existed from the time of his youth. "My father brought me to

Madrid when I was ten years old. After much... *convincing*... from my mother, he introduced me to important people."

"She must've been a much better convincer than me then."

Antoine laughed, poking her. "I don't know how many times we have to go over the fact that *convincer* is not a word."

"It is now! We've *both* used in a sentence."

"She was definitely a good *convincer* where my father was concerned. All she had to do was mention something one time and he moved the heavens and earth to make it happen. There, now all *three* of us have used it." Laughing, Jonas pointed to a small building. "El Gallo y Toro. The Cock and Bull. I had my first taste of wine in *that* very tavern. I got drunk off of one glass."

"*That's* the name? I'm pretty sure they mean chicken and beef, but... the translation gets lost in the shuffle." Dusty's eyes were like saucers, staring at the building as they passed by. "That's *not* the image floating in my mind."

Dumbfounded, Antoine thwapped her arm. "*Dusty!*"

Laughing, she turned, nudging him. "Well, it's *not!*"

Unable to keep a straight face, Jonas shifted in his seat, laughing. "Trust me. The first time I heard it, I thought my father was taking me to a... different... sort of establishment. The food there hasn't changed in over six hundred years."

"Holy olé! It's been open for *that* long? Can you imagine being born into *that* lifestyle and never knowing anything else but? I don't know if it would be memorable or boring!"

"I find it inspiring that people wanna keep things the same for generations." Antoine also stared out at the building. "Too many Mom-and-Pop stores die out because the spoiled kids don't wanna keep it going. Too much work or something."

"I wouldn't know what that's like." A hint of sorrow crept into her light tone.

Reaching over, Antoine squeezed her hand. "You'll *always* have us."

After softly smiling at him, she focused her attention back out the window. Spain did something strange to her emotions as she fought the sudden urge to become a bawl bag of tears.

The vehicle continued through the small town. "Many businesses in this area have been open for at least two hundred years." As they passed the *Toledo* sign, Jonas happily looked at the green landscapes filled with livestock; visions of happier times flooded his head. "Welcome home, Diego," he whispered.

"Did you know that the earliest recorded history of Toledo comes from the Romans? They captured this Iberian city in the year one-ninety-two BC. Being in the center, its location would stop invasions. It was the perfect defensive spot, being on a hill with deep water on three sides. When the Roman Empire fell, the Visigoths moved in. Their rule was short, but they left behind the laws and a centralized government that's used to this day," Antoine told them.

Unable to keep from smiling, his sudden lesson in history brought her out of her remorseful mood. "*Always* the professor."

"Learning never hurt nobody," he huffed.

"*Anyone,*" she corrected, poking him.

The journey wound through several old villages, some unchanged. As they looped around an old brick road, the car stopped – they arrived at their destination.

Jonas glanced around, grief tinting his voice. "They're right. You can never go home again."

Hearing the pensive tone, Hooch jumped onto his lap, slobbering all over his face.

Tackling the endearing poltergeist, Jonas couldn't help but feel better as he gave him a good belly rub. "Oh, you're such a good boy! Who's a good boy!"

Rubdown complete, Hooch jumped up eager to go, unearthly tail thumping everyone.

As Antoine battled the swiping apparition, Dusty opened the door. "Come on, Hooch. Let's go check things out."

Invitation accepted, he bolted from the vehicle. Even a phantom dog loves to get out and run back and forth at full speed every once in a while.

While Hooch frolicked, Dusty investigated the burned-out shell of a five-hundred-year-old Nobleman's hacienda. Crumbling walls, thick with vines, reached for the clear blue sky. Jonas led them on a tour of what remained, reliving the last dinner he shared with his beloved mama. As he finished, there were no tears this time just a far-away stare into the dark part of his past when they stopped in what was once a grand dining room.

While thumbing over a time-worn relic of a forgotten age – a dinner table scorched and burned – Dusty glanced over at Jonas. "There's been something clawing at me since we shared that vision. *Who* killed your mother? Did ya ever figure out who shot the arrow? I mean, to shoot it through a window like that *had* to take some skill."

"And *hit* someone." Doubt edged Antoine's tone. "It's one thing to shoot an arrow all willy-nilly into the sky and hope it lands somewhere. It's another to actually hit what you're aiming at."

Jonas looked off to the horizon. "Don't know."

"You never thought of finding out? Maybe exacting revenge?" Dusty ignored the "Don't push him!" look in Antoine's eyes. "As long as I've known you –" her words ceased for a moment as shock registered. "W*ow!* It *really* hasn't been that long but… it seems a *lot* longer. Like… I've known you my entire life!"

Looking over the charcoaled ruins, Jonas rolled his shoulders. "That was a *whole* different situation. With all the political battles going on back then, we never knew *who* ordered the assassination. Royals fought amongst themselves for different reasons. First and foremost, power. Being of royal blood – never mind how far *down* into the family tree roots we went – put a target on our back."

Scrunching up her brows, Dusty let out an exasperated breath. "The village didn't hold you in high esteem? Hell, when it got around that royalty was living within their ranks, why didn't they use you to get in good with the king? Wasn't that the big hoopla back then? Who could kiss the most butt and receive the most reward?"

"Yeah, but we were caught somewhere in between."

"Meaning?"

"My father was the lowest man on the royal totem pole, so he didn't have *any* pull with the king. He was just another nobody. Mooching off his blood relation. Doing a menial job that any peasant could do. Collecting gold for his deeds. If the king overtaxed the village – never mind that *we* paid them too – the villagers harassed us. It isn't like today's politicians, with all their loopholes. Any time the king passed some bullshit law, the village looked at *us* as if *we* cast the deciding vote… even though we had *nothing* to do with it. My father took a lot of their complaints to the king, but that just pissed him off."

"So then… being royal didn't help?"

"Nope. It made things worse. On both sides."

Antoine kicked at a piece of blackened wood. "Why didn't your family live in the castle?"

"My mother. See, dear old dad had quite the reputation for being a womanizing rouge."

"Hence the whore house," Dusty interjected.

"Exactly, but with all the courtesans running around the castle, he didn't have to go any further. All they required was a trinket or two to keep them happy. My mother didn't want to *see* any part of it. Rumors of him parading around town with this woman or that she could ignore, but actually witnessing it… another story entirely. My father *begged* her to live within the security of the castle, where he spent much of his time, but she refused. He even tried to get her to move into one of the houses on the other side of the barrier. It was just too close. They compromised. That's why we were located way back here… away from everyone… but people love to talk. She wanted me to live a normal life – as opposed to a spoiled-rotten one of royalty – but that was impossible. It was either the life of a prince… or a pauper." Glancing around, sadness registered across his face. "Neither seemed appealing. I've always believed *this* was an act to show the royals that if they could get to the lesser nobles in the family, they could easily get to the crown itself."

Antoine stared around the room, watching the events unfolding within his mind. "What a cowardly thing to do! Oh sure, it's easy to take out a mother and her child… unguarded… defenseless… but go up against an army? Good luck. I wonder if anyone ever suffered for this? Other than your father, I mean."

"No clue. It took all I had to survive when my father cast me aside. I had to learn to live off the streets, which isn't as easy as romantic novels make it sound."

"Doesn't sound very romantic to me." Walking back outside, Dusty watched Hooch running as Jonas joined her. "I'm just surprised you didn't look them up, doing a little research into who it was, make their generations suffer for it. That's all. I mean, after what you did to your own father, one would expect a little payback."

"Dusty, some things are just too painful to –" Antoine's eyes widened, snapping to Jonas. "Wait! *What* did you do to your father?"

When Jonas didn't answer, Dusty did. "Found him in a whore house years later. Killed him."

"What?! Your own flesh and blood?"

Not wanting to continue diving into a part of his history that cut like a knife, he pointed off to the distance. "Dusty can explain it to you later. Come on. I'll introduce you to mi Madre."

8

A few hundred feet to the west, they arrived at a small fenced in cemetery. Several old stones lay on the ground, broken, scrubbed blank by time. One, in the left corner still intact, had centuries of overgrowth hiding it from the world. Jonas got on his knees, pulling the thick vines away, as Dusty and Antoine pitched in to help. Even Hooch. It didn't take long to expose the deep carving on the stone.

Rising, he crossed himself, speaking in perfect Spanish. "Hello, mama. It has been forever since I have visited. Please forgive me. Much has happened, and I did not want you to see me like this. I hope you will forgive me for what I have become and for the suffering I have caused. As much as it pains me to say… I do not believe we will see each other in the hereafter. I am bound for another place, altogether. However, I hold your memory in my heart and always see you in my dreams. Mama, these are my friends,

Antoine, Dusty, and the little guy, Hooch. We are working hard against an evil, the likes of which the world has never seen. I will need your love and guidance to be strong enough to do what I must. I hope you are still proud of me. When you look down… smile… remember me for who I once was. Your little boy who loves you more than life itself… to this very day. Mama, Dusty reminds me of you, in many ways. Strong. Vital. Loyal. She is the glue holding our little group together. You would love her as much as I do. Much time has gone by, but I think of you every day. When I leave here, I do not know if I will be able to visit again. I am not long for this world, but just know… with everything that I am… I will always be your Don Diego Ramirez. I love you. Be well, mama."

Antoine bowed his head, sighing at the loving words spoken with such raw emotion. It showed a side of Jonas that the professor didn't believe existed anymore… until that very moment.

When Jonas stopped talking, Dusty kissed her crucifix, before hiding it under her shirt again. Turning, she left the little circle and headed over to the wildflowers growing at the edge of the woods. Her mind a million miles away. After searching the area, she found a stone sharp enough to dig into the earth. Getting down on her hands and knees, she started edging around a clump of flowers, tilling up the soil until she had the root and all.

Watching her, Antoine's brow rose at the kind gesture. He had not seen *that* side of Dusty, in all the time he knew her. It made him smile. The much-needed vacation showed a human side to a creature who long ago lost that part of himself. It also exposed the gentle side of a woman who had buried her feelings with all of her memories. With Dusty's attention elsewhere, Antoine, reached over, tapping Jonas on the shoulder.

Jonas turned. "Yes?"

The professor inclined his head toward the car. "I wanna discuss the scroll with you, but I don't want Dusty to hear, in case she suddenly decides to shift back into work mode."

Understanding, Jonas followed the old man to the car.

Kneeling in front of the weathered stone, Dusty used the rock to make a hole big enough for the different colored flowers. They would bloom yearly if she did it right. Bringing over the pretty light pink and deep purple plants, they added some much-needed life to the neglected sight. That vision showed into Jonas's soul and how much he adored his mother and how deeply she loved her only child. Experiencing it through his eyes dug into her conflicted heart. Never knowing a mother's love hurt more than she let on. After all, the unending training taught her to show no pain or emotions. Not even if it felt as if her spirit shattered. The only time she felt *true* love… in that shared vision.

Placing the plants around the marker, Dusty alternated the colors while speaking softly. "Hello, Isabella. I hope you don't mind if I call you that. Mrs. Ramirez just seems too formal for everything that your son and I have been through. Besides, the memory that Jo-… *Diego* shared with me, I feel like I know you personally. I know you see what your son has become. Being a God-fearing woman, who loves and cherishes the Lord as much as I do, you've probably stopped looking down on him from heaven due to his actions. Don't worry. As you know, the Lord puts people in other's paths for a reason. I was put in his to help him find his faith… so he can see his mama again." Once she planted the flowers, she wiped the dirt off the slab. "We'll keep him on the straight and narrow and make sure that he's still the same boy that his mama loved. I only wish I had a mother look at me the way you looked at him." Sighing softly, she brushed the tear from her eye.

Hooch whined, his slobbering tongue helping get rid of the evidence of the tear.

After reassuring him, she turned back to the grave. "Isabella, you should be really proud of Diego. Given the hard road forced upon him, he fought demons… came a long way. I believe *that* is in part due to your wonderful job raising him into the fine man that I proudly call my partner. Just don't tell him I said that, or I will deny… deny… deny. What he has become is no fault of his own. I blame his worthless father, who I know you loved deeply, but even *you* had to have cursed him when he blamed his very own son for your death… when it was *his* own doing that caused your untimely demise. Don't worry. I'll watch out for him. It was really nice meeting you." That said, she leaned up, kissing her fingers, placing them on the cold rock. "Rest in peace, Isabella Ramirez," she whispered in perfect Spanish, slowly walking away.

Off in their own little corner, Jonas looked at Antoine. "So, what do you have, pops?"

"Well, I think we'll be able to beat Sethy-poo to the punch this time. Since I don't have to translate anything, we just have to figure out the damn riddle. I don't wanna say anything else right now, in case… well in case *someone's* listening, know what I mean, Vern?"

Giving the old man a chuckle, Jonas started back to the grave.

Antoine stopped him. "You may have eternity son, but she does not," he whispered in Spanish.

Jonas nodded. "I know, Antoine. And that's what scares me."

"Are you afraid of losing your immortality… or *her*?"

Before Jonas had time to think of a lie, Dusty joined them. "So, who's ready to eat?"

"Me!" Antoine clapped his hands. "About damn time. I was beginning to think you were gonna landscape the entire area! Though, it does look nice, I must say. You added life to a neglected eyesore. Good job." Then he turned to Jonas. "I *am* still starving!"

"I'm feeling kinda hungry too. Can't live off jelly beans for long. What about getting some Caparrones? I can't leave here without trying them. Especially after that memory where you fed them to me… or rather teased me with just a taste." Dusty wiped her hands down her jeans, leaving streaks of brown embedded into the black denim material. A smile on her dirty face. It looked as if she just finished playing in the dirt with gobs in her hair, on her clothes, and halfway up her arms.

Antoine stared at her in surprise as if she had just risen from the grave. "You're not gonna wash up first?"

Looking down at her appearance, she flashed a grin at Antoine before glancing around. "Oh yeah. Sure. Which way to the bathroom… oh right… there isn't one here. However, I'm sure where we're going, they do. I mean… *lots* of places have moved into the proper century with… indoor plumbing… sinks… you know, things necessary to help me clean up."

Reaching over, Antoine patted her down, knocking off as much as he could. His actions sparked a dust cloud, as if opening up an ancient mummy's coffin. "Good Lord, child. How did you get it all over you? Good thing you don't get this messy when you eat."

Unable to stop from laughing, she shook her head. "Hooch thought we were playing a game and started kicking it on me."

"Good thing we're in the middle of nowhere and no one saw dirt just flying at you from the ground. That might be a little harder to explain." After he finished, scowling, he looked her up and down. "Well, *that* will have to do. It's much better than before, but you *really* should stop off at the bathroom and clean up first. You look like you just dug yourself out of a grave."

"Yes, daddy."

9

After Antoine managed to get as much dirt off Dusty as he could, he hopped into the backseat. Dusty climbed in after him with Hooch deciding to rest on both of them, hoping they both would give him a good scratching. After all, he just played in the dirt as well.

After munching on a handful of jelly beans, she winked at Jonas. "Ready to go."

"After this trip, I'm gonna be addicted to those dang things. Gimme some." Holding out his hand, Antoine waited while she handed him the bag. "They may not be healthy, but you're right about one thing."

"What's that?"

"It stops hunger pains from eating away at my insides."

"Keeps the blood sugar balanced too."

Turning around to face them, Jonas smiled, reaching out his hand as well, taking a turn at digging into the candy. "Next stop… Casa de Ramirez."

After swallowing, Antoine dug a finger into his mouth, prying a stray piece off his teeth. "So, inquiring minds would like to know how your family started a restaurant?"

"That is a long and twisted story. The short of it, after my father exiled me from the family, one of his brothers opened a small roadside place for travelers to eat." Turning, he popped a few beans into his mouth. "He often spoke of opening a restaurant and it was the only way he could leave out scraps of food for me to find without visibly going against my father's wishes. Some days I got it, others someone else did, but it kept me alive until I could fend for myself. It's hard to do much when you're fighting an infection on your own… and you're still just a boy. He kept it going and grew it into one of the finest restaurants in all of Toledo. I never forgot his kindness."

Leaving the bag on the console, Dusty grabbed another handful, popping them into her mouth. "And it's been around all this time?"

"Oh yes. Even though I haven't been back in centuries, I've *always* kept an eye on things and made sure that it remained solvent."

Her brow shot up, questioningly. "Oh? What *exactly* did you do?"

A sly grin played across his face, making his eyes glisten with flecks of gold. "Deva isn't the *only* one with deep pockets. During hard times, when war or natural disasters struck the area, I made sure that my uncle's restaurant always had the funds to see them through. There's a reason no one has developed on the plot of land that my family's house sits on." Winking, he turned around just as they pulled into the parking lot. "And here we are."

The vehicle pulled to a stop, parking in a reserved space. Once Dusty stepped out, flavorful aromas almost knocked her down. She inhaled deeply. "Oh, my word! Do you smell that? What *is* that? Now, I'm *really* hungry. I hope they have Caparrones."

"I wouldn't have brought you here if they didn't. This place was handed down from generation to generation and they still have all my mother's recipes, though I'm not sure how they got them. It's close to her cooking. Only *I* can tell the difference." After Antoine exited the vehicle, Jonas instructed the driver to keep his eyes peeled for *unwelcome* guests.

Looking to Hooch, she smiled. "Sorry boy. You need to stay here with… this guy."

Groups of people sat at the different tables in the outside garden area, chatting and laughing softly with each other while enjoying their meals. Entering the crowded Cantina, Dusty noticed the mixed décor right away. Save for the beer taps, lights, and an ATM machine, she swore they stepped into the late seventeenth century. Tapestries hung from the old stone walls, embroidered with countryside scenes depicting life in another era.

Delightful scents wafted from the kitchen. Antoine closed his eyes. A look of pure bliss spread across his face. The hostess led them to a table in the back – one for reserved guests. Upon the wall, a painting of a nobleman, his beautiful wife, and handsome young son looked down at them. Jonas chose the first chair which put his back to it.

Passing by the different plates of food, the underlying scent of spice assaulted Dusty's nostrils, tempting the inside of her nose. After a quick trip to the bathroom, she took a seat at the table. "I can't wait to bite into a Caparrone."

After setting the menus down, the hostess left them with the usual, "your waitress will be right with you."

Her eyes shot to the life size painting, instantly recognizing it from his vision. "Jump back! Wow. It looks so real. I can see why you wouldn't wanna be reminded of how things were. It looks just like it did back when you were a boy."

Taking his eyes from the delicious morsels, Antoine glanced back to Dusty. "Whatever are you talking about? Though I'm sure they keep a few things, this place is most definitely of the modern day and age."

"The painting. It's him and his family."

Peering closer, Antoine's eyes widened. "Well, what do you know about that? It is!" Turning back to the menu, he picked it up, shaking his head. "Now, onto important matters. After starving me for two days, I feel like I could eat everything on this menu, so picking just one thing is gonna be quite hard."

Giving it the once over, Dusty shrugged. "I don't care to see the menu. I've been dying for a Caparrone. If I don't have one now, I never will."

Glancing through the list of options, Jonas did a double take. "Things *have* changed a bit. Just in case the traditional dishes are too spicy for your tastes, you can always go with an American favorite." He winked at Dusty with a sly grin. "How about a cheeseburger? But, if they're using local beef, the taste won't be what you're used to." Glancing over at Antoine, the old man poured over the menu like an editor looking for punctuation errors. "See anything interesting?"

The professor peeked over the top. "Yes, but I'm looking for a dish called *one of each*. They need to have a sampler meal that allows you a bite of *everything*."

Shaking his head, Jonas chuckled. "Put it in the suggestion box."

Returning to the laminated pages, Antoine sighed. "I wonder if they have a to go section." His eyes darted back to Jonas. "You know… for later."

The waitress appeared, standing slightly to the side of Jonas with long brown hair, captured in a neat ponytail, reaching the middle of her back. A pair of expressive, deep brown eyes sparkled as she introduced herself. "Welcome to Casa De Ramirez," she said, her exceptional English leaving only a subtle hint of Spanish accent. "I'm Isabella. May I start you off with something to drink?"

At the mention of his mother's name, Jonas turned his head, blinking in surprise, unable to take his eyes off her. The girl looked young, no more than twenty, but with a striking resemblance he instantly recognized. For a moment, he saw his beloved mother. "What would you suggest?"

Looking down, she smiled softly. "We have an excellent red wine."

"That sounds most inviting," he said, regaining his composure. Looking at his friends, he wondered if they even noticed. "It's very good."

Tilting her head, Isabella studied his face. "You have been here before, Señor?"

Turning back up to smile at her, he nodded. "Yes, but not for a very long time."

"You look strangely familiar."

Looking back to the menu, he gave a lift of his shoulder. "I have one of those faces."

"Perhaps." She turned to Dusty. "Señorita?"

Taking her eyes from the menu, Dusty's breath caught in her throat as the woman's face came into view. She could be his mother's twin. Coughing to hide the shocked expression, she patted her chest. "Oh, excuse me. Must've had some dirt still in my lungs, I guess," she pointed to a section on the menu. "I'll try the red wine also, thanks."

"Good choice." Seeing Dusty's reaction, Jonas tried hiding his smile in a drink of water.

Isabella turned to Antoine. "Something to drink, Señor?"

Still pouring over the menu, he appeared indecisive about two choices before pointing at one. "I see you have Alhambra Mezquita. I'd like a cold bottle of that please."

Breathing in the luscious scents made Dusty's stomach growl loudly. Her eyelids fluttered with anticipation. "Red wine goes good with Caparrones, right?"

Jonas nodded. "The Ramirez red wine goes with anything. Even cheeseburgers."

"*Caparrones?*" Isabella's smile widened. "Very few people order that anymore. Luckily, my brother, Diego, is our chef and *always* has some on hand. This recipe has been handed down. They are *delicious*."

Hearing his own name, Jonas nodded in respect. Grinning slightly, he held up two fingers. "Make that *two* orders, please."

After mulling over every dish and ingredients, Antoine set his menu to the side. "Well, leave it to me to be different. I'd like to start with a plate of Pintxo's and a bowl of Gazpacho."

Crossing his arms over his chest, Jonas leaned back in the chair. "Are you *sure* your stomach can handle that, Antoine?"

Patting his stomach, he snorted. "It handled ten Bhut jolokia's. I'm sure it can handle your Gazpacho."

Taking up the menus, Isabella disappeared around the corner but soon returned with their drinks. "Your meals will be ready shortly." She placed a basket of warm Spanish pan rolls and honey butter on their table. "Anything else I can get for you?"

Glancing from the painting to Isabella, Dusty arched a brow. "Well, slap my mouth and call me stupid! You look just like that woman in the painting! Are you related, by chance?" Even though she knew the answer, she still had to ask.

Isabella blushed, the color enhancing her beauty, then looked at Dusty in confusion. "Señorita, no! I would never call you stupid or slap your mouth." Shock soon turned to a smile as her eyes lit up like twin candles, focusing on the painting with such love and adoration. "Si, I am. My papa named me after Señora Isabella Ramirez… a great woman… and my brother after her son. A tragedy happened to them long ago and this is his manner to pay respect. What better way to keep showing appreciation but to keep the family name alive? My family traces its roots to her. According to legend, Juan Sanchez Villa Lobos Ramirez, her brother-in-law, started this place, five hundred years ago. I often find myself daydreaming about living in that wonderful time, curious of how it would've been."

Glancing down, Jonas adjusted his napkin. "I'm sure it wasn't as grand as paintings and stories portray." Winking up at her, he smiled to soften the harshness of his words. "But I'm also sure that had *you* lived in that time, your father would have had his hands full with suitors, noble and otherwise."

Trying to hide the flirtatious giggle, she put a hand up to her lips. "Señor, you are too kind." Her smile faded as she stared at him and then the painting and back again. "Forgive me, Señor, but you look very much like the boy in this painting. Is your family from this area, as well?"

"Yes, but my ancestors left… probably not many years after that painting was done."

Staring at her, Antoine became interested. "You say that the woman's brother-in-law was named Juan Sanchez Villa Lobos Ramirez? Does the phrase *'there can be only one'* sound at all familiar to you?"

Shifting her baffled gaze from Jonas, who was trying to stifle a laugh, toward the professor, she cocked her head to the side. "Why… *no* Señor, it doesn't. Should it?"

Giving her a wink, Antoine smiled. "No, it's just some old man's fantasy. Pay me no mind, dear. I get this way when I haven't been fed in a few hours."

Just as bewildered as Isabella, Dusty took another sip of wine, before pointing at the menu. "Do you think we could get some of those nachos with sour cream and all the fixings with guacamole on the side? That might help with the zoo sounds coming from this table before too long."

"Chiliango nachos!" Her face beamed. "They are *soo* delicious. I will get some for you right away!"

As Isabella vanished around the corner, Jonas hit Antoine in the shoulder lightly. "*There can be only one?* Are you serious? That young woman has probably never even *heard* of Highlander, let alone understood the reference."

Laughing, Antoine looked at Dusty, knowing that she too had no idea what they were talking about. Before he could give Jonas a reply, Isabella returned with a steaming plate of fresh nachos and several cups filled with different salsas and guacamole.

Setting the plate in the center of the table, she smiled. "Your meals are on their way."

"Thank you very much!" Grabbing one of the crispy nachos, Dusty dipped it into the maroon-colored salsa. "Oh my God. This is paradise on a platter."

As promised, their main courses soon arrived, and they busied themselves in the flavorful meals. The Caparrones were so close to his mother's that Jonas flashed back for a moment. Words like "delicious" and "amazing" were the only ones spoken as they spent the better part of an hour in culinary Eden.

Taking a sip of wine, Jonas carefully set the goblet aside. "As good as this is, and as much as I appreciate both of you indulging me this little side trip, we need to start talking about where we're headed next." Turning to Antoine, the professor seemed to be in a food coma. "So, tell us what you have. Other than indigestion."

Frowning, the old man stuck out his tongue. "I've eaten everything from the nastiest bugs, to the finest Caviar but I have to say that this meal is in my top three of all time." Taking a deep breath, he leaned back in his chair, having a pull from his beer. "Well," he began, setting the bottle down, "we know it's English… so there's that."

Taking the last nacho, Dusty scraped the remaining guacamole from the cup before shoving it into her mouth. "From what I've been able to gather, the dam isn't in the UK. The one that looks the closest, so far, is the Hoover Dam. I can't be sure, yet. You pulled me away before I could double check."

"Well, if everyone is ready, we can head back to the hotel." Jonas turned to Dusty. "I know you're *dying* to get back to work. But in all seriousness… thanks for taking the vacation. It meant a lot to me."

Downing the rest of her spirits, she set the chalice on the table before smiling at him. "Believe it or not… it meant a lot to me too. Now… I don't have to *wonder* what Caparrones taste like… I *know*. It adds more meaning to the memory too."

"Wait. *My* memory? You still see it?"

"Yeah. Like it was my own."

Jonas furrowed his brows. "That's odd. Usually, the recipient only holds onto it during the transfer, but it quickly fades when the connection is broken. After that, remembering *anything* about it is impossible. Too cloudy to recall any details."

Dusty shook her head. "Psh! Someone fed you a mess of horse feathers. Not even. I can see and feel everything like it happened *to* me. The emotions. The pain. The slightest detail in the dining room floor to the delicious steam rising from the pot. Everything. It's like… it's etched into my brain."

"Hm. That *is* odd."

Not paying attention to their conversation, Antoine called Isabella over. "I want one of those nacho platters to go. The biggest ya got." Settling back, he patted his stomach. "Man can't live off jelly beans alone."

10

Once back at the hotel, Dusty imagined a thousand sand fleas burrowing into her skin. Possibly remnants from digging in the dirt but it still gave her the heebie-jeebies thinking that anything would be setting up shop on her body. "Okay team, y'all are gonna have to give me a couple of hours to clean up and soak in that massage tub."

Jonas's brow rose. "*A couple of hours*? I know women like to freshen up, but… don't you think that we-"

"Look Sparx, we took almost a *whole* day walking down memory lane for you. I'm still covered in dirt and Lord knows what else. All *kinds* of things live in the dirt. The bathroom at the restaurant wasn't good enough to clean… everything… just the dirt under my nails so I could eat. I haven't had a good bath in what feels like ages. I am taking one *now*. Like I said, I will see you two in a couple of hours."

He looked at Antoine for help.

"Not getting involved in this one, son. You're on your own." Antoine raised his hands and headed to his room.

Huffing out an impatient breath, Jonas shrugged. "Fine. You go play little mermaid. I expect you to be shining… or looking like a prune. After that, *no* more breaks!"

Biting back the retort of not needing his permission, she forgot all about it as the aromatic aroma of bath oils filled the air. Since the evening Jonas – the animal expert – walked into her office, late, starting off on a bad foot, she barely had time to jump in a shower and rinse the day's sweat off. Sinking into the soothing heat, she felt her body relax. The pulsating jets worked magic on sore muscles, but nothing could touch the heartbreaking question rolling around in her mind.

Which one of us is gonna survive this?

Her heart shattered at the real possibility of losing someone else.

Shaking off the worry, a stray memory surfaced of another, happier time, in a different tub.

…

"Are ya gonna soak in there all night, or am I gonna have to come in and get ya?" Travis anxiously walked into the room. "We got places to be and things to see." Stopping short, he leaned against the wall, a devious grin lining his lips. "Then again, I kinda like what I'm seeing right now."

Pulling the bubbles closer to her body, Dusty sat up, leaving nothing for his viewing pleasure but suds saturating her feminine curves. "Good, because everything else can wait. This bath is so warm... very inviting... don't ya think?"

"Woman! Don't think I won't pick you up and carry you to the bed. Bubbles and all. It'll make a mess but be well worth cleaning it up!"

Playfully winking, she motioned to the tub. "Ooh, I think this is plenty big for the *both* of us."

"True. If we pile on top of each other."

"If you can find me in the bubbles... I'm all yours."

"Promises, promises," he told her, peeling off his shirt. "I'll believe that when I don't have to hogtie ya to the bed to see ya. Ya know I'm crazy about you, Dusty. You're the *onliest* one I ever gave a rat's ass over. So why ya gotta do me like that?"

Raising a leg out of the water, she ran her fingers down it in a teasing manner. "Because you like hogtying me to the bed."

"Damn right. Ya can't run out on me then." Watching her, he unbuckled his belt. "Keep up the teasing and I'm gonna give it to ya good."

Winking, her finger traveled further down with a sexy moan. "Promises... promises."

...

The knock on the door brought her out of the daydream with a start. Remembering the good times put a smile on her face, but it didn't last long with the memory of him shooting her, overriding the happiness, replacing it with heart-shattering pain.

Antoine stood outside the bathroom door – after losing a two-out-of-three game of rock, paper, scissors with Jonas – and gently knocked again. "Dusty? You okay in there?"

Washing the tears away, like Antoine could see through the door, she cleared her throat. "Yep. Just enjoying the quiet. Did you take a bath, yet? This thing is *wonderful*. It makes me wish for the days when things weren't so... rushed."

Sighing deeply, he closed his eyes in silent prayer. He heard the emotion through her teasing. As much as he hated to drag her out, they still had a deadline. "Yes, I did. I know! It felt so good. Made me all tingly when I got out. But… um… I hate to bother ya, but… we *really* need to know where that dam is. Jonas and I are just going back and forth with ideas, but… *you're* the only one who saw it, so that means we can't even *guess* to the next location. Umm… so… can ya… like… put a spin on that bath? We *really* need to get back to work on this."

Fighting back the urge to selfishly stay in the tub all night, she groaned. "Yeah. I'll be out in a minute."

"Okay. Ya want me to make ya a cup of coffee? Sounds like ya might need it."

"Yes, please. That sounds heavenly. Just… don't let Jonas fix it. I'm not in the mood for mud. Thanks."

Since arriving in Spain, a whole cluster of raw emotions attacked her like heat missiles seeking out the closest warm body. It put her on high alert and near tears at the drop of a hat. Luckily, her training taught her to ignore such things. In the solitude of the bathroom, she didn't hold them back any longer. Putting her hands over her eyes, she silently cried for the loss of someone who meant more to her than even she realized. As her shoulders rocked with silent sobs, tears washed down her face. After a few minutes, she sucked in a deep, ragged breath. The despair savagely raped her soul, fueling more salty tears as if the man had died in a bloody war. Then again, in a way, he did.

Wearing clean clothes again, towel-drying her hair, she sat on the couch going through the dam websites, searching for the image embedded in her mind. As promised, a cup of steaming coffee – flavored just how she liked it – sat beside the laptop. Taking a sip, she once again focused on the pictures. While the boys played an engaging game of chess, Dusty looked for that shiny needle, in a haystack of porcupine quills, to jump out and smack her.

Before long, it did just that. "I found it!"

Jumping up, Antoine disrupted the board, spilling pieces onto the floor, preventing Jonas from 'checkmating' him. "You did?"

Grumbling, Jonas leaned down, picking up the pieces. "Sore loser."

Racing over, Antoine looked at the monitor. "Which one is it?"

"*This* is the one I saw." Dusty pointed to the screen. "In fact, this is the *exact* image! It has the same water trickling down the concrete side. It *is* the Hoover Dam."

After setting the queen back on the board, he glanced at Dusty. "Are you *absolutely* positive?"

Giving it another once over, she nodded. "Yep! It's the Hoover Dam. From this shot alone, you can't tell which it is, but since it's looped in with the pictures that this person took while there... it's safe to say it's the same one. That's it!"

"Huh. Go figure. Does anyone else think it's strange that two of the stones are in the United States? I mean, what happened to sharing the wealth?"

Antoine pointed to the picture. "Who's to say what went through their minds back then. It would've been nice if the quatrains were back-to-back though. Would've saved time and money on flights. Going back and forth is ridiculous."

"If I could go back in time, I'd smack the shit out of whoever wrote these." Jonas groaned, running a hand through his hair. "Pack up. We can figure this out once we're in the air. I'll call Deva and let her know that we need the jet. Back to the States we go."

Dusty packed up the laptop and scattered papers. "This grab and go existence sucks."

"I'll be glad when I can actually unpack." Antoine helped Dusty gather up the clutter. "Good thing the 'wrinkled' look is making a comeback. I don't like being unfashionable."

Once they had everything in place, Dusty zipped the laptop case. "We can stop and get you an iron if you like?"

"No. We better not take time out for something that I probably don't even need. Especially with that stone waiting for us back at home." Antoine's lips pursed. "If Seth doesn't get there first."

"He won't." Glancing at his watch, Jonas gave the professor a slight grin.

Lifting a brow, Antoine ceased all actions, giving him a quick glimpse. "Wanna let the rest of us in on how you know that with *such* certainty?"

"Not yet. Call it a fall back plan."

On her hands and knees – doing a final walk through, checking for any stray items – Dusty peered over. "What *sort* of *fall back plan* are you talking about?" As he continued keeping secrets, it took all she had to bite her tongue. It wasn't the time or place to kill the white flag treaty… just yet.

Jonas started to say something before thinking better of it and punched a number on his phone. "Can't say right now. The fewer people who know, the better." Winking, he brought the phone to his ear.

Antoine looked over. "Oh, thank Deva for those scrumptious delights in the car. They were to die for!"

Deva answered on the second ring. "It's about time! Did you enjoy the only vacation you will be allowed until the completion of this mission?"

"It was," glancing at Dusty's rear in the air, he smiled. "Restful."

"Good because there will be *no* more downtime until these stones are found."

"We were still working. We know where the next stone is."

"Ah. Well, don't keep me waiting. Good news, I hope?"

"Define *good*."

"Jonas, I am a busy woman and do not have time for guessing games. You are not the *only* ones with deadlines. There are many players behind the scenes. Get to the point."

"When Seth held the stone, he got a vision of the Hoover Dam, so… we're headed back to the States." The long pause that followed made Jonas check to make sure the call didn't drop.

"And *how* do you know what Seth saw when he held the stone?"

Once more he shot a glance at Dusty scouring over the room with a fine-toothed comb. "Dusty saw it, actually. When she held the stone, *she* got an image from it too, but we're not sure how to figure *that* one out."

"I am going to *assume* that it slipped your mind the last time we spoke. Do *not* let such an oversight *ever* happen again. Are you *sure* she saw the image that he did? Mortals *cannot* see nor feel *anything* when holding those stones. To them, it is like holding a rock. That is *only* for the supernatural."

His own thoughts ventured into the same as Deva's. "I know."

"Your partner is an interesting mortal indeed. I can see why you… and Seth… are so… *attracted* to her."

He cleared his throat. "Dusty zeroed it down to the Hoover Dam."

"Really? And she is *quite* certain of that?"

"Yes. She's the *only* one who saw it, so only she could determine the exact location."

"Hm. Odd that there would be two stones that close to each other."

"That's what we said too."

"And she is *absolutely* positive that it is the same dam? My sources tell me that Seth went to China. *Why* would he go there if the next stone is back here?"

"A bit of misdirection."

"Misdirection?"

"Did I ever tell you about being a magician in Vaudeville?"

"Well, hopefully, you can do more than pulling a rabbit out of your hat," she snapped. "Regardless, be careful, Jonas. Seth is *not* one to play games with. Need I remind you of how testy he can be when crossed?"

"Nope. I remember quite well."

"Well, keep in mind one important detail… it is not *you* who will suffer for any unsuccessful trickery."

Understanding her meaning, he continued watching Dusty. "I'm well aware of that."

"Good. As long as you understand the ramifications of your actions. Also, this will be the last time you get to use the jet."

"If it's too expensive, I'll pay from now on."

"Jonas, darling, stupidity is not a good look for you. The measly amount so far has barely put a dent in my account, not that it is any of *your* concern. What you need to worry about is Seth finding you. Using the jet makes it a lot easier for him to track your every location. In fact, *anyone* can. All they have to do is look at the flight plan. They are not under lock and key, you know."

"Can't the captain lie and say he's going somewhere else?"

"No, darling. That would take a lot of manpower to falsify records in airports and captain's logs and... well... you do *not* want the Federal Aviation Administration snooping around over faulty logs."

"True. That would bring in too many alphabet groups."

"I have been working on a new mode of transportation that will solve all your needs in one swoop. No need to keep calling me because soon... I will be out of reach for a brief spell."

"Business or pleasure?"

"Both. But this will ensure that you can manage things on your own. I must warn you, though, the accommodations will change slightly, but it *will* be necessary. It will make it harder for him to steal it from you if he has no idea where you are. Remember, he has *two* now. Do not forget, the more he acquires, the *stronger* he becomes."

"I'm fully aware of the obstacles we must overcome. What sort of *new* transportation and accommodations?"

"You will find out soon enough. The jet will be ready for boarding when you get there. I will have the pilot wait until the last possible moment to call in his coordinates, but that's the best I can do."

"Oh, before I forget, Antoine wanted me to thank you for the delicious sweets in the car. The man is a bottom-less pit and they helped."

"Jonas, do I strike you as a powerful vampire who *caters* to human pets?"

"Well then... who did?"

The call ended.

"Jet's on standby." He slid the phone into his pocket, curious who stocked the car with snacks. Not in the mood to hear arguments, over things he had no control over, he didn't mention the unknown future accommodations. "Are we ready?"

"Ready as we'll ever be." Dusty headed out the door carrying her bag and a few of Antoine's. "I'll be glad when this is over. I'm gonna do nothing for a week."

Antoine followed her out. "Stop your lying. You can't sit still that long. It would drive you crazy."

"You know me too dang burned well, Antoine."

"That I do, Dusty. That I do."

11

Xiluodu dam

The Xiluodu Hydropower Station on the Jinsha River in China stood six times higher than Niagara Falls, with a double-curvature arch 937 feet tall. Seth walked around the middle of it, inhaling deeply with a confused scowl on his handsome face. "Something's not right." Furrowing his brows, he hopped down off the arch. Bending, Seth touched the cool ground, pausing for a moment, before looking around, shaking his head. "Hmm. Something is *definitely* not right."

His mother arched a thin brow while pocketing a sparkling gold watch, happily relieving the four guards – now nothing more than mangled corpses – of their valuables. "Son, what are you talking about? I sense nothing out of sorts."

"You wouldn't. You're too busy committing petty larceny." Turning away from her, once more inhaling deeply, his eyes roamed the area. "With every stone, I could sense it without knowing *exactly* where it rested. I could *feel* it. This time," once more he placed a hand against the dam's cold concrete, pausing as he tried to focus, before turning to her in bewilderment. "This time I got nothing."

"Look at the size of this thing. If it's buried *too* deep, you wouldn't–"

As his phone rang, Seth raised a hand silencing his mother before glancing at the lit screen. "Why, hello, Charles. I assume you have news for me?"

"Yes, yes!" came the excited reply.

After a moment of silence, annoyance tramped across his features. "I'd like to buy a vowel."

"Oh. Forgive me. They just boarded Deva's jet. The flight plan says they're on their way to China."

"Now *that* is the best news I've heard all day. Well done, Charles. Well done."

"Thank you. What should I do now?"

"Sit tight. I'll send for you if you're needed. Enjoy a bit of Spanish cuisine." Not waiting for an answer, he disconnected the call, slipping the phone back into his pocket. "Well now. It seems the Scooby gang is headed our way. Suppose I'll let *them* do all the hard work and reap the fruits of their labor… again." A brow rose as the mournful wail of a harmonica broke his thoughts. Turning, he saw an old black man leaning against the railing.

As the last notes rang out and echoed away to nothing, he tipped his black Pork Pie hat. "Evening." Eyeing the dead guards, he smiled. "Late night snack?"

Stepping protectively between the man and his mother, Seth narrowed his eyes. "Old man, I don't know how you got up here, but I *do* know how you're getting down." Taking a step forward, he found he couldn't move as a weathered finger wagged at him.

"Now *that's* not very neighborly. Here I come to do you a favor, and you try to do violence on me. What has the world come to?" Sighing, he placed the harmonica in its case, slipped it into his coat pocket and smiled. "Seems to me you have a bit of a problem, son."

"And what might that be, not that it's any of your business… Mister…?"

"Bishop. Harley Bishop. But you can just call me Harley. As for your problem, well… let's just say that what you're huntin' ain't here. You been played, son."

Seth felt his blood boil. "And just what do *you* know about what I'm hunting?"

"Oh, I know the *whole* story from… way back. Before you was even born. What shoulda been a simple deal, turned into a cluster fuck of biblical proportions. Just can't trust nobody, can ya?"

Making a note to deal with Charlie in a very brutal manner, Seth shook his head. "Apparently not. So *why* are ya willing to help?"

"See now, I gots me a few horses in this here race. Yes, sir. Don't matter who they are, but I know if you stay here *too* long, the other sides gonna get to that stone first. Then you ain't *never* gonna find it." Placing a palm on Seth's face, his eyes burned into the old vampire's core. "And I can't have that."

In 3,000 years, Seth hadn't felt stark fear. This old man's searing touch reminded him just how powerful a tool it could be. "You have my undivided attention… *sir.*"

"Good. Now, contrary to your bad intel, the white hats ain't headed here, *buuuut* I assume you realize that now. They're headed back to the good old U.S. of A."

"I don't suppose you could be just a *tad* more specific, Harley?"

"Use your head, boy! I ain't here to tie your shoelaces and make sure you put on clean underwear."

Remembering what the second stone revealed, his lips pursed. "There are a *lot* of dams over there. The odds of getting the right one is about eighty-four-thousand to one."

Grinning, Harley tilted his head a bit. "That's why they call it gambling." Tipping his hat, he looked over his shoulder with a wink. "Ma'am." Smiling back at Seth, he clapped the vampire's shoulder. "Good luck, son. I know you'll make me proud." Taking a few steps away, he turned and bowed. "As you were."

Released from the invisible hold, Seth lunged, finding nothing but air. Steadying himself, he leaned against the railing, stroking his chin. After a moment, his lips curled up in a grin. "Gambling. Las Vegas. Hoover Dam." Clapping, he eyed the empty space which Harley previously occupied. "Well played. Well played, *indeed.*"

Still trembling from the experience, his mother rushed over to him. "Do you know who that man was?"

Nodding, Seth patted her head. "I sure do." His grin evaporated. "I want you to go home. *Stay* there until I call for you, understand?"

Slightly thrown off balance, she pointed at the dam. "But I can be of use. I can–"

"*You* can be of use by doing as you're told for once. Things are about to get a bit nasty, and there's gonna be a ton of collateral damage. I don't want *you* in that group."

"I don't understand. If the dark one is going to help us, then–"

"*That's* what concerns me. If *he's* involved in this," his eyes scanned the night sky, "you can bet your ass that so is *He*... but where?"

12

Swaddled in the comfort of the jet's seating, Antoine relaxed. "At least now we know where we're going *before* solving this riddle. Within the New World... *obviously* that's the United States... but how they knew of its existence, back when this thing was created, is beyond me."

"What? Is *everyone* here a heathen?" Wide-eyed, Dusty frowned at Antoine. "God knows *everything*. He knew there was gonna be a United States created before someone said, "I wonder what's over there." Though, I have a feeling our country plays more into the *end* of times than anything else. The world is getting weirder by the day!"

"Yeah, but *God* wasn't the one who wrote *this*." Antoine pointed down to the quatrain. "Besides, I don't think He knows 'everything' because people have free will. He knows the way that things are *supposed* to go, but if people don't follow the path He's laid out for them... *everything* changes, and it affects more than just that person. Religion reminds me of that Sims game."

"I don't have time for games. What are you talking about?"

"It's an interactive role-playing game that allows the gamer to play God."

"*How* do they play God, exactly?"

"Sims are supposed to be people living in a virtual world."

"A virtual world? Like… with cities, cars, babies?"

"Exactly. Well, they choose the actions of the Sims in their game. They wanna make sure their Sims do things to get further along in their job, have families, don't cheat, make money… and so on."

"Sounds kinda boring to me. Spend your life sitting around watching virtual people living a life?"

"Well, lots of people feel the same way you do. That's why a lot of them choose to torture them, killing a bunch at one time by having them cook on a cheap stove that catches on fire, and thus… kills the sims in the house."

"What?! They actually *kill* these virtual people? *That* doesn't say a lot about the gamers."

"True, but religion's a lot like that game, if you think about it."

Dusty's blank stare spoke volumes. "Not following."

"In the game, you lay out a path for the people… or *Sims* in this case… to follow, but they will always do their own thing, *unless* you take away their free will."

"You can do that?"

"Well… sure! All you do is tweak the settings and you can control every move they make. However, *when* you give them the ability to think on their own, they flirt with people who aren't their prospective others, cheat on their spouses, lie, don't go to work, don't do their homework, stay out later than they're supposed to, ignore the family."

"So… like *people.*"

"Exactly. Now, when something happens that stops them from taking an action, they look up and bitch to the heavens, like the gamer is the one that caused the problem. It's the same with people. They're always blaming God for every little thing that goes wrong in their lives when it's their own stupidity, and bad choices, which get them into a mess. Then they pray for an escape, blaming God when things don't just fix themselves right away."

"I never knew you were a gamer."

"Gabby and I dabbled with it. It took her mind off the pain."

"Ah. So, what's the object of the game?"

"To win," Jonas snorted.

"Wrong. Not *all* games have a win or lose approach." Antoine turned back to Dusty. "Lessons aren't learned by the easy path."

"*Exactly!*" Dusty shouted, before casting a faraway glance off to the right. "I think. Anyway, God knows the way things *should* go as long as they don't allow evil to block the path."

Having heard enough, Jonas groaned. "Okay, can we set Sunday school aside and get back to the quatrain, please." Picking it up, he read aloud. "Within the New world lies the third brother. From wickedness and iniquity should the intended journey. One half and twenty-seven leagues Northwest to KXTA, it rests one half league beneath the false water. His skills tested to their limit, by eyes hidden and not, the intended will only know a short respite when the beast again steals victory."

Antoine nodded. "As we learned from the other quatrain, *brother* would be the stone."

"From wickedness and iniquity should the *intended* journey?" Looking between them, Dusty heaved a sigh. "Is that telling us *anything* new? I mean… this trip has been evil all the way around. Don't tell me this is a recap."

Laughing inwardly, Jonas shook his head. "I *don't* think that's what it's saying. It reads more like directions. From wickedness and iniquity should the intended journey. It's more like… a starting point. What town is more wicked and immoral than Vegas?"

"Washington D.C.!" Antoine's eyes sparkled.

Laughing, Dusty nudged the professor's side. "Behave!"

"Somehow, a *dam* fits into all this, so I *doubt* it's D.C." Jonas's tone grew serious as he got more comfortable, stretching out his long legs.

Dusty and Antoine exchanged irritated looks. "That's a joke, Sparx. Jeezy-Peezy."

Not amused, Jonas crossed his arms over his chest. "We don't have *time* for humor right now."

Antoine scoffed. "Son, there's *always* time for humor."

Something changed. He felt it in the air, like a gentle pulse of the first breeze ahead of a raging storm. A sense of urgency. It put him on edge. Clearing his throat, he went back to the quatrain. "One half and twenty-seven leagues Northwest to KXTA. I don't suppose *either* of you know how far a league is?"

Dusty shot him an irritated look. "Not a clue."

Throwing his hands up into the air, Antoine pointed to himself. "Hello? Language professor here. The origin of the word 'league' is from the fourteenth century and is Middle English. It's a Gaulish unit of distance equal to one point five Roman miles. A square league, as a unit of land measure. The second Italian definition of *working together often in secret* came about in fourteen-twenty-five to fourteen-seventy-five. I could get further into it, but since we're *soooo* pressed for time, it's just under three and a half miles."

After a slightly peeved staring contest, Jonas nodded, doing the math. "So, we head Northwest for about ninety-five miles, until we reach this... KXTA." Eyeing Antoine, he tilted his head. "Okay language professor. What language is *that*, and what does it mean?"

"KXTA?" Pursing his lips, Antoine shook his head. "Not one I know, that's for sure. I don't think it's a real word. I mean, why have it in all caps? Unless of course they were shouting, then–"

"What about a radio station?" Dusty interrupted. "I mean, all radio station names have four letters, and they're all in caps. It might look funny if they weren't."

"True," Antoine began. "Like WKRP in Cincinnati."

"Never heard of it. Then again, it *could* have something to do with the whole proper noun and capitalization... I suppose." Both men looked at her as if they'd found the missing link. "*What*? Chances are it's *not* a radio station. Just offering up an example. It sounds better than *they might be shouting*! Then again, it could also be an airport identifier too. Now, having traveled around the world... *many* times... I've become pretty familiar with most of them. I have *never* heard of one called KXTA."

"We'll figure that out when we get there. According to the writing, the stone is," another bit of quick math caused Jonas's brow to crease. "About a mile and a half under the false water."

"*False* water? What the *hell* does that mean? The water in the Hoover Dam is real." Crinkling her forehead, she groaned. "These riddles are cryptic as hell. I hope it's not telling us that it's *under* the Hoover Dam."

Jonas picked at a bit of lint on his pants. "I don't think so. Hoover Dam is a little under forty miles southeast of Vegas. The scroll tells us to head northwest. Don't forget, what Seth sees from each stone isn't the *exact* location of the next one, but just a general idea. He saw *part* of a dam. There are *too* many dams in the world to narrow it down, so the way I figure it... he'll bide his time, see where *we're* going before he moves in."

Antoine grabbed a cookie off the tray in front of him, shaking it for emphasis. "Yeah, but that *last* part is very telling of the future. I don't like it *one* bit. Beast steals victory tells me that Seth is gonna steal *this* one too!"

Dusty huffed, watching the crumbs fall onto the floor. "Why is he even looking for it then? Hell, all he has to do is follow us around the world and *swoop* in and steal it. Ya know, for someone *sooo* powerful, he's not impressing me in the slightest. It's too easy. We're doing all the work *for* him!"

"Not this time." Setting the quatrain back in its protected sheath, Jonas stretched back. "Antoine, have you seen Raiders of the Lost Ark?"

The old man grumbled. "Only about a hundred times. They got *sooo* much wrong in that film, but it's a fun popcorn flick. Why?"

Irked, Dusty looked from one to the other. "Did you two do *anything* other than watch movies your whole lives? I swear. You guys *really* need to broaden your horizons."

Ignoring her, Jonas continued. "Remember the scene where Indy and Sallah were trying to figure out how long the staff of Ra should be?"

Antoine's eyes widened. "Yes, *that's* one thing they screwed the pooch on. The staff is actually supposed to be-" His jaw fell open.

"Are you telling me Seth's looking in the *wrong* place? *How* do you know that?"

"My fall back plan." Glancing at his watch, Jonas looked out the window. "We've got a few more hours until touchdown. Why don't the two of you get some sleep. That way, when we land, we can hit the ground running."

The professor yawned. "Okay, *just* a catnap though." Curling up to the window, he closed his eyes. "Wake me if anything exciting happens."

Dusty sat looking out the window at the passing clouds, a distant expression in her eyes, her hand lightly stroking Hooch's fur. Turning, she glared at Jonas hard enough that he might think he kicked her dog.

"Not tired?" he asked, knowing full well the answer to that question.

"*Not* important. *Why* do you constantly hide stuff from me?"

Confused, he blinked. "What are you talking about? I'm not *hiding* anything from you."

"Really? Okay. So then tell me about this 'fall back plan' you mentioned. I'm pretty sure I've been to *every* meeting and I'm not aware of *that* one. Did I miss a memo?"

"It's not *time* for you to know about that. Trust me. It wouldn't do you *any* good to know it yet."

"*I'll* be the judge of that. Now, *what* is it?"

"I'll tell you in time. It's better for you *and* Antoine if you *don't* know. I don't want to take the chance that Seth *might* be able to get the information from you."

"From *me*? Sparx, *no* one can get into my head without me allowing it. Not you, Bacchus, or *even* Seth, for that matter. So, anything you tell *me* is very safe, stored in my mind. So, *what* is this plan?"

Pursing his lips, Jonas eyed her. "Okay. Let's go with that. No one can get into *your* head. Say I tell you what this plan is. Seth manages to kidnap both you *and* Antoine. Knowing he can't read *you*, Seth tortures the old man, making you watch until you can't stand it anymore. Would you be willing to sacrifice Antoine's life, to keep that secret?" Giving her a moment to process that, he shook his head. "Of course not, but what if you *were*? The blood doesn't lie. In that situation, all Seth would have to do is drink from you and he'd have a front row seat to that *very* conversation… plus any other we've had. So, you are *just* going to have to trust me on this."

Even though he was more right than wrong, Dusty wasn't ready to drop it. "*Trust* you? That seems to be your *fall back* on everything. You ask for my trust, yet you've lied to me *so* many times already! Each time you do, you apologize, promise not to do it again, and then turn around and do it *again*! And *every* single time, I trust you at your word. Why the *hell* should I chance that again? I'm not a friggin' welcome mat and I'm not naïve. You're keeping stuff from me and I wanna know what it is."

"Dusty, I-"

"Don't 'Dusty' me. Am I or am I not your *partner*?"

"You know you are."

"Then start *acting* like it. You can't pick and choose what you're gonna tell me. Partners don't work that way. You talk about trust like it's a commodity to give and take at will. It's not *me* that hasn't trusted *you* and been lied to time and time and *time* again! It's *you* not trusting *me*."

"It's not that. It's just-"

"I don't wanna hear *why* you're keeping shit from me, Sparx. It's all bullshit," she barked. "IF Seth's gonna try something like that, he would've already done it! Besides, he can get into *your* head faster than he can mine. All that other gobbledygook is just *that*. I can keep secrets better than the three of us here, and yet you *still* refuse to trust me with something that could be pertinent to this case."

"Is *that* what's bothering you? It's not pertinent to the case."

"Again, *I'll* be the judge of that. Tell me what it is."

"Look, you're going to have to be kept in the dark a while longer. You'll understand when the time comes."

"Is that so? In case you haven't gotten it through your thick head yet, *you're* not the boss of this mission." Pulling out her necklace, she flashed it at him. "*This* is something *highly* important to this whole thing… though I haven't a clue what. Being the protector of it, that means you need me *more* than I need *you*."

"I doubt you're going to throw everything away on a temporary secret. Stop acting like a child."

"A child? Is that so? Flip the tables, Sparx."

"Meaning?"

"Let's say that Antoine started keeping secrets from you but told *me* everything that he knew. What if he and I started working together and left *you* out because… well, we didn't want Seth to get into *your* head and figure out what's going on. What if *we* started giving *you* only half-truths and innuendos? How would *you* feel?"

"That's *not* what I'm doing."

"The hell you're not! I'll tell you how you would feel! Screwed with a barbed wire coated dildo and no Vaseline!"

He arched a brow. "Interesting analogy."

"You know what I mean. For all of us to be able to give one hundred percent to this, it helps if we *all* are kept informed on *every* step of this 'life or death save the world' fiasco. Otherwise, someone could get killed." Glancing over at Hooch, she sighed. "In fact, *someone* already has."

"You're just going to have to trust me. I'll tell you when the time is right."

"Again with the trust. Well, Sparx, *that's* not good enough. Not *this* time. Since you can keep me in the dark, how much do you *really* need me on this fucking thing? Looks to me like you can do it on your own!"

"Dusty, you know better than that. *Everyone* on this mission is needed because we all do our own thing. Antoine translates. I figure out the riddles. You," he paused. "You can find a crumb of bread in a sawdust factory. Not to mention, you're unlike any mortal I've ever met. I doubt anyone else would've been able to handle a portion of this. I need you to trust me."

"No, Sparx. It's the other way around. *You* better start trusting *me* if you wanna keep this… *partnership*… and I use that term loosely…

together. Keep it up, and we'll go our separate ways to find the damn stones… and Antoine comes with *me*!" That said, she unbuckled her belt and went to the furthest seat away.

Growling, Hooch followed, giving Jonas the evil eye as he passed.

Jonas couldn't tell her about Charles F. Thomas, Officer of the Law – now eternal bloodsucker – lumbering around as one of Seth's minions. Knowing her, she'd put one of those wooden rounds in his chest and take his head or try and adopt him to the crew. That would interfere with allowing Jonas to fulfill his promise to Charlie and relieve him of his immortal burden, but they weren't close to that train station, just yet. He couldn't take the chance – better to brave her anger.

Still infuriated, Dusty stared out the window. A pair of green eyes caused havoc, tossing out memories of better times along with the gorgeous man starring in every one of them. Travis. For having such an airtight mind, *he* had no problems finding his way in, lurking in the distance, goading her with his presence. Taking out her phone, she sent a text, finding it comforting that Jonas looked at her curiously.

Dusty: Care to tell me what's going on?

Travis: You'll understand when the time comes.

Dusty: When the time comes? What the *HELL* is that supposed to mean?

Travis: You'll understand everything, including things you didn't realize that you needed to understand, when the time is right.

Dusty: Don't give me that shit! Is that question just too hard for your imbecile brain to compute?! Let's try something easier. *Why* did you betray me? Why? If there was *one* person in this world, who I never would've expected in a *million* years to ever betray me… *you* were that person. And you did! You were working with Seth? *SETH*? What the fuck?! Are you two old chums now? Getting ready to go fishing at the old crawdad hole?

Travis: A case of being in the right place at the right time, needing something from each other. I never wanted to hurt you. You might find this hard to believe, Dusty, but I truly love you.

Dusty: *Love*? You fucking *shot* me! If *that's* your idea of loving someone, I'd rather you hate me… like *I* feel about *you*. Hate you. Though, I don't think that's a strong enough word. Why, Travis? That's all I want to know. Fucking *why*?!

Travis: Because I love you. You don't believe that, and how could you, but I do. You'll understand in time.

Dusty: Fuck you. Don't give me that fucking shit! I'll understand everything my ass. For your information, moron, you were the *one* person who I thought I could *MAYBE* love a little bit. I guess you know *that's* gone. Burned. Destroyed. Buried under a mountain of rocks. Good luck trying to dig *those* feelings out.

Travis: I know you don't mean that. By the way… did you enjoy your trip to Spain?

Dusty: Was there a message in skywriting about us going to Spain?!

Travis: (Kissy face emoji with lots of red hearts.)

Dusty: (A line of turds.)

Travis: See you soon, love.

Dusty: For your sake, I hope not.

As Jonas looked questioningly at her phone, she merely slipped it back into the case. Resting her head against the window, she drifted off to restless sleep.

13

The look on Sir G's face told of his growing frustration at his young protégé. "Dustina, we're not getting anywhere with your training. You're so upset about the death of your parents that your sentiments are getting in the way."

"I can't help that. They died! I think about them and," tears welled up in her eyes, "it makes me sad."

"I know." Running a gentle finger across her forehead, he pushed a stray strand behind her ear. "It's normal to have those feelings. You *should* feel sad, but that's *why* I must take them away from you. A good knight doesn't allow emotions to get in the way of her job. Unlike myself, you can't just turn them off as you need."

The waterfall threatened to cascade down her face as her pleading eyes snapped to his. "No! Please! Don't do that!"

"You've given me no choice."

"I'll be good! I promise! I won't think of them anymore!"

Sir G shook his head, emitting a soft sigh. "It will be better if you don't remember them. At least for *now*. In the future, they'll come back, when you're better able to deal with everything. After you've had training on how to shelve your emotions until needed. There is a way, but it's a slow process."

She could taste the salt as the tears coursed down her face. "Why?"

"This is going to be your first key to understanding. Even though I'm going to strip your memories of your parents and your upbringing *and* this conversation, I'm going to install… keys… for lack of a better word… of all your memories so you can understand. As you need them, you'll remember events. As certain things happen, they will trigger the other keys that I will install for *that* certain memory."

"I don't understand."

"I know you don't, but when you remember it, you will."

Crinkling her brows together, she nodded, even though the look on her face told him she didn't understand a thing. "Okay."

Sitting down at the table, he pulled her chair closer. "My putting this barrier up is going to help you with training. Not having your emotions will make you a stronger warrior and prepare you for all the fictional madness set to come your way."

Struggling to keep the tears at bay, she wiped at her swollen eyes. "What's… fictional?"

"Make believe." Resting his fingers on her temples, he looked deeply into her eyes. "I *wish* it didn't have to be this way. Before I do the first key, I need you to understand. When you start opening them, it means that I am no longer in this world to help. You will be *totally* on your own against the evil. Pay attention. Be careful who you trust. As I told you, you were *born* to this position. It wasn't an accident. You are the last one of the 'de Jardiner' clan and *they* have always been the keeper of the necklace. Your parents had no clue when they created you, but the handlers in the background knew. We've been pulling the strings for decades."

"Why?"

"Because of the threat of something happening that is bigger than humanity. You see, I am extremely old."

Dusty looked at him. "You don't *look* old."

Laughing, he gently mussed her hair. "Thank you! Trust me. I have lived more lives than you can even begin to imagine. I've been watching out for your lineage for as long as this became my mission. Even before I became what I am today."

Fixing her hair back in place, she cast a shy glance up at him. "A… bodyguard?"

"Of a sort."

Lowering her eyes to the bulky piece of jewelry, she touched it with her finger. "What does it do?"

Lifting the cross off her chest, he eyed it as well. "*This* necklace has a power that will play a big part in stopping a horrible prophecy. Once all the puzzle pieces fall into place, it will trigger a reaction in you that will help you fight… let's call it a beast."

The frightened unasked question, *'What kinda beast?'* stamped across her forehead in bold red letters. "A *beast*?"

Seeing the scared little girl before him, he touched his hand to the back of her head, pulling her forward to plant a soft kiss on her forehead. "You are so young. So young. Then again, it seems that all the players in this war started out young." Pulling back, he looked down at it again, embossed with the symbol of the Knights Templar. The red cross. "You'll know in time. There's no guarantee it will happen in your lifetime, and if it doesn't… then we'll find you a husband and have you pass this down to your firstborn… and the whole thing starts again as it has for many millennia."

"So… I'm not the first?"

Sir G broke out in unbridled laughter. "Heavens no! We've guarded this necklace since we found it. Its power is one that can make or break the world for the person wearing it."

Still confused, she merely nodded.

His hands fell away to relax on his own thighs. "One day, it will be up to *you* to save humanity. It's our job… the Knights Templar… to make sure you're ready for that fight. You are the youngest knight we've ever trained. Good. Evil. Kind. Wicked. It won't matter. The entire world will count on *you* for their survival. *This* is your first key. You were born for *this*. I know, it's confusing now, but as I said, certain events will trigger these keys. They will open the door for you to understand. For now, though, I need you without emotions. They get in the way. Tug at your heart. If you don't have memories of a mother wrapping her arms around you when you fall and skin your knee, kissing away your booboos, or a father who tucks you in every night with a story, then you can concentrate. Once you open *this* key, slowly but surely, you will remember everything and why it's important that you do. Now, be a good girl and close your eyes."

Pouting, she did as he instructed. With just the soft touch of his fingers, a great steel wall slammed down within her mind. Nothing could get in or out; loving memories stored away until the future called for them.

Pulling back, Sir G's tone took on a harshness. "Your training will start every morning at dawn. When the rooster crows, that is your signal to get out of bed."

Gone were the tears and inquisitive "why me?" sobbing child of earlier, replaced with a young obedient soldier; a lump of clay ready for molding. "Tell me what to do."

"We need to teach you how to put a barrier in your mind so that no one can get in. I can help, but you need to do it on your own for when I'm not around. Can you do that for me?"

Nodding, she watched him. "Yes, Sir G. I'll try."

"No. No *trying*. You *must* do this. There is no good in trying when you don't succeed. The world's fate rests on your ability to block everything from your mind. Now, let's begin."

…

Feeling her pain, Hooch whined, putting his head in her lap. Her fingers gently massaged him as they both drifted back to sleep as if magically.

"She's right, ya know."

Hearing that familiar voice too close for comfort, Jonas's head spun around to the seat across the aisle, seeing Seth sitting there with one leg dangling over the armrest. "Seth?"

"Working partners shouldn't keep things from each other. It's a bad look. You're supposed to be working together on this. Might help ya find that stone faster, I might add." Seeing Jonas's eyes turning red, Seth waved a hand. "Calm yourself, son. You should know by now that I'm not *really* here."

Minus the elaborate settings, it reminded him of the times Bacchus visited. Antoine, Dusty, and Hooch slept, as the stars slowly moved past the window; all indicators that this wasn't just happening in his mind. "How?" Jonas asked, settling back.

"The 'how' ain't important. Technical mumbo jumbo. Borin' really. What *is* important, is *why*." Glancing around, he let out an admiring whistle. "I see Deva hasn't lost her sense of style." Tilting his head, he reached around the side of the seat beside him and felt around for the slight depression. Pressing it, a hidden compartment beneath the seat slid open, revealing a sealed bottle. With a smile he brought it up, cracked the gold seal, dipped a finger into the maroon-colored liquid and suckled the blood off his fingertip. Cringing, he capped the bottle and replaced it. "I'm gonna have to speak to her about her *disgusting* culinary choices."

"Is there a point to this visit, or are you just lonely?"

"Oh, Jonas. I'm *never* lonely. You know that. I always have *plenty* to keep me company. Why, take your friend, Officer Thomas, for instance. At this *very* moment, he's providin' me with a *wealth* of entertainment. Would you like to see?"

Before he could answer, a horrific scene formed before him. Charles F. Thomas – officer of the law turned vampire, killer of innocent children – being torn to pieces by hordes of fang boys and girls. As bits of flesh flew everywhere, amid the primal sounds of hungry vampires, Jonas noticed Charlie's eyes looking in the direction of the sleeping Dusty. As the last bit of life left those dull orbs, Charlie mouthed *thank you* to Jonas, before he exploded in green flames, taking most of his assailants with him.

As the vision dissolved, Seth narrowed his eyes at Jonas. "Well, *that* was unexpected... and messy." Tapping a finger against his chin, his lips pursed in thought. "Let's see now... first, you plant some false memories inside old Charlie. Ones that send me to the other side of the world. Then you deny me the pleasure of seein' him die slowly. I see I'm gonna have to up my game. So much the better." Looking over at Dusty, his lips curled into a grin. "She's so purty when she sleeps. And vulnerable." As he started to rise, his body slammed back into the seat. Struggling proved useless, and he turned to Jonas. "Fine. We'll call this one a draw then?" Feeling the push against his body lift, he reached into his pocket and tossed Jonas a small box tied with a purple ribbon. "For you. Souvenir from... your *old* neighborhood." His form became transparent, then re-coalesced for a moment. "Oh, one more thing. I *know* where that next piece is. Hoover Dam. Apparently, my victory is *highly* anticipated by a particularly *important* entity. One who's willing to toss a bone my way, now and then. Last one there buys dinner." Winking, he vanished.

His visit left Jonas with more questions than answers, but with the knowledge that the all-important entity, tossing out bones, gave Seth bad intel. One question burned hotter than the rest as he went to open Seth's gift. *What the hell slammed him in his seat? It wasn't me! I wonder if–*

"We'll be landing shortly. It's a pleasant seventy-three degrees, humidity a dry twenty-three percent. The forecast high for today is one hundred nine. Please make sure all personal items are accounted for. Buckle in. Thank you for flying LaDevia Air."

Jonas watched Antoine, Hooch, and Dusty rouse from sleep as he shoved the box into his pocket. The professor cracked his neck, yawned, and turned, before buckling in. Dusty stretched, buckled her seat belt, then turned with a confused expression on her face. When her eyes met Jonas's, they changed to daggers. So much for thinking she would let the issue of his *fall back plan* drop. Not that it mattered anymore, but he would surely catch hell for the end results when she found out about his part in it.

14

As they arrived at McCarran International Airport, one by one they stood, stretched, and made their way to the steps. Being the first one out, Jonas stopped to speak to the captain while Hooch, Dusty, and Antoine dragged behind, grabbing their luggage.

"I *know* you heard our argument," Dusty whispered.

Antoine nodded, gathering his things. "It was kinda hard not to."

"I say we give him a taste of his own medicine."

"What do you mean?"

"I *mean*, we start telling him half-truths and just keep it to ourselves. We tell each other what we find out but leave him in the dark. We'll just tell him, 'You'll know in time' and show him what it's like."

Stopping short, Antoine stared at her with wide eyes. His jaw dropped open as if her head spun around like the exorcist. "Girl! Have you lost your mind? You sound like a child in the midst of a temper tantrum!"

"Keep your voice down," she shushed, glancing at Jonas, still deep in his own conversation. "We don't know what they're talking about, now do we?"

Looking over, Antoine eyed the two. "Well, no."

"And we won't ask. We never do. Unlike *him*, we figure if we need to know, he'll tell us, but he's not doing that. He never tells us a dang burn thing! He's keeping secrets... from *us*. The team. Regular secrets that *don't* involve the mission... are fine." Shouldering her bag, she continued, thinking about the dark recesses of her mind she had yet to divulge. "But when he's keeping stuff from us that involves this mission? That's wrong. So, I say we give him a dose of his own medicine."

"You're probably right... about the whole secret-keeping thing." There were a few of his own he kept closely guarded.

"You know I am! So, let's give it back to him. Maybe when he sees how annoying it is, he'll stop and bring us into the *full* circle of trust. None of this halfmoon crip-crap."

Thinking about her suggestion, Antoine scratched at the growing fluff on his chin. "That's gonna interrupt our chemistry. It's hard to work in conditions where no one trusts each other."

"Yeah, but that's not what's happening here. *We* trust him totally, telling him everything, but *he* doesn't trust *us*. At least not *me*. I see you two with your heads together, talking softly, and neither of you tell me what you're talking about. It won't be any different than that."

Actually, it would. They were discussing her, but *that* can of worms needed to stay closed. "Okay. If it will get you to exit the plane so I can, then I'm for it. But, if it starts to interfere with the mission, it stops. Ya hear me?"

Smiling, she leaned over kissing his cheek, grabbing the other bag. "That's all I ask."

"Kids," he muttered following behind her.

As they approached, Jonas arched a brow. "Glad to see the meeting's over. Are we ready to begin?"

"We just wanted to give you time to finish yours." Her words were like ice as she walked down the stairs.

Jonas shot Antoine a quizzical look, but the professor just waved a hand. "Don't ask."

Entering the airport in the wee hours of the morning, they found the terminal fairly empty. Most of the people nursed hot coffee, watched TV, or read the latest horror novel. Others tried their luck at the slots, losing their paychecks faster than they earned them.

Noticing Antoine sniffing the air, Jonas chuckled. "I don't think you're going to find much to eat at this time. Maybe a taco, or some fake nachos."

"I'll pass. After what we had in Spain, I'm spoiled. What time do you think the buffets will open?"

Shaking his head, Jonas took out his phone. "I need to call Deva. She mentioned something about alternative transportation."

Antoine arched a brow. "What *kind* of alternative transportation?"

"Not sure. Knowing her, it could be bicycles." Seeing Antoine's horrified expression, Jonas laughed. "I'm kidding."

"Ass," Antoine grumbled.

Dusty looked down at Hooch. "Stay. Guard Antoine." Then she looked at the other two. "I'll be back. I have to find the ladies room."

"You should've gone on the plane," Antoine chastised, glancing over the pamphlets in the tourist section.

She stuck her tongue out at him. "I didn't have to go then, but I do now."

Jonas looked over. "Are you sure you don't need an escort?"

"I think I can go to the bathroom by myself without any incident, Sparx. I've been doing it alone for years."

"Fine. Don't be long."

"Long as it takes." Turning, she headed off around the corner.

Chuckling, Antoine bent down in pretense of tying his shoes, giving Hooch a quick pet. "You stay with me, boy. Mommy be right back."

That dream had Dusty's mind off in a million different directions.

What the hell does it mean? A first *key? How many are there? Jonas is still keeping secrets. Don't even get me started on Travis doing the same thing. Not to mention Deva always keeping us in the dark. I don't even wanna think about what Bacchus is keeping from us. The only one upfront with everything is Antoine.*

Lost in her thoughts, looking down at the ground, she didn't see the man until they bumped into each other.

"Oh, I'm sorry," he said with a deep French accent, gripping her arms, making sure she didn't fall. "My apologies. I am such a klutz. Are you okay?"

Surprised at first, Dusty locked eyes with the attractive stranger with light brown hair and matching eyes. Smiling, she shook her head. "I'm fine. I'm so sorry! That was totally my fault. I was looking down at the ground and not paying attention to where I was walking… or who I was walking into."

"That is okay. I am in a hurry. Flight boarding. As long as you are okay?"

"I'm fine. Thanks. You have a safe flight."

"You as well," he said, rushing off toward the gate.

She in turn slipped into the bathroom.

Jonas placed the call to Deva which she answered on the third ring.

"Jonas, I've been expecting your call."

"We're in the terminal at McCarran. We need a good shower and comfortable beds. What hotel are we going to this time?"

"There won't be another hotel."

"Excuse me?"

"You heard me. We are going to have to bring in another sort of lodgings."

"What other sort?"

"An RV. You will be more self-sufficient that way. With you taken care of, and able to do things on your own, I can get a few… overdue visits out of the way. The driver will be there to take you to… your new home."

"Our… *home*?" She didn't answer, but he heard a click as the call ended. Pocketing the phone, he looked around, arching a brow. "She's not back yet?"

Antoine shrugged. "Long as she's been gone, I'd say it was a little more than a tinkle. So, what was that all about? I could only hear one side and it didn't sound too good to me. Do I wanna know 'what other sort' means?"

"If we need to fly again, we're going to have to do so incognito… or in an RV."

He looked like a puppy being given a new command. "I'm sorry, did you say… RV? As in… recreational vehicle?"

"Sure did."

"I know they've come a long way, but I have *yet* to see one that flies."

"No, they don't. At least, I don't think they do. We need to get from Point A to B without being followed. There's no way to fake our flight plan without getting a bunch of government intel involved, so we'll have to travel by land. We need to be in stealth mode… more or less."

"Well, that's true… I suppose. No one would think to look for us in an RV. Might take a lot longer to get to point B though."

"True." Looking around, Jonas glanced at his watch. "How long has she been gone?"

"About… fifteen minutes? Ish? It was when ya got on the phone with Deva."

"Hm. Let's go and check on her."

"Remind me not to take a shit around you. I'll be in there for a half hour… at least."

Dusty reappeared, looking at the two. "Okay. Where to now?"

Turning, Jonas gave her the evil eye. "Good timing. We were just about to come looking for you."

Antoine put the pamphlets in his back pocket. "Yeah, there's been a change in plans, apparently."

Her gaze cut to Antoine. "What sort of… *change?*"

"Apparently," Jonas cut in, "the powers that be are tired of everyone tracking us where we go so other means have been brought in. Seth can't steal the stone if he has no clue where we are. Deva said something about the driver taking us to our new home. No more hotels or her jet. We will be traveling by land now."

"By land?" Dusty looked confused, staring from Jonas to Antoine.

Before they could answer, the driver approached dressed a lot differently than the others, sporting raggedy jeans, a T-shirt, flannel over shirt, denim jacket, cowboy hat, and a pair of dirty work boots. Gone were the Armani suits and shiny shoes. "Jonas Sparx, Deva sent me. I'm… Zeke. Follow me."

Grabbing what little baggage they had, he escorted them outside to a fresh-off-the-lot black 2014 Dodge Ram 3500 dual diesel truck – a far cry from the Land Rover and Rolls. The running board on the sides would help them climb up into the tall vehicle made for towing and going places the other vehicles couldn't. After securing their baggage, they headed out.

15

Several miles into their trip, Zeke pulled off onto a few intersecting crossroads which led to their new *accommodations*. "Deva shelled out some bucks for this baby. It may not be the posh hotels you folks are used to, and you'll have to do your own cooking, but at least you won't be followed all over creation. Oh, and one more thing. You will all be in the RV while I'm driving. That's a bit illegal, so if I get pulled over, be quiet. Deva said any tickets, or fines are coming outta *your* pockets."

Jonas smirked. "That sounds like her."

Looking at the 34-foot family-sized RV with a cream exterior and dark-tinted frameless windows, Antoine appeared ready to fall over in a dead faint. "We're going to be in *that* thing? While it's *moving*?! And here I thought you were *kidding* about an RV!"

The memory of her slamming him into the wall over a little joke, caused Jonas to scratch at the back of his head. "Deva doesn't joke. Trust me. I found that out the *hard* way."

Seeing the monstrosity, Dusty's mouth fell open as she stared in disbelief until Antoine reached over and pushed her chin up. "Close your mouth, you'll catch flies."

She pointed in shock. "*This* is how we're gonna travel? Do you know how much gas that thing burns? It's gonna take us *forever* to get *anywhere*! It's like-"

"Well, actually, it's the truck that's gonna burn the gas, but what do you expect? It's a house on wheels." Antoine finished her sentence.

"Exactly. Camping in *one* place might be okay, but we have to live in it while it's moving? That might prove to be difficult. I do believe we've been downgraded." When the truck stopped, Dusty hopped out, walking around, checking out the size of it. "It's huge. How is no one gonna find us in this?"

"Because no one will think twice about a man who looks like he's going camping," Jonas replied. "Think about it. All this time we've had limousines, jets, five-star hotels, and have been seen in the latest trendy restaurants."

"I happen to like those, thank you very much," Antoine mumbled under his breath.

"So did I, but who in their right mind would think we would ever stray from that," he beat on the side of it, "to this? No one will be able to track us now." Jonas ran his hand over the 'Made in U.S.A.' sticker on one of the wheel hubs. "God bless America."

"Well, look at the bright side of this." Antoine shoved his hands in his back pockets, rocking on his feet with a broad smile on his handsome face. "At least we'll be on the damn ground and won't have to worry about 'a little turbulence' that just pops out from nowhere."

Dusty glanced around the wooded area surrounding them. "That's true. We just have to worry about deer now."

As his stomach growled, Antoine looked down. "Shh. I'm sure there's something in this beast to munch on."

Laughing, Zeke set about hooking up the RV to the truck's fifth wheel. "No turbulence, but you might feel a bump if I run over an Armadillo."

Losing his smile, Antoine moved to Jonas's side. "I'm not sure I like this fella."

Clapping the professor on the back, Jonas winked. "Better an Armadillo than a person." Looking over at Dusty, he tilted his head. "Well, what do you think?"

Knocking on the side of it, she gave him a cockeyed glance. "It's built like a tank!"

"Hopefully, it's more comfortable than one," Antoine muttered.

Putting his arm around Antoine, Zeke grinned. "That's relative. I sleep upside down, hanging by my toes from a rafter. Just like *all* vampires do." Giving Jonas a wink, he headed for the truck, expertly backing into the RV's hook up.

Glancing at Jonas, the professor shook his head and headed over to Dusty. "Nope. I didn't need to hear that, no sir. Uh-uh. Lost Boys. I'll never sleep again."

"Lost boys?" Holding up a hand, she shook her head. "Never mind. I'm pretty sure that has something to do with a movie." Huffing out a breath, to match the rolling eyes, she pointed to one of the creased sections. "Is this one of those rooms that slides in and out?"

"Yep," Zeke answered, sliding out of the truck. "There are five slide outs built into this baby in case you need more room. And please don't slide 'em out while I'm driving. Plays hell with stability. I figure since there's only three of you," noticing Hooch's indignant look, he smiled, "I'm sorry, *four* of you... it'll be big enough on its own."

Antoine pointed to the three 20-pound propane tanks. "Can we use those while we're driving? Are we allowed to cook? I mean... I understand we need to stay hidden, but can we do those things while we're moving?"

"Like use the bathroom?" Dusty tossed in her two cents worth, feeling the urge coming on.

"The bathroom, yes. You can use that whether it's moving or not. With the inverters in place, you can use the electricity all day long. I can run the generator while we're driving. As for the cooking while driving..." Zeke shrugged. "It depends. If you were trying to cook baked beans or soup, that could be messy if I start going up or down hill and you're not paying attention. Over bumpy terrain could be problematic as well, but it should be fine for everything else. There are anchors for the crockpot and pans to make sure that they don't move and are fastened in place."

"Crockpot?" Antoine and Jonas said at the same time.

"Deva's thought of everything. If there's something special you wanna eat, or need, just let me know. I'll make sure you get it. Ready to see the inside?"

"Might as well." Still not as onboard as the others, the grumpiness on Dusty's face leaked out in her tone.

Zeke gave them the grand tour, showing off the sparkling kitchen, dining room, two bedrooms – with one being a studio theater – and bathrooms. "Are there any questions?" Everyone shook their heads. "Okay. I'm gonna get us on the road. We're on a tight timeline. It's gonna be a little bumpy to start, but once we're on the asphalt, it should be smooth sailing."

Dusty motioned to the large shower in the full bathroom off to the right. "Well, if I go playing in the dirt, at least there's running water."

Once Zeke left, and after Dusty used the bathroom, Antoine shook his head, taking the four steps up to the front room; the one Zeke called the 'theater' section. "Have you seen the movie RV about a dad who took his family on vacation in one?" Looking around, he noted the two pull out sofas situated around an electric fireplace. A variety of DVDs surrounded the big screen TV.

Unable to hide the chuckle, Jonas looked over with a gleam in his eyes. "Him trying to drive the RV from the windshield. Priceless. *Hilarious*. Robin Williams outdid himself."

"Personally, I thought his best was Aladdin. *No* one could do it better."

Looking up, Jonas appeared in deep thought. "I dunno. Will Smith might be able to do it justice, but you're right. No one could *ever* be as funny as Robin. The way he did all those voices… the man is a genius."

Seeing Dusty rolling her eyes, Antoine continued. "Any who, back to what I was getting at. Remember what the people were like in those RV campgrounds they parked in?"

Looking over, quite concerned, Dusty glanced from one to the other. "Fill in those of us who have better things to do than watch movies. What *kinda* people are we talking about? Criminals? Killers? People on the run?"

Turning with his mouth agape and brows furrowed, Antoine stared at her in complete astonishment. "We *really* need to get you out of the office. *No!* They're the friendliest group of people. Well, I'm sure not 'everyone' is, but they were in that movie. But… they were also the *nosiest*, trying to be too nice, helping each other out, getting all up in everyone's business."

"Oh. Not sure that would be the best thing if people got *too* curious. Then again, Zeke said we would be living in this thing *while* he's driving, so not sure we're gonna be stopping anywhere." Dusty glanced out the window watching the scenery pass by. "Good thing these are so dark and tinted, no one can see inside. Speaking of those… parks. *Do* we have to stay in one?" Her eyes turned in Jonas's direction.

"No clue. I'm sure Deva thought of that." Jonas shrugged. "I hope."

Antoine sat down on one of the black leather couches. "Well now… as far as mobile homes go… *this* is pretty nice. Did *you* give her a list of movies?"

Glancing over the selection, Jonas shook his head. "No. No idea where they came from. If she knew they were here, she *probably* would've had them taken out. After all, *nothing* is supposed to stop us from searching for those stones."

As her eyes traveled around the room, they settled on the men staring at her. "Oh, hell no! You're not gonna sit here and watch movies when we could be working. I agreed to a vacation – which is over – but I did *not* agree to stop working and watch a bunch of make believe."

"Ooh! Speaking of great movies," reaching into his back pocket, Antoine pulled out a pamphlet he picked up from the airport. "Guess what's close to where we're going? After all, we still have to eat. Plus, I have been *dying* to see this place! It's on my bucket list and it would be a shame to not grant an old man his last wish, right?"

Unsuccessfully, Jonas tried reading the waving card in the professor's hand. "What are you going on about? I can't see it with you waving it like that."

"Remember the movie 'Independence Day' when Russell Casse was in Little A'Le'Inn telling everyone about his alien abduction?"

Jonas nodded. "Yeah."

"*That* restaurant. We're headed in the same direction, as far as I can tell."

Dusty arched both brows, the irritated expression told of her disbelief. "Little Alien? Is that a real place?"

"Yep. It's actually, Little A Le Inn. The restaurant they used for a scene in *Independence Day*."

"That's what I said. Little Alien."

"No. Little Ale-" Ignoring her, Antoine turned to Jonas. "The producers of the show presented the town of Rachel with a time capsule – that they can't open until twenty-fifty – and installed it at the Inn."

Huffing out a groan, Dusty looked around the room, mumbling under her breath. "And *that's* more useless information that really doesn't concern me."

Sitting up, excited, Jonas did not share her thoughts on the matter. "Oh! No shit?"

Looking at the pamphlet, Antoine nodded. "It's not quite three hours away in Rachel. It opens at 8 and I do believe… it's on our way… but… if not… maybe we could take a pit stop and get something to eat there. I hear their Alien burgers are to die for, but I'm sure breakfast will be just as yummy! You know me… always thinking about food!"

"I'll let Zeke know. From the looks of it, you're right. We *are* headed in that direction anyway."

"Sounds gross. I'll stick with cow meat, thanks." With a disgusted huff, Dusty shook her head. "You two and your movies, I swear. Hell, if someone were smart, they would make a movie about *our* lives. I'll bet it would be the most exciting thing out there."

"Spoken like a woman who's *never* watched a movie." Standing, Antoine went down to the kitchen area. Opening the cabinets, he pulled out a big bag of Cheetos. "Well, we've *definitely* had better, that's for sure. Who gave her the grocery list, anyway?"

"If there's something you want, just let me know and I'll get Zeke the list," Jonas told him, taking out the movie. "I say we should show little Miss naysayer just what we're talking about with the *best* movie."

After rejoining them, Antoine clapped, looking at Dusty. "Yes! It can be the start of something that will add fun in your life. Lord knows, you need it."

It took a little bit of convincing, but finally the three sat down to watch *Independence Day* for the three-hour drive. No sooner did it start, Dusty fell asleep while Antoine and Jonas laughed, joking with each other while munching on Cheetos.

16

Following in a rental car, Travis watched the little blip on the computer screen, making sure to keep a few cars behind them. "An RV, huh? Well, that might've fooled the others, but not me."

Turning up the radio, he began singing along, patting the steering wheel to the beat. "On the road again. Just can't wait to get on the road again. The life I love is making music with my friends. And I can't wait to get on the road again. On the road again. Goin' places that I've never been. Seein' things that I may never see again. And I can't wait to get on the road again. On the road again. Like a band of gypsies, we go down the highway. We're the best of friends. Insisting–"

As his phone rang, he touched the Bluetooth in his ear. "Knight. … What? No. I beg to differ, sir." Reaching over, he turned down the radio. "I would think it would be obvious, but in all the time we've had it, we still have no clue what that thing is. … There's only a *possibility*. It's nothing definitive. Then again, nothing ever is. However, if we get rid of the *one* person, who has been in contact with something just like it, who *might* know what it is, then anything it has to tell us will be lost for good. … Yes sir, it was *identical*! The writing might've been a little different, but it was the same thing. … True, I *could* have, but that would've blown my cover and we wouldn't be tracking her and the others right now. She would've lost us just as easily as they did the other tail. … I understand that, sir. … Yes, but- … I want it on record that I *totally* disagree with that plan. Killing her will *not* help our situation at all. Need I remind you about what is at stake? … Emotions have *nothing* to do with this. I have never let them interfere before and they won't now. … I'm insulted that you think me so weak as to allow a mere woman to stand in the way of my job. Have I ever let you down before? Well, have I? … Exactly. I won't now either. … Yes, even if *that* has to happen. … Thank you. I'll check back later after I have the package in hand."

17

The enclosed, uninsulated porch held just a small prison cot in the corner – more like a gym mat with no padding. The two blankets folded at the foot of the bed – one thick and one thin – helped with the temperature outside. Dusty had use of a makeshift bathroom, consisting of a bowl, rag for cleaning, and a five-gallon bucket for a toilet, with her being in charge of disposing her own waste. Off to the side sat a spare bucket to wash her clothes and hair. She learned quickly how to keep things clean at an extremely young age.

Her meals never changed; pieces of fruit, and water for breakfast, vegetables, and water for lunch, which made her look forward to dinner – a piece of meat, bread, and water. A hose ran from the outside faucet to her 'bathroom' supplying her with all the water she could drink. In case she wanted more to eat, a bowl of fruit sat beside her cot, but never anything else. One time, her aunt tried giving her a bite of something sweet. Before she could even taste the cream filling, her Uncle Thaddeus slapped it out of her hand.

The big window, leading into the kitchen, didn't have any curtains for privacy. It also allowed her to witness what she didn't have. The woman she knew as *Aunt Meg* doted on her two cousins, plying them with hugs, kisses, and spoiling them rotten with brightly, colored gifts. She witnessed many joyous festivities while studying from the confines of her springy cot. Holidays passed her by. *Santa* dropped off numerous bounties for every member, except her. She didn't matter, though she did get an extra piece of meat with dinner. To the outside world, she didn't exist. That window made her watch others divulging in sweet candy and cakes that each festivity brought about.

Her birthday never changed. She didn't get to blow out candles, or eat sugary goodness baked just for her. No one allowed her to tear open beautifully wrapped presents, hoping something good was inside. Her uncle tossed in a bag with two of each: sweatpants, sweat jacket, pairs of socks, underwear, T-shirts, and tank tops. For running outside in the winter, she did get a new coat each year, but only because she outgrew her last one. Waste not, want not, her old clothes became new rags for cleaning purposes when they no longer passed as legitimate attire. Then her old holey cloths went right into the trash.

Anytime she thanked him, he set her straight with a solid backhand across the face. "You're not worthy of a gift. It's something for you to wear. *Necessities*. People don't give clothes as a gift. It's an excuse to give you something you need. No need to sugarcoat it with you. It's *not* a gift."

She never had a hug or kind word. Anything that could illicit an emotion, her uncle strictly forbade. No cakes, cookies, pies, or snacks allowed. At first, missing out on the delicious looking treats upset her, but later, she preferred it. It meant she didn't have to be around other people, finding solitude more to her liking.

On one of his few trips to visit, Sir G took a seat opposite her. "I am pleased with your progress thus far. You have exceeded my expectations. Today, I am going to teach you how to keep everyone out of your head. I want you to visualize a wall in your mind. It needs to be bulletproof, shatterproof, something that can't be torched."

Furrowing her brows, she looked up at him with her head canted to the side. "Why?"

"Because you can't let *anyone* know what you are thinking or doing. It's for your safety that no one be allowed to break into your mind. When you get older, I won't be able to watch out for you. You'll have to do things on your own. Trust no one, only yourself. Your life and the lives of millions of people will be counting on your ability to close off your thoughts." He motioned to her. "Now, do it. Keep me out."

Squinting, she tried visualizing a wall in her mind that would stop him from getting through. Being so young, not knowing the ways of the world, it confused her about *bulletproof*, but she gave it her best. However, her mind replayed the delicious looking cupcakes sitting in the window, distracting her.

"Sweets like that are just wasted carbs and make you fat. You become addicted to the sugar, like a drug, and it will own you," Sir G told her. "You disappoint me, Dustina. That wall has to stop *anything* from getting out and *anyone* from getting in. It must not allow any memories to squeak out." Walking to the back door, he motioned for her to follow. "Come with me."

Stepping outside, she noticed a running track in the back yard, stretching from one side to the other. "What's this?"

"*This* is going to be your punishment. When you fail at your mission, you will quickly run around this one time, not stopping until you get back *here*. Each week, your laps will grow by one. *If* you can do what is asked then you will not run, so it's in your best interest to *always* succeed." He pointed. "You failed at keeping me out. Get to it."

As she ran around the track, Sir G's voice sounded off in her head. "Key number two. Even though you are eminently important to this prophecy, you *can* be replaced. The key is that necklace. Trust no one else with it. You've had the training to handle the power that it will grant the user. Superman. Remember your daddy telling you about that? That is because, he was the firstborn 'de Jardiner.' Though he didn't know *why*, he recalled that we told him it would make him *Superman*. It will do the same for you. Now that *you* are ready, we stripped him of the necklace, and it is *your* responsibility. It has always been the firstborn and you are the last of your bloodline. It is always that way. We planned it like that for a reason. Only one family to keep track of, hidden from prying eyes that mean you nothing but harm. Safety for the world depends on you. *You* will be the key to stopping what is going to happen. But remember, *no* one else must be the keeper of the necklace. Only you. If you are opening the keys in your mind, then it's happening and after decades of waiting… the inevitable has occurred. May God walk with you on this life-or-death journey. Now, a memory for a reward."

In a blink, her father leaned over, tucking the covers under her. Toys and stuffed animals of every make and color lined the pink shelves on the wall starting with her second favorite. A little periwinkle table sat in the corner, surrounded by pictures lining the walls, showing off her latest talented designs. Clutching a floppy-eared white dog close to her chest, she kicked her feet in excitement. "Daddy, tell me a story."

Robert de Jardiner hopped in bed beside his daughter, wrapping his arm lovingly around her shoulder. The love he felt for her leaked through in his warm smile. "Okay. What would you like to hear *this* time?"

Looking up at him, she grinned. "How you and mommy met!"

"Again?"

She nodded. "Yes. It is the best story. Pleeeeeeeeeease."

He could never resist those amber-colored eyes and laughed softly. "Okay, okay. You win! It was like any other day. The birds sang a glorious song as I hummed my way to the train. Being early, I still had plenty of time to just enjoy the nature around me. A beautiful woman stood at the train station, tapping her foot impatiently, constantly looking at her watch. That poor woman had been running late all morning long. Apparently, she overslept after hitting snooze on her alarm." He leaned down, whispering. "She still does that to this day. That's why we have *two* alarms, with one across the room." Wiggling his brows, he sat back up amidst her giggling. "Anyway, we stood there trying to act like we didn't notice each other. Two men started harassing mommy, touching, and prodding, making her uncomfortable. She asked them to stop but they just laughed… so I leaped in to rescue her."

"Like Superman?"

"Shh! Don't give away my identity. If everyone knew that Superman turned in his cape for the love of a woman and a beautiful daughter… there would be eeeeevil pounding on our doors."

She giggled again as he tickled her.

"So, after I saved her from the two men, she looked up at me with dreamy eyes and called me her hero. Well, I knew I just *had* to take her out. We went to dinner that night and every night for a month. After that, we were married and moved in together and shortly… the light of my life was born… Dustina Elizabeth de Jardiner."

"I love you, daddy."

"I love you too, Dusty. Never forget how much we love you. No matter what happens in your lifetime… you are always loved." Hugging her tight, he kissed the top of her head before jumping out of the bed, once more tucking her in. "Now, go to sleep, silliness. We have big plans tomorrow. We're going to Disneyland!"

"I can't wait!" Pulling the blanket up to her chin, she grinned up at him. "I'm gonna shake Mickey's hand harder than anyone else ever has! After all, I'm Superman's daughter!"

"Then close your eyes so tomorrow hurries up!"

...

"We're here!" Zeke called out as he stepped inside the RV.

Startling awake, Dusty groaned, stretching, before letting out a yawn. A new memory. A new piece to the puzzle. A new reason to be emotional. "Y'all go in without me." She fought back the threat of tears. "The movie put me to sleep. Besides, I'm not hungry. *One* of us has to get back to work if we're *ever* gonna find that flipping stone."

Zeke looked at Jonas. "If you don't mind, I'd like to go in and check this place out too. Independence Day is my favorite movie of all times."

Glancing from him to Dusty, Jonas arched a brow. "Are you sure you won't join us? I don't like leaving you here by yourself and it's not fair to make Zeke stay and babysit."

"*Babysit*? I'll have you know that I managed to actually live a life before vampires plagued my existence." Growling, she motioned them out. "*Go*! All of you! Who the hell is gonna figure out I'm in an RV, of all places? Stuck in the middle of *nowhere* at that! I'll be fine. It would be nice to get a few moments by myself anyway. Y'all are always around. I need some '*me*' time!"

Shrugging, Jonas nodded his head to Zeke. "Sounds like you're joining us this morning."

"Yes!" Zeke fist bumped the air. With the surprised glance from Jonas, he reeled back his enthusiasm. "I mean, I can't have you going out... unguarded... so this is a good thing."

Feeling quite insulted, Antoine huffed. "*Fine*! Don't have to tell us twice that we aren't wanted."

"It's not that." Her tone instantly calmed, pulling him in for a hug. "Please, don't *ever* think that." She clutched him tightly, even though it made her want to break down in tears.

Feeling the urgency, Antoine held her close, concern lacing his tone. "Oh, honey, I'm teasing. You know how I am. Trust me, I know better than that. What's wrong? You look... a bit... frazzled."

"I've just been having all these weird dreams. My childhood training. What it all meant. Last night... I had a dream about my father. My *real* father. A hint about the life I had before being drafted into this prison. A reward of sorts. I don't understand that either, but… I don't know why I'm having them now when I've never dreamed before. Not until we went to Spain… but they're annoying. I just need a few moments by myself to collect my thoughts. That's all."

Feeling as if someone punched him in the gut, Jonas turned a troubled glance in her direction. "Dreams? Spain? *When* exactly in Spain?"

"Hell, if I know. I don't keep a diary of dreams."

"*Try* to remember."

Riled, she glanced over, shaking her head. "Which word do you *not* understand about how I *never* dreamed thus no need to keep a diary of them?!"

"Then you should have *no* trouble remembering the day you started."

Seeing the look on his face, she mumbled inaudibly before throwing up her hands in defeat. "*Fine*! It was… um… the day we went to visit your mother. *That* was the first dream. I don't recall ever dreaming before that. About *anything*."

The feeling in his stomach moved up to his chest. "I… see."

Placing a hand on her hip, Dusty glared. "Why? Did something *else* of importance happen that you've decided to keep from us? Something go wrong with your *fall back plan*?"

"No. Nothing of… *importance*." *At least, I don't* think *it was of importance,* though he began to wonder if maybe Garrick had another reason for wishing to be dead. He needed to research those memories for more information.

"Oh? But *something* definitely happened, right?"

Glancing away, he shrugged lightly.

"You've *got* to be kidding me! *More* secrets? I'm tired of all your damn secrets, Sparx! When I start keeping them from you, I better not hear one word about this partnership you always throw in *my* face."

"I don't throw anything in your fa-"

"Get out! *Everyone*! Get out and leave me alone to think! I'm tired of seeing the same faces over and over! Hooch is here if someone comes!" With as much strength as she could muster, she pushed Jonas across the floor. "Go! All of you! *Out*!"

Turning, he stomped out the door, pushing the other two in front of him. "Fine! Let's go, guys! It will be a better time without grumpy puss bothering us and not knowing a damn thing about what we're talking about. We *won't* bother bringing you back any food either!"

"Good!" She yelled after them. "I'll eat Cheetos if I get hungry! Unlike you, I'm not picky!" As soon as the door slammed, Dusty threw herself onto the couch, allowing tears to finally fall, gripping tightly to the throw pillow. Her father loved her. He truly adored her. He looked at her like the sun rose and set in her eyes. It made sense why Sir G had to take away her emotions. Had he not, she never would've gotten anywhere, stuck on the couch, crying into her pillows, over the loss of what she used to have, but would never experience again. Someone so wonderful cut out of her life without ever getting to say goodbye.

Hooch danced around and over her, trying to wipe away the tears, not sure what happened.

Before walking off, Jonas turned back to glance at the RV. When Zeke first pulled into the restaurant, he had to park around the side of the building so they could easily get back out onto the road. At the same time, he needed to be careful not to block the heavy flow of traffic the little store generated with daily tours. That put the RV door on the opposite side, away from the diner. They couldn't do anything about it without drawing attention. Then again, as Dusty screamed in his ear, no one would realize they were in an RV, in the middle of nowhere. Still, he didn't want to leave her behind. Something bothered her more than she let on, but he couldn't get inside her mind to figure it out. He should stay and get to the bottom of it. Then again, if he went back inside, she would chew him up and spit him out.

A bit of the conversation with Deva, on the first day of his training, popped into his head.

Shaking her head, she laughed softly. "Your weakness shows. He will use it against you."

"Since when has caring become a sign of weakness? How can you be sure he'd use it against me?"

Her eyes bore into his. "Because I would. The difference is Seth likes to play games. I don't." Shaking her head once more, she laughed harder. "Usually, our death is because of a mortal? Ridiculous. She should be food, not a romantic interest. Out of all the females, why on earth would a male vampire look to a human female for a love interest? For a second time." She looked at him, waiting for an answer.

At that moment, he would rather stand up to Deva, in all her anger, before walking back in to face Dusty. Deciding to put off World War III for another day, he ignored the little voice in his head, screaming at him to stay with her.

In her present condition, he wasn't about to drag her, kicking and screaming into the restaurant. Upon winning the argument with himself, he huffed out an exasperated breath of uncertainty, and headed into the busy diner.

Following a good cry, Dusty washed her face before picking up the laptop. Time to get back to work. After lighting a cigarette, hoping it would calm her nerves, she began searching for anything that involved KXTA. As the search engine pulled up a few sites, she blinked at the evidence on the screen. "You *can't* be serious."

It only took five minutes of sleuthing for her to figure things out. Getting ready to head into the restaurant and join the men – loaded with valuable information – she checked herself in the mirror. Usually, she didn't feel the need to look at her reflection, but she didn't want anyone to know about the tears. Wiping off all evidence, she fluffed at her hair. It looked like she stood in the middle of a windstorm, but she didn't care about impressing anyone. The way things were going, everyone was going to be dead soon anyway. There seemed to be no stopping Seth. Her stomach stabbed at her with the first sign of hunger pains. She could feed them the new information and indulge in alien burgers at the same time.

A knock at the door pulled her attention. Figuring Jonas returned to apologize, or sent Antoine to do it, she put the cigarette in the ashtray, racing to the door. "You guys aren't gonna believe what I just found! We've been thinking about this all wrong! I looked up-" Opening the door, her heart lunged into her throat as she felt the penetrating sting of a dart. "Travis."

Winking, he put the tranquilizer gun away. "Told you I would see you soon. I *always* live up to my promises." As she fell forward, over his shoulder, he grinned. "You're always falling for me." Closing the door, he quickly rushed to his car. "It's about time I swept ya off your dang burned feet. I've been trying since we were kids."

Growling, Hooch lunged out the door but hit the ground, going right through Travis. Shaking off his confusion, he jumped up, snapping at his heels, but didn't make contact. Every action had little effect on Travis as if he wasn't even there. As a last-ditch effort, he tried materializing as Bacchus taught him, but the poor dog made no more than a slight puff of dust over his boots.

Putting Dusty in the car, Travis pulled the seatbelt over, snapping it in place. Just to be on the safe side – having been on the wrong side of that fiery temper – he pulled out the handcuffs, snapping them over her wrists. "Can't have you fighting me, now darlin'." Leaning down, his thumb gently brushed against her cheek. "I *do* love you, Dusty. I just hope I can make you understand that. I would never, in a million years, no matter if the president *himself* gave me the order… do *anything* to ever intentionally hurt you."

After a quick kiss, making certain all body parts were inside the car, he closed the door. Rushing to the other side, he hopped in. Whipping the vehicle around, he headed back out onto the unpaved Old Mill Street, before making a quick left onto NV-375. "Sorry, honey, but some very important people want to meet you." Picking up the phone, he dialed a number, clicking on his Bluetooth. "Ma'am, I have her. I'm bringing her in now. … Yes ma'am."

18

Just north of Las Vegas in the Great Basin Desert, along Nevada Highway 375, lies the rural township of Rachel. Due to many cameo features in several Science Fiction movies and TV shows, it made the top local tourist trap drawing young and old alike to the quaint little city. The same happened to Roswell, New Mexico. People loved the unknown enough to investigate the possible existence of that which could never be… or could it?

Earthlings welcome!

The hot spot, previously known as the Rachel Bar and Grill, Little A'Le'Inn stayed afloat in the small town as a fun size bar, restaurant, and motel for over 20 years. At that very moment, Jonas, Antoine, and Zeke played out beloved scenes from *Independence Day*. They weren't alone in their acting debuts. Most of the visitors, dressed in the latest alien attire – sporting green hair or crazy makeup – had fun with it as well; earning a groan and an eyeroll from the locals trying to enjoy their breakfast in peace. A few recorded the strangest looking because "no one is gonna believe this shit" and needed proof. Some boasted about how they had experienced an alien abduction of their own and used that knowledge while creating their "out of this world" costume. Everyone claimed to have witnessed an unidentified flying object, showing pictures and/or video on their phones of little blips in the sky that could be anything.

"Everyone's trying to get outta Washington, and we're the only schmucks trying to get in!" Antoine could barely say the statement without laughing.

"You didn't think they actually spent ten thousand dollars for a hammer and thirty thousand for a toilet seat, did you?" Zeke added, pointing at Antoine.

Jonas leaned in, wiggling his brows, darting his eyes between the two men. "If you're so smart, tell me something. How come you go to M.I.T. for eight years to become a cable repairman?"

Not to be outdone, Antoine switched gears and grew instantly angry like flipping a switch. *"That's right!* That's what you get! Look at you! Ship all banged up! *Who's the man? Huh? Who's the man?* Wait until I get another plane! I am going to lower your friends *right beside you…* and what the hell is that smell?!" Many of the people nearby broke into laughter, giving him a round of applause for his rendition of Captain Steven Hiller arguing with the downed alien, before knocking him out. The professor gave a slight bow before turning back to his table.

Jonas joined in with the applause. "Looks like you missed your calling, professor."

"Bah! I like to watch it, but I'd never wanna do it. I'm not an actor."

Zeke leaned in looking from one to the other with an embarrassed expression on his face. "Oops."

Getting an eyeful of their surroundings, Antoine turned back around blinking. "What? What's oops? Oops is not a good word when we're running from Seth and his minions. Did you forget to lock the doors or something on the truck?"

Flashing a grin, Zeke continued. "What do you mean, *oops*? *Some jerk put this...* Don't say *oops*. *There. What do you say we try that again?* Yes, yes. Yes. Without the *oops*. That a way."

"Whew!" Relaxing, Antoine allowed the instant high alert to his system to flow out with laughter. "*They're bringing us in.* When the hell was you gonna tell me? *Oops.* We're gonna have to work on our communication." Antoine wiped at the tears in his eyes. "That sounds like a few of *our* conversations."

"I ain't heard no fat lady!" Jonas lifted his hand in the air as if saluting the building. "*Forget the fat lady. You're obsessed with the fat lady. Just get out of here!*"

Antoine buffed his nails on his shirt. "Good God! I've been sayin' it. I've been sayin' it for ten damn years. Ain't I been sayin' it, Miguel? Yeah, I've been sayin' it."

Jonas chuckled. "Think he's been saying it?"

Looking at the two of them covertly, Zeke nodded. "For ten *damn* years!"

After the fit of the giggles passed between the three of them, Antoine pointed around the room. "To think... we're sitting in the *same* location as that movie. I can't *wait* to taste the Saucer Burger with fries. I wonder if they'll taste any different than a regular burger and what the special sauce might be."

Folding his napkin on his lap, Zeke grimaced nervously. "I just hope it doesn't have to do with alien... uh... well... *you* know."

Cringing, Jonas leaned over, lightly nudging Zeke. "I don't think we have to worry about alien DNA. Probably just a regular burger and fries. Old Bay. It probably has Old Bay on it. Anytime there is a special sauce, it's usually made with Old Bay."

"Or Thousand Island dressing," Zeke nodded.

Jonas chuckled. "Yeah, or that. Ya know, I gotta say... you are the *best* driver we've had this entire time."

"Bout time Deva gave us one that seemed more human than the rest."

Mimicking Antoine's action, Zeke buffed his nails on his shirt, winking at him. "Why... thank you, sir. It's all part of my charm." With a sudden strike from under the table, he glanced down. A smile traced upon his lips as Hooch headbutted him. "Hey boy. What's the matter? Did your mom kick you out too?" Reaching his hand down under the table, he stroked his head, while glancing around the restaurant. "I wonder what made the director pick *this* place?"

Taking in all the alien paraphernalia, Antoine couldn't help the grin from spreading across his face. "Why, of course, it had to do with aliens. I mean, look at the gift shop. Aliens used as mannequins wearing T-shirts. Where else but the Alien Inn?"

Having no luck with Zeke, Hooch then headbutted Antoine, growling, tugging on his pant leg, trying to pull him out of the chair.

"Whoa, boy! What is *wrong* with you?" Seeing his frustration, Antoine glanced out the window at the RV. "Ya know... this isn't like Hooch. He's bothered about something."

Concerned, Zeke looked at the RV through the mirror at the back of the bar. "Is it too much to hope that she pissed him off too? Kicked him out?"

A disturbed expression crept onto Jonas's face as he stared out the window. "No. One, this dog can do no wrong in her eyes, and two... he would *never* leave her side. Not even in death."

"I dunno. Tonight, she's in her own element. I've never seen her quite like this before. Not sure what happened in Spain, but it's got her in a tither." Arching an inquisitive brow, Antoine turned a perturbed glare back to Jonas. "You'd tell us if something happened, right?"

Did something happen? Vampire things were still considered *his* business and nothing, really, that had to involve any of the others. Then again, spilling the beans about one thing would lead to another and soon there would be this whole Domino effect with all his lies dancing out into the open like a Broadway musical. He didn't want to deal with that. He didn't like lying to her, but he had no choice in the matter. Still, he had to wonder... *did something happen?* "What?! Antoine, please. I have to hear it from her. I'd rather *you* didn't start on me too. You *know* I would tell you if something important happened."

His play on words didn't appease Antoine as his eyes drifted back to the RV. Something wasn't right. He could feel it. "Don't get in a huff. I have to make sure. After all, we *are* a team and I just find it odd that she started remembering things while we were in Spain. I mean... what does *your* past have to do with *her* memories?"

Jonas blinked out of sight.

Glancing around a bit concerned, Antoine cleared his throat. "Let's hope no one saw that."

Turning the corner, the waitress stopped at their table with a tray. "Here we go. I hope we didn't keep you waiting too long." Setting down the plates of piping hot food, she blinked seeing the empty spot. "Where did your friend go?"

Spotting the restroom sign behind her head, Antoine pointed. "Bathroom. He'll be back."

Turning, she did a quick check, arching a brow. "Odd, I didn't even see him pass by me."

Standing, Zeke gulped down his Alien Amber Ale. "He's sneaky like that, but something pressing has come up and we need this to go after all."

"Oh. Okay, I'll take care of that." She picked up the hundred-dollar bill off the table. "I'll just get you your change and bag this order to go."

Reappearing behind her, Jonas cleared his throat. "Nope, that's for you. Keep the change."

"Aaah!" The sound of the man's voice in her ear made her jump near out of her skin causing her to fall backward.

Jonas caught her, setting her right. "Are you okay?"

"Good Lord! He's right! You *are* sneaky." Trying to calm the racing of her heart, she put a hand protectively on her chest. With the shock out of the way, she blinked down at the bill in her hand. "Wait. Did you say… keep the change?"

"Sure did."

"Are you positive? I mean… I know people always talk about that big tipper, but I never met one… until today!"

He winked. "You deserve it."

"You are too kind! Thanks for the tip! I'll get your food in bags right away." Flabbergasted, she disappeared around the corner with their food, barking instructions to expedite their order to go.

Once she drifted out of earshot, Jonas groaned. "*Now*, I see why Hooch is upset. We got *big* problems."

"I don't like the sound of that. What do you mean *problems*?" Antoine stood up quickly, downing his drink.

"What do you mean *big*?" Zeke glanced at the RV.

Jonas chugged down his drink too. "Let's get the food first, so we don't make a scene that might need explaining later."

Once they had their takeout in hand, the waitress gave them a refill on the drinks as well, the four of them headed back to the RV. "Everyone just walk at a normal, mortal pace." Even though he wanted to zip back over, Jonas couldn't help but notice the crowd of people. "We don't need the townsfolk swearing that aliens came in and ate and just disappeared out of sight. Appearances and all that."

Antoine nodded, picking up the pace. "Mortals can walk faster than *this*! Now, *what* has you and Hooch in such a mood?"

Rounding the RV, Jonas held the door open for the others. "I've checked this place three times over. She's gone."

"Gone? Oh, Deva isn't gonna like this!" Running a hand nervously through his hair, Zeke looked toward the surrounding mountains. "Do you think *maybe* she went for a walk to cool down? I mean, it wouldn't be out of the question. After all, she was *highly* agitated about *something*."

Longing for it to be that simple, Jonas pointed to the counter. "I wish. That cigarette left burning in the ashtray tells me someone… or some*thing*… interrupted her." Reaching into his pocket, he pulled out her phone. "Also, there's this."

"Her phone?" The shock reached Antoine's eyes. "Lord have mercy! That child would never go *anywhere* without that thing. It's like her jelly beans."

Looking at the phone in Jonas's hand, Zeke glanced around the dining room for any clues. "Where did you find it?"

"At the bottom of the stairs. That tells me someone took her, and it fell out in the struggle. But who could find us? We're in the middle of the desert… in an RV… at an alien restaurant!"

Thinking over the possibilities, Antoine gasped. "Good Lord. I'll bet it was that Travis character."

Whining, Hooch headbutted Antoine, making him bend down and pet him.

"I know, booboo. We're gonna find your mama." While trying to comfort the frazzled dog, he looked up at the other two. "Travis seems to be able to do things most people can't! You don't think… he's still working with Seth. Do you?"

After putting out the smoldering filter, Jonas turned back to Antoine. "Seth doesn't work well with others and he can't *stand* mortals."

"Then *why* is he making *us* do all the dirty work?"

"I don't think Seth would get anyone to kidnap her though. He wants this stone quickly. He doesn't want to play games to get it."

"As much as I hate to say this," Zeke huffed out an exasperated breath, shaking his head. "You *really* should call Deva. It would be better coming from you… than me."

"I would, but she basically told us that we're on our own. She's… taking care of *other* things. This one… *we* have to figure out. That's why we're living in *this* thing, which I have a feeling if we were in the jet, *no* one would've gotten to her!"

"Okay then. Where do you want to start?"

Standing, Antoine stared at Jonas as if he just escaped from a mental ward. "On our *own*?"

"We don't need Deva for *everything*. Hell, it might surprise you to know that before she came along, I handled a lot of things on my own."

Antoine scrunched up his face. "Not like this."

"*Exactly* like this. This isn't my first rodeo with Seth." Looking at Hooch, Jonas bent down, touching the dog's head. "Hooch. Find Dusty. Find Dusty, Hooch."

Sniffing the ground, it took a moment before he bolted for the road, hot on her trail. As the others followed closely behind, he stopped short. Sniffing from one side to the other, he reversed gears, once more in hot pursuit before stopping and looking from the left to the right with a disoriented expression on his face. Stopping, he looked from one to the other before sitting down. Whimpering, he turned his head back to Jonas and howled.

Taking a deep breath, Jonas let it out slowly. "He lost her scent."

The fear of never finding her clung to Antoine with razor-sharp talons. "That probably means she's in a car. Like I said, it *has* to be Travis. No telling how far away they are by now. He could've gone in any direction. The question is, why? *Why* would he kidnap her after trying to kill her? Wouldn't he just shoot her and be done with it?"

The hurtful words earlier, between him and Dusty, replayed in Jonas's mind like a scratched CD. "Let's find out." Dialing the number for Travis, he silently counted the rings, waiting for someone to answer. When the voicemail kicked in, he ended the call with a resigned sigh. "He's not answering. Now what do we do?"

"Perhaps *I* can help."

Hearing a familiar voice, Jonas pivoted around, his eyes turning crimson. "What are *you* doing here?"

Francis de Molay held up a hand. "We are not here to fight. We are here to help. Sir Garioch informed us of the error of our ways, and we are deeply sorry for putting you through what we did. We were misinformed. Putting all that aside, we can help you. We've been in training for this day for more years than you've been alive."

"You hide your age well."

"Not me, *personally*. The Knights Templar."

A frustrated growl rushed from his throat as Jonas took a step forward. "We don't need your help. You 'helped' us enough before. We can do this on our own."

Getting between them, Antoine placed a hand on Jonas's chest, stilling any further actions. "Put your pride away, boy! Our girl has been Dusty-napped. I don't think it would hurt to have God's army on *our* side for a change. Every little bit helps. Remember, the big man puts *everyone* in our path for different reasons. Some are just there for a test to see if lessons were learned. Others are there to help us get over something, offer support when needed, or keep us informed. And if that's not enough, sometimes, *we* are the test. Are you *really* going to look a gift horse from God in the mouth?"

Looking from Antoine to Francis, Jonas exhaled slowly. "Fine. You're right. I'm going to try and get Deva on the phone and tell her what happened." Impatience tinted his tone behind flatlined lips as Jonas jabbed the air at Francis. "Remember one thing, *knight*. If you give me *one* bit of trouble, and it won't take much, I will snap your neck before you have time to twitch. Do you understand?"

Biting back the retort, Francis bowed his head, though the challenge remained in his gaze. "I understand."

Antoine's brows notched up before he winced. "*Deva*? I'm glad *I'm* not making that call." Turning to the newcomer, he outstretched his hand. "Hello, allow me to *officially* introduce myself. I'm Professor Antoine Dubois. Linguistics Professor. Consultant to many alphabet groups. Riddle master of this journey. Pleasure to meet you."

Francis bowed his head in respect while clasping hands for a friendly shake. "Sir Francis de Molay of the Knights Templar. Nice to meet you as well."

After trying to call her twice, Jonas groaned. "She didn't answer."

"You *just* said that she told you she wouldn't be available," Antoine reminded him. "We had to figure out things on our own. Hence the utmost importance of this tank on wheels."

Running an impatient hand through his hair, he shook his head. "Yeah, but something's wrong. She *always* answers when it's me, no matter what is going on, because she knows just how important this mission is to *everyone* in the world. Mortal *and* immortal alike. I wonder what she's up to now."

Antoine crossed himself. "Probably nothing good."

19

The Arizona desert, 5 miles outside Deva's Castle.

The fierce heat rippled off the sand, creating a surreal kaleidoscope of the barren desert. It looked like waves of fire spanned across the scorching ground. With a grin creasing his face, Seth eyed the area. "This is almost like home," he mused, drawing a hand through his hair.

"*Why* have you summoned us here?"

Turning, Seth eyed the two figures before him. "I have my reasons, Kanis." Furrowing his brow, he noted an absence. "Don't you always travel in threes?"

"Garrick is... *missing*. I cannot locate him, nor can any of my children. He has not passed through Amelia, yet I fear he is no more."

"Well that just breaks my heart." Smiling, he turned his attention to the female clinging to Kanis's side. "Amelia, darling. It's been too long. Still kissin' the wrong ass, I see." Giving her a dismissive wave, he turned back to Kanis. "It would seem our dear Jonas has gotten more powerful than I anticipated. Apparently, the lovely

Deva did more than provide him with a few meddlesome tricks. I wanna know *exactly* what she gave him."

"More powerful? I do not understand."

"I paid Jonas a visit on Deva's plane. Long story short, when I tried to get up, he stopped me. Normally, I could understand that, but I wasn't *really* there. If you catch my meaning."

The Russian vampire's eyes narrowed. Feeling Amelia's grip on his arm tighten, he gave her a reassuring pat on the hand. "That is not possible. In our astral form, the physical world cannot affect us. There is no spell she could have taught him to keep you at bay."

"Are you callin' me a liar?"

"No, no. Not at all, it is just that—"

"Enough. It happened. I wanna know *how*, so we are gonna pay 'Castle LaDevia' a visit."

"Oh really?" Amelia piped up from behind Kanis. "Ya just gonna walk up to the front door and knock?"

Squeezing Amelia's hand to silence her, Kanis shook his head. "Ignoring the hundred or so guardians, I doubt that she will be willing to share that information, *if* we get to her."

"Deva's not home right now," Seth replied, shooting Amelia the evil eye causing her to hide behind Kanis. "She's over in jolly old England, dealin' with a… long-standin' *personal* matter."

"I see." The tone in his voice and look on his face reflected that Kanis did not 'see' anything. "Still, we cannot simply walk right in and—"

"Oh, ye of little faith." Looking up, Seth extended his arms to the sky. "Setua aken topeth ha." Grinning, he watched as the heavens darkened. Hordes of ancient demons rose from the ground, screaming toward the castle. "She's not the *only* one with a bag of tricks." He turned back to the pair. "And Amelia… if you *ever* get snarky with me again, you're gonna wish you never had a tongue."

Taking a step between them, Kanis shielded Amelia. "She will remain silent."

"See that she does." Turning back, he smiled as the sounds of carnage reached his ears. "Now then, who's up for some barbecue?"

As the massacre reached her ears, Amelia whimpered. "Oh no. Not again." Her body flung straight up into the air, as if hoisted by an unseen arm, before slamming back into ground with bone-breaking speed.

Once more, angry, powerful vampires cut down in their prime raped her body to the core, twisting and pulling at her limbs as if trying to rip her apart. Enraged souls, not wanting to go to their final resting place, thrust into her, marking her essence with their fiery scrawled names. Some wrote them in her flesh from the inside out.

Continuously picked up and thrown to the ground, she couldn't heal fast enough to mend the broken bones, punctured lungs, or cracked skull. Seth thoroughly enjoyed the show while Kanis feared she might not be able to make it through this one. Too many at one time could be devastating, even for her.

As the last vampire shadow crashed into her body, she lifted up once more, arms and legs being pulled outward, before dropping to the ground in a heap. Curling in a fetal position, blood tears streaked down her cheeks as she slowly began the healing process.

Not wanting to appear weak before his sire, Kanis smirked down at her. "Very good. Now, clean yourself up."

Seth golf clapped. "Very nice. I do appreciate a little entertainment while killing. But if *all* vampires pass through her at death, and she hasn't felt Garrick, then it only stands to reason that he is still among us."

"But I cannot reach him. The sire bond has been severed."

"Maybe he's learned a few things over the years."

Kanis blew out an irritated breath. "Garrick? He is *very* loyal to me and to the mission. He would *never* stray. No. There is something else going on."

"Worry about that on *your* own time." Seth headed toward the castle. "We have *other* things to tend to."

Slowly trailing behind, Amelia stood, wiping the blood from her nose,. "One would think I would be given some extra powers when they all passed through me, but no. Just pain and suffering. Next time, a little warning would be nice."

Kanis shook his head, warning her not to get uppity with Seth.

Seth growled. "Darlin', if I have to repeat myself, what just happened will feel like a tickle fest compared to what I will do."

"Forgive her. It was too much at one time. That is all."

"Keep your pet in line, Kanis. Any more lip from her and I'll rip them from her face."

"Understood."

20

The inner workings of Deva's castle were enough to confuse the best tracker. The doors opened to plush carpeting; walls filled with majestic blood-splattered design – stained with the massacre from Seth's minions. Winding stairs dead-ended at walls, long corridors stopped at doors which opened to more empty hallways, giving the impression that rooms shifted their locations.

Surrounded by the vampire holocaust his demons wrought, Seth stood in the middle of the great hall, admiring their work. "Effective." He kicked a smoldering skull aside. "Messy, but effective."

Looking around at some of the destroyed medieval tapestries hanging on the stone walls, Kanis gave a derisive snort. "Aristocratic drivel." He ran a hand over one of the more colorful selections. Turning to Seth, he inclined his head to the floor. "I mean no disrespect, but how do you intend to locate the spell you are seeking, given that there is no one left to interrogate."

"You never learned to think outside the box, have you? Deva would *never* trust a spell that powerful to her flunkies." As Kanis still appeared confused, Seth rolled his eyes, pointing to the small blinking red light, pulsing in the corner of the high ceiling. "I'm gonna assume somewhere in this castle is a control room of sorts. A place where she can see every nook and cranny. Inside and out. Rather than go room by room, let's find *it* and just see what our absentee hostess is hiding."

The blur of three vampires moving at top speed looked like tracers from an acid trip, as they covered the vast expanse in seconds. Kanis found it in the Oratory – Deva's private chapel – hidden behind a false wall. Filled with all manner of high-tech surveillance equipment, his brow narrowed at the blank screens. Closing his eyes, he called to Seth and Amelia.

Appearing on either side of him, the pair took stock of the situation.

"I take it this is command central. Interesting hiding place she picked." Seth's brow knitted. "I so hate this electronic age. What happened to good old handwriting? Why, I remember when a person could just break the lock on a chest, go through the papers inside and find out what they wanted to know. Now it's all… this." Eyeing Amelia, he stepped aside, motioning to the control panel and two keyboards. "Time to earn your keep darlin'."

Sitting down, she took a moment to assess the situation before flipping her hair back. "Talk about top notch tech! Course, I'd expect nothing less from *her majesty*." Booting the system, she turned to the men behind her. "This'll take a speck of time. I'll let you know when–" Interrupted by a beep from the console, Amelia turned back to the screens. 'Password Required' flashed across all of them, as she tapped a long nail against the smooth, marble countertop.

Noting her hesitation, Seth leaned over her. "Problem?"

"Possibly. It would seem that our queen isn't ignorant of computers and what is necessary to hack into them. There is definitely *something* here that she wants to keep secret… but she failed to realize *I* am better than that." Tapping a few keys brought her into the system configuration as she examined the coding which popped up on the main monitor. After minutes of scrolling through various numbers, letters, and symbols, she stopped, pointing to one line in particular. "Ooh. Well, our dear Deva *is* a bit paranoid." Spinning around in the chair, she nervously looked up at Seth and Kanis. "I can't hack this system. I actually *need* the password."

A dark brow rose over Kanis's left eye. "I have seen you crack passwords before. What is so difficult *this* time?"

"I could try, but it would take a lot more time than we probably have. *This* system is set up to only accept *one* password. No mistakes allowed. One wrong letter or symbol and the entire system will be *destroyed*. That means we get just *one* shot at this. If I don't put in the right password the first time, the whole thing locks down and self-destructs. Now, I'm sure she has a backup, but I'd bet a fresh virgin that it ain't here in the castle." Glancing between the men, she put her hands in her lap. "Both of you know her better than I do. Any ideas what she might use for a password?"

"Drake," Kanis offered.

Glaring up at him, Amelia shook her head. "Her sire?"

"Yes. Why not?"

"Because it would be something that few would know about her. A secret. Hell, the whole vampiric world knows about her hatred for her sire. As much as she loathed the man, I *seriously* doubt she would use his name. Too easy. That'd be like you using 'Blood' as your password without zeros for the O's."

"Well... that *is* my password."

Letting out a burst of laughter, Seth clapped Kanis on the back. "You always were good for a laugh."

Blinking, Amelia shook her head. "No. It would be something that means a lot to her."

"You two sit tight. Don't touch anything. I'm gonna take a walk around. See if anything strikes me as a possibility."

Once Seth disappeared, Amelia smacked Kanis in the arm. "You did *not* use 'blood' as your password, did you?"

"I was in a hurry."

"Blood? *Really*? Didn't I tell you to use letters, numbers, *and* symbols?"

"I was going to change it... eventually."

"As soon as we get back. On second thought, *I'll* change it for you. If some of those files fell into the wrong hands..."

As Seth wandered around the castle, his mind traced back through the memories he and Deva shared. Nothing stood out until he came across a tall curio cabinet, filled with trinkets and small sculptures.

Opening the door, he removed one of them. A certain remembrance eased its way into his thoughts as he turned it over in his hand.

...

Castle LaDevia 1947

Seth pointed to a carving of a beautiful ebon horse. "What is this?"

Deva's face softened as her eyes fell upon one of her prized possessions. "When my parents were alive–"

"I didn't ask for story time. I just want to know what *this* is."

Her eyes hardened as lips flatlined. "So then shut up and listen. You get the *whole* story whether you want it or not! Don't ask a question if you can't handle my answer! *As* I was saying… my father used to bring home horses to train. They were going to be used in our royal army, so they *had* to be the best." Reminiscing brought a smile to her lips. "Oh… they were *exquisite*. All regal. Muscle bound. Just *gorgeous* animals. There was one that gave everyone a hard time. The most beautiful Andalusian stallion I'd ever seen. His color was bold. Black. Not a patch of shading anywhere. They tried taming him. Everyone who got too close was thrown against the wall and damn near trampled to death."

"Sounds like my kind of beast."

"Well, my father did not share your sentiment. He was having him put down if he couldn't be trained in a week."

"A whole week?" Sarcasm laced his words. "I would've given them a day."

"Unlike you, my father was very fair. He felt that should be enough time. There was something special about that horse. I could feel it. Sneaking out of the castle, during the changing of the guards, I headed to the stables. I talked to him for hours, feeding him sugar and carrots. After a few days, he trusted me. Actually looked forward to my visits."

Wiggling his brows, Seth grinned. "I so look forward to our visits as well."

Rolling her eyes, she poked him. "Knowing his time was drawing nearer, I had to put a plan together to help him. He needed to be tamed. Once we were out of the stables, he tried bucking me off, slamming me into the fence. He did everything possible to get me out of the seat. He couldn't. I tied my hand to the saddle and couldn't get off if I wanted to. We were making so much noise that a crowd gathered outside the fence, watching, screaming at me. It didn't take long before he calmed down. I tamed him. Though my father was *extremely* angry, he gave me the horse. That horse never allowed *anyone* else near him without my permission. From that point on… we were inseparable."

"You must've cared a great deal for him."

"I did. He was my first pet… of a sort. When I became queen at such a young age, he carried me into battle, protecting me, putting his own life in danger many times. I rode him in parades and festivals." Her expression darkened. "Just after Drake turned me, I tried to retrieve him. I snuck into the royal stable, but he sensed my new life. Tried attacking me. I realized that the horse would never let me ride him again and was going to set him free. Just as I got the gate open, Drake showed up. To keep control over me, and as a warning what he would do to those I cared for if I didn't listen to his every word… to make sure I had nothing left to cling to… he killed Luciferous. Made it look like a pack of wolves and forced me to watch. I can still hear his screams as his minions ate him alive."

"Luciferous?" Seth asked. "Odd name for a beloved royal steed."

"To other people, he was the devil. He would just as soon kill them before letting anyone ride. I was the only one. My father hated the name, but what was in a name? He allowed it. After all, I was his pride and joy… and just as stubborn as he."

…

As the memory subsided, Seth headed back to the control room. "Try Luciferous." He wrote it on a small slip of paper, handing it to Amelia.

"Luciferous? That's an odd name. Do I wanna know?" She turned to the keyboard.

"No."

"If it doesn't work though, it ain't my fault."

"Fine."

Bringing up the password screen again, she typed in the word. Hovering her hand over the enter key, she glanced at Seth. "There's about a hundred things that could go wrong here, even if the word is right. Is it all caps? All lower case? A mix of both? And if it is a mix, which ones are upper and which ones are lower. The 'l's' could be lower case 'l's' or–"

"Just press the damn button."

Backing to the door, Kanis stood ready to make a hasty retreat in case it didn't work. He wouldn't put it past Deva to set up a surprise or two.

Biting her lower lip, Amelia pushed *the damn button*. The screens went black for a moment, then lit up with surveillance footage. "*Sweet.*"

Leaning closer, Seth reviewed the monitors as Kanis eased forward. Most showed dead vampires in every shot with blood soaking the walls as if they exploded.

Pointing to one of the screens, Amelia looked up at Seth. "I think your fun boys missed one."

Within a corner of one of the lodgings, magical writing littered the walls, ceiling, and floor. Chey stood, sword in hand, ready to fend off any attack.

Kanis scoffed. "What a sniveling coward. I am surprised Deva tolerates having such a creature in her employment. Look at her hiding. I will dispatch this one with–"

"I don't think so." Seth placed a hand on Kanis's chest.

"Why didn't your demons attack *her*?"

"*That* could be the answer." Amelia pointed to the scribble on the walls behind the woman. "But... why would Deva go through so much trouble for *one* person."

"I don't think that's it at all. Look behind her."

"What is that?" Kanis peered closer. "Is that... a *door*?"

Barely perceptible, the outline of a door appeared. "She's not hiding. She's guarding something. And seeing all the magic charms of protection, it's something *extremely* valuable indeed." Pointing at the screen, he turned to Amelia. "Where is that?"

"Lower level. East wing. Looks like the door leading down to the undercroft... or cellar." Amelia pointed to the identifying marks from the camera.

"*That's* where we're going." Seth pointed as the three of them vanished in a green mist.

One by one, they appeared around the woman. Seeing Seth, Chey growled. "You!"

"Why, hello, my dear. And who might you be?" Seth asked, wearing a charming smile on his handsome face. As the woman confronted him, his face lit up like a Christmas tree. "Oh, my word! Is that you, Chey? It's good to see you again. What? No tea this time?"

"I should have guessed something bad plagued the castle. You always do come in with a bang... or a splatter of blood and death." Chey leveled the business end of the sword at Seth.

He placed a hand over his heart. "Now, Chey, that's not very hospitable."

"Who is this woman?" Kanis asked, disgusted at her appearance.

"Who is this? Surely you heard of the illustrious Chey. The woman who raised Deva. Drake changed her too. Long story and we don't have time, but she's *especially* important to Deva. I would say that we have ourselves quite the bargaining chip." Seth turned back to Chey. "We're not gonna hurt you. Just looking for information."

Spitting at his feet, Chey held her ground. "I'd sooner die, then give ya the time of day, monster."

"That can be arranged. Course, that's not *my* preference. I'll get right to the point. Your mistress, the lovely Deva, has a spell. A very potent one which affects us in our astral state. If you'll kindly hand it over, my associates and I will be on our way, and you can get back to doing... whatever it is your duties call for."

"Yer looney. Magic don't work on us in that state. Ya wasted yer time coming here."

"Well since you're so adamant about that, you won't mind if we waste a little more and have a look at what's behind door number one?"

Backing up, Chey held the sword raised over her head. "Over my dead body!"

"You seem bent on dyin', darlin. Since you do, I'm gonna assume there's something *incredibly* special behind that door. So, I'm gonna have to insist." With a motion of his hand, Chey's body crumpled to the ground.

Amelia's lips turned up in a pout. "Damn it! I wanted that one."

"Relax. I didn't kill her. You might get your chance, but we may need her. For now, let's go exploring."

As Seth reached for the door, Amelia blocked his way. "What are you doing? Aren't you worried about all the magic around the door?"

Giving her the evil eye, he pushed her from the opening, slamming her into the wall. "For being the archivist, you haven't learned much, have you? These ancient symbols aren't *just* to keep us out, but also to keep whatever is down *there* from getting out." He ran his finger over one. "A powerful spell at that. What does dear Deva fear will get loose… and why?"

Opening the door, they made their way down a set of narrow steps, to the vaulted cellar.

Kanis waved a hand in front of his nose. "Disgusting. It smells like decay in here."

Amelia felt the assault to her sinuses as well. "What could be so important down here? How could Deva live with this stench. I thought she had more class. Apparently, I was mistaken."

Seth ignited a few of the torches lining the damp walls. "We *all* lived like this at one point." As they reached the floor, he looked around the vast expanse of unending walls. "This smell is to drive others away. It's a deterrent. A clever ruse. Spread out and see if you can find anything."

Amelia found it. An oblong coffin sealed with silver straps. It rested upright, leaning against a dripping wall. Running her hands over the raised symbols, her eyes widened, before jerking away from the burn. "Inanna." Her words were barely above a whisper as she slowly backed away. Coming to an abrupt halt against Kanis's chest, she spun around. "We have to get out of here," she pleaded.

Seth popped around the corner. "What's all this about leaving? I have not dismissed you yet."

Amelia pointed a quivering finger at the coffin. "Inanna." Her voice shook as badly as her finger.

Looking over at the casket, Seth smiled. "Well now. I think we can forget about that spell for the moment." Walking over, he ran a hand over the same symbols Amelia had. "This is *much* more impressive."

"It is my turn to be confused." Kanis eyed the ornate box. "*Who* is Inanna?"

"It's a sad state of affairs when your pet knows more about our history than you do, Kanis. Inanna. The Goddess of fertility and war in ancient Sumer." Seth continued inspecting the casket. "When I was a boy, there were stories about the Sumerians. Hell, most of the modern religious tales are nothing but re-pukes of Sumerian lore. Inanna was one of the most important deities they had. Though she's gone by other names throughout time, you might know her as Katherine DuPont."

Kanis tilted his head. "Jonas's Katherine?"

"The same."

"What would a celestial being want with Jonas Sparx of all people?"

"That… is a good question."

"And why would *she* be here? With Deva, of all people, in care of her resting box?"

"I don't know." The lie slipped from Seth's lips as easily as his name. "But I simply *can't* allow this find to languish here." With a snap of his fingers the box vanished.

"*No!*" Amelia screamed out in fear. "You can't free her. I–"

"I can do whatever I want." Seth interrupted. Turning, he eyed Kanis. "I thought you disposed of the vampire council?"

Kanis nodded adamantly. "I did."

"Well, you missed one. I want both of you to return home and guard Katherine's body. Make sure no one touches her. Am I clear on that?"

They both lowered their heads, but only Kanis responded. "As you wish. What will you do?"

"There's still a small matter of this spell. I want it." He cracked his neck, glancing up the stairs. "Since I now have something Deva wants…" He grinned. "We can barter."

Taking a step back, Amelia's eyes widened. "You're going to face her? After what you did *here*?"

"Yep. It's time we cleared the air about a few things. Now go. And remember what I said. *No* one comes near that box."

Bowing, the two vanished.

Seth summoned Chey, reviving her. As she regained consciousness, he smiled, seeing the hatred in her eyes. "Hi there. Remember me?"

21

Unlike the timber frame of American houses, the 1930 3-bedroom, detached, bungalow sat isolated off by itself. A long driveway led up to a circular arc guarding double front doors. A faded sign in the driveway pointed to a dirt path, leading around back for servants and deliveries. An attractive couple entering the residence ignored the all-but-forgotten sign. After all, it was *their* home.

"I didn't think that twat would *ever* shut up. I mean, how many times can you listen to the same prattle before it's acceptable to rip off her head and shove it up her fat ass?!" The beautiful woman dropped the keys on the circular, medium antique mahogany, Drum end table by the door. The cheapest article of furniture in the house, it ran a cool $4,000. "Blah, blah, blah. I wish we didn't have to be so… accommodating of her wishes."

"You must calm that hot head of yours, Agnes. We need her… for a little while, yet. She is so *very* influential, and we can use that to our advantage. The way her lips moved, constantly, never stopping, she reminded me of a hungry bird." While removing the brown herringbone wool cap from his head, he laughed. "Just kept her mouth open like waiting for food. Then again, all the winking she did in my direction, I do believe she wanted me to get frisky with them."

As he helped her remove the wool shawl from around her shoulders, she laughed. "Walter! Now *that* I would have paid to see! Lady Evelyn Isabella Elizabeth Johnson turning up her nose while getting down and dirty on her expensive white shag Kerman Persian imported rug!" Removing the light blue wool fedora bonnet from off her head – accessorized with black fishnet, topped off with a black bow – she placed it in the closet by the door. An assortment of oversized hats snuggled within; the ridiculous ones reserved for weddings per British customs. Closing the door, she stood in front of the rectangular mirror, repositioning her auburn hair back into the tight bun. "Then again if that would've stopped her yammering... I had to stop myself from tossing in a piece of meat or one of her God-awful cucumber sandwiches. I mean, who thought putting salad on bread was a good idea? Next, she will be out in the yard, finding the best tufts of green grass to splay between two slices with some honey mustard, calling *that* a meal. Disgusting, really."

After hanging the jackets on the coat stand by the door, he winked, brushing down his deep brown hair. "Agreed. A sandwich needs some sort of meat in it to be called satisfying. The bloodier the better." Laughing softly, he swatted her behind while turning right into the main room.

"Funny. I don't recall *jam* being labeled meat, but I get your point." She turned in the opposite direction, into the kitchen – peppered with black and white everything from expensive appliances to a shiny marble floor – and opened the refrigerator. "I'm going to get a cup. After all that hobnobbing, it couldn't hurt. Would you like one?"

"Um. Y-yes." His voice sounded shaky and guarded. "H-how about something different from my norm. I'll take... O-negative. I'm feeling a little... stiff."

"Well, aren't we fancy?! Since when do you want the good stuff? It must be time for a celebration. I think I'll join you! Might need to ring up the blood bank for delivery later." That brought about an amused cackle from the kitchen. "Wait, did you say... *stiff*? Ooh, is that a hint at your mood? Oh, goodie! Be sure to stay that way and I'll take full advantage of it tonight." After popping two china cups into the microwave for a minute, she sauntered back to the living room. Stepping through the door, she came to a whiplashing standstill as gray eyes widened, seeing the unnerving sight ahead that turned her blood to ice. "*Deva!*" Her mouth hinged open as shaking hands threatened to drop the cups to the floor.

Walter could not control his snappish tones while rolling his eyes; the only thing he could move on his body. "Agnes! Are you stupid?! How many times did we go over our code? Did you forget about that? When the *hell* do I *ever* take negative blood? It's too alien for me. You know that!"

His finger-pointing voice brought her back to the present. "Code? What code?" With shaky hands, to go with her trembling voice, she set the cups down. "Bollocks! You mean the one you spoke about eons ago? Oh sure… like *that* was the first thought in my mind while going to the kitchen for a cup of… tea."

Finding their tiff quite enjoyable, Deva offered a wave from her position on the comfy sofa. "Hello, love. I *hope* I haven't come at an inconvenient time?"

Clearing her throat, the woman smiled nervously, shaking her head. "N-no. We were just about to have a spot of blood-infused tea. Would you like a cup?"

Grimacing slightly, Deva glanced at the offering. "*Mortal* blood-infused?"

Arching a well-manicured brow, the woman's offended expression carried into her tone. "Well, of course. What else is there?"

Waving a hand at the absurd notion, Deva leisurely stretched out on the sofa in to the soft cushions. "I'm not sure *why* your question surprises me."

"We were not expecting you."

"No, but any *other* vampire might've had an *inkling* I had arrived. Then again, you both have grown quite serene in your environment. Forgetting any and all danger that might befall upon you. Cocky lot you rich, snobby vampires are. It might've been easier on you to escape before walking in and finding me getting comfy on your awfully expensive couch, which is… quite cozy, I might add. Maybe I'll confiscate it for payment in making me track you down. This little side trip has cost me much in time that I should not have dallied, but… *some* things are worth a few trinkets, wouldn't you say? As you may have heard, I am incredibly busy. I don't have time for such dollying as this. Then again, *you* made it too easy for me… but… when you nibble from rats, you gain no extra powers at all."

"Um." The woman didn't know how to respond.

Clapping her hands together, Deva stood, brushing down her black leather pants. "Sir Walter Dumfries and Lady Agnes Shultz of Blackhall. Well, they do say that Edinburgh is the millionaire's hotspot for the UK. And look at you two. Living large on the west side of Edinburgh. Aren't you the latest dapper residents? You've actually made the wealthiest list. Hobnobbing, I do believe that is the term you so eloquently used, with the insanely rich – quite the play on words there, if you get my meaning – has made you weaker. You believe all the chatter about what you deserve… are *entitled* to… just because you have a little extra change in your pockets. I wonder if they would think the same if they knew *how* you stole those riches?"

"You're one to talk," Walter barked, trying to fight against the magical spell keeping him still.

"Oh, darling. I acquired my billions the hard way. I earned them. I created an empire with supply and demand. You… you made yourselves easier targets. Just once, I would like someone with skills to challenge me. Just once."

Walter struggled against the invisible hold. "Release me and I'll *show* you skills!"

"*Show* me the skills and release yourself."

Swallowing hard, Agnes took a step backward with a nervous giggle. "To what do we owe this unexpected… pleasure?"

"*Pleasure?*" Walking around the man, Deva draped a finger over his firm shoulder. "Doubtful." Turning to Agnes, she smiled. "By now, you've heard the rumors. You do know how our sire died, correct?"

Unable to hide his immense disdain for the woman, Walter growled. "Yes."

Shushing him with her eyes, Agnes sounded more cheerful about the matter. "Of course. The moment it happened. We knew it was you. You didn't exactly hide that fact."

Looking from one to the other, Deva nonchalantly rolled her shoulders. "I hadn't learned how yet. You see, Drake lied to me just as he did to you two. Did you know his real name was… brace yourselves… *Merlin*?"

"He was our sire and *that* was the only thing that mattered!" Walter roared, still trying in vain to move. "We were supposed to protect him, not kill him!"

"*You* didn't have to live with him. He did not take everything that you hold near and dear to your heart and destroy it because you did not love him back!" Deva sounded off, the outline of her blue eyes glowing red.

"I always said, if anyone could take him out, it would be you. Why should I care *who* he was? Wait. What?" Agnes couldn't hide the stunned expression on her face, or from her tone, as she turned toward Deva. "*The* Merlin?"

"That's right. I didn't find out until I drained him and stole his powers. *All* of his powers. The man had a goldmine of magic spells. Do you know, when you practice magic, it actually latches itself into your blood? With a mortal, it drains them of their very essence. It is why young witches look so old without the use of a youthful spell. When I took from him, I had a whole book of shadows just there in my head. Spells for every occasion in case I needed them. Perfected. Down to the tiniest ingredient, or the much-needed words for the desired effect."

Walter seethed. "*Why* are you telling us this? Just do what you came to do already."

In a blur, Deva appeared in front of Walter's face, laughing. "So impatient you are. Another thing I learned, any thoughts you have also are burned into your blood. Memories. And I learned how to find them. So, I will know everything without you having to lie to me – a little something I picked up after offering mercy in the past." Running a gentle hand down his face, she tweaked his goatee, tugging on it lightly. Walking around the room, she admired the costly paintings on the walls. They had acquired some original works of art. "Some people only want a stay of execution to try and catch me at a bad time. He could've lived a long life, but he didn't want mercy… apparently… he wanted my death. Of course, that was not one of the options."

Agnes tried wrapping her head around the fact that the famous Merlin, the magician, rebirthed into a wickedly, evil vampire sired her. With a shake of her head, she put the past on the back burner as she returned to the present situation at hand – her impending death. "I can imagine he was loaded with a wealth of information. I promise you. *I* don't want your death. I just want to be able to live and not worry about looking over my shoulder. You did me a favor when you killed Drake. Before you came along, *I* was the one he tortured." Not really, but she hoped it might draw Deva into a sisterly sort of bond, thinking they both were dealt the same tragic fate.

Walter spat on the floor. "*I* do not want your mercy. If you do not kill me, I *will* kill you. *You* broke our rules, our laws, our way of life with the killing of our sire. Now, you will suffer for it."

"You sound just like him before I ended his life. He was in a similar situation as you. Unable to move. Spouting off rubbish that he could never do in a million years. Tell me, have you sired many children?" Holding up a finger, she put it to his lips. "Never mind. Don't tell me. I want to be surprised when I drain you of every drop. Such big talk from a man who can't move." She turned a knowing gaze toward Agnes. "*You* may leave. If I ever see you again or catch wind of you plotting against me, I will not show mercy a second time when I hunt you down. Do you understand?"

Looking to Deva, Agnes slowly nodded before turning sad eyes back to Walter. "Goodbye, my darling. I will always love you."

"You're… leaving me?" His eyes practically bugged out of his head in surprise. "Together, we can defeat her! She can't fight us both!"

Deva continued watching Agnes, studying her actions and tone of voice. "Says the man who literally can't move anything but his head."

Agnes's eyes darted from Walter to Deva and back again. "I have no qualms with her. I meant what I said. She did me a justice by getting rid of Drake. After he tired of her, I would've been the one he came back to. No thank you."

"You're just as despicable as she is! Go! Get out of my sight, you slut! You were only good for one thing anyway."

Deva's laughter echoed around the large room filled with the finest that life had to offer. "Wow. You really *do* sound like Drake. It might be that you have lived your full life… and death will be your *only* salvation."

"Goodbye." Agnes exited the house, turning off the emotional feelings connected to it, pulling the door closed behind her.

Walter screamed after her. "You know how to beat her! We talked about this! Get back here, you coward."

Moving to the corner of the room, her back protected by the wall, Deva counted on her fingers before motioning a hand in the air. Everything slowed to a crawl, including Agnes lunging at her with a wooden spike, aimed right at her heart. "You underestimated me. That will be your death as well. Did you ever hear about who I was before Drake changed me into a monster? I was a queen. I conquered many armies because I could tell by their words. Their tones. Their actions. I knew when they were lying. Pity. You could've walked away from this alive… in a manner of speaking. But now-" Quicker than the human eye could see, Deva chained the woman to a chair with glimmering links. The spike having disappeared from sight.

As the silver burned into her flesh, Agnes screamed out in pain, anger, and fear. "No!"

Wincing, Deva watched her reaction. "Silver is *not* your friend. So… you believed me to be as big a fool as you? You honestly thought I would buy your horrible acting? There are better roleplayers in Washington DC. Now *that* is saying something. After all, they don't use a jackass for a symbol for nothing."

"Please. I'm sorry. I had to try it. I promise, if you let us go, we won't bother you," Agnes pleaded.

Once more, Deva waggled a finger at her. "Fool me once. No. You *had* your chance, and you blew it. Now, you're going to end your own life."

"No. Please. Not that." Unable to fight, the woman brought a nail over her wrist, slicing deeply before repeating the action with the other side. Sitting back, she dribbled into the container on either side of her. "I'm… not healing! Why am I not healing?!"

"I did mention the *enormous* book of shadows in my head, correct?"

"Let her go!" Walter yelled. "It's me you want. Not her."

"That *was* the case until she tried attacking me. Vampires do *not* want mercy. They would rather die than be pitied or proven incapable of dealing with the fact that someone much younger is much more powerful. Waste not, want not. Supply and demand." Turning to the man, she motioned to his companion. "It's a brand of vampire blood. You see, when a vampire drains another, they get their powers. Our venom sac releases when the last drop of blood is spilled. Well, you two have been feeding off mortals for your whole existence, so you don't have anything that I don't already possess. However, with the venom mingled in your blood, it will deliver a 'kick' to those who drink it. Almost like the energy drinks for mortals. Maybe you'll have something they don't. It's my new line of vampire blood. You get a little something with every vial. No telling what. Talk about a *real* blood-infused cup of tea."

"You will not get away with this! Our children will hunt you down."

"Good! I am always in need of more for this new brand. Now, what to name it? Vampire Kick? Vampiric Surprise? One Hit Wonder?" Laughing softly, she shook her head. "No doubt my advertising agency will think of a grand name for it. It has been in the making for several years. You see, after the first two hundred or so vampires, I stopped draining them for myself. I saw a money-making opportunity, along with the chance to rid the world of vile creatures, so, I drained them for others. But, before you die, I have to let you in on a little secret. Drake said the same thing. Word for bloody word. It's amazing how you sound just like him! But *that's* not the secret. Do you wish to know how I found you?"

"I don't care!" The anger showed in his glowing red eyes.

"Well, I am going to tell you anyway. It took *numerous* centuries because *I* had to search. You were hidden quite well among the rich and famous. Possibly never would have found you if not for a mutual friend of ours. *He* gave me your new name and location."

"*What* mutual friend?" Walter asked, watching his loved one quickly drained of her blood. "Why isn't she healing?"

"Silver. It renders vampires useless. Your healing abilities no longer work."

"But *you* touched them!"

"I've had centuries to get over the… *allergies*… associated with it." Pausing, she winked. "And… in answer to your question… Seth."

His brow furrowed. "*Seth*?! I thought he was in torpor!"

Once again, Deva's genuine laughter filled the room. "Oh, I am having more fun than I've had in… well… too long to count! I am amazed at all the vampires who never do their research! Well, maybe not *all*, but you *obviously* haven't been paying attention. Unfortunately for you, the mainstream media doesn't dabble in vampiric reporting, otherwise, they would've brought in the headline breaking news." Pushing an imaginary pair of glasses up the bridge of her nose, she took on the part of an American news reporter. "In the news today, the vindictive Kanis – who killed the vampire council in the 9/11 tragedy – released the mighty Seth from torpor, offering him three virgins to regain his full powers. Even though everyone says they don't know why, our sources tell us that it has to do with the Bloodstone prophecy. Stay tuned for more on this late-breaking report… that will be the start of a real apocalypse."

"The prophecy?" Walter gasped. "That's… not real."

"Says the creature that most mortals don't believe in. It is just as real as you and I. It started some sixty some years ago, when the vampire council, through Kanis, had Jonas put Seth in torpor. Though, we find it odd that he couldn't do it himself. Don't you think?" Shaking off the American skin, she winked at him. "Seth hasn't been in torpor for almost a year now."

"But… why would Kanis have Jonas capture him just to set him free again?"

"You'll have to ask Kanis. Oh, wait. You won't be able to. Unfortunately, you won't be around."

Watching the woman he loved for too many centuries to count, die, he shook his head. "*Why* would Seth give you *our* names?"

"I'm sure it had to do with something evil within his plans. For whatever reason, he wanted me out of the country and not because he owed me. Though, I highly doubt the man has an honest bone in his body. Sometimes, to get what you want, you do things you wouldn't normally do."

As Agnes died, her eyes rolled over and every drop of blood stopped as the clear venom seeped into the container, intermingling within, causing steam to rise for a moment.

"No," Walter gasped.

"*That* is going to give someone a burst of speed when needed, with a thrown in spell for good measure. It's up to the vampire using it if they wish to redefine it and keep it as their own or use it and discard it. If they're fools like you, chances are, they won't know *how* to do that. More money for the cause as they get addicted to it."

"You killed her!"

"We all have our parts to play in this fight to the finish. Yours is to die so someone else can live. And to be quite honest, she killed herself and that's what her children will see." Within seconds, he found himself in the same situation. "Just as you're going to do as well." Suddenly a rush of thoughts filled her head as her phone sounded. Pulling it from its case, she held it to her ear. "This better be good. … What do you mean it went offline? That's not possible. … I'm almost done here. I have two more for the warehouse. Get the shipment ready. The new brand is ready to go live. … Good. It will be worth the wait." Ending the call, she looked at Walter. "If you could speed this up, I am wanted elsewhere."

"You shouldn't trust Seth," he told her, his life fading quickly. "He only cares about himself."

"Darling, I found that out when he and I dated so long ago. Of course, little did Seth know, I was only with him to get information for a friend. Talk about having a date from hell. I could barely contain the smile on my face when I told him that we were better off as… *friends*." She shrugged. "So, don't worry your gorgeous head about it. I do not now, nor have I *ever* trusted Seth. That's like walking into a poisonous viper den and trusting that none will bite you."

"He," his words stopped as the last drop of blood released the venom followed by the steam.

Capping off the supply, she smiled at his corpse. "Thank you." In the blink of an eye, the silver containers disappeared. Turning to the bodies, she decapitated both, setting her head in his lap and vice versa. "*That* will have Scotland Yard chasing their tails." Taking out a vial, she sprinkled it on the bodies before setting them on fire. "There will be *no* coming back from *this*." That said, she torched the house before heading out. "Two down… twelve to go."

23

It didn't take long for her to return home. She knew Seth had big plans and needed her out of the country, busy with her own affairs, because he never offered valuable information free of charge. He always collected. Before Deva hit the castle perimeter, she realized the high price of her leaving the castle. Souls of the dead cried out with the all too familiar scent slapping her in the face. Death. *Real* death. In a blink, she stood outside the castle.

It once stood regal, moving through the test of time, drawing many tourists who took pictures from a distance of the white bricks sparkling in the sunlight. Sometimes, danger can be found in many beautiful places. Now, the blackened stone crumbled with the mighty battle that took place as if many wars happened over night. Her trusted guards lay mangled at her feet, mutilated beyond recognition. A great power decimated everyone within sight.

Narrowing her eyes, it didn't take long to figure out the responsible party, but why? Looking around with a mixture of horror and anger, a sudden thought struck her between the eyes. "*Chey!*" Bounding into the castle, she stopped short as blue eyes took in the blood-splattered walls. A more terrifying thought surfaced. "*Katherine!*" Turning, she moved quicker than a lightning bolt. Seeing the opened door fueled her rage. Rushing to the protected room holding Inanna, she found it no longer contained the box or the woman.

Seth leaned back against the opposite wall with arms crossed over each other. "Welcome home, darlin'. It's about time you returned. I wondered if I was gonna have to send out a smoke message for you. Oh. Sorry for the mess, but you know how these parties can get," he winked, "outta hand."

Suspended within a magical cage overhead, Chey lowered her gaze at Deva's entrance. "Forgive me, my Queen. I've failed you."

Taking in the surroundings in a second flat, Deva waved a hand up to Chey. "Nonsense. You did no such thing. Let me deal with the troublemaker and I'll see to getting you out of there." Glancing from Chey to Seth, she arched a brow. "Party? Looked like a hell of a banger. The invitation must've been delivered about the same time you sent me out of the country. Release her."

"You cut me to the core with your blatant accusations! I did no such thing! You needed valuable information. I had it. I cannot be responsible for your untimely actions, Deva, nor the repercussions of them. Always trying to throw the blame around instead of bathing in it. Tsk. Tsk."

"What do you want, Seth? I'm in *no* mood for games."

"A pity. You know how much I love playing." Giving her a wink, he pushed off the cold stone, moving toward Chey. "Now, I *suppose* we could toss insults and barbs at each other 'til the cows come home, but neither of us has that kind of time, so I'll come to the point. You have something *I* want. I have something *you* want." Glancing at the caged woman, he gave her floating prison a small nudge. "I believe we can come to an agreement of sorts, without resorting to all manner of nastiness."

"*Without* resorting to nastiness. What do you call all *this*?"

"Nothing more than a calling card, darling."

"I'll remember to return the favor next time I visit *your* home." The challenge hung between them. "You have *stolen* from me, destroyed *numerous* works of art, *killed* off my *whole* crew... but yet, *I* have something *you* want? Well, please don't keep me waiting a moment longer. I'm on pins and needles about what this... *thing*... is. Enlighten me so we can get on with it, or are you waiting for me to *guess*?" She continued glaring a hole through him. "It could take a lot longer than either of us have time for."

"A spell," he replied, still eyeing Chey. "A very... *particular*... spell."

"A spell? Stop speaking in riddles and get to the point, Seth. I did tell you how busy I am, did I not?"

"One that you gave to our dear Jonas but have neglected to pass out to the masses. It can affect even a powerful vampire such as, well, *me*, in my *astral* form."

Confusion registered on her face. "*Astral* form?" Her eyes darted from one point of the room to the other before resting back on Seth. "Not possible."

"Oh, it is *very* possible. See, I paid Jonas a visit on your plane, and... by the way, *where* did you get that *awful* tasting blood from?"

"Seth," she warned.

Smiling, he took another step toward her. "You're right. Cut to the chase. I tried to get out of the seat to have some fun with his delectable partner and found myself shoved back down in it. I couldn't move until I agreed *not* to hurt her then the force released me."

Glancing off to the side, Deva grinned. "Interesting."

"Now, we both know that's not *really* possible. Or at least I didn't *think* so, but your student seems to have exceeded his expectations. Now, you give me that spell, I'll release your little maidservant here, and we can all get back to our regularly scheduled apocalypse."

"You did all *this* – threw a bloody temper tantrum like a five-year-old brat – over a spell? A *spell*, Seth? You will get the bill when I have to start training people. You know... I would tell you to use your head but being in torpor must've killed a few hundred brain cells. There *is* no spell, that I know of, that can stop us when we're in that state. None. I did not teach Jonas anything of the sort. Like I told you before, he was a *horrible* student. It took *weeks* to pound the *slightest* bit of information into his head, and it wasn't the Harry Potter school for the stupid."

His lips pursed. If this had been any other vampire, he'd laugh in their face, but he knew Deva all too well. He never caught her in a lie, therefore, trusted her more than others to be honest with him. "I see. Well then I'll just have to wring it out of dear Jonas's blood, when the time comes."

"Whatever you must do. Now, are we finished? If so, I expect you to clean up your mess before you leave."

"I'm not a janitor. Clean it yourself."

"Fine. See yourself out before I change my mind."

Looking around, he let out a deep sigh. "I suppose there's nothing left to say." With a twitch of his wrist, the cage closed in around Chey, slicing the poor woman into pieces.

"Chey!" Deva half growled in shock, anger, and sadness. Seeing the silver cage collapse into itself, the blood and vital organs dripping from it, tore at her heart. Fighting the urge to race over and try and put her back together – not that she could – the blue in her eyes turned to flames of hatred.

With a nod, he waved his hand. Nothing happened. Shaking his head, he shot Deva a deathly glare. "You *don't* wanna do this."

"I don't?" She giggled viciously, her tone reflecting the restrained emotions. "I am not Jonas, *nor* am I Chey. You and I were *never* really enemies, but as of *this* moment, we are. You will pay for what you did today. Return Katherine, or I will destroy *all* your children until I find her. You did this temper tantrum over a spell? Sethie-Poo," she took up the stance, motioning to him. "Come and get some and let's see who walks out of here." Motioning her hand, she sent him flying into the wall as she did Jonas not so long ago.

Slamming against the cold stone with a dull thud, he rose, giving her a derisive snort. "All right then. I'm your huckleberry."

"Please. Kilmer did it *much* better."

Raising his hand to the ceiling, she flew up into it. Dropping to one knee, he slammed his palm into the floor crashing her onto the cold stone. "I *hoped* we could be friends. After all, you seem to have an open spot. *Obviously*, I was mistaken."

Hitting the ceiling felt bad enough, but then he slammed her body almost through the aged stone. Wiping blood from her nose, she stood, shaking off the stars surrounding her. The intense pain ravaging her body fueled her rage as the healing slowly began. Concentrating on the sorcery keeping him tied to the castle interfered with her ability to heal quickly. "*Friends*? You wouldn't know the meaning of the word."

"Oops… too soon?"

Pushing back a stray piece of hair from her eyes, she motioned to him. Lifting her finger up, she twirled it in the air, sending an F-5 tornado screaming in his direction, picking him up, and turning him into a live video game of breakout. "I have *more* than enough now."

They volleyed spell after spell, each increasing in power and damage.

"*Enough*!" he said, rising unsteadily from her last effort. Broken and enraged, he dragged a hand across his bloody lip. "This ain't gettin' us *nowhere*." Coughing up another wad of goo, he spat it out onto the floor. His body began to heal, albeit far slower than usual, as he held up his hand to her. "I say we settle this old school. No tricks. No hocus pocus. Vampire to vampire."

Grinning, she winked. "Ooh, *now* you're speaking my language. I'll be sure to give Kanis your regrets at not being able to say goodbye yourself… when I rip off his head and take back what is mine." She pointed, offering a devious grin. "Do you need a break, old man? Maybe five-minutes before we continue?"

Giving her a salacious leer, he cracked his neck. "Break *this*." With a lunge, he flew past, his nails slicing open her face. Landing on the other side, he bowed, licking her hot blood from his fingers. "Mm. Been far too long since I had *that* taste. I must admit. It's quite addicting."

Feeling his talons raking through her flesh sent an intense burst of pain throughout her body. Shaking it off, she didn't take her eyes from him. Blood trailed down her face as flesh threatened to seep between the deep gashes. Turning her head, she grinned. The words she told Jonas, during training when he battled ten vampires at one time, echoed within her enraged mind.

"You will heal. Harness the rage and turn it around. Yes, you feel it, but don't show it. Use it. Never show any emotion no matter what war is raging inside you. Do not let your opponent know how much he or she has wounded you. It will just give them fuel for the fire. Instead, do not allow yourself to grieve until you have won the match. Use it to fuel your own rage and destroy them."

"Mm, you're trying to seduce me! No thanks. That's like reusing old trash!" Lashing out with her leg, she donkey-kicked him into the wall, only this time, her secret weapon – the same wooden spear used on her sire – went after him, burrowing into his heart. After all, he didn't say they couldn't use weapons.

Impaled against the wall, he couldn't help but manage a weak smile. "Nice. You should come work for me."

"I'm too *good* to work for the likes of you."

"I can–" his speech gurgled as blood filled his mouth. Summoning all he had, the lance shook a bit, but remained steadfast in the wall. No strength, magic, or trick could release him.

Turning, she reached up, unlatching the silver broadsword from the wall. The steel glistened in the dim lighting before the tip struck the floor, too heavy to grasp. The combination of the fight and keeping the spell active weakened her. Dragging it behind, she started moving toward him, sparks flying in her wake.

His expression flattened. "Now, let's not do anythin' hasty."

"Hasty? You should've thought about that before your actions today. I always did say you were too stupid for your own good. Looks like it will finally be what kills you."

Watching her advance, Seth summoned whatever power he had left, to no avail. "I could use a bit of assistance here," he managed to get out, as she drew closer. The eerie wail of a harmonica broke the silence, growing louder as he grinned. "I believe we're about to have company, darlin'. Why don't you be a good girl and put on a pot of tea?"

"I'll get right on it. As soon as I sharpen my blade on your skull." Standing in front of him, using all of her strength she lifted the sword. "Take just a few seconds."

"I'm afraid you don't have a few seconds," came a voice from behind her. "In fact, I've seen *enough* of this."

The sword wrenched from her grasp as Deva went flying into the opposite wall, plastering her there, unable to move.

Harley Bishop shook his head, glancing up at Seth. "I see you're a bit hung up." Reaching up, he yanked the lance from Seth's chest. Holding it in his hand, he admired it. "Very nice work."

After dropping to the concrete floor, Seth grabbed it from Harley's hand. "One good turn deserves another." Flinging it at the now frozen Deva, he watched as it zeroed in on its mark.

Seeing the weapon approaching, she smiled, winking at him, waiting for death to finally remove her from the picture.

"And we'll have no more of *that*." Harley snapped his fingers. As it touched Deva, the weapon crumbled into sawdust, floating harmlessly to the floor.

Seth, having fallen to one knee, eyed the man. "Why'd you do that? We could've been done with her!"

"Not time yet, boy." Grabbing Seth by the collar, he yanked him up. "Time you got back to work." Glancing over his shoulder, he gave Deva a wicked smile. His eyes showing his true form as he tipped his hat. "Ma'am."

And with that, the pair vanished from sight.

24

No longer anchored to the wall, she slipped to the floor. Those eyes. Only *one* being could do that. Summoning every strength of power left, Deva tried healing herself. Nothing. Her usual means of recovery failed. Crawling over to Chey's remains, she closed her eyes as blood tears fell. After allowing herself a few moments to grieve, she sat up, wiping her face. Enraged, she called out to the one person who could help. "*Bacchus!*"

The ancient vampire appeared beside her. "Try to have a nice quiet dinner and–" his mouth fell as he beheld the scene of battle. Glancing down at Deva, and Chey's remains, he dropped to his knees, examining her wounds. "What happened? *Who* could do this to *you*?" In his mind, only one person could have come close to causing this much destruction in Deva's castle.

"Seth."

"As I feared. Why? If he had *any* friends in this world, I'm sure he thought of you as one."

"Bacchus, Seth and I were old bed mates, thanks to you, but we were *never* friends."

He watched Seth around her and knew better but felt they didn't need to harp on that subject. "What brought on this horrid act of violence? What could you have done to anger him?"

"Nothing. He claimed while he was in astral form, Jonas stopped him from getting to Dusty. He thought *I* taught it to Jonas and was adamant that I give it to *him*. IF a spell like that existed, I would know of it. There is none. Nothing can touch us in that form. It angered him that I could not give him what he asked," tear-filled eyes turned to the destroyed cage, "so he killed Chey."

Looking over at the mangled remains, he rested a hand on Deva's shoulder. "I am so sorry for your loss. I truly am. I know how much she meant to you."

"She raised me when my own mother cast me aside from jealousy of the strong relationship I had with my father. Drake changed her to keep me in line. She never deserved to live this life. After killing him, I tracked her down. It was easy. I have made sure she lived a wonderful life. Her mind… slightly touched… from Drake's actions. He allowed his minions to use her for any and all of their sadistic desires. It saddens me deeply about her loss." Shaking off the sorrow, she looked up at him. "First, we battled with magic until that proved to be no good. I had him staked to the wall in the same manner I did with Drake. As I headed over with a sword to cleave his body in half, a visitor popped in."

"A… *visitor*?" His brow creased. "I neither saw, nor felt, any of this. Tell me about this strange person."

"He has a very powerful ally on his side," twisting her body, she winced in pain. "A harmonica-playing black man. He's more magical than Drake could *ever* hope to be. I'm not sure what he did.

I can't heal on my own. He threw me into the wall and my powers disappeared. Seth tried killing me, but he stopped him. He's not 'helping' him in that manner." After a coughing fit, she spit out the blood. "You'll have to continue without me. I'm not going to be around much longer."

"A black man playing a harmonica? Did he have a white kid playing a guitar by his side down at the Cross Road?" Seeing the look on her face at his ill-timed movie reference, he bowed his head. "Never mind. Bad joke." Laying his palm over her forehead, he felt the life slipping away from her. "No time for magic. We're going to have to heal you the old-fashioned way." Deva would become privy to things she shouldn't know, but desperate times called for desperate measures. Opening his wrist with a thumbnail, he brought it to her pale lips. "Drink," he whispered.

The smell of his blood made her fangs descend. The rich flavor filled her mouth, causing her to moan seductively. She never experienced any feeling that took her to such heights. The orgasmic taste… the sweetest… most addicting. The businesswoman in her could see the dollar signs that *this* alone could bring before the bloodlust trance took over. Once healed enough – that it didn't feel like her insides were busted – she pulled back. After he helped her stand, she canted a crooked head up at him. Grasping his face, squeezing his cheeks together, she growled. "Someone has been keeping *important* secrets. You *know* that's not nice."

The wound closed, as he gently removed her hand. "I don't know what you're talking about. I'm an open book."

"Open book, my royal ass. I say we go somewhere and talk about what I saw."

His smile hid far more than his words, as he glanced around. "Would you like some help cleaning up?"

Fighting back emotions, she shook her head. "No, I just want to burn the place to the ground. I have other homes that no one knows about and more people. Seth doesn't realize the army I have collected over the years who are extremely loyal to me. Chey deserves to have her remains burned. She's been tortured enough."

"You'll do no such thing! I've grown rather fond of meself, thank you very much."

Hearing what couldn't possibly be, Deva spun around, followed quickly by Bacchus. She stared in shock at the woman before her. "Not possible."

Seeing the disbelieving look from the pair, Chey winked. "Wha? You two think that you're the only ones with a bit of mumbo-jumbo?" Leaning down, she blew over the remains on the floor causing them to reform into the image of Chey before rising off the floor, floating back into her body. Closing her eyes, the woman gave a small shudder. "There now. Feels good to be whole again."

"What the bloody hell?" Rushing over, she pulled the woman into a hug, a blood tear of happiness washed down her face. "What just happened?"

Chey hugged her back. "One of the easiest spells in the world is the cloning spell. You see, I'm not as touched in the head as I let on, but no one ever concerns themselves with the crazy person in the room when they really should."

"You mean… all this time you *haven't* been crazy?"

Smiling again, she shook her head. "All this time. Like I said, when people *think* you're nutty, no one ever is concerned that you're in the room, listening to all their plotting and planning. They don't think of you as a problem." She looked at Bacchus. "Seth sent Katherine off with Kanis and his lap dog, Amelia. They're guarding her with specific orders not to let *anyone* come near her."

"I had a feeling." Winking at her, he clapped his hands. "Very impressive, Chey. I must say, I underestimated you as well."

"Thank you. That was the plan. I knew some day it would come in handy. There is always a reason for someone to be in existence. Why do you think I did so much reading in my room? I learned spells and at night… did a little hunting on my own. Remember, Drake was *my* sire too. I learned a lot from you," she said, turning to Deva. "I drained many weak vampires, working my way up to more powerful ones. Oh, the lap dog is terrified of you… oddly enough… so is Kanis."

"Kanis and I have an old score to settle from long ago when he destroyed the vampire council, and, in the meantime, turned the world into a nuthouse over who did and didn't do it. Some claimed the president at the time helped plan it screaming about it being an inside job. Others claimed enemies did it. Ridiculous really. If they only knew the *whole* truth. Both sides are terribly wrong, but they will never agree."

"You two get on about your business, I'll take care of the 'clean-up' here."

Deva shook her head. "No. You see, Seth believes you are *dead*. We can use that to our benefit. If we do not keep up the farce that you are, he will come after you, especially after what I have planned. He also knows that I am going to retaliate over being robbed *and* your death. If I don't, he will question why. I have an underground palace much like the Garden of Eden with an army protecting it. You can be my command there. However, you will need a makeover and a name change."

"I have always wanted to be called Deztiny. Deztiny… Darkstorm! Call me Dez for a nickname."

"As you wish. From this day forward, you will be known as Dez. I will get the paperwork together, so you have the proof behind the name. America is tricky about the whole identification thing. Can't buy liquor or cigarettes without it. Can't do any business without the proof that you are who you claim to be. The only thing you can do without proper identification, in certain places, is vote in a Democratic state, but that's about it. Luckily, their petty political wars don't involve us. Good thing for them. We've got our own to contend with. But you will still need identification."

"Yes! I mean," she winked at her, "if you're sure."

Smiling, Deva nudged her. "Absolutely! I believe your talents can be used elsewhere. Standing by my side as we take back over the organization." Motioning around her, she turned to Bacchus. "Do me a favor. Burn this castle to the ground. Everything of importance has been duplicated. I did not keep originals in my home that people know of. I learned that lesson thanks to nine-eleven. You don't get to be a rich business mogul by playing it stupid. I don't want anyone finding any of the dead bodies here. Burn everything about it to the ground with a fire that can't be extinguished until the last ash has floated off."

"Why can't *you*? It's just a simple fireball spell combined with lava."

Shaking her head, she looked between them. "I don't know. My magical powers are in limbo, for some reason. I can't even do any spells. Whoever that old man was… he did a number on me. But I don't need magic to handle what must be done."

"Very well." With a swipe of his hand, the three of them vanished as molten lava consumed the castle. A roaring inferno that no one could put out, until the last stone crumbled into ashes, floating off into the breeze.

25

Clean. Train. Read the Bible. Study. Just a normal day. Alone in her prison of a room, Dusty quietly did her schoolwork. She often heard arguments from the main house. Her 'uncle' had taken up drinking as a pastime and her 'aunt' wanted no part of it. Usually, Dusty blocked out their petty arguments over everything from loneliness to money, but this time, they spoke about *her*.

"This situation requires a gentle touch… understanding. I can't just throw pads at her with instructions and not give her a hug! This is a trying time in a young girl's life. She's probably confused. I know when it happened to me, I thought I was dying! *I know what she's going through*," Meg screamed.

"No, you don't!"

"Yes, I do! I've been in her shoes! I go through this once a month! You don't! You don't have a *clue* what it means!"

"You have *never* been in her shoes! Dusty's been handled a lot differently than most children," he explained, his voice tight. "She doesn't think like most others. She's not whiny, needy, and doesn't expect a lot out of life that she hasn't earned."

"But it's not right! I want to hug her! I refuse to keep treating her like this!"

"You have to," Thaddeus told her. "She's not *allowed* to experience anything that'll trigger emotions… at least not yet."

"Then you should've brought in a boy."

"The final stages could not be won with a boy."

"Tad, when a young girl steps into adulthood, it's a very emotional time. Her hormones are going crazy right now and that will happen at least once a month. It's nature. Unavoidable."

"Then she'll learn from it."

"Is she a prisoner?"

Thaddeus looked in at Dusty. "No. Not... *exactly*. We are protecting her from the outside world."

"Then why do we treat her like one?"

"I told you why!"

"I'm tired of this way of life! Why can't we do *real* things? Most regular people take a vacation! Their kids go to public school. They aren't homeschooled! This *isn't* normal!"

"Bullshit. More and more are homeschooling their children nowadays to keep them safe! Most have *no* clue what's happening around them, while others just prepare for the worst."

"I'm sick to death of living like this," Meg yelled. "Every day it's the same thing. Over and over! Why?! How long will this last?"

Thaddeus dismissed her with a wave of his hand, taking a deep swig from the flask. "You *know* why we have to do this! We *have* to protect the girl. She's essential to the future of all mankind. I can't tell you any more than that. People *have* seen her, so what sense would that make if we have three children, but two go to public school while one is tutored? That would send up red flags and bring unwanted attention our way."

"If she's *that* important, then why do we have to treat her so badly? The poor thing has lost her parents. We, as her caregivers, are not allowed to give her a simple hug? I feel so sorry for her. She's turning into a young woman and all I can do is give her the materials she needs with explanations on how to use said things, but I can't hug her?" Shaking her head, Meg choked back a sob. "You don't understand because you're a man, but she's just a little girl coming into womanhood. She's got to have questions! This is a hard time in a young girl's life, Tad!"

"If you don't show a child emotion when growing up, they will not have them as adults! Enough!" He bellowed, backhanding her. "I'm tired of explaining this to you over and over!"

Watching her aunt hit the ground, Dusty jumped up, rushing toward them, stopping short at the door frame. The number one rule keeping her in place; *stay out of the house.* Balling up her fists, she could only watch.

"Stop harping on things that we have no control over! I can't do anything about any of this! I have my orders."

Lying on the ground, she brushed a hand across her cheek, glaring up at him. "I warned you what would happen if you *ever* struck me again."

As if seeing his actions for the first time, Thaddeus cried, rushing to help her up. "Oh my God!"

"Get away from me!"

"I'm so sorry. I'll never do it again. I don't know what came over me! Do you really think I like any of this? It's my duty! Please… forgive me."

Pushing him away, she picked herself up off the floor, rubbing her face. "You're nothing but a drunk. I don't know *why* you are so hell bent on keeping that poor girl in chains, but you need help. I can't help her, but I can sure as hell help myself and my children! Boys, in the car."

Tad took a deep breath. "I'm sorry! Please, I've had too much to drink. Don't do this! They will kill you if you try and leave!"

When he grabbed her, she balled up her fist and punched him. "Death would be more welcome than living this life. I *warned* you." As the boys went out the door, she turned, shaking her head at the little girl. "May God always stay with you, Dusty." The glare relocated to her husband. "May you burn in hell, Thaddeus. My attorney will be in touch." That said, she stormed out the door.

Rubbing his bruised cheek, he downed the contents of the flask, fighting back the tears, giving Dusty a death stare before moving into his room.

After finishing chores, schoolwork, and her mental homework, she tidied up like Meg explained and then went to bed. Their argument still on her mind. Something about what Meg said dawned on her.

This isn't normal!

Snuggled up under her blanket, her eyes barely closed before she felt herself being lifted up and tossed. Flying through the air, caught off guard, she hit the wall with tremendous force. Her forehead bounced off the floor causing a goose egg to form. Little blue and pink stars danced around her. They were so pretty. Something hard struck her in the leg, promptly bringing her back to reality. *Ouch!* After getting struck across her legs, arms, side, and in the head, she jumped up into a fighting stance, trying to focus. When her eyes accustomed to the darkness, she saw Thaddeus standing in front of her, swinging his belt – buckle first.

"You bitch!" Thaddeus bellowed. "It's all *your* fault!"

Sleek as a cat, she jumped out of the way, the clasp slamming into the floor hard enough to leave dings in the wood. Calculating his movements, she dodged the weapon. With accurate skill, she wrapped her hand around the leather, yanking it from his hand, tossing it a safe distance away. "Uncle, what's wrong?" As he lunged for her, she side-stepped, delivering a Karate chop to the back of his neck, sending him to the floor. "What did I do?"

"I lost my wife and kids because of you!" Jumping up, he kicked out his foot, slamming a boot into her face.

Excruciating pain and rivers of blood exploded down her cheeks as once more those pretty stars threatened to send her into the void of blackness. Unable to see anything but a red smear, she held out her hands in front of her. "Uncle, stop! What are you doing?"

"What I've wanted to do since you first came into my house." Reaching down, he grabbed her by the throat, slamming her into the wall, holding her there. His face contorted with rage; he leered from behind cloudy eyes. "So, you're becoming a woman, huh?"

Reaching down, he grabbed her right thigh. "Let's just see what sort of woman you are."

Unable to breathe, she struggled, kicking, before uttering her last dying breath. "Sir G, help." In the next second, she hit the floor. As her lungs greedily filled with oxygen, she began coughing. On the verge of consciousness, she felt someone picking her up, carrying her, and then laying her back on the cot. Her clothes shifted – pulled up and then back down. She had a broken nose and many bruises forming.

"I'm here, Dustina," Sir G whispered, checking her for damages. "This is going to hurt." He set her nose.

The pain almost made her black out as she screamed.

Grabbing a clean rag, he gently washed off her face. "I'm sorry. *No* one will *ever* hurt you like that again."

Tears poured down her cheeks as – for the first time in her miserable young life – she just wanted to die. As he lifted her to a sitting position, she pushed him away. "Leave me to die. I don't want this anymore. It's not normal."

"Nothing in this life is *normal*. We are all trained to believe and act a certain way until it *feels* natural. You get used to the status quo until it becomes your *routine*. It's called conditioning." Holding a glass to her lips, his voice, stern but soft, coaxed her into obedience. "Drink. This will make you feel better."

"No."

"Dustina! *Drink*."

Having no choice, she consumed the thick and disgusting mud-like substance. It filled her mouth, making her cringe, leaving a metallic aftertaste. Shaking her head, she tried pushing it away. "Ew. No."

"I know. It's an acquired taste, but drink. It will help you heal faster. You need it."

After getting the mixture down, her body began to feel better, but it also made her want to sleep. Laying her head back on the pillow, she snuggled under the covers again. "Thank you, Sir. G."

Leaning down, he kissed the top of her head. "I will be back in the morning to see to your memories. Sleep for now, my darling girl."

Being between sleep and awake, her ears picked up the distinct sound of commotion – loud banging, screaming, thudding – happening in the house. She hoped Sir G bounced her uncle around like he had done to her.

Closing her eyes, Sir G's voice sounded off in her mind. "Sleep, Dustina. No one will ever hurt you like *this* again."

'Wake up, Dusty!'

26

The sudden bolt of a killer headache jarred her back to reality. It felt as if her head had been split in two. Immediately reaching up to massage painful temples – and make sure it didn't crack apart – Dusty found she couldn't bring her hands up higher than her chest and heard an odd, familiar clanging-like noise. *Where have I heard that before?* As she struggled to wake up, her other senses took charge. She could feel movement as if a car driving. She heard a voice too. Male.

While working with the CIA years ago, she found herself in the dreadful predicament of being taken against her will – knocked out with Chloroform – for one of the tests they put her through. When she woke up, she had this same experience. Barely on the verge of consciousness, she tried remembering her last action.

Through the fog she saw different events taking place. Her father tucking her in as a child. Antoine hugging her. Jonas yelling at her. Her pushing him out the door of the RV. Checking the laptop. A knock at the door. Travis. *Travis?!*

Forcing her eyes open took a lot of effort as she had to fight through the cloudiness trying to keep her asleep. When she finally managed prying her eyelids open, and her eyes adjusted to the brightness, Dusty stared down at the cuffs securing her to the seat belt. *What the...?*

'Focus. Concentrate. Be aware of your surroundings. Remember your training.'

"Yes ma'am. If there is anyone on this planet who can identify it, Dusty can. I'll keep you posted." Travis ended the call, sliding the phone into his pocket.

Giving him a side-eyed murderous glare, Dusty struggled to be free. "Travis? What the hog-tying crap is this? What are you doing? Are you still being Seth's bitch? Is this another prisoner exchange?"

"Ah! You're finally awake! Worried me. Thought I might've overdosed you."

"Cut the chit chat. What the *hell's* going on? What *thing* am I supposedly the only one on the planet who can identify? What is *it*?"

"Well, when we were doing that 'prisoner exchange,' as you call it, I noticed the stone in your possession. You remember that?"

Still trying to free herself, she scoffed. "The bane of my existence? Kinda hard to forget. What about it?"

"We have something… similar."

All actions stopped as her eyes widened, drawing in a short breath. "I don't think I heard you right. Probably something to do with this migraine of a headache. Did you say that you have one *identical* to it? Like… its *twin*? Are you sure?"

"Yes."

"Where?"

"Safely secured in a well-guarded holding area. It's been at Area Fifty-One. They found it while digging out the crash in Roswell. That's when they concluded that aliens brought it with them."

"Of course. Why didn't I think of that sooner? If something can't be explained, it's *got* to be aliens and must be stored at Area Fifty-One." Huffing she rolled her eyes into the back of her head before focusing on Travis.

"Area Fifty-One is *not* just about aliens. It is an open, practical, adaptable battle area to administer testing strategies development and advanced training. Now, back to the topic at hand, it just looked like a strange rock to me, but the geologists studying it over the years claimed otherwise. Seeing that you had its equal, well… I figured you would be the best one to translate it."

"What do you mean 'translate' it? How does one go about deciphering a rock?"

"It has faint writing on it."

Lines appeared in her face as brows crumpled in the middle of her forehead. "Writing? What sorta writing?"

"We've had every language professor in the world trying to interpret the strange symbols. No one has a clue. The only thing we've figured out is that it's not of this Earth. Not since the beginning of writing anyway. We've had it for about seventy years now. The only reason we took special interest in it again is because you had one just like it."

"And... what makes you think that 'I' can figure it out?"

"I gotta tell ya... there are a lot of people interested in meeting you."

"Yeah, I'm the belle of the ball lately. Answer my question."

Chuckling, he pointed ahead. "Nope. We're out of time. We have arrived at our destination."

Looking up, she got a glimpse of their surroundings. Groom Lake road. Miles and miles of desert sand. Two signs on either side of the road threatened deadly force if anyone without authorization entered the forbidden zone. As they did, two armed men approached on both sides of the car. After checking his badge, they allowed him on his merry way.

"You know, for this to be some secret military facility, I expected a little more than a dirt road leading into the mountains. Talk about boring."

Travis laughed. "This location is perfect. You would think no one would ever guess in a million years what lies beneath the soil."

"Then how does *everyone* know about it?"

"Whistleblowers. UFO fanatics. Science fiction movies that like to assume what we do here. All of them don't have a clue. Hell, there are things happening here that *I* don't have clearance to see, and I have Top Secret Q clearance."

"And they're okay with you bringing me into the fold?"

"As I said, there are a *lot* of people interested in meeting you."

Nodding, she looked back out the window. Not quite a mile down the road, they came to a thirty by forty-foot building with a black and white barrier, dressed up with red flashing lights, blocking the road. The guard shack.

The on-duty lookout walked over and after a short show and tell of the "Top Secret Q" badge, the gate lifted. Passing by the KXTA airstrip, Dusty noticed predator drones, sitting at the ready, behind a chain link fence. Armed guards stopped them at every checkpoint.

When they finally came to a stop, Travis took off the cuffs. He knew Dusty well enough to know, at that point, they wouldn't be necessary. He piqued her curiosity. Holding tightly onto her arm, they stepped into the facility's main elevator.

Dusty watched the lit panel go from numbers to a mixture of numbers and letters. "Wow! How far are we going down that the letters are duplicated?"

Silence met her question. Once it stopped, he pushed her toward the stairs leading down.

We're still going down? Where the hell is he taking me?

'Pay attention.'

While descending, Dusty heard strange inhuman sounds followed by chilling screams. "What in God's name is that?"

"God didn't make *those* things. Don't worry about it. Not your concern."

"Why not?"

"You don't have the proper clearance."

Rolling her eyes, she continued walking. "Whatever. I miss your sexy accent. Now you sound like every other boring-ass man... *amazingly* easy to ignore."

Poking her, he turned on the southern charm. "I doubt that. You know I'm *always* on your mind. You just don't wanna admit it."

Groaning, she took a deep breath. Slowly releasing it, she pivoted around with a dreamy expression in her eyes, registering all the love she felt for him, catching him off guard. Stepping closer, she gently ran a finger down his cheek, outlining his jawline before lovingly moving her hand teasingly through his hair. While dating, he called it her "usual signature move" before kissing him, though she didn't follow through this time. It did what she hoped. Turned him into an unarmed mound of confused putty in her hands as he appeared frozen in his tracks – unable to move lest he break the spell.

"Mm. *There* you are. *My* Travis. The part of you I find *so* irresistible." Her eyes darted from his eyes to his lips as her head moved in sideways motions as if going in for a deep, passionate kiss, only stopping herself before allowing such actions. She was so close, she could feel his breath on her lips, tingling them, making her want to dive in.

'Focus!'

Letting out a soft breath, she smiled. "If only you knew how much I have missed you. Before all this happened, just your mere presence made me quiver. My heart soared to new levels I didn't think possible. I could see the two of us... standing in a church... before a preacher. Antoine the only person on my side. I saw a whole life pass before my eyes. Our children. Grandchildren. The two of us rocking on a porch together. Me, fat with gray hair. You, skinny as a rail missing hair. My impossible dream." Slapping him hard across the face, she took a step back, glaring at him. "That was then. Now... you're on my hit list. Thank you for breaking that sticky sweet, annoyingly disgusting nightmare in the making." She confused him even more and it showed through his bewildered expression. "You broke whatever spell that voice had on me the moment you shot me. Now? I can't stand you. No. That's not strong enough. I *hate* you. I want *nothing* to do with you, so thank you! I will now be able to sleep at night without you bugging me!" Turning back around, she began walking again.

Travis stood in the same spot looking dumbfounded. He didn't quite know what to say. He had the same dream, only his didn't fade. He pushed her forward. "Keep telling yourself that."

At the bottom of the stairs, one guard stood at the main door. After flashing his special I.D., they were allowed through. It led to a long corridor stretching as far as the eyes could see and then some.

"Talk about an ant hill for people."

"You don't even know the half of it," he said, urging her forward.

"Uh-huh. Travis, I've tolerated it this far because I have got to see that rock. However, if you keep pushing me, I'm gonna kick your ass as I have done in the past, so fucking knock it off!" Passing doors on either side of them, all her training piped in and she noticed the high tech means to get into them. *All this for a rock?*

Stopping at one of the more secure doors, he punched in several numbers on the keypad. Giving Dusty a wink, he leaned into the eye scanner before speaking into the voice recognition module. "Travis and Dusty will be happily married one day."

The door opened.

Blowing out an annoyed breath, she shook her head. "Not if your life depended on it." Once inside, she saw the Plexiglas-looking casing with the stone positioned in the middle of it. Breaking away from him, she rushed over. "So, it's been here this *whole* time?"

"Don't touch the Polycarbonate Panels!" he screamed, making her stop on a dime. "If anything, and I do mean *anything,* disturbs that container, this place will drop into shutdown. Everything is trigger sensitive around here."

"Nothing like making things more difficult than they need to be."

"Your tax dollars, hard at work."

Walking around the chamber, she peered through the glass. "I can't be sure, without touching it, but it looks like the other one."

"Yeah, so what is it? Is it alien? If so, where did you *get* the other one?"

"It's… a long drawn-out story." Glancing over the frame at him, she winked. "I'm not sure you have the proper clearance to understand it all."

"C'mon, Dusty. Stop playing games. I've seen things that would shock you to the core. Trust me. I can understand *more* than you think."

Shrugging, she arched a brow. "Then *you* should know what it is, Mr. High and Mighty security clearance!"

"Dusty, just tell me."

Once more, she looked at the covering. "I can't be sure if it's the same thing without holding it."

"Not possible."

"You mean to tell me with all your *clearance* you can't pull some strings? How am I supposed to tell you *what* it says without touching it? I *might* be able to get some key information from it, but I *have* to touch it."

"Why? Many people have and got nothing. I suggest you find another way."

"Come to think of it," she tapped a finger against her chin, "it's doable, but there's only *one* man on Earth who *might* be able to answer your question."

"Who?"

"Antoine. We need Antoine, and he won't come without Jonas."

Travis adamantly shook his head. "Negative. It was hard enough getting *you* in here, much less two other… people. Need I remind you that this is a *highly* secured military facility? A huge secret that no one even believes exists. If anyone even hints about this place, we scream out *conspiracy theorist* which then makes them a laughingstock. I can't just let more people in here to verify the existence of something that isn't supposed to be. The less who know about us the better!"

"I hate to tell you, but *everyone* knows of its location." Giving him *the look*, she pointed at the rock. "You wanna know what that writing says? Well, *I* can't tell you. *Jonas* can't tell you. The only one who can… is Antoine. He's had a lot of experience with… *this*."

"*You* held the other one. You know what it is. Tell me! We *have* to start trusting each other."

"I'm sorry, I was way over here and missed that bit. Did you say… *trust* each other? Need I remind you that you *shot* me?! It wasn't *me* trying to kill *you*, though over the months I have wanted to. *You* tried killing *me*! That does *not* equal trust. In fact, it's just the polar opposite!"

Taking a deep breath, he pursed his lips before letting it out slowly. "I can't believe I'm going to do this, but I need your trust. I didn't try and kill you."

"Yes, you did. I was there. I remember the pain in my side *very* intensely."

Taking out his knife, he moved closer, holding up his hands. "Look, if I wanted you dead, you would be. My aim isn't off. My love for you hasn't clouded my abilities to do my job. I pinged you with a tracker. How do you think I knew your *exact* location? I'm just going to remove it."

"A *tracker*?" Seeing the knife, she hesitated for a slight moment. She knew the man could shoot a fly off the side of the barn from a hundred yards. Turning, she lifted her shirt. "Okay, so *why* did you do that?"

"Because it was the easiest way to track you down." Running a hand over her bare skin, he blinked, trying to find the wound. "Are you sure I hit you?"

"Yes. Trust me. You did."

"I don't even see a mark." Taking out a hand-held metal detector, he held it up to her. "Good thing I have this."

"What is *that*?"

"The same thing they use at the county courthouse to make sure no one has a weapon, only smaller. The difference in theirs and this one, it locates trackers… and bugs. It'll be easier to get it out, versus me just cutting into your side."

Furrowing a brow, she glanced down at his hand. "Yeah. Easier. I don't want you playing butcher on me."

Once he discovered its exact location, he took the knife, making a small incision, and scraped out the tracker. Showing it to her, he motioned to the seat. "It was just inside the epidermis, which explains why there wasn't a mark, or hardly any blood. It's like… pushing a needle through your flesh. Unless you go too far, there isn't any blood."

"Oh." *So, that's why there wasn't any blood and no wound. Now it all makes sense.*

"Okay, so... come clean with me, Dusty. *What* the hell's going on?"

"You're not gonna believe me."

"I'll believe *more* than you think."

Omitting the part about the stone, she told him everything that happened until that very point.

After processing the information, he took out his phone. "This better *not* be a trick."

"We have to start trusting each other. Where did I hear that?"

27

After Zeke relocated the RV to a spot not as busy, Antoine dove into a giant bag of Cheetos, groaning. "Though this place is pretty nice... for an RV and all... I must say I've had better meals."

Pulling a yellow legal pad closer, Jonas continued going over the quatrain, making notations. "Well, get used to it. Apparently... *this* is our new home until we finish our mission."

"I guess it could be worse. They could have us camping out in tents." Antoine shoved a handful of golden puffs into his mouth, taking a step toward the dining room table. "Now, what's going on with the quatrain."

Glancing up, Jonas waggled a finger at him. "Noooo sir, Mister. You don't come *near* these with those yellow fingers. You stay over there."

"Jonas, being that I'm a highly respected language professor, I have handled my fair share of National treasures – that you could only *dream* of seeing, much less touching – so I think I know how this works."

"Hmm," he continued writing down notes. "Okay, but if there's any yellow on them, I'll direct Deva to *your* doorstep. I'm pretty sure they will have to go into the vampire archive museum... or something of importance, as a warning to others... *without* yellow staining. Now, help me figure this out. We know the stone isn't *under* the dam."

Francis walked up munching on a sugar cookie, looking from one to the other. "Why do you say that?"

"Dusty saw the Hoover Dam in the vision, but it's not under it." Jonas pointed. "The quatrain tells us that much."

"Vision? *What* vision?"

Leaning back, he intertwined his fingers together, putting his hands behind his head. "She was holding the stone in her hand and saw a man's face."

Francis's blue eyes gleamed with curiosity. "A man's *face*. Whose? Someone she recognized?"

"Not from what she said."

"If she saw the Hoover Dam and a face, am I to assume that he was standing *on* the Hoover Dam?" Taking another bite, he focused his gaze on Jonas.

"No. It's a little complicated. When Dusty held it, she saw a face. Later on, after Seth held the stone, she saw the same thing that he did. A dam."

"How does a mortal see anything that is only visible in the supernatural realm?" Finishing his cookie, he wiped his hands over the sink.

"Maybe she has some hidden gift."

Arching a brow, Francis turned to him. "A gift?"

"Yeah. You know how some people talk to the dead, while others have visions of the past, present, and future? Maybe *that's* why she's so special," Antoine added. "And... considering she's the *only* one who saw it, she's the only one able to find it. Do we know if she's on point? *That* remains to be seen. At this stage, we can only hope."

"Can we focus here?" Jonas asked of the two, pointing to the quatrain. "I believe that 'from wickedness and iniquity' is giving us the starting point we should go from. Almost like directions."

"Oh! With all the excitement, I forgot to tell you!" Antoine pointed to the laptop. "Dusty found KXTA. You guys aren't gonna *believe* what it means."

"KXTA? Oh, that's easy. It's-" The ringing of Dusty's phone cut off Francis's words as they all glanced at it in surprise.

Looking at the screen, Jonas quickly answered it. "If you harm *one* hair on her head-"

"Save the threats, *fang boy*," Travis growled. "She's here. Safe."

"And just where is *here*?"

"Area fifty-one."

Pulling the phone away, Jonas blinked, staring at it as if it had just turned into a snake and bit him before putting it back to his ear. "*Area fifty-one?*"

"Yes," Antoine, Francis and Travis all said at the same time.

"Dusty said she needs you and Antoine. There's a little… *puzzle* for you to solve," Travis continued.

Looking around at the other two, he scoffed, shaking his head. "Sure thing, Knight. We'll just waltz on in. What floor?" Sarcasm laced his words.

"I'm not kidding, Sparx. I'll send a guard to meet you. He'll bring you right down."

"How do I know this isn't a trick."

"You don't, but you also don't have a choice. *Not* if you wanna see Dusty alive again."

"Let me talk to her."

It took a few minutes before he heard her voice on the line. "Yeah, so much for that *alone* time."

"You don't say? Are you okay?"

"As well as can be expected. He knocked me out with some dart that gave me a killer headache. One good thing about this… he helped with the mission."

"What? How does kidnapping *you* help with anything?"

"The stone is here."

"Excuse me?! *There*?! Are you sure?"

"Looking right at it."

"How the hell did it get *there*?"

"You know how stupid the government is. If they can't tell what it is, it must be *alien*."

"Ah. Makes sense now."

"So, look. I can't understand the writing on it."

"It has writing?"

"Yep. It's too faint. I finally convinced him that Antoine can read it and knowing Antoine wouldn't come without *yoooou*, I talked him into you too."

"I see. The Knights Templar sent a few of their best to help."

Part of the memory flooded her mind again. *"One day, it will be up to you to save humanity. It's our job… the Knights Templar… to make sure you're ready for that fight."*

"They're… *helping*?"

"Yes. Earlier they… well… a big misunderstanding… apparently."

"Well, they're gonna have to stay put. I mean… adding more people is definitely pushing it. It's at three, if you count me. I don't see anyone here agreeing to allow a whole slew of people to walk into the most secret military base in the world… that I know of. I'm sure there are others that are just as strongly guarded."

"It's not as secret as they think."

"We had that discussion."

"My spider senses are tingling."

"Your… *what*?"

"I just *know* this is a trap of some kind." Sighing, he ran a hand through his hair. "Fine. Tell Travis to send a car."

"I ain't your secretary. Tell him your *damn* self." Exhaling an annoyed breath, she handed the phone back to Travis. "It's for *you*."

Crinkling his brows, he took it. "Trouble in paradise?"

"Shut up." Turning back to the stone, she stared at it. "I guess they could be twins, but I don't remember any writing on the other one."

"Are… you talking to me?"

Once more, Dusty groaned. "No, I'm speaking to someone more intelligent than you. Myself." Turning back to the case, she continued trying to work out the puzzle. "In fact, if I remember correctly, it had a smooth surface. So, the million-dollar question, what makes *this* one different?"

Holding back the chuckle, Travis spoke into the phone. "Okay. I'm going to text you the coordinates to put into your GPS to get here. Do *not* go past the no trespassing signs. A car will come and pick you up from there."

"Why not go past the signs? If you're expecting us, that shouldn't matter, right?"

"Because it will take too much shit for me to get you out of the doghouse. If you cross that line on your own, they *will* stop you at gun point, with all legal rights to shoot to kill. They will immediately confiscate your car, going through it with a fine-toothed comb. Any cameras or phones on you will be confiscated, and you *won't* get them back. Then the local police will hold you for seventy-two hours before allowing you *one* phone call. And it's all legal. So, just wait until they come to escort you over the line."

"Seems a bit much for people who aren't hiding anything."

Travis groaned. "*No* one said we're not hiding anything, but it's *what* we're hiding that people wouldn't understand. Not even you, bloodsucker."

"No crossing the line. Got it." Hanging up the phone, he turned to Antoine.

"Let me guess. That was Travis. He has Dusty and the stone. Am I right about that?" Antoine closed the bag, placing a clothespin over the folded end, shoving it back into the cabinet.

Looking over, Jonas nodded. "Very perceptive."

Turning on the tap, he washed off the orange/yellow staining on his hands. "Might I ask *why* the stone is at Area Fifty-One?"

"From what Dusty said, if the government can't identify it then it's alien. Where do they store most alien things?"

"Meh. That's a myth. Did you know that they created Area Fifty-One during the Cold War between the US and the Soviet Union as a testing and development facility for reconnaissance aircraft? The U-2 spy planes from the fifties comes to my mind. It originally opened in nineteen-fifty-five, but the official acknowledgement only came through the CIA in… August of two-thousand-thirteen if memory serves me correctly. They use it to develop aircraft. Many believe that a lot of the UFO claims are simply those crafts in flight. Why else would they be around *that* military base?"

"Mhm. Well, we don't have time for a history lesson. We are needed on that base."

Turning off the water, Antoine spun around in shock, splashing liquid droplets in all directions. "Who is *we*?"

"You and I." He turned to DeMolay. "The rest of you stay holed up here. The less people who know that you're helping us, the better for all concerned."

DeMolay shook his head. "Yes, but we could help."

Jonas jerked his thumb at Antoine. "Sorry. It's just him and me."

"As you wish."

Wiping his hands on a dishtowel, Antoine narrowed his eyes. "Wait, why am *I* supposed to go with you? Fighting is your thing. I'm just a language professor. Surely, they ain't gonna just let us waltz onto that base of our own accord."

Jonas chuckled at Antoine's contradictory words. "From what Dusty said, she finagled Knight into believing that you can read whatever writing is on the stone."

"Writing?" Antoine looked surprised. "What kinda writing?"

"Didn't have time for a heart-to-heart, ya know? Both Dusty and Travis said to bring you. I'm only going as your bodyguard… apparently."

Putting the towel back on the cabinet hook, he nodded. "Okay. I guess we're going to Area Fifty-One then. I'm gonna be damned disappointed if I don't see a little green man and a spaceship."

Jonas headed to the door. "Everyone else, just make yourselves at home. If you get hungry… eat. I need to go and tell Zeke about the change in plans."

Francis pursed his lips. "I wish we could go with you. I don't trust this situation. The beast is tricky."

Pausing, Jonas turned to him. "I know. We don't have a choice. There's no way to get into that complex without permission."

"I understand. We will fire up the grill for dinner while you're gone. Give the impression that people are actually camping here."

"Sounds good. I'm sure Dusty will be hungry."

Antoine snorted. "*Excuse* me! You keep forgetting about little ole me! I'm about to wither away to nothing. *Cheetos*," he huffed. "They *aren't* very filling."

As Hooch started to follow, Jonas bent down, touching his head. "Hooch, stay. Guard the place."

Shaking his head, he howled.

"I know, you don't like being away from Dusty, but you *can't* go with us. We'll bring her back. I promise."

At the mention of his mistress's name, he leaned up, licking Jonas's face with a whimper.

"I know, boy. I miss her too."

28

Startled by Jonas rapping on the truck window, Zeke dog-eared the page of the book in his hands before lowering the glass. "You really *have* learned a lot from Deva," he said, turning in his seat. "No one gets the drop on me, but you managed it with ease. What's up?"

"Change in plans. You, Antoine, and I are taking a little side trip." Raising his hand to stop any questions, he shook his head. "Don't ask. You're going to drop us off and come back here. I need you to watch over our guests. Make sure they don't get any hero-like ideas." Seeing the book in Zeke's lap, he motioned with his head. "Good read?"

"So far," he replied, showing Jonas the cover. "New Stephon Queen novel. This one's about–"

"Thanks, but I'll wait for the Blu-Ray. They always make movies out of his books." Giving a chuckle, Jonas glanced around the desert. "If we aren't back by sunrise, you call Deva and let her know… well… she'll no doubt understand."

Zeke narrowed his black eyes. "Look, I've been working for Deva for the last three hundred years. Not that she gave me much of an option." Adopting a British accent, he gave his best imitation of her. "You have a choice. Work for me or die. And be quick about it, I don't have all day." Winking, he smiled a bit. "I'd gotten used to this undead life after a few centuries, so I signed up. It's been good and I don't want to see it all go to hell. Did you know that she hands out gifts on Christmas day? Believe that shit? An all-powerful vampire, treating those who work for her like they are more than cattle. I doubt *Seth* will be that generous *if* he manages to pull off this prophecy of his. You need to stop him… at all cost. Many of us are counting on you. There won't be any gifts from Scrooge."

"Son of a bitch!" Jonas reached into his pocket. Pulling out the ribbon-wrapped box Seth gave him on the plane, he turned it over in his hand. "I'd forgotten all about this." Untying the bow, he gently removed the lid. His eyes turned to blazing coals seeing the small name tag with 'JENNY' embossed on it. Rage shot through him of a sort he never experienced before and the ground beneath his feet began to rumble. "I will kill you, you bastard!" he screamed. The truck and RV shook.

As the small quake subsided, Antoine flew out of the trailer rushing over to the two of them. "What in God's name was that all about? Is Seth here? Was that an earthquake?"

Taking the name tag, he clipped it to the inside of his shirt. Glaring into the professor's face, Jonas snarled. "He just made this personal."

Weary lines appeared on Antoine's face making him look ten years older. "*Just?* Son, he made this *personal* weeks ago when he killed Hooch."

"Now it's double."

29

Unending miles stretched out before them, when Zeke pointed to a stop sign covered with alien-themed stickers. "I think we're headed in the right direction."

As they passed a white padlocked mailbox with a drop box underneath it, Jonas turned in his seat. "Okay, Professor. You seem to know everything. What's with the strange mailbox in the middle of nowhere?"

"Local cattle rancher. It's his mailbox. Back in the day, it was black. Alien enthusiasts – some call them conspiracy theorists – would rifle through his mail, looking for military secrets. After all, as you pointed out, it was just a black mailbox in the middle of nowhere. It got their overactive imaginations on high alert. You see, his ranch is miles away. Maybe this is the furthest the mailman can go? Who knows? Well, he probably got tired of having strangers going through his mail, so he put in a padded mailbox they couldn't break into. The one underneath... probably so people can still leave ET a note." Shrugging, he looked out the window. "Or so goes the rumor." Looking at the GPS, Antoine noticed that it read *Groom Road.* "You know that Area Fifty-One is on Groom Lake which is just a salt flat, right?"

Recognition littered Jonas's face as the corner of his lip lifted slightly. "False water. *That* line makes sense now."

"You're pretty smart for a vampire, but do you know the myth *behind* Area Fifty-One?"

Jonas glanced over his shoulder. "Let me guess... you're going to tell us something we've never heard before."

"As I said... pretty smart." Like a well-versed tour guide, Antoine cleared his throat. "Basically, in nineteen-forty-seven, an alien craft crashed near Roswell, New Mexico. Those in charge sent the wreckage and the alien bodies... possibly even survivors... to Area Fifty-One, but they didn't call it that in forty-seven. The engineers there did reverse engineering on any unknown craft. Not to mention, shortly after that, we started producing our *own* advanced technology. U-2 spy plane that looks like a UFO. *Supposedly*, it's the military themselves who created the stories about the little green men, but it all boils down to H.G. Wells."

"If you say so, Professor. If you say so."

"That's why it's called a *myth*. Thanks to the odd men in black who visit people who have encountered UFOs, some believe, others… not so much." Glancing out the window, he looked from one side to the other. "I think it's odd the way this dirt road cuts through so much public land. You would think the government would find an isolated place where no one else lives – maybe even a deserted island." Behind them, he spied nothing but a cloud of dust.

Fourteen miles down the flat desert road, signs marked the edge of the base; simple red and white placards forbidding entry and threatening six months jail time, and/or $1,000 fine, not to mention that deadly force *would* be used. Men dressed in camouflage, brandishing fully automatic weapons, stood beside a white truck.

"I don't see a line, but you better stop before crossing those signs." Jonas pointed ahead. "They are perpendicular to each other. That *could* be what Travis meant."

Stopping the car, Zeke's eyes widened as he peered through the windshield. "*This* is our destination?"

Also eyeing the surroundings, Jonas mumbled under his breath. "That's what the man said." Opening the door, he stepped out. "Well, I guess we've been in worse places."

Antoine followed, staring hard at the men. "Nope. I have to say that *this* trip is the *worst* one so far. I thought the pyramid was bad, but… nope. *This* one takes the cake." He pointed at both of the signs, the 'I don't believe this shit' exclamation highlighted on his face. "*Those* signs don't exactly make me feel warm and fuzzy, and those *soldiers* look like they mean business. I gotta tell ya, Jonas… I *don't* like this."

"*Neither* do I." He could smell it. "Change in plans, Zeke. Stick around for a bit. Might need you here after all but stay clear of this place." Silver everywhere. Possibly the military knew vampires roamed the Earth. He wouldn't put it past them. Deva's brutal training made more sense. At the time, he thought she got off on torturing him.

...

"I can't make it stop!" Sitting in the tub of water, Jonas screamed as the silver pellets ate away his flesh. "I'm not strong enough!"

"You sound like a little girl." In a high-pitched falsetto tone, she offensively imitated him. "*I can't make it stop! I'm not strong enough!*"

"Please, Deva, I can't do this!"

"*Please, Deva, I can't do this!*" Rolling her eyes, she got right in his face. "*Can't* seems to be your favorite word. I'll bet your *pet* would handle this a lot better than you!"

"Of course, she would! Silver doesn't bother *her*!"

"Listen to you. Get a grip. You've been pampered your whole bloody vampiric life! Protected by your sire in *all* things that make you a moron."

"You mean turned me into a bloody addict!"

Waving her hands dismissively, she put them both on the bathtub edge. "Yes, and *that* made you easy to control. Kanis only *threatened* you with a bath of silver, and you walked willfully behind him, doing all his bidding, just so you didn't suffer."

"How do I make it stop?"

She tapped his head. "Turn it off."

"What?" His eyes widened in shock.

"Turn off the pain. With that ability, you turn off the effects of it eating your flesh."

"That's ridiculous! It's not my *mind* making this happen! It's disintegrating my flesh!"

"Jonas, you have *got* to be the most *stubborn* student I've *ever* had. You only *think* it can do this much damage to you and that's why it can. You've programmed over time to be fearful of it and therefore, you make the situation a lot worse than it is."

"What?!"

"When a mortal is bitten by a snake, no matter whether it's poisonous or not, they can *make* themselves go into cardiac arrest over worry that it 'might' have been poisonous and it 'could' have hit them with a kill shot. Never mind that *most* snakes don't do that so they can reserve their poison for when it's really needed. Mind over matter, Jonas. It works for vampires just as much as it does for humans." Shoving her hand into the water, she grabbed the silver pellets, bringing them out, proving she suffered no ill-effects from it. "Use it!"

"How?"

"Ignore it. Think of it as warm water. That's all. You're taking a bath. Don't see it as silver. Fool yourself into what you *think* it is and it will actually change what it is… not physically, but how you *think* it affects you. These marbles in my hand do nothing to me. They are pretty little beads. Nothing more. Nothing less. Mind over matter, Jonas. It works. Turn it off… *now*!"

…

"Yeah, well, I hope they get here soon." Antoine ran a hand through his hair, taking a few steps back, looking around like a tourist. "They're looking at me like I'm a burnt piece of tender chicken. You know how white people love eating burnt food. I like mine nice and tender, almost raw. Just a little pink, but not bloody."

Jonas smirked. "So do I. Only, the bloodier, the better."

Putting a hand on his hip, Antoine eyed him up and down with a sarcastic glance. "I'm sure, but you're also *not* your average white guy, now are you?"

Laughing, Jonas shook his head. "Touché."

Not long after, Travis pulled up in a jeep, hopping out, and speaking to the men in the white truck. After the discussion, the men got into their vehicles and headed down the road. Travis walked over to Jonas and Antoine. "Change in plans. After what Dusty told me, I figured I'd better come and get you. Let's go."

Quickly rushing over Travis's 'line' to the jeep, Antoine climbed into the backseat. "I can't help but think I'm breaking *into* prison when I should be running far *away* from it."

Walking beside Travis, Jonas growled low in his throat. "This *better* not be a trick, Knight. I promised to kill you if I saw you again. I never break my promises." *Well, just once… or twice…*

"I don't like this anymore than *you* do, but Dusty insisted. You *know* how she can be."

"That I do."

"Yeah, but you *don't* know what a wildcat she is in bed," Travis said, eyeing him. "*I* do. Remember that, *vampire*. I can give her *everything* that you can't. Love. Marriage. A family. I have to admit, I *was* jealous of you. After all, who wouldn't be. I mean, look at you. I doubt there is any woman in the world who would kick you out of their bed." Seeing the satisfied gleam in Jonas's eyes, he went in for the kill, diving back into that southern charm. "Until she told me you're a vampire… and how much she *loathes* every inch of you."

30

Once they made it past all the checkpoints, Travis flashing his high clearance identification card, they came face to face with Dusty.

After Antoine hugged the very breath out of her, he instantly checked her over for injuries. "Thank God, you're safe! I've been worried sick. I mean, you are okay, right? He didn't hurt you, did he?"

"No, he didn't hurt me, but look!" Rushing over to the case, she held her hands out, stopping anyone from getting too close. "Look but don't touch. Apparently, it's an *unbelievably* bad thing. It causes a shut down."

"Almost like Indiana Jones." Antoine focused on the stone.

"Who?" Waving her hand, she pointed. "Never mind. Check it out. *This* one has a faint bit of writing. I don't remember the other having *anything* like this. I knew if *anyone* could read it, *you* could."

Walking over, he pulled the loupe from his pocket, turning to the stone. "Hm. Interesting. It's still too faint for me to see. It's like… someone walking in the sand… an hour ago… through a blistering wind."

Groaning unhappily, Travis looked at Antoine. "So, *you* can't read it *either*?"

Slowly turning her head in his direction, Dusty stared at him as if she just found the town's missing idiot. "Wow… can't get one over on *you*, can we, Travis? You're quick."

Walking by him, Jonas cheerfully mumbled. "Welcome to the club. Seems she loathes *you* just as much… if not more."

Antoine's voice sounded discouraged. "There's not much to *see* to be *able* to read it."

Ignoring Jonas, Travis sighed. "So then, how are we going to find out what the damn thing is?"

Jonas examined the case. "I can't believe it's been here this whole time."

"Recovered during one of the Roswell excavations. They found part of the ship buried deep and this with it. At first, it looked like part of the alien ship. All of a sudden, this… writing shows up. None of us could see anything that resembled a letter, so once more we thought… aliens."

"It's not anything from outer space." Walking over, she joined Antoine. "This is actually part of the stone that Cain used to kill his brother Abel."

"*Dusty!*" Jonas scolded. "*Why* are you telling the enemy vital secrets? In the movies, this *never* ends well for the heroes!"

"*This* isn't a movie," she shot back. "He *needs* to know the truth."

"How do you know we can trust him?"

"Because I know."

Irritated, Jonas tilted his head. "He shot you! Damn, if the best way to build your trust is to shoot you, you should've told me weeks ago! I would've shot you first thing!"

"He didn't shoot me."

"I was there! Yes, he did!"

"No, he tagged me with a tracer." Walking over, she picked up the small device, showing it to Jonas. "*That* was why there wasn't a lot of blood. It was just on the inside of my skin."

"Oh!" Antoine sounded relieved. "Whew! When there wasn't any blood, I was beginning to think there was something kooky about you."

"You and me both, Antoine," she grumbled. "You and me both."

Travis stared at her in shock. "Excuse me? Go back to that other thing you said."

"What *other* thing? A lot of things have been said here today. Be more specific."

"Cain and Abel? Like... from the Bible?"

"No. The twin brother farmers in Cider Lake," her sarcasm-laced words dripped with honey. "Of course from the Bible! I... kinda... left something outta the story I told ya earlier. Seth is after *this*. If he gets this one and the last one, because there are four and he already has two, it will give him enough power to destroy mankind."

"You knew this when you traded the stone for my life?"

"Yes, we *all* did."

"And still, knowing what *could* happen, you gave it to him anyway?"

"It was only the second one. We were hoping to stop him from getting the last two."

Swallowing hard, the realization of the devastating part he played dawned on him, and it bled through his facial features. "I thought it was just a stupid rock. How did you get involved in all this?"

"Oh no. I have told you-"

"A lot more than you should have." Jonas interrupted her, staring at the stone.

Eyeing him, she turned back to Travis. "Time for *you* to start answering *my* questions. What the hell is going on! You've been on your phone talking to... I assume your boss. I want to meet him... or her."

"No can do."

"What?! You said you brought me here so important people could meet me. Well, bring them out! I told you *everything*. You better not be playing me again, or I'll rip your heart out of your chest and shove it up your ass."

Jonas crossed his arms over his chest, smirking. "She'll do it. She knows how."

Dusty got in Travis's face, an imposing finger poking his chest. "Now, I *demand* to know *who* is behind this and *why*!"

"Dusty, you don't understand. It's not-" just then his phone cut him off. Taking it out of his pocket, he answered. "Knight."

"Bring them down," the voice said before disconnecting.

Putting his phone away, he shook his head. "You asked for it. You got it. It's time you met my boss."

Once more they stepped into an elevator. Travis slid a key into the slot and then hit the button to take them further down. Each of them stood in silence. The three on one side glared at Travis as he returned the stare. When the doors opened, they stepped right into an office. Exiting the hoist, Dusty came face to face with her own image.

The woman stood, walking around the desk. "Hello, Dustina."

31

Driving up to the North gate, General Tom Daniels stopped his vehicle at the guard station. Lowering his window, he eyed the young man waiting to receive his credentials. Handing over the ID, he shifted that ever present stogie from one side of his mouth to the other as the soldier ran the small card through a handheld device. After a few seconds, it beeped, and a green light came to life as the gate slowly opened.

"Afternoon, General." The man handed the card back. "I need to inform you that we have company."

A silver brow rose as he removed the cigar from his lips. "*Company*? At a highly classified military base?" Pursing his lips, Daniels glanced at the building in the distance. "On *whose* authority?"

"That would be Mister Knight, sir."

"I see." Daniels turned back to the man. "I don't suppose you got any names?"

"No sir, but I can tell you they were an odd-looking pair. Two men. One, an older black man and the other a white guy. Tall, with real pale skin. Like he hadn't seen the sun in a while. Oh, and earlier Mister Knight brought some woman here. Real pretty one, too."

Tapping the ash from his smoke, he nodded. "Looks like Mister Knight and I are gonna have a little talk about chain of command around here." Stroking his chin, he gave the man an imposing stare. "Nobody gets through this gate in either direction, you got that! I don't care if it's the God damned President of these United States. *Nobody* enters or exits. Is that clear?"

The soldier furrowed his brows, darting his eyes back and forth. "I… I have to confirm that order with the director, sir."

Daniels eyes narrowed. "What's your name, son?"

"Private first-class Edward Cullen, sir," he replied, snapping to attention.

Why am I not surprised? "Well, private first-class Edward Cullen, how would you like to wake up in Afghanistan tomorrow morning?"

"N-no sir. I wouldn't like that at all."

"Then you'll do what I tell you without question. Is that understood?"

"Yes SIR!"

"Good. Now assume the position."

Stepping aside, he clicked the safety off his weapon, ready to guard this post with his life as Daniels drove through the gate. Picking up the car phone, he pressed a button.

"This is Travis Knight. Leave a message."

"Bullshit!" Hitting another button, he waited for an answer.

"Headquarters."

"Daniels here. Locate Travis Knight, pronto."

"I'm sorry General. Mister Knight is in a private meeting with the director and can't be disturbed. Should I tell him you called?"

"No. I'll find him myself." Disconnecting the call, he parked the vehicle, got out and walked to the front of the building. Waiting for the security system to acknowledge his presence, he glanced around. The heat from the desert rippled off the ground in waves, causing the sand to look as if it were moving. A small hidden door slid open, followed by a soft, computer generated, female voice.

"Please insert identification credentials now."

Sliding his card into the slot, the machine pulled it in.

"Credentials confirmed. Welcome, General Thomas A. Daniels. Please lean forward for retinal scan."

Rolling his eyes, the General bent over, placing his left eye into the optic comparator.

"Ninety-eight percent match. Thank you, General Thomas A. Daniels. Using your full name, rank, and passcode, please speak carefully into the microphone for voice recognition."

Removing the cigar, he groaned, wanting to punch the irritating machine. "Thomas Andrew Daniels. General. Delta. Omega. Nine. Six. Tango. Five. Sierra. Seven. Seven."

"Identity established. Full access granted. Have a wonderful day, General Thomas A. Daniels."

"Liberals," he grunted. The door opened and he stepped inside. "That damn thing *had* to be designed by liberals. Next thing you know, they'll be demanding a urine sample."

"Christ, Tom. Don't give them any ideas," came a voice from his side.

Turning, Daniels smiled at General Lucas Fallon. They had been assigned this duty together, and in the span of twenty years became close friends. "Lucas, I'm gonna blow that damn thing up one day."

Laughing, the two clasped hands.

"I was headed to the commissary for some lunch," Fallon said. "Join me? My treat."

Daniels laughter died out as he shook his head. "Another time. I got a few problems to deal with and they won't wait."

"Well paint me in a rainbow and put a pussy hat on my head. Tom Daniels turning down a free meal. I never thought I'd see the day." Winking, Fallon clapped his friend on the shoulder. "I'll have a second order of ribs, just in your honor."

Watching him walk away, Daniels smirked. "You just do that," he muttered, turning to get his bearings. Deciding to use the stairs instead of the complex's elevators, he barked odd orders to each guard he came across at every level.

"I want you to guard these stairs. If anyone... or *anything*... comes up them that isn't me... shoot."

"Yes sir."

"Secure this door. Don't let anyone in or out of it."

"Yes sir!"

"See this spot on the floor?"

"Yes sir?"

"Guard it with your life."

"Sir, you want me to guard a spot on the floor?"

"You got a hearing problem, mister?"

"No sir!"

"Then guard it!"

"Yes sir!"

Reaching the level with the stone, he approached the guard at the door. "Stand aside, soldier. I need to get in there." Stepping forward, he tilted his head when the man didn't move.

"Sorry sir, I can't allow anyone in there. Director's orders."

"Is that so? Well, we don't wanna disobey the director now, do we son? I understand she's in a meeting with Travis Knight and some… guests. Is that a fact?"

The guard shook his head. "I wouldn't know for certain sir, but from what I've heard, yes."

Daniels smiled a bit, his eyes moving toward the director's office. "I wonder what all the hush-hush is about. I'd give a month's pay to be a fly on the wall in that room."

32

The office appeared to be a home away from home with all the modern-day conveniences. A refrigerator stood in the corner of a make-shift kitchen, opposite a full bathroom with shower and tub. A shine to the glass over the cherry wood desk top reflected the fluorescent lighting. Security screens lined the entirety of one wall, while a 40-inch flat screen TV hung from another. The shag, plush blue carpet under their feet appeared to be fresh from the store.

"*Dustina?*" Jonas looked from the woman back to Dusty. "*What* is she talking about?"

Dusty hadn't heard that name except in her dreams. "How do you know my name? Everyone has ever just called me Dusty."

The woman smiled. "I remember the day at the hospital when your daddy put that odd name on the birth certificate. It didn't go over well with your mama."

Confusion traced across Dusty's face. "What?"

"I'll never forget that day as long as I live. Your mother was furious. She wanted to name you Annabelle Dixie… or something like that."

Antoine tried hiding the giggle behind a cough. "Annabelle Dixie??"

Turning white as a sheet, Dusty felt an adrenaline rush hit her nervous system. She lightly swayed back and forth, struggling not to black out. "Who *are* you?"

"My dear! You look white as a ghost." Rushing forward, the woman helped her sit in a chair, grabbing a cup of water, handing it over. "Here, drink this. It might help." Wiping away her own tears, she smiled. "I'm your aunt, Claudia de Jardiner. Your father's baby sister."

Antoine whistled. "Well now! Talk about a plot twist!"

Travis raised an eyebrow. "Ma'am, do you think this is a wise course of action?"

Dusty glanced at Travis. "You knew this? And you didn't tell me?!"

Looking from the director to Travis, Jonas smirked. "Well, look who's spilling secrets now."

Not sure what to think, Dusty looked back at Claudia while shaking her head. "How come I don't remember you?"

"I wasn't around much. Julianna and I didn't get along… like… at all. Your mother was a bit of a prissy one. Always had to have things her way. Your father was so smitten, he spoiled her in every way possible just to see her smile. Well, I'm the stubborn one of the family."

Antoine looked from one to the other. "I guess that's where Dusty gets it from."

Claudia agreed. "Most likely. I wasn't one to just fall in line, so I wasn't allowed over for visitation, but it wasn't from lack of trying. Roger and I were close. For some strange reason, Julianna tried stopping all communication between us. It worked… for the most part."

"Why didn't you come and find me then? Sir G from the Knights Templar took me to… I don't know who he was. They claimed he was my uncle. I lived in a prison. With nothing but training my whole life. I finally escaped."

Sir G? Garrick? What other hidden layers are associated with Garrick? Did I even know him at all? Jonas pondered.

Claudia wiped at her eyes, blowing her nose. "I thought you died with your parents. When the house caught fire, it took years before I realized that you didn't. When I finally found the hidden files, I realized that there were only three bodies ever found. Your mother, father, and unborn brother. If you had died too, where was your body?" Leaning on the front of her desk, she motioned to the back of the room. "Please, help yourself to a cup of coffee, a Danish, or doughnuts. I can't tell you how happy I am to see you." Once more she dabbed at her eyes.

"When you realized I was alive, why didn't you come and rescue me? The man who raised me was-"

"Not your uncle. I looked for you. I searched from one end of this world to the other. No school records. Adoption papers. Nothing to tie you to the de Jardiner name. As the years went on, I began looking through social media and face recognition. Nothing. No sign of you anywhere."

"I don't understand." Jonas shook his head. "*Why* was he raising her? Why didn't you? I would think with you having enough clearance to get three people in here that you could find a safe place for your niece."

"It wasn't that simple. By the time I realized that Dusty didn't die, she was in the C.I.A, going by the name of Garner. There are still many things that you don't understand. Believe it or not… Dusty had a normal life at one time. Roger and Julianna de Jardiner-"

"Jardiner?!" Jonas glared at Dusty. "It seems someone *else* is keeping secrets as well."

"It was necessary," Dusty told him, shrugging. "One of the things drilled into my head – tell *no* one my real name. No one."

"Not even me?" Jonas felt a slight twinge from the deception. "And you gave *me* shit for keeping secrets."

"Yours far outweigh mine!" Turning to Claudia, she motioned to her. "Please, continue."

Snagging a Kleenex out of the container, she blew her nose again, taking a deep breath. "I just can't believe you're finally here. I have longed for this day, but I couldn't just rush into your office and blurt it all out, you'd never believe me. Your parents loved you so much. Do you remember them? At all?"

"I'm only now getting bits and pieces of my memories back."

"Oh, they loved you as much as, if not more than, any parent loves their baby. You had dressers and closets filled with the cutest little girly clothes, and enough toys to supply a large day care, but there were odd things that happened up until your birth and then after."

"What do you mean?"

"Before you were conceived, your father had a chance encounter with an old man. Maybe *chance* is the wrong word. There really is no such thing, after all."

"What was so special about this old man?"

"Well, for starters, to hear Roger talk about it, the man was a bit eccentric. He wasn't supposed to tell a soul, but he told me. Maybe it was because he sent me an email that no one found out about it. I didn't have this job at the time, but I was working my way up. So, our secret way of communicating was to send pictures to each other with writing on it. NSA can pick up words. The computers are trained to target certain words, but they can't do that with pictures. And no one could figure out our code. We started it when we were kids." Sighing, she walked back around the desk, sitting down again. "Anyway, he promised Roger money… a lot of it. Enough that he would never want for anything again. The old man told him that his wife was going to get pregnant and they were going to have a daughter. Even suggested what to name her, though it was more than a suggestion. It was all part of the deal."

"Why?" Dusty looked stunned. "Why was it so important that he named me Dustina?"

"I don't know. He did make him promise to never tell a soul about their pact. If he did, terrible things would happen to his family."

"Money with strings attached is never a good thing," Antoine said, sitting on the edge of his seat, munching on a jelly doughnut.

"True, but of course, Roger didn't believe him, but what harm could it bring? He agreed. No papers or contracts. Just a simple handshake. He thought it was just one crazy old, eccentric millionaire throwing away his millions on some fantasy he genuinely believed. I only wish it had been that easy. You see, Roger *did* get the money promised. Every last cent. And they did have a little girl, but…" Turning to the wall, she motioned to the big screen TV. "Let's watch."

…

"Oh, honey, stop!" Julianna laughed, her brown eyes dancing as she watched the two of them. "You'll spoil her!"

Roger wiggled the six-month-old little bundle, all dressed in pink, high above his head. "Little girls are made to be spoiled. Aren't ya? Aren't ya, Dusty?" Bringing her down, he blew raspberries on her stomach as she grabbed his hair in a fit of laughter.

She grumbled. "I still can't believe the nurse let you get away with giving her that awful name."

Bringing her over to the highchair, he shimmied the baby into it, strapping her down before locking the tray in place. "You want some Cheerios, don't ya, baby girl?" Grabbing the box out of the cabinet, he stopped short, giving his wife *the look*. "And what is wrong with Dustina Elizabeth de Jardiner? I went to school with a kid whose parents named him *Sunshine,* so I think it could've been worse." Scoffing, he threw his head up like a proper snob. "I think the ladies at the high society ball are going to rave over our little girl." Walking back to the highchair, he plopped a kiss on top of Dusty's head. "She's gonna get far in college too, just on that name alone. I can see the diploma already… Dustina Elizabeth de Jardiner… M.D."

"Dustina! Who names their little girl *Dustina*?!" Reaching into her jacket pocket, she snagged out a couple of jelly beans, popping them into her mouth. "What century is that from?"

After putting the box away, he took a deep breath and turned, smiling at her. "It's…" his hazel eyes darted to the left. "Umm."

Dusty beat on the tray, grabbing a handful of cereal, shoving it into her mouth, cooing with delight.

"Yes? I'm waiting."

Holding his hands out to his sides, he winked at her, giving his best Italian accent. "Fuhgeddaboudit. What does it mattah? I like the nickname Dusty." Reaching back, he smoothed down the hairs on the back of his neck as a shiver took hold.

"You could've just named her Dusty then!" Laughing at the accent, she took a sip from her glass of orange juice. Swallowing, she glared at him, pursing her lips. "Okay, I know that look. Who was she?"

Tilting his head in confusion, he raised both brows. "Beg your pardon?"

"The woman you named our daughter after."

Smirking, he slid in behind his wife. "Damn! You found me out. She was a pretty little filly we used to bet on at the track. We called her… Dustina… because she was guaranteed to leave you in the dust." Leaning his head down to her neck, he nibbled on her flesh.

Laughing, she elbowed him in the chest. "I'm serious! *Where* did you get that name?"

Looking off to the side, he cleared his throat. "You know how I told you that I inherited money from a rich uncle that you never met?"

"Yeah," she glanced over her shoulder at him. "What about him? Is this like… some family name or something?"

Sighing, he almost looked relieved as he nodded. "Yeah. I was making an old man's dream come true by carrying on the family name. Don't you feel ashamed of yourself… making fun of a name that's been in my family for… decades?"

"I can see why *that* name didn't last through the ages."

"Why you," he tickled her until she laughed before wrapping his arms around her stomach, kissing her neck. Watching their little girl eat, he rested his chin on her shoulder. "She's going to be a big deal someday."

"She already is." His wife leaned back against him, nodding. "But we're supposed to think so. We're biased where she's concerned."

33

"*Where* did you get *that*?" In shock, Dusty looked at the man who could've spit her out. Seeing how loving her parents were and how much they adored her brought a tear to her eye.

"Roger had wired his house with security cameras. They were hidden. No one knew that the smoke detectors held recording devices. When he died, suddenly, I got years of footage. It was like... he knew something was going to happen and wanted someone to know about it. When I came to the last day... I understood. Six happy months soon turned into six blissful years. It was right before your seventh birthday when Roger was forced to reveal the truth," Roberta told her, motioning back to the screen.

...

The two-story brick home had an L-shaped staircase leading to the upper floor. The house was decorated in vivid colors with pictures on the walls depicting a very loving family.

The front door flew open. Julianna entered, slamming the door behind her. Stomping up the stairs, she stormed to her bedroom, flinging open that door as well.

Watching the rather odd entrance, Roger raced up after her, thoroughly confused. "Honey? Julia? What's going on?"

In the bedroom, the walls came alive with beautiful red roses and purple violets. The fluffy bedspread matched, coordinating with plush lavender carpeting. "Don't speak to me!" She screamed loud enough to wake the dead, grabbing a large suitcase out of the closet.

"Honey, what's wrong? Where are you going?" he asked, seeing her packing.

"Don't you *honey* me! I'm going anywhere I can away from you!"

Not sure what he did, he unpacked her clothes, putting them back in the dresser, as she continued shoving things into the case. "He's kicking you again, isn't he? I swear that boy is gonna be a-"

Spinning around, she slapped him across the face. "*Lies*! You lied to me! Well, I'm not in the mood for your games or any more of your damn lies!"

Stunned, he took a step back. "Jules. Talk to me. Why are you so upset?"

Stepping over to the bedroom window, she drew back the sheer curtain, pointing at Dusty playing in the backyard. "So, you named Dusty after someone in your family, correct?"

Clearing his throat, he swallowed hard. "Yes."

Crossing her arms over her chest, she spun back around. "*Which* family member had the name?"

Shrugging, he looked to the side. "I don't know. My uncle never told me."

"Your *uncle*, huh? Funny thing happened today. I ran into your sister. We got to talking about Dusty and that odd name. Without realizing why, I started questioning her about your family. She told me your mother was an only child, and your father had two brothers. One was murdered in prison, where he was sent for bond fraud, and the other was just a street bum. According to her, your dad was the only *decent* man in your family, and I'm beginning to believe that now more than ever!" As the color drained from his face, she glanced at her suitcase, eyes stinging from the tears. "You have ten seconds, Roger. After that, I'm gone and I'm taking Dusty and our son with me."

"Okay. I'll tell you everything." Sighing, he took her hands. "You're right. It's not a family name."

"Five seconds." She yanked her hands away.

"Remember the night I came home with the suitcases filled with money and you were waiting for the cops to arrest me for robbing a bank?"

Slowly nodding, she wiped her eyes. "Yes. The day I found out I was pregnant. I was so scared I was gonna have to raise the baby by myself because you were going to jail."

"I didn't lie. I didn't steal the money. It was given to me."

"From your rich uncle?"

"No. *That* was a lie."

Breaking off a sob, she threw her hands up in the air. "Was our whole marriage one big lie?"

"No, no baby! *Nothing* about our marriage was a lie." Getting down on his knees, he gently pressed his head against her stomach. "I love you. I want to spend the rest of our lives together. I want to sit out on the porch and watch you fussing over our great-grandchildren." Taking her hand, he kissed the top of it.

"Love is trust, Roger." She eased her hand away. "And you aren't doing a good job of earning mine back. *Where* did you get that money?"

Sighing, he pushed off his knees. Walking to the window, he looked out at Dusty. "It was a hard day at work. We had the real threat of a hostile takeover looming over our heads. Well, it happened. Just like every other one, they retained all the executive positions, but the middlemen and the low men on the totem pole… we all got canned."

Her brow furrowed. "You… lost your job? You told me because of the money you *retired* early. *Another* lie."

"It was the only way to explain it all." Still looking out the window, he nodded. "I know. I'm sorry. I felt like such a failure. I didn't know what to do. We had *just* started talking about having a family. You weren't working, and even if you were, I wouldn't have allowed you to take care of me." Taking a deep breath, he continued. "They let us go as soon as we got there that morning. I drove around for a little while, searching desperately for another job. I scoured the newspapers. I went on a few interviews, but I was too overqualified for everything."

Running a hand through his hair, he sighed. "After a while, I went into this bar, sat down, and ordered a beer. I didn't know how long I could make our savings and checking account stretch. We had the mortgage on the house, two car payments, and we had to eat. Not long after, this old guy came over and bought me a drink. He said I looked like I had lost my best friend. I told him no, but I sure as hell was about to *disappoint* her. I spilled my guts about what happened at work. How my whole world was coming apart at the seams. How I couldn't figure out a way to break the news to the love of my life."

Glancing down at the floor, she inhaled deeply, before looking back at him. "So, after hearing your hard luck story, he just… offered you all that money?"

"Nothing's ever that simple. He started spinning a story so farfetched I wanted to get away from him. The only thing that kept me listening, I could tell that *he* believed it. He told me I could have wealth beyond a king. Right then and there. I just had to do one little thing for him. He told me you were pregnant. It would be a girl. All I had to do was name her Dustina Elizabeth. When I asked him how he knew that he just smiled, put his hand on my shoulder and told me that my bloodline was going to be part of some ancient prophecy. That – just like others in my heritage – she was chosen."

Her hand went to her belly, moving in small circles. The life growing within had become active again, and she winced, feeling a foot hit one of her lower ribs. "Chosen for what?"

He shrugged. "I don't have a clue. I thought he was just some eccentric old man, so I told him I would do it. He said when she was ten-years old, that's when she would be called to guard."

"To guard what from who?"

"Not who," turning to look at her, he winced, "but what."

Her brow rose. "What?"

"Monsters." Tears streamed down his face. "We're supposed to turn our little girl over to another family so that they can train her to fight monsters."

She snorted. "Over my dead body."

A man appeared in the doorway, leaning against the jamb. "Cheeky, but if that's the way you want it."

Rushing over, Roger put himself between the stranger and his wife. "How did you get in here?"

The man chuckled. "You live in a very safe neighborhood. You're home. Nobody locks their doors when they're home. Not that it would stop me, but…"

Julia stared at him with wide eyes. "Who are you?"

"I'm the one who told your husband what would happen if he ever spilled the beans about our little agreement."

Looking from the young man back to Roger, she huffed. "He doesn't *look* like an old man."

Roger's eyes narrowed at him. "The night I spoke to him, he didn't look like this."

Laughing, he shrugged. "It suited my purpose to tug at your humanity. To let you believe you were just granting a wacky old man one last wish. Getting wealthy in the process."

Julia's eyes filled with fear as she heard Dusty downstairs.

"Mom! Can I have some cookies?"

Her head snapped to the little girl's voice. "Stay downstairs, Dusty! I'll be there in a minute."

The camera showed Dusty thudding up the stairs and down the hall before slipping past the man standing in the doorway. Stopping short, she turned, giggling. "Sorry. Mom says I need to be polite." She stuck out a hand and smiled up at the man. "I'm Dusty."

The man's eyes lit up and a grin crossed his face as he took her hand. "Manners are exceedingly rare these days, Miss Dusty. I'm Duncan Garioch, and it's a pleasure to meet you."

She giggled again and turned around to Julia. "Can I have a cookie? No, wait. A brownie with chocolate chips." She rubbed her belly, closed her eyes, and let out a satisfied, "Mm." Turning around, she looked up at the man again. "Would you like a brownie, Mister Gariouch? My mom makes the absolute bestest!!"

"Oh, I *love* brownies," he told her. "Especially with big chocolate chips, but I'm afraid we don't have time for that right now."

Roger tried reaching for Dusty, but the man grabbed her, pulling her back against him. "Please! Don't hurt my little girl."

"*Hurt* her?" His head shook. "Not for all the money in the world." He put his hand over Dusty's head, and her expression went blank. "*Three* more years. You could have had her for three more years, and one day she simply wouldn't have come home from school. Another sad statistic of child napping. A case never solved, but you would have a healthy, strong son, and you could have lived your lives out in comfort. No money worries, none of the usual day-to-day drama that people go through, but you just couldn't keep quiet." He looked at Roger. "What happens now is on your head, Roger de

Jardiner. Dustina, I need you to go downstairs and wait for me. We're going to meet your new parents."

Her smile returned. "Okay." Turning, she skipped down the hall and back down the steps.

Screaming for Dusty, Julianna ran after her.

'Mister Gariouch' thrust his hand into her chest, removing her heart and dropping it onto her writhing body. Enraged, Roger shrieked, racing after him only to bounce off an invisible wall. "Your wife is the lucky one, Mister de Jardiner. She died quickly." Taking out a red cloth, he wiped the blood off his hands. "You, on the other hand, are going to die screaming in agony from fire."

Roger tried to move but found his body anchored to the floor. Looking up at the man, he sobbed. "Why?"

Shaking his head, Duncan sighed. "It's the only way to protect your little girl. We can't chance anyone finding out about her until it's time. You humans are so weak. Your minds can be read like a newspaper. I wish it could be different. I don't get any joy from this, but I don't have a choice. May God forgive me and have mercy on your soul. Let us pray. Please Lord, forgive Roger and Julianna for any sins they may have committed. I ask that you take them into your loving arms and show them forgiveness. They were part of something they had no choice in. I beg of you to allow them to walk into the sunlight of your gardens. I ask in the name of your son, Jesus Christ. Amen." Bowing his head, he looked once more at Roger, pursing his lips, before raising his hand. With a twist of his wrist, Roger's neck broke, killing him instantly. "I cannot allow you to suffer for something that is not of your doing." Walking over, he closed Roger and Julia's eyes. "Walk with God." That said, he stood, turned, and moved quickly down the stairs. "Burn it. Make sure the girl sees. She has to remember that her family was killed in an accidental blaze. Once her training begins, I'll make sure she doesn't remember anything else… until she absolutely *has* to." Looking up at the smoke detector/camera, he winked. "'ello mate. It's *your* turn to watch out for her. *Don't* disappoint me."

…

The screen went blank. Jonas sat dumbfounded. "Garrick," he whispered. His last visit, pleading for Jonas to end his life, made a lot of sense. He did it to protect Dusty. The thing he didn't understand, how did Garrick know that Jonas would be in charge of her safety and watching the security footage?

Roberta turned back to Dusty. "*That's* when they took you to the knight to guard over and train you. God chose you to be the guardian of the necklace. It has to be our lineage that guards it against all evil… and you *are* the last daughter."

"Yes, but what is so important about this necklace?"

34

When Dusty uttered *necklace*, the place came alive with a vivid red color as the lockdown klaxons filled the base. Confused men went into battle-ready mode while the room blinked like some 70's discotheque. Roberta's eyes instantly went to the monitors on the wall. Flipping between the displays, she stopped at the room where they kept the stone. A decapitated guard lay crumpled in front of the door, a trail of blood leading to his head on the other side of the room – lifeless eyes staring in shock at the camera. Gasping, she switched to the interior view; a destroyed case, stone missing, and the backside of a man walking away. As he turned around, they saw the face of General Daniels.

Roberta blinked. "*Daniels*?! That's not possible."

"What the hell?" Travis jumped to his feet. Pulling his weapon, he checked the clip, then slammed it back in place. "I don't know why *he* would steal that stone, but I have to stop him before he gets out of the complex."

Knowing they might never find the stone again if it got out, Jonas stood as well, glancing to Antoine and Dusty. "We might want to provide some back up."

Antoine groaned, shaking his head. "Now just a minute! I think we should let Mister Knight here handle this on his own. I mean this *is* what he's trained for, right? Besides, my blood sugar is falling to dangerous levels." Turning to Roberta, he smiled a bit. "I think I'll grab a Danish over there, if you don't mind."

Falling in line behind Roberta, Dusty pulled her gun. "Grab it to go, Antoine. C'mon. Let's get that stone!"

Antoine grumbled between bites. "I swear you'd think the world was gonna end. When this is over, I'm gonna turn my phone off, lock my doors and sleep for a week."

"Why would Daniels take the stone? I don't understand this." Stepping out of her military-issued pumps, Roberta reached for the door. "This just doesn't make sense. He *knew* it would put us in lockdown." Flinging it open, she didn't waste any time waiting for the others as she raced up the stairs two at a time.

"More reason to get up there then," Dusty agreed, hot on her heels.

Reaching level fourteen, Travis took point. "Everyone stay behind me. Daniels is a crack shot. If he takes me out, you might just have to," looking to Jonas, he paused. "Well, you know what to do, right?"

Jonas's lip curled in a grin. "So, you want me to let him shoot you first, right?"

"Smart ass." Travis plastered his back against the wall, rounding the corner. Seeing Daniels exit the room, he leveled his gun. "Stop right there, Tom. Hands where I can see them. Turn around slowly, or you're dead."

As he did, the general's form shimmered into Seth within the blinking lights.

"Oh shit," Jonas whispered.

"Why, hello darlin'." Seth looked directly at Dusty.

The stunned expression on her face leaked out into her words. "You?"

"We have *got* to stop meeting like this. People are gonna talk." After winking at her, he glanced at Travis. "Mister Knight. So good to see you again. I'd love to sit and talk, but I'm a bit pressed for time, so…"

Jonas lunged but even with his speed, he grasped only air. Landing hard, he jumped to his feet at the loud sound of boots heading toward them. "Shit!"

Turning to Dusty, Roberta motioned. "No time for family reunions. You guys *have* to get out of here. People will ask too many questions that can't be answered."

Dusty glanced around at their surroundings. "Yes, we've got to get back to our… lodgings. What's the fastest way out of here where no one will see us?"

Confused, Antoine glanced around the circle. "*Why* do we have to rush? He's already got the stone. Can't we take our time going back? I never got to eat that wonderful burger… those Cheetos aren't-"

"Because *he* knows where the last stone is." They could hear the echo of hurried footsteps around them. Dusty looked at her aunt. "We need to move. Besides, I, for one, don't feel like answering a bunch of questions and don't feel like being 'debriefed' over this stone-walling crap. Trust me… the government is very picky about their 'secrets' and we don't want to be holed up for that."

Roberta nodded. "She's right. I wouldn't be able to stop *anyone* from keeping you in quarantine – an excuse to scare you – for the debriefing of, 'you never saw this, you were never here' type thing." She pointed to a door. "Through that door is a tunnel that will take you back up."

Hearing the boots closing in, Antoine looked at Jonas. "Umm… sounds like we don't have time to use the door. Can't you just, I dunno, vampiery us outta here?"

Jonas's brow lifted. "Do I look like God? I can zip *myself* out, but as for all of us, no. I don't have that particular skill, yet. *If* it even exists."

Antoine frowned. "You're so damn negative. Can ya at least try? Who knows, maybe you have it, but it only works under stress and…" Glancing over Jonas's shoulder, he shook his head. "I'd say we're all about to be stressed to the max."

"Bacchus was able to zip me and Hooch back to my house and then him and me back after the burial." Dusty glared at Jonas. "*Try!*"

Roberta shook her head. "I'm staying. It might be better to have *someone* with a high-level security clearance to assist you later. You never know when you might need it. Besides, no one would *dare* argue with me." Pulling Dusty into a hug, her face softened. "You have your father's eyes and your mother's cheekbones. I'm glad I got to see you once more."

Dusty hugged her back. "It won't be the last time. You have my number."

"And I will call to check up on you too." Releasing her, she took a few steps back. "Now, go, all of you. I'll misdirect the troops."

Travis looked down, pursing his lips for a moment, then back up at Roberta. "Burn me." The meaning clear.

Roberta nodded in understanding. "As you wish. Now go!"

Closing his eyes, Jonas tried to access a power or spell that would bring them to the outside.

Without warning, they suddenly appeared inside the truck, much to Zeke's surprise. "Shit!" he said, looking to Jonas. "How in the hell did you-"

"Drive!" Jonas barked, just as shocked as Zeke. "Get the hell out of here, now!"

Being plopped into the backseat of the truck, on the laps of a stunned Antoine and pleased Travis, Dusty tried righting herself. "Well, could be worse, I guess."

Travis wiggled his brows. "Speak for yourself! I kinda like my spot."

Antoine rolled his eyes. "Oh Lord, take me now."

35

As the sound of alarms blasting off around them, Zeke drove faster than speed allowed, kicking up a dirt trail. No one bothered to follow them as all the sentries headed in the opposite direction. No doubt to search for the missing people running around the secured base.

Before long, they arrived back at the RV.

As the truck rolled to a stop, Dusty raced for the RV's door. "Be right back. My bladder is about to explode."

Exiting the vehicle, Antoine headed for the kitchen. "That's a little more than I needed to know. I guess it's back to Cheetos for me. I'm gonna starve to death eating nothing but Cheeto-" Eyeing the takeout bag from the restaurant, his eyes glistened. "Ooh! My burger." Picking it up, he held it to his chest. "How I have missed you, mon Cherie." Popping it into the microwave, he mumbled. "I swear, y'all are trying to starve me for *real* this time around."

Travis went for a tour of the RV. "I kinda expected something different but, this isn't bad. Do you know how expensive this thing is? I know of houses that don't cost this much! You guys have some deep pockets."

Stepping out of the bathroom, drying her hands, Dusty looked over at Travis. "Well, I guess it's lucky that you're really one of the good guys."

"Told ya so." Winking, he leaned down to kiss her. "It's about time you know. I have missed-"

"Not *that* good." The hand on his chest didn't deter him as much as the stormy glare in her eyes.

Wiggling his brows, he put his hand on hers, lightly massaging the top. "Not that good *yet*. You *know* you can't resist my charms."

Pulling away from him, she rolled her eyes. "Trust me. I can." Turning to DeMolay, she eyed him warily. "So… from what Sparx told me, you're trustworthy now? Not trying to kill us in our sleep? Even though, I do believe they call that *more* than just a misunderstanding. More like attempted murder, but who keeps track of a silly thing like that."

Lowering his head, he nodded. "Please forgive me. Had I realized who you were, I would have never acted in such a rash manner." Reaching out to touch her necklace, he smiled. "Perhaps you would allow me to hold onto this? Just for a time."

Slapping his hand away, her eyes narrowed. "You can't help us with a broken hand, or a missing arm. Since I was seven years old, *this* has been in *my* care. A drunken knight from your organization held me prisoner because of it. Don't push it. No one touches it but me. End of discussion on *that* topic." Eyeing him curiously, she kissed the necklace before placing it back inside her shirt. "What do you know about this, anyway? Who I *was*? What do you mean by that?"

Holding up his hands, he backed away from her. "Of the de Jardiner clan."

"*Why* would that have mattered?"

"Your family is one of the oldest in our order and that necklace has been passed down in your line since it was found. As for *why* it is so important," he shrugged. "We do not know."

"That seems to be the general consensus. *No* one knows *why* it's important, just that it is. My life's been ruined because of it. So, excuse me if I'm curious about its origins." Sighing, she looked down and then back up. "But we did find out some information. However, all that can wait till later. The first order of business. Seth got the stone."

As the microwave dinged, Antoine retrieved his steaming burger. "Mmmm. Smells so good." Unwrapping it, he took a bite. "This sure as *hell* beats Cheetos."

Jonas rolled his eyes. "I don't know how you don't weigh five-hundred pounds."

Sticking out his tongue, the professor waved him off. "High metabolism. Besides, I work harder than you think I do, and we haven't eaten in hours. *Hours*! You act like I've been munching on jelly beans all day!"

"Whatever. Anyway, as Dusty said, Seth has number three now, so we have a prob-" His eyes turned golden and a snarl curled his lip. "We have company."

After checking his weapon, Travis headed to the door. No matter the bad blood between them, he trusted the vampire's instincts. As he took a step forward, Jonas stopped him with a hand to the chest.

"Not your kind of company." He turned to the RV's door. "*Mine*."

Before Jonas could get the door opened, Dusty had her own weapon out – loaded with silver bullets. Instinctively, she yanked Travis behind her before standing beside Jonas.

Glancing to his side, he smirked. "You do like to live dangerously, don't you?"

"Partners. Remember?"

Rolling his eyes, he opened the door, his jaw immediately dropping. "*Katherine?*"

The beautiful woman looking up at him smiled. Her long dark hair trailed down to curve around her breasts as big blue eyes stared up at him. "Diego! Oh, thank God I found you!"

"I go by Jonas now. Jonas Sparx. I thought Seth killed you two hundred and fifty years ago. How are you here right now?"

"I wished he had. It would've been easier. He and his minions put me in Torpor. It's not a fun state. Your mind still functions. You can feel everything. The hunger never stops. It's like starving to death, only you don't die." Brushing a hand through her hair, she eyed Dusty's gun warily. "May I come in?"

Holding the door open, he pushed Dusty's gun away. "I'm sorry. Yes. Please. Come in. Is there something I can get for you?"

"I would love some O-Negative."

Jonas chuckled. "I don't have that, but I do have something that will make you feel better. Come and sit down. Get comfortable and then we'll talk." Turning, he noticed the concerned looks from everyone in the room and the angry glare from Dusty. Eyeing the gun still in her hand, he took a step forward. "No one touches her." His eyes relocated to Dusty's. "Not even you."

As he threw her own words back at her, she scoffed, holstering her weapon. "Whatever."

Rushing back to his things, he returned with a small tea bag. Heating a cup of water in the microwave, he steeped the bag in it. The liquid turned reddish-brown. After a moment, he handed it to her. "Here, drink this. My very own blend. It will make you feel a lot better."

Accepting it, she took a sip, marveling at the taste. "Oh, that's good."

Leaning against the wall, Dusty stared at the woman. She didn't even budge when Travis put his arm around her shoulder. "Sparx, you should introduce your… *friend*… to us."

Returning the glare, Katherine arched a brow. Sad eyes gazed at Jonas. "*Friend?* Have I been downgraded to friendship now, Diego? I mean… Jonas."

Looking from Dusty back to Katherine, Jonas fumbled for the right words. "Well… um…"

Setting the empty cup down on the table, Katherine turned, wrapping her arms around him. "Oh, my darling. How I have missed you all these years."

Just her touch brought back so many memories. He wrapped his arms around her, holding tightly, gently running his hand through her hair. "I missed you too. I thought I lost you."

Nibbling on the inside of her cheek, Dusty motioned to Jonas while pushing Travis off. "Okay, Sparx. We've been through the charade of people not being who they claimed to be. So, are you gonna tell us who this woman is, or do we have to guess? I'm not in the mood to play games nor do we have that kinda time. Or we can just leave you here to catch up and go on without you?"

Biting into his burger, Antoine mumbled, "Sounds like someone's jealous."

Travis nodded. "I think you're right, Antoine."

"Jealous? Need I remind you that Seth… *twice* now… has appeared to us as someone else. We just lost the third stone as he took on the mirage of some high-falutin' general. Not to mention how he killed my dog! I lost Hooch," hearing a whine, she glanced down, "well, the *living* version of him… because we took it for granted that the person was who they claimed to be! No, this has *nothing* to do with jealousy. I don't feel like losing anyone else close to me. *How* do we know we can trust her?"

Drinking in the blue from Katherine's eyes, Jonas looked back to Dusty. "I trust *her*," he pointed to Travis, "as much as *you* trust *him*. Need I remind you that he shot you? It doesn't matter whether it was a tracker or not. He still shot you. Katherine has *never* betrayed me in all the time we have been together."

"The *old* Katherine, maybe, but how do you know she's the same? A lot can happen in two hundred and fifty years." Shaking her head, she pointed from one to the other. "Travis has proven that *we* can trust him. However, I don't know who this woman is! You don't know if she's some plant that Seth sent our way either. Hell, for all you know, it's that freak playing some bullshit game to find out where the last stone is. None of us know what he saw when he held it! Or, for that matter, she could be sent here to keep us from finding the last stone by distracting you!"

Travis nodded. "She's got a point, Sparx. You two may have been something back in the day, but this isn't that time. I find it odd that she just shows up out of the blue and knows where this RV is. The only way *I* was able to keep track of y'all was the tracer."

Antoine nodded, between bites. "I hate to say it, Jonas, seeing as how you *really* care for this woman, but Dusty and Travis both have good points. We're in the middle of nowhere. How did she find you when others of your kind can't? It's too convenient."

Thinking over those words, Jonas released a deep sigh, turning to Katherine. "They're right, my love. I've been fooled before by Seth. I need to make sure it's really you."

"How?" Katherine asked, confused. "Seth kept me prisoner all this time, locked in a coffin. Only recently did he bring me back but kept me chained. I was too weak to fight at first, but he left me with some idiot. Amelia. She slipped up and I got away."

Pointing to her arm, he nodded. "Let me read your blood. Blood doesn't lie."

Katherine sighed. "You don't trust me?"

Shaking his head, he touched her face. "I do. I trust you with all my heart. You know that. We loved each other so much that we blood bonded to one another."

Finishing the last of his burger, Antoine paused at the trash can. "Blood bond? What does that mean? Is that anything like blood brothers?"

"Not really. It's marriage between vampires." Jonas looked deeply into Katherine's eyes. "We were happily married for over one hundred years."

"Married?" Wide eyed, Dusty couldn't hide the astonishment in her tone. "The two of you were *married?*"

Katherine looked at Dusty. "*Are* married. Vampires don't divorce. We stay married until one of us dies."

Antoine turned up a half smile. "Con… gratulations?"

Jonas lovingly brushed his fingers through the strands of her hair. "I searched for you. Never gave up. Not until Kanis told me you were dead."

"I know."

Still annoyed, Dusty stomped a foot, calling attention back to her. "Sparx, I'm happy you're reunited with your true love, but we still want proof she is who she claims to be. I lost my dog because of your believing a charade. I'm not losing anyone else."

Turning back to Katherine, Jonas nodded. "She's right." Once more, he pointed to her wrist. "May I?"

She held out her wrist. "If you must."

Sinking his teeth into her wrist, the blood filled his mouth and took him from the present to a past long forgotten.

36

Eighteenth century London. A time of extreme class separation, except regarding death. Dead bodies, mostly the poor, littered the streets. No burial, just greedy scavengers picking the bones clean. The rich, privileged to die in their homes, fared no better.

Diego Ramirez sat in a claw-foot bathtub filled with steaming water. "Darling, what would you like to do tonight?"

Katherine entered the room showing off her pastel-colored mantua with a closed petticoat and open-fronted bodice. "Somewhere that I can show off my darling new dress. Isn't it beautiful?"

Watching her, he smiled. "It is very nice, but it would look much better, crumpled up in the corner of the room… on the floor."

Messing with the elbow-length sleeves, she scoffed at him. "Diego! This dress cost too much to *ever* see the floor." Spying him in the tub, she grinned. "Then again," sitting on the edge, "we could just stay in and cuddle."

"Maybe you're right, we should go out and show off that darling new dress of yours, that you will probably only wear once before purchasing another. Maybe take in a show."

"You'd rather do that than use our fingers to explore every crevice of our bodies?"

Grinning, he reached up, pulling her in with him. "We can do that any time. We've got *centuries* to be together. I'm *never* letting you out of my sight."

Laughing, she kicked her feet, struggling to get out of the tub. "*Diego*! You've ruined my dress! Now, I have to change."

Pulling her closer, he buried his mouth into her neck. "And here you were talking about cuddling. Make up your mind woman."

Turning, splashing water onto the floor, she wrapped her arms around him. "Well, I guess it wouldn't hurt… and then go out. Besides, I'm getting hungry."

His eyes flashed crimson. "*Now* you're speaking my language."

…

Pulling his mouth from her wrist, Jonas laughed. "Oh my God. It *is* you!" Looking at the others, he beamed. "It's *her*! She has a memory in her blood that only she and I would know!"

"And there's no way to fake a scene in blood?" Dusty asked a bit surprised.

"None," he told her, still looking at the woman beside him. "The blood doesn't lie. I never thought I would see you again. I've missed you so much." Pulling her into his arms, the two shared a kiss of longing.

Watching the make out session on the couch, Travis cleared his throat. "Um, does anyone else feel like a peeping Tom at this point?"

Cleaning up his mess, Antoine shook his head. "I don't see nothing. In fact, I'm about to get busy on the new quatrain. Just had to eat first because I'm not on a diet."

Seeing the rather loving embrace, Dusty growled. Pointing to Travis, she nodded her head in the direction of outside, as she slipped out the door, cigarette in hand.

Travis followed her. "Well now. Are things *always* this interesting around here?"

"*This*? This is nothing. It gets better and worse by the day." She lit a cigarette, offering it to him. "You still smoke?"

Taking it, he grinned. "Does a bear shit in the woods?"

"I don't know." Lighting a cigarette for herself, she glared at the RV. "I think it's too neat." After taking a drag, she cringed. "Must be stale."

"Spoken from a woman who hasn't seen bear scat!"

"No. I'm talking about this whole thing."

"What do you mean?"

"Remember that job we worked on together. I know you remember it. The one where the guy did the thing with the kid."

"Oh, *that* narrows it down."

"Lord, what was that file called? Sand… the Sanders custody case! Remember that one?"

Taking another drag off the cigarette, he shook his head. "Not really. Refresh my memory."

"Prominent banker, or some position high up in the bank. Messy divorce. Custody battle. Each labeled the other unfit to raise the little girl. Dad had her for the weekend. Someone kidnapped her. He couldn't remember the clothes she wore. His story changed three different times. Yet, he recalled exactly what she ate that morning, the conversation they had before leaving for the store, what cereal she just *had* to get because she loved that one above all the others. He even remembered the exact time they left. It seemed too neat."

"Oh yeah," he nodded. "He had his girlfriend dressed up in a costume who took the kid out of the store. The two were going off together to raise her. I remember that. We had to stake out the guy for a week before he took us to her location. What about it?"

"*That* reminds me of this."

"How so?"

"It's too neat. I mean… here we are in the middle of nowhere… and she finds him?"

Eyeing her, he took another drag while rolling his shoulders. "Well, he *did* say they were blood bonded together. Maybe they can sniff each other out?"

"Maybe. But explain this. If she could easily find him and knew his exact location from 'sniffing him out' as you claim… why didn't Jonas know who stood behind the door? Before he opened it, he had *no* clue who it was. If that was true, he would've sensed her… but he didn't."

Glancing down at his feet, he kicked at a rock. "Hm. You've got a point." Looking up, he refocused on her. "But he just read her blood *proving* her identity because only the two of them shared that memory, and blood doesn't lie… *supposedly*."

"So they say. I don't know. I don't trust her."

Taking another drag, Travis looked her up and down. "Dusty, are ya sure you're not just… jealous?"

"Jealous?!" Glaring at him with daggers shooting out of her eyes, she put a hand on her hip. "*What* would I have to be jealous of?"

"You've been his sole focus this whole time."

"Not exactly."

"Any fool can see that it's obvious there's *something* going on between you two."

Scoffing, she shook her head. "That's ridiculous."

"No. I see it. I can't exactly put my finger on it, but there is definitely something there. I can see it when the two of you look at each other. It's like you love to hate each other… or hate to love each other."

Taking a drag off the cigarette, she used her other hand to run it through her locks, layering it back in place. Once more she cringed at the taste. "Yuck." Tossing it into the tin coffee can for butts by the door, she turned back to Travis. "Quit being stupid. He's my *partner*. We're supposed to love hating each other. Nothing more. Psh, I can barely stand him half the time."

"That's what your *head* tells you, but your *heart* screams something else altogether."

"No, my heart is already taken by some other fool. I'm not jealous of anything that has to do with Sparx."

"Really? Your heart is taken? By whom?"

"I haven't totally forgiven him yet. I'll let him know when I have."

He grinned. "Okay, if it's not jealousy, then what is it?"

"I told you. I don't trust her. My gut tells me something is totally wrong with this *whole death do us part*, lovey-dovey crip-crap they're trying to shove down our throats."

Travis took another drag off the cigarette. "You mean the way Sparx doesn't trust *me*?"

"You've given him plenty of reasons *not* to. He almost killed you when you shot me."

"What about you? Do *you* trust me now?"

Cocking her head from one side to the other, she mulled over his question. "Meh, I guess."

"You guess?"

"Well, knowing you didn't *actually* shoot me, makes me stop thinking of places to bury your body." Gripping his shirt collar, she pulled him closer. "Heed my words well, Travis. If you *ever* lie to me again, you won't have to worry about Sparx." In the distance, a mournful howl split the early evening air, followed by several more. "What is up with that?! Dang burn wolves seem to follow me everywhere!" Dusty's eyes scanned the never-ending expanse of desert. "Seems like wherever I go, there they are."

Travis's gaze followed hers, his brow narrowing. "There *aren't* any wolves around here. Coyotes, yes, but no wolves." Turning back to her, a grin creased his face. "Maybe you're being followed by a pack of werewolves. I mean hell… we got vampires, so why not?"

"Travis Knight, don't you *even* go there. I got enough problems without having to deal with *fictional* bullshit."

Taking a step closer, he reached down, running his hand over her cheek, bringing out that southern charm. "Wait a minute. Let's get back to that mention of your heart already being taken. Does this mean that you've forgiven me?"

Smiling up at him, she poked him in the stomach. "You and that damn accent. How can you turn it on and off like that?"

"Born with it. It's easy to just sliiiiide right back into it, like a comfy old pair of shoes. You didn't answer my question."

"Maybe," she teased. "It's that damn accent."

"*Just* the accent, huh?"

"Well, I do have to admit," she looked him up and down, "you do look *damn* good in those jeans."

Grinning, he leaned down, pressing his lips to hers. The instant they touched, an electrical current passed between the two and she wrapped her arms around him, sharing a kiss of desire.

God, he feels so good.

Lost in each other, taken back to another time and place, Dusty remembered when they happily did this very thing. His hands roamed over her backside, pulling her tightly to his body. She pushed in molding comfortably to his frame. The perfect fit. Then again, they always did fit exactly right.

"Ahem!" Antoine cleared his throat.

The sound of someone spying on them in a tender moment, caused the two to separate as if suddenly allergic to the other.

Looking up at Antoine, with a guilty expression on her face, Dusty couldn't help but notice behind him. Jonas still sat on the couch with an unmistakable glare, shooting daggers at her. "Yes?"

"I hate to interrupt another session of *The Love Shack on Wheels*, but is this the way the rest of the trip is gonna be? Kissing in here. Kissing out there? Everyone unable to keep their hands and lips off their prospective others? If so, I'm gonna ride with Zeke! I mean, I hate to break up all this loving and all, but I got some important, breaking news."

"We… came out for a cigarette, knowing how much you hate them."

"You have invented a strange new way to smoke, I see."

"What's your breaking news?" Shoving a hand into her bag of jelly beans, she chewed on the mouthful as she headed into the RV.

"This quatrain has language I've never seen before. At least... I don't *think* I have. I don't even know if it's from this *planet*."

"What?" Dusty quickly moved inside.

Travis trailed behind. "That's not possible."

Following Antoine up to the area dubbed the 'TV room', the eight of them stood around the quatrain as the professor pointed. "Anyone have any clue what language this is? I mean... I can try and find out, but I've never seen anything like it before."

Examining it, DeMolay shook his head. "Nor have I."

Dusty stared hard at the scroll. "This looks vaguely familiar... ish. I don't know why. I feel like... I've seen this before. Not sure where though."

Travis stared at it, stroking his chin. "I know what it is." They all turned in his direction. "Aliens." He grinned. "It's *got* to be aliens."

Everyone but Jonas laughed. "Get serious. This is no laughing matter."

"I dunno. *I* thought it was funny," Dusty teased.

"*You* would." Jonas pointed at the table. "How can we figure out *where* the next stone is if we can't read the damn quatrain?"

"Excuse me." Bacchus appeared behind them to the surprise of everyone. "Perhaps *I* can help with that."

37

With the sudden arrival of Bacchus just popping in behind them, startled knights drew their weapons, ready to attack. Instinctively, Jonas and Dusty stood in front of Bacchus, shielding him from the others. Once getting over the shock, DeMolay stopped the knights with a raised hand, motioning them back into place. Jonas and Dusty glanced at each other in complete shock. They acted as one, in complete harmony, as if one mind between them. Turning away from each other, they separated almost as quickly as Dusty and Travis had earlier.

Falling back on the couch, Antoine clutched at his chest, trying to keep his breathing under control while Dusty fanned him with some RV magazine. "Bells. I'm getting the lot of you necklaces with bells for Christmas. I'm getting *too* old to be scaring the *daylights* outta me! I don't have *that* many more years to live! I'd like to *not* have it snuffed out with *heart failure!*"

"My apologies. I did not mean to frighten." Bacchus bowed slightly.

"Well, you're a bit late for that!" Antoine continued to breathe quickly. "I think I might need oxygen. I swear you're trying to kill an old man! A little warning would be nice."

Dusty groaned. "Stop milking it, Antoine." Rolling up the magazine, she bopped him on the head. "He apologized already."

Turning in a complete circle, eyeing the interior, Bacchus smirked. "I see you've been downgraded slightly. Although I must say, this is by far the roomiest recreational vehicle I've ever been in."

After giving Dusty the stink eye, Antoine nodded, caressing his chest. "Far as the accommodations, they work, but I do miss the fine dining we've grown accustomed to."

"Cheetos ain't cutting it?" Dusty teased, nudging Antoine.

"Hush you, or I won't make you anymore of my heavenly delights when we get back to reality, after all this… what did you call it? Oh yeah. *Crip-crap* plays through."

Catching sight of Katherine, Bacchus narrowed his silver eyes slightly. "Inanna. A pleasure to see you again. I trust your little rest has rejuvenated you?"

"Never mind that." Stepping between Katherine and Bacchus, Jonas tilted his head. "I'm sure you didn't just show up for a grand tour of our new mode of transportation. You said you could help, so get to the point."

"Just a dead-aim minute," Dusty said, squeezing past Travis. Looking at Jonas, she pointed to the woman behind him. "*You* call her Katherine, now mister 'I show up whenever I feel like it, but never call first,' calls her Inamma? What gives?"

"*Inanna*, my dear," Bacchus corrected, emphasizing the 'N's'. "*Inanna*."

"In... what the ho-bag ever." Crossing her arms over her chest, she didn't take her eyes off Jonas. "Well? We're all waiting."

"Inanna. The Sumerian Goddess of love, beauty, sex, desire, fertility, war, justice, and political power." Antoine stood at Dusty's side. "The Babylonians and Assyrians called her Ishtar. She and her brother Utu were the bringers of divine justice. One myth has her-" Realizing all eyes had turned to him, the professor smiled. "Sorry. Rambling old man here." Returning to his place, he shrugged, turning back to the scroll. "As you were."

Dusty gasped. "You're married to the Sumerian Goddess of love?"

Jonas cut her a quick glance. "It's... *complicated*."

"*Complicated*?! Why didn't you share *that* bit of info with me when you were telling me about your *mortal* marriage?"

Arching both brows, Katherine moved into Jonas's sight. "*Mortal* marriage?"

Glancing from one to the other, he shrugged. "Like I said... complicated."

"We'll discuss these... *complications*... later," Katherine replied, shooting him *the* look.

Bacchus kept his gaze trained on Antoine. "*You* seem to know an awful lot about the Goddess. Most humans have little interest about ancient times, especially their... *myths*."

Grinning, Antoine glanced up. "Hello? Professor here. It's my *job* to know these things. I studied the Sumerian language, so obviously I'd know about their myths, Gods, and Goddesses." Pursing his lips, he handed Bacchus the scroll. "I have *no* idea what language this is in. Since you're so old, how about you give it a shot?"

Taking the scroll, Bacchus nodded. "You *wouldn't* know this language because when this was written, you were just coming out of the trees. It's Atlantean."

Silence fell over the group as they all turned to Bacchus.

Huffing out a breath, Dusty put her hand on her hip. "Coming out of the trees? Well, that's insulting. I don't care what scientist claim… I ain't related to no dang monkey and I'll be damned if I *ever* swung in a tree."

DeMolay hadn't taken his eyes off Bacchus since he just appeared out of thin air. "Perhaps you can explain what you mean. Atlantis is a fictional city that sank to the bottom of the ocean… if *that* is who you mean."

"That, my dear man, is precisely who I mean." Bacchus shifted his weight, leaning against the small countertop. "Much of what mankind considers *fiction* has its roots in fact. Time has a way of lessening the memories, until all that remains is a foggy notion of some fable told around a fire. Take us, for instance. Most humans think we are nothing more than whispers in the dark. A way to keep children in line. Of course, as some of you now know, we are as real as it gets."

"So, Atlantis exists?" Antoine asked, lifting a silver brow.

Turning to the professor, Bacchus winced. "Not *exactly*. It's complicated. Like Jonas's relationships."

"Do y'all *ever* give a straight answer to *anything*?" Dusty looked between Jonas and Bacchus. "I'm about two breaths short of taking Travis, Antoine, *and* Hooch and walking out that door, if I don't start getting some *clear* answers."

Hugging her from behind, Travis couldn't hide the smile on his handsome face. "I love it when ya talk dirty," he whispered in her ear.

Frowning, Dusty elbowed Travis in the ribs. "You shush. I'm serious."

Bacchus pursed his lips. "Very well. Atlantis *did* exist with a population more advanced than even yours is now. Impressive, but arrogant. They sought to help mankind flourish. Unfortunately, a powerful vampire caught wind of their plans and assembled hordes of his kind to bring war to the Atlanteans. It raged for months, with *both* sides suffering enormous losses." Pausing, he huddled within himself a moment before looking at Dusty. "Realizing the futility of it all, this vampire called upon ancient powers. Bringing the sea to bear upon the island, it consumed it."

"Wait a minute," Jonas interrupted. "I know that legend. A small city on the island with a population anywhere from ten thousand to fifty thousand. They *all* died?"

"Yes, most of them perished, but try a population of *one-hundred-thousand*, Jonas."

"*Most?*" Antoine tilted his head.

Bacchus nodded. "Around a hundred managed to escape, including Tyrian, their leader. Allow me to show you." Holding out his palm, an image of a man's face slowly formed.

"Well put me in the electric chair and spin it around!" Dusty whispered, her eyes widening. "That's the face I saw!"

"When did *you* see Tyrian?"

"When I first held the stone in Egypt. It felt like I stepped on a live wire."

Antoine winced. "Yeah, she looked like she was in some sort of trance if I remember correctly. It lasted a few minutes."

"That's the face I saw!" All eyes turned to her as the image faded away. "Whaaaat?!"

"Interesting." Bacchus eyed her up and down while stroking his chin. "You must have some connection to Tyrian."

"Great." Travis ran a hand through his hair. "Just what I need. *More* competition."

"You said that's what he looks *like*," Jonas interjected. "Present tense. Does that mean-"

"Yes, he's still alive, as are the hundred who escaped with him." Looking at the scroll, he handed it to Antoine. "I cannot read what is written here, but I can take you to one who can."

Taking the scroll, Antoine slid it back into its sheath. "Count me in. Any chance to learn a new... or in this case *old* language, I'm all in for." Setting the sheepskin in his backpack, he narrowed his eyes at

Bacchus. "So, you didn't tell us what happened to the vampire responsible for the death of Atlantis."

Bacchus glared, his eyes turning a shade of crimson that made even Jonas flinch. "You are looking at him."

"Jumping serial killers! Well, that paints a whole other picture of you, Bacchus… and it's not nice." Shaking her head, Dusty looked around the room, snatching up her backpack. "Oh well. What's done is done. Travis, did you pack your undies? Sounds like this is gonna be a long journey."

Bacchus shook his head. "No. Not everyone. Just Dusty, Jonas, and Antoine. That's it."

Antoine headed to the bathroom. "Y'all settle this. That burger didn't agree with me after all the *good* food I've had. I'll be in the can if anyone needs me."

Jonas shoved Katherine behind him. "No way, Jose. Katherine comes along, or I stay right here."

Dusty turned on Bacchus. "Excuse me? One thing, you forgot Hooch. He goes *everywhere* with me. No argument."

Travis looked around confused. "Hooch? Not to bring up a sore subject but… ain't he dead?"

Ignoring Travis, she continued. "Second, if Seth knew for *one* instant that Travis is now part of this team, he'd snatch him up and use him as a hostage for real! Unlike *you*, I *refuse* to have anyone else dying over what I could've saved. It's not happening for all the tea in China. If you want me to go, he comes too, or we'll stay here, and I can catch up on those movies that everyone talks about. And that is *not* up for debate. Period. End of discussion."

Jonas pointed to the woman beside him. "Katherine escaped from Seth's clutches once, he *won't* let that happen again. She's on board to guarantee her safety, if for no other reason."

"Your dedication to your romantic interests is admirable, and in any other circumstance I'd allow it. However -"

"*Allow* my ass!" Jonas said. "You don't have a *choice* here. I'm getting tired of being told where to go, what to do, and how to do it.

If you want us to risk our lives any further, it's time *you* gave in a bit."

Travis applauded. "You tell him, bro. Go team Jonas."

Pointing over to the movies, Dusty winked at Travis. "Well, looks like we're gonna be watching movies. Sparx, I guess you two are with us, huh? Good. You pop the popcorn. We'll pick out the movie. Travis, which one of these is best?" Turning, she ran a finger over them. "Wait, is Hooch here? I'd love to actually watch it this time. Does it just say, *Hooch* on it?"

Hearing his name, Hooch came forward, tongue wagging.

"You both are being unreasonable." Bacchus growled. "Where we are going is *not* exactly the Bahamas. I, Jonas, and Katherine won't have an issue, but you, Travis, and Antoine will. Besides, vampires are not exactly... *welcome* there, for *obvious* reasons. We may not even get an audience with Tyrian so the fewer that show up, the better."

Shrugging, Jonas headed to the kitchen area, turning to look at Dusty, walking backward, he smiled. "You two like butter on yours?"

"And salt." Travis waved a hand. "*Lots* of salt."

Dusty continued looking through the movies. "Bacchus, *we* have been put through the ringer on this mission of death, because so far... that's pretty much all it's been. We've been shot at. Locked in a pyramid. Forced to give up our lives as we were so happily unaware of the crap going on. We've been put on a time restricted schedule that didn't even allow us to enjoy all these sights we're seeing. Now, either *those* two join us, or we're gonna sit down and watch a whole *slew* of movies. Your choice. Which will it be?"

"And forced to live in this trailer!" Antoine's voice shouted from the bathroom. "Eating Cheetos and burgers which, by the way, are *not* helping my constitution. When I'm done in here, y'all *might* wanna let it air out for an hour or so. I'm about to call the Guinness Book people. That last turd was a world record holder."

Jonas chuckled. "You sure you want to take Antoine?"

Glaring at Jonas, Bacchus shook his head. "I could just take you, Dusty, and Antoine with a snap of my fingers."

"Go ahead. Apparently, *I* can zap a number of people from one place to another now, as well. So, you go ahead and do that. I'll just zip us right back here."

"Oh? And *when* did you develop this amazing talent?"

"Back inside Area fifty-one." He snatched out the popcorn jar. "Like you said. They'll come when I need them."

Throwing up his hands, Bacchus gave in. "*Fine*! We'll do it your way. Just remember, I *warned* you."

Travis's face fell. "Wait… you mean I don't get to have any popcorn?"

38

"Are you certain this plan to distract Jonas is going to work?" Kanis asked, as Seth examined his prize. "He has gotten more powerful it seems, and perhaps he will -"

"Are you doubting me, Kanis? I hope not, cuz if you are, I might get offended. And you wouldn't like me when I'm… *offended*." Turning the stone in his hand, he examined the shallow etchings on it. "Now let's see where we're off to next, shall we?" Placing the stone in his palm, he extended it out and waited. As the others had, it produced a floating image. "You gotta be shittin' me. Water, *again*?" The image of a vast ocean filled his field of vision. As if an eagle taking flight, he flew over the calm sea, stopping when a landmass appeared. A man's face materialized, bearded and stern, a crown of gold upon his head and in its center, a brilliant beam shot forth. Seth's eyes narrowed. "I've seen that face before," he said, remembering his encounter at the Sphinx. "Though he didn't have a beard."

Standing next to Kanis, Amelia's eyes grew wide, her grip tightened around his arm. "The crown of Zeus," she whispered, unable to tear her gaze from the face.

As the image faded, Seth turned to her. "Why, Amelia, my dear. You look like you've just seen the ghost of your daddy. Care to share?"

Amelia swallowed hard. "Some Greek myths were lost to the world, but those of our kind who lived among the people, preserved them in our archives." Releasing her hold on Kanis, she moved toward the stone. "One spoke of the crown of Zeus being stolen by the Atlanteans, and in his rage, the God ordered Poseidon to destroy Atlantis. He did so, but Zeus's crown was lost. It was said to be stronger than even his lightning bolt, maybe the very source of his power." As she reached for the stone, Seth snatched it away.

"That's a very entertaining story," he said, putting the stone back into his pocket. "I hope there was a point to it?"

Shaking off the supernatural pull, Amelia nodded. "Myth has it that the Atlanteans hid the crown inside the statue of Zeus they had built and placed in the great hall. When Poseidon raised the sea against the island, it sank as well." Looking up at Seth, her lips curled into a smile. "The crown's power came from the last stone. We need to find the ruins of Atlantis."

Seth rolled his eyes. "Why of course. I'll get right on that." Shaking his head, he plopped down in the large chair behind an old desk. "It appears we're gonna have to let the Scooby gang find the last one as well."

"Do you want me to have them followed again?" Kanis asked, reaching for his phone.

Seth waved him off. "No, that won't be necessary this time. I got it covered. And *this* time, they won't even see it comin'." Drumming his fingers against the desktop, his lips pursed. "Shall we see how our guest is doing?"

Descending three flights of stairs, the trio stopped in front of General Daniels. Shackled by his wrists to the stone wall, his chin rested on his chest, eyes closed. Lines of dried blood crossed his pale face.

"Wakey, wakey," Seth said, giving him a few slaps on the cheek. "I thank you for choosing to stay with us here at Sundown Motel, but I'm afraid it's check-out time." Smiling as the General's head slowly rose, he removed a white cloth from his pocket and wiped off the man's face. "I apologize for the over eagerness of some of our staff. It's so rare we actually have guests here. I'll be sure to speak to them about their behavior. I do hope you'll find it in your heart to give us a four-star rating on Priceline." Dabbing off a bit of scabbed-over blood from Daniel's chin, he tossed the cloth to the side. "There now. All clean and shiny. I'd like to personally thank you for the use of your image. It came in very handy, yes sir. Now, anything you'd like to say before you depart?"

Daniels snarled, hate showing through bloodshot eyes. "Go to Hell!"

"Tch, tch. You have it all wrong, my friend." Grabbing him by the chin, Seth squeezed and leaned in close. "I intend to bring Hell up here." With a twist, Daniels neck snapped like a dried twig, his hanging body going limp. "Well, *that* was boring," Seth remarked, glancing over at two of his children. "Get rid of this," he ordered, then turned back to Kanis. "I'd say we have about a week before our intrepid detectives locate the last stone. I want you to find out where Deva's holed up. Her and I have… unfinished business."

<h2 style="text-align:center">39</h2>

Rummaging through what little debris remained of Deva's castle, Harley shook his head. "Smart. Get rid of the evidence. Not bad. You could've left behind some gold," he grumbled, kicking aside a few small rocks. As he started on the dirt road leading away from the place, a tumbleweed rolled by, stopping in front of him. His dark eyes narrowed as it burst into flame. "Really? Ya know, writers might call that a cliché, and not a good one, at that."

A low rumble came from the sky, as jagged spikes of electricity jumped between the clouds.

"Spare me the light show. I've seen it all before and, truth be told, it's a bore."

"We had an agreement," came a deep voice from the tumbleweed. "No direct interference."

"No choice," Harley answered, removing his hat, and running a hand through sparse gray ringlets. "She was gonna kill him. Besides, *I* ain't the only one tiltin' the chess board here." Narrowing his eyes, he placed his hat back on his head, adjusted the brim, and glared at the bush. "Am I now?"

A moment of silence told him all he needed to know. "From this point forward, we let fate decide the outcome, agreed? Either they win and survive, or they don't."

"Fine. You know the only reason I agreed to this? Hell is *mine*. I don't need some charlatan tryin' to take my place. If he didn't plan on destroying the whole human race, I'd be his biggest fan."

"One more thing. Give Deva back her powers."

Harley shrugged. "Don't know what you're talkin' about." A searing bolt threw him a few yards backward. "Okay, okay! I'll give the little bitch back her bag of tricks. Geeze, somebody needs a Netflix and chill night," rising, he dusted off his suit.

The flame dissipated from the tumbleweed and it rolled on its merry way.

"Yeah, I hope ya get hit by a semi," Harley grumbled as he cracked his neck and vanished into the blackness of night.

To Be Continued…

Hi, I'm Sam. The 'Beach' in "Walker and Beach." I know, it sounds like a Law firm or a publishing company. (Don't I wish.) I just turned 60 this past July, and now that I've entered the winter of my life, I figured it was high time to reach for my dream of being a published author. Better late than never.

I've always been an observer of people. 'Wallflower', to be frank, but that has given me a great insight into the human condition. People will say all manner of things, when they don't see you as a threat, or don't see you at all.

So welcome to our author page, where Lisa and I will keep you abreast of how our joint effort, The Bloodstone Chronicles, and our solo projects are coming along. For now, be good, be safe, and be real.

Visit my website: Sam Beach | Walker & Beach (wixsite.com)
Follow me on Facebook: https://www.facebook.com/sbeachauthor/
Subscribe to my blog: Blog | Walker & Beach (wixsite.com)
Send emails to: sunofabytch@gmail.com

Why you want to know about little ole me, Lisa Walker, is mind-shattering, but here it goes. Born in a town, in the middle of the U.S., with a mom and a dad. Being the oldest, I ruled the scene... until others invaded. They say that everyone's life is a story all its own. If I ever got around to writing mine, it would be held in the fiction aisle. Drama. Comedy. Horror. Unbelievable. It's a wonder I escaped it much less lived through it, but enough about that!

The writing bug attacked every organ in my body right after I turned twelve. I had a blast creating stories, characters, situations for them to work through. My mind dove into the criminally insane, the helpless victims, the abandoned brokenhearted. Quite addicting. Playing 'what if' turned into me writing for hours on end. Thank God for the computer! No more wasted paper. Don't like something? Delete it. Voila. Magic.

I have to be creating or editing something. Websites. Blogs. Stories. Characters. Worlds. It's nice when one finally comes together enough to take shape and then need editing... and more revising... over and over 100 times or more. Ah, the life of a writer. Glamorous, eh? I love it. Hope you enjoy reading it as much as I slaved... err... loved writing it! Thanks!

Visit my website: L. Dee Walker | Walker & Beach (wixsite.com)
Follow me on Facebook: https://www.facebook.com/L.DeeWalker/
Send emails to: TorturedTales@gmail.com

Made in the USA
Las Vegas, NV
08 June 2021

24416788R00138